Strung TOGETHER

KASHA THOMPSON

Copyright © 2026 by Kasha Thompson

Cover design by Qamber Designs
Cover Copyright © 2026 by Honey Blossom Press LLC
Print book interior design by Qamber Designs

Honey Blossom Press
www.honeyblossompress.com
@honeyblossompress

ISBNs: 9781967565320 (trade paperback), 9781967565337 (ebook)
Printed in the United States of America

HONEY BLOSSOM PRESS

For everyone who kept the show going with duct tape,
hope, and a little bit of magic.

This one's for you.

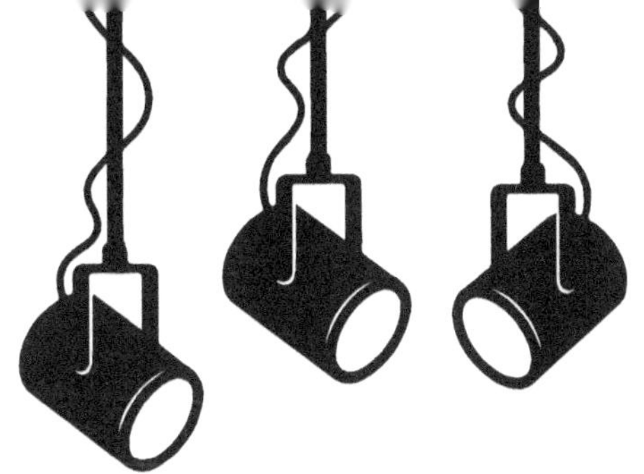

CHAPTER 1
Letitia

"WHAT'S WRONG, AALIYAH?"

"Hi, Gus. I didn't get invited to Nala's birthday party."

"I see how that could make you really sad."

"It does. Everyone was invited but me."

"Do you know what Grumpy Gus does when somebody hurts his feelings?" Gus rubbed his furry yellow paws together.

"No. What?"

"I eat half of their sandwich right out of their lunch box."

My eyes shifted from Gus to our director off stage. "How does that help?"

"It stops my grumbling tummy and sends the other person on a fruitless search for their missing lunch. It's a win-win all around."

"Can we cut?" I called out, breaking character.

Diego Torres, the director, approached the set. "What's up?"

"Uhm, I don't think we want Gus teaching a bunch of kindergarteners to become petty thieves."

Stanley Dinkle, the puppeteer for Gus, cleared his throat. "This is how we practiced it in rehearsal."

"No, it's not. Your line was, 'I just let it roll off my back.'" I knew his lines and mine because any time there was a break, I'd read the scenes—all of them. It helped with memorization. "I'm just not sure Grumpy Gus is the best monster to help Aaliyah with this specific problem."

"Are you trying to cut me from the scene?" Stanley was a Juilliard-trained actor and talked with a South African accent, even though he was born and raised in Detroit. Every chance he got, he let people know he once starred in a movie with Robert DeNiro. He'd say, "Bob almost stole my wife."

"No. I just think you're better suited for another scene that doesn't include the need for emotional intelligence."

Before Stanley could object, Diego spoke up. "Let's take fifteen and then regroup." He patted Stanley on his back. "You're doing great, buddy." Stanley walked off the set grumbling under his breath. Diego turned his full attention toward me. "Letitia, you know Stanley likes to improvise."

"I do, but I just want the best product. Our kids deserve it. And teaching them to shank their enemies isn't exactly on brand."

"I hear you. I'll talk to Stan."

"Thank you. We can still try his take, but I think we should have the original option just in case it doesn't work out."

"I'm going for a smoke."

"Those things will kill you."

"Life is slowly killing us. What's the point?" The vape pen was already hanging from his lips.

I stared at Aaliyah, the brown felt puppet that was still on my hand. "You get it, right?"

"Of course I do, Letitia," I said to myself in Aaliyah's unique, bubbly voice.

I'd joined the cast of *Jellybean Junction* three years ago, auditioning more times than I'd like to admit before being hired. The show had been on the air since before I was born and was a toddler rite of passage. Growing up, it was in heavy rotation, and I secretly continued to watch it while other kids my age were into *Forever Summer*, *Chad Tries Everything*, or other popular tween shows.

Back then, my parents were concerned there was something wrong with me. But now we know I just had a deep love of all things make-believe and a fascination with the relationship between the felt characters who seemed so real and the people who brought them to life. Working on this show was a lifelong dream, and now I was a full-time cast member looking to leave a lasting legacy.

The soundstage for *Jellybean Junction* was located in Harlem, New York. I was a transplant from Connecticut, but after five years I considered this city my home.

In the breakroom, I propped my puppet up on the counter and made myself a cup of coffee. It wasn't unusual to walk in a room and find a puppet sitting unattended on a chair or lying on a table. At night, it could get kind of creepy when you thought you were alone and then peeped a pair of lifeless yet eerie eyes staring at you.

"Did you hear?" Joseline Lucas, the office assistant, swept into the breakroom out of breath.

"Hear what?"

She beamed in the knowledge she would be the first one to share this information. "They hired a new puppeteer."

"We don't have a budget for yarn when the puppet's hair needs maintenance, but we can hire a new employee?"

"You'll never guess who it is." She really relished her role as the office gossip.

"Who?"

"Rustin Hayes."

"*U-turn* Rustin Hayes?" My eyes grew into saucers.

"That's the one."

Rustin Hayes was a legend in the game. He had his own indie puppeteer studio. He'd written, produced, and starred in *U-turn*, an adult Broadway musical featuring puppets. I'd also auditioned for a role in that production and never received a callback. Why would Rustin Hayes come to work on *Jellybean Junction*?

"I think your intel is unreliable. Junction couldn't afford Hayes."

"Then why is he in Brea's office signing the contract as we speak?

"Like right now, right now?"

Joseline sported a cocky smirk. "It's okay. I know you want to hightail it over there to see for yourself."

Of course I wanted to meet Rustin Hayes. He was a role model for an up-and-coming puppeteer like myself. "I don't even care, but... It just... Stop looking at me like that."

"Let's go." Joseline grabbed my hand and led the way. We dashed down the hall, jumping over cords and narrowly missing the open vending machine door. In the administrative wing of the building, we stood outside of Brea's office trying our best to ear-hustle. I could make out laughter and a deep male voice saying, "This will be fun," or maybe he said, "Have you ever tried dim sum?" Either way, Brea Sinclair, our showrunner, was talking to a man.

"How long have they been in there?" I whispered.

"He came in about thirty minutes ago."

"Alone?"

"What did you expect him to have, an entourage?"

"Kind of." A rib-tickling image popped into my head, and I tried to hold back a giggle. "What if his entourage was made up of puppets." Covering my mouth, I did my best to cackle in silence.

"How is that funny or practical?"

"Okay, not practical, but it's funny."

"Uhm…no."

"That's why you work in admin and not in the writers' room." The door abruptly opened, giving Joseline and me zero time to look like we weren't snooping. From my crouched position, I stared up at Rustin Hayes. *The* Rustin Hayes. "I found it," I called out, flashing the earring I'd covertly removed from my ear in my hand.

"You did? Great." Joseline understood the assignment.

Popping up, I straightened my skirt. "My bad. I dropped my earring, but crisis averted. We found it." I made a big show of displaying the gold bamboo earring to Brea and Rustin.

His brown eyes settled on me. "Good thing you found it, because if not, you'd have to spend the day walking around with one door knocker, and that would be ridiculous."

"And completely asymmetrical. He gets it." I pointed to him and laughed.

Brea's gaze pinged from Joseline to me. She wasn't buying our bullshit, but she painted a smile on her face. "Rustin, you've already met my assistant, Joseline, but you haven't met Letitia Vincent, one of our talented puppeteers."

Rustin extended his hand, and I slipped mine in his. "Nice to meet you. I've heard good things," he said.

"Yeah. Nice to meet you too. When you say you've heard good things—"

"Your reputation precedes you."

"I have a reputation?"

"Yeah. People say all kinds of things about you."

"Hopefully, it's all good things."

"Mostly."

Mostly? What the fuck was that supposed to mean?

Rustin turned to Brea. "It was good meeting with you. I'm looking forward to this new endeavor."

Brea was all teeth and gums. "Me too. See you soon."

He left the small, cube-filled room and disappeared down the hall.

"What was that about?" My mind was racing with a laundry list of questions.

"Why were you two huddled at my door?" Brea asked.

"Earring. Remember?" I tapped my earlobe.

"People who sneak around fishing for gossip have to pay the toll."

Nodding in agreement, I said, "Done. I will buy your first drink at happy hour on Friday. Now, spill."

Brea was my best friend. When I started working here, we immediately clicked. She was several years older than me. Our relationship was giving *big sis, little sis* vibes, which I needed after moving to New York and knowing no one. Brea had taken me under her wing. She got my quirky sense of humor—most people didn't— and she was ten times cooler than I was.

Her style included timeless statement pieces, while most of my outfits were thrifted. Brea owned a beautiful condo on the Upper West Side, and her wife was a famous ob-gyn, which was crazy because I didn't know you could get famous for administering medical care. Maybe Mother Teresa and Florence Nightingale were the two exceptions. Brea didn't need to work but preferred staying busy, so she'd landed at *Junction*.

"Mr. Hayes is joining the staff," she announced.

"Told ya," Joseline chimed in, returning to her desk.

I followed Brea into her office. "Did he lose a bet or something?"

"No. He heard we were dealing with threats to shut us down."

"I thought you said those threats were all smoke."

"I said that so you wouldn't freak out."

"*Should* I be freaking out? Brea, I just bought an apartment."

"*Jellybean Junction* has been on the National Community Network for close to fifty years. We have some staunch supporters, and we won't go down without a fight."

"So, there's going to be a fight? I'm not good with my hands."

"And that's why we hired Rustin."

"We have one-ply toilet paper in the restrooms. How were we able to afford Rustin Hayes?"

"The cheapo toilet paper, watered-down coffee, and the air conditioning set to only kick in when temperatures reach over eighty all helped."

"We have people in costumes sweating their balls off, you monster."

"This is a good thing. It ensures we all have jobs…at least for the next few months."

"Very funny." I laughed, but Brea didn't join in. "Why aren't you laughing?"

"I'm laughing on the inside."

If Brea thought we'd be okay, I trusted her. The alternative was obsessing over the possibility of the show going belly up. And the chances of that were like being killed by a meteorite. Have you met someone who died by a meteorite? No. Then I rest my case. This show would be around long after I retired. And thanks to Uncle Sam, that would be thirty or forty years from now.

I flipped through a binder on her desk filled with fabric. "So, Rustin… He's taller than I expected."

"He's also fine as hell."

"I guess if you go for that type."

"What type is that?"

"You know, perfect teeth, hard body, a mustache that connects. No tan line on his ring finger."

"I noticed that too."

"Not that I'm interested, 'cause he's clearly not my type."

"Yeah. He looks nothing like the brothers you usually date."

That felt like an insult. "Are we still on for dinner tonight? Because I really need a home-cooked meal."

"Yes, but maybe if you unboxed the cookware I gifted you, you'd be able to make your own meals."

"I'm working on it. I just moved in."

"You closed two months ago."

"Yeah…just moved in." My eyes shot wide open. "Shit. I left Aaliyah in the breakroom."

"Puppets are like Gremlins—you can't feed them after midnight, never get them wet, and don't leave them alone."

"That's not one of the rules," I said, rushing out of her office.

Brea and Sandra's apartment was a stunning space with magnificent views. When I dreamed of living in New York, this was the home I'd envisioned. As an adult, I now understood a home like this was reserved for the uber wealthy, and since I didn't get adopted by Lionel Richie, I'd ended up with a studio apartment. Don't get me wrong, I loved my place in Morningside Heights, and I was blessed to be able to afford anything in this market. My home may be modest, but once I fixed it up, it would be cozy and, more importantly, all mine.

"The tickets go on presale in a week. I want to be close but not standing close," Sandra said.

"I've been to standing concerts, and the trick is to wear good shoes. It isn't about fashion; it's about stamina and good arch support." I shoved a brussels sprout into my mouth.

"We should get seats together and hire a car for the night," Brea suggested.

Anjeni concert tickets were going for close to one thousand dollars a pop. I was part of the fandom, but I was also house poor. "I'm going to have to sit this one out. My budget does not include concert tickets. Maybe an indie underground nightclub where the entrance fee is ten bucks, but stadium tours are a no-go."

Sandra brushed my words aside. "We can cover you. I know you're good for it."

"That's sweet, but actually I'm not."

Learn from my example: get you a friend or two who are financially secure. I never had to open my wallet when we went out to brunch. It was as close to being a kept woman as I would ever get.

"Everyone gets a bit thrifty after a home purchase. This too shall pass," Brea said, doing her best to reassure me. She was probably right, but right now, spending unnecessary funds was a hard no for me. I went on dates for the free meals. If there was a love connection, that was just a bonus.

"So, tell me about Rustin. What was he like?" Sandra asked.

"He looks like a baby," Brea said.

"What is he, twenty-nine?" Sandra poured me another glass of wine—the good kind, not the cheap-o stuff.

"Yeah, something like that."

"Did you two talk about *U-turn*?" I wanted to get to the good parts.

"I mentioned how much I like it, and he seemed to be embarrassed by the compliment."

"I auditioned for a role—a minor role—a few years back."

Sandra narrowed her eyes. "You would've been perfect for that musical because you're not afraid to look dumb."

"Gee, thanks."

"It was a compliment. Too many actors and performers are more concerned with how they personally look rather than what's best for the character."

My cheeks flushed from the kind words. I would never admit this publicly, but I *loved* compliments. It could be as simple as "nice dress," or a remark about my penmanship. If your opinion of me was favorable, I was likely to keep you close. Maybe because compliments were in short supply growing up. "Tell us more, Brea."

"Obviously he was familiar with *Jellybean Junction*—I mean, who isn't? And he had nothing but praise for the show and cast."

"Did he say why he was interested in joining said cast?"

"No. For the most part, we kept it light."

"Hopefully he understands his place in the food chain," Sandra said.

"What do you mean?" I asked.

"He just can't come in on day one swinging his dick around and making demands. There's a hierarchy."

"Yeah, sure, of course. And when you say hierarchy, what do you mean?"

"Brea's the showrunner, so the buck stops with her. Yeah, he's the producer, but Brea is well versed on the ins and out on set, and he should defer to her—at least until he gets his footing."

"He seemed like a man with big opinions," Brea noted.

Sandra didn't back down. "He may have a ton of ideas, and it's possible they're all great, but it all needs to be run by you first. Because he's Rustin Hayes, he definitely has more cache than, say... Letty or Grumpy Gus."

"Now hold on. What about seniority? Doesn't that count for something?"

"Seniority kind of gets thrown out the window when you hire the Michael Jackson of puppeteering."

"I thought Jim Henson held that title," I said.

"Modern puppeteering. Does that make you feel better?"

No, it did not. I was just getting into a groove. Aaliyah was a popular character—the first Black female puppet in *Jellybean Junction*'s long history. In the writers' room, I finally felt comfortable enough to speak up, and some of my suggestions were getting incorporated into scripts. The wash day episode was all me. Our ballet class episode was also a Letitia Vincent original. Diversity was encouraged at *Jellybean Junction*, and I was forging a path of inclusion.

Growing up, I'd loved this show despite never seeing puppets that looked like me. Now, all these years later, we were closer to representing the world we lived in, which was why I was so passionate about the show, knowing little girls who looked like me saw themselves in Aaliyah. And if one little girl or boy looked at me and was inspired to pursue puppeteering, then my work was done. Because oftentimes we needed to see it to know it was possible.

Brea patted my arm in an attempt to reassure me. "I'm teasing, sort of. Don't worry. I'm positive Rustin will fit right in. And sure, he'll make some waves, but we're talking kiddie-pool–sized waves, not ocean tsunami."

CHAPTER 2
Rustin

"WHY IS THERE a cart filled with arms and legs in the entryway?"

"I'm about to load those up and take them to the theater. They'll be out of sight in ten minutes," one of the interns said.

"Thanks. Appreciate it." There was always something being prepped for transport—costumes, puppet parts, or scenery.

"What are you doing here?" Omar Mendoza, my best friend and business partner, asked.

"Can't I just stop by for shits and giggles?"

"No, because your presence makes people nervous."

"That sounds like a them problem."

Thread and Thespian Studio was located in Crown Heights, Brooklyn, founded eight years ago in my apartment with me pitching the idea to Omar while flipping through my multi-slide vision board. My goal was to cultivate a space for creatives in the puppeteering and animation sectors to thrive. Yes, we were behind the scenes, but we put our hearts and souls into the creation of these felt thespians. Puppeteering was my life's blood, and I wanted skin in the game.

Sure, I could work for one of the major studios, get paid beaucoup bucks, and just rest on my laurels, but where was the fun in that? I didn't want other people deciding my future, shooting down my ideas, or limiting my potential. My eyes were bigger than my stomach, and that made executives scared. Instead of taking a chance on a new original property, studio heads preferred repetition. Audiences loved that dinosaur movie last year—let's make ten more of those. As my own boss, I could greenlight new and exciting projects and take risks. And, truth be told, I didn't play well under others' authority.

"How'd your meeting go yesterday?" Omar was scrolling on his phone. When he died, he'd probably still be clutching his cell phone with an unfinished text flashing on the screen.

"It was promising. The showrunner was nice enough. The studio was well loved." I motioned for him to follow me to the food lounge.

"Is that a nice way of saying it's falling apart?"

Biting down on an untoasted Pop-Tart, I nodded. "Let's just say it's obvious they are on a shoestring budget."

"Yeah, and hiring you is about to put them in the poorhouse."

I kissed my teeth. "Trust, they couldn't afford me. That's why I lowered my rate."

"What do you mean? The man whose motto is 'Hustle until your money makes money' took a pay cut?"

"I'm just doing a little charity work for the greater good."

Omar eyed me skeptically. "You always have an end game, and you never do shit out of the kindness of your heart."

"That's a lie. Some things you can't put a price on."

"But?"

"Let's just say I'm keeping my options open."

Jellybean Junction was an American staple. Even with calls to defund the National Community Network, there was still major juice in the property. Like most kids, I'd grown up on the show, and in a time when quality educational programming was lacking, *Junction* was a godsend. I wasn't trying to disrupt that, but I did have strong ideas on the future of the show and ways to make it more sustainable.

The show had a Black female puppet, Aaliyah, but not a male one. My puppet, Jabari, which was being created specifically for the show, would bring balance, and it would create interesting scenes among the school-aged puppets. I also planned to introduce Jabari's father because I truly believed in positive images of Black families, and a Black father in particular was much needed.

"When do you start?"

"Next week. But I'm going to attend their happy hour on Friday."

"Look at you participating in shit." He tagged me on my arm.

"Shut up. I prefer to meet the cast in a relaxed setting. First days are stressful enough. At least I'll experience first-day jitters in a casual environment with a glass of liquor in hand."

"They are going to hate you."

"What do you mean? I'm a likable guy."

"Did somebody say lickable?" Rory Simmens said in his goofy stage voice, appearing out of nowhere with an unfinished puppet in tow.

"You and the puppet need to get out of my face." Puppeteers were never considered the cool kids, myself included. Often I had to soft-pedal my zeal because if you let me loose, I'd bore you with the history of puppeteering and its impact in Hollywood. Hiding how weird I truly was had spared me plenty of ass whippings growing up.

"I know when I'm not welcome," the puppet addressed Omar and me before Rory walked off.

"This is why people don't like us," I said, "because we insert inanimate objects into human conversations."

"And that is exactly how you're going to bomb on Friday night. I'm calling it. You're not good at peopling. You're like a human doppelgänger who malfunctioned while downloading code."

"We all can't be attention whores like you, my friend."

"Why I gotta be a whore?"

"Because you spread easy and often—just hugging anybody, shaking random unwashed hands, kissing strangers on the mouth." I walked away laughing.

People liked to call us the brain and the bronze because I was considered astute and Omar was six foot five. But Omar was more than just the muscle. He was the person who told me I was tripping when I stepped too far out of line. His honesty kept me grounded when I attempted to bite off more than I could chew. More importantly, on occasion, he indulged my delusions, especially when a big payday was attached.

The inbox on my desk was stacked with items for me to review. Taking a seat, I spent the next few hours approving fabrics and signing paperwork. Between this studio and my musical, I barely had time to catch my breath. My days were meetings, pitch sessions, writing, and trying to remember to eat. Adding *Jellybean Junction* to my already-packed schedule was asking for a one-way ticket to an IV drip and in-patient treatment for exhaustion. But I'd never been one to turn down an opportunity. I could sleep when I was dead. Right now, it was all about making it into the history books. In one hundred years, when people discussed the art of puppetry, I wanted Rustin Hayes to be referred to as a modern-day pioneer.

Plus, it was *Jellybean Junction*. My parents had watched the show as kids, I watched the show, and hopefully one day my future children would have that same experience. Who didn't love Lulu Lark, a cheerful musical bird that helped kids with numbers and letters? Or bookworm Oliver Oats, who always had a story to tell? My favorite, Rosie Riff, beatboxed and taught kids about rhythm and poetry.

The show got a lot of flak—people claimed it was old-fashioned, insisting today's kids were more interested in playing games on their phones or watching short videos online, but I knew that was a lie. *Jellybean Junction* was constantly innovating, and with the introduction of new characters like Aaliyah and the grandfather she lovingly called Pops, a world of new possibilities had opened, and I wanted in.

On Friday evening, I rolled up to the Honey Well, a nondescript bar in Harlem I would've missed if it weren't for the curved arrow pointing at a door. Before entering the building, I closed my eyes and took several deep breaths. In between, I mumbled a familiar reminder: "It's just a few hours, and by nine o'clock, you'll be back home in bed rubbing your feet together." Reaching for the door handle, I paused and whispered, "Don't be weird. Don't be weird. Don't be weird."

"Oh, you should definitely be weird," a soft voice called from behind me.

Speaking of weird, Letitia Vincent was just inches away from me. Her hair had a wild, untamed quality about it, but it was clear the style was a choice—one that made her stand out. Some people you could size up immediately, but this woman was a puzzle with her bangles, graphic T-shirt of *The Electric Company,* and bell-bottom jeans accentuating curves that were difficult to ignore.

"Hi. It's just that I don't like to show my neuroses in mixed crowds."

"Everyone who works on the show is a little off. I guess you kind of have to be if you spend most of your day with your hand stuck up a puppet's ass."

"That's one way to think about it."

"I'm just saying, being the new guy can be hard, but we're a pretty forgiving crowd."

"Just want to make a good impression. Is that stupid at my big age?"

"No. It would be strange if you didn't want to—like if your goal was to leave a sour taste in everyone's mouth, that would be odd."

I'd never been one to shy away from the weirdos and freaks, and it was clear Letitia fit comfortably in that category. Black nerds were part of an elite club because it didn't matter what hood you grew up in—being Black and a nerd was never considered cool. "Let me buy you a drink."

Her face lit up. "Oh, you're buying drinks. The crew is going to love you."

"Oh no. FYI: I'm buying *you* a drink. Just you."

"Okay. I like it. Fuck them. Cheers to you."

Inside, we made our way to the bar, where I opened a tab for a beer for me and a drink by the name of Dave's Lookin' Ass for Letitia.

"Is this the usual happy hour spot?" I asked.

"Every Friday without fail—well, one time we all got food poisoning…"

My face telegraphed my surprise. "Ouch."

"Day-old sushi. It was a mess. But other than that, we're pretty regular."

"Note to self: avoid sketchy platters of sushi lying around in the office."

"It wasn't sketchy—maybe it tasted a bit off. But hindsight is twenty-twenty." She bopped to the music playing so loudly it was difficult to hear. "So do you hate all happy hours or just this one?"

"I'm not really a gather-after-work-and-drink-with-coworkers type of guy."

"Antisocial. I can dig it." She leaned closer, yelling into my ear, "I'm the opposite of that."

"So, social?"

"Yeah, but let's go with the word *gregarious*. It rolls off the tongue better."

"You're very talkative."

"Well, we're strangers, so there's so much to learn. I don't know if you like pie or cake, or if your go-to dance move is the sprinkler, and you don't know—"

"Whether you take pauses in between sentences."

She took a long sip from her glass, scanning the crowd before turning back to me. "I do. You get what I did there?"

"Yep. I caught it. It's great." She was cute—a motormouth with the biggest brown eyes I'd ever seen, but cute.

"The last guy they hired didn't last three months."

"And you're expecting me to suffer that same fate?"

"No. You look like a guy who's up for a challenge."

"I once auditioned for *Outlast Island*."

She did a double take. "Really?"

"No. That's a lie. I just lied."

"It that something you do a lot, the lying?"

"No. Only when I'm trying to come off as more impressive than I am."

She pressed her hand to her chest. "Are you trying to impress me?"

I nodded. "Kinda sorta."

Letitia took another sip, and I was rewarded with a bright smile, a nod, and a view of her phat ass as she walked away. Damn, she was a nice surprise. The memory of her lingered long after she'd left, the corners of my mouth twitching into a smile at the thought of her. I wasn't antisocial, but I liked people in small doses. Intimate dinner parties were preferred over a night at the club any day. I was the guy who showed up to the grocery store right when it opened to shop in peace and avoid the crowd. If I RSVP'd, eight times out of ten I wasn't showing up.

It was my worst trait. I wasn't a homebody—I was just absolutely okay with being alone. Movies, museums, restaurants. I was a party of one. Solo dolo. The only company I needed was my own. But I must admit, Letitia was a nice distraction. She was bright and airy in a world where everyone took themselves too seriously. Okay, we get it you're an aerospace engineer, but are you down to play Racoon Tycoon or nah?

"You made it." Brea approached, arms spread wide. I didn't realize we'd reached the point of mandatory hugs.

"I'm not a hugger, if it's all the same to you."

"No problem. My wife is the same way."

"Yeah? How long have you been married?"

"Nine years."

"That's cool. Marriage is cool." And this was exactly why I didn't do happy hour, because I ended up looking like an idiot.

"Have you had a chance to meet anybody?"

"I bumped into Letitia on my way in."

"Hopefully she didn't scare you off."

"No. Actually, she was very kind."

"Well, come, come. Let me introduce you to the others." I followed Brea through the crowd and to a small outdoor patio area sandwiched between brick façade brownstones. She clapped, drawing attention to herself and me. "Announcement: As some of you already know, we have a new member joining our team. All, I want to introduce you to Rustin Hayes. He needs no introduction, I'm sure, but I'll give it a shot. Rustin is a genius, and his studio Thread and Thespian has worked in television, stage, and film. Speaking of the stage, Rustin is the brainchild behind *U-Turn*, a revolutionary musical starring an all-puppet cast. We are so happy to have you on our team, and I'm excited to witness all we can do together."

The cast broke out into not-so-quiet whispers.

Brea patted me on the back. "Please feel free to speak."

"Uhm, thank you. I fear that introduction was more than I deserved. I'm just so excited to be a part of *Jellybean Junction* and to work with a cast and crew that's fighting the good fight and doing the much-needed work for the children in our community. I look forward to getting to know each and every one of you."

At this point, you'd expect applause, or at the very least murmurs welcoming me, but my new team seemed stunned silent. Was my addition really that off-putting? Not trying to brag, but I was a pretty big deal. So, attaching myself to the production could only be seen as a good thing—worthy of applause, raised glasses, and enthusiastic handshakes.

"Yeah, Rustin. Welcome to *Jellybean Junction*. Woot, woot, woot, woot." Letitia was in the back attempting to hype up the crowd.

A man raised his hand, and Brea called on him.

"Hello. My name is Stanley Dinkle, and I'm the puppeteer for Grumpy Gus and several other side characters. Are we getting fired?"

"Uhm…no." I looked at Brea. "No?"

"No one is going to be fired."

There was a lone hand clap in the back from Letitia. "Yay! That's good news, 'cause layoffs make me sad and potentially homeless. So up with job security. I think in honor of Rustin joining the team, we should all buy him a drink."

"Oh no, not all of you," I said. "That could be dangerous and potentially lethal."

"You're right. I didn't think about that. I'll do my part and *not* buy you a drink, but Stanley really should because he's the *Jellybean OG.*" Stanley flashed her a pissed expression. "Maybe we should sing the theme song as a welcome."

"No." The cast and crew downvoted that suggestion in unison.

Undeterred, Letitia began to sing, "Hop on board, come take a ride. To a magical place where fun's inside." The groans drowned her out. "No? Okay. Maybe later."

I leaned toward Brea and asked, "How many drinks has she had?"

"Just one. That's all her. We don't allow her to have sugar on set."

CHAPTER 3
Letitia

I FOUND MYSELF in the puppetry and costume design department tinkering with Aaliyah. Puppeteers had to have knowledge in a little bit of everything. You needed to be able to create a compelling character, understand camera angles and timing. Even though I was never on camera, I needed to be able to act, because tone and delivery of lines mattered more than anything. Right now, I was styling Aaliyah's hair.

Most puppets had a fixed appearance—they wore the same outfits and rocked the same hairstyle. What made Aaliyah special was her ever-changing style. One episode she'd have afro puffs, the next, curls with ribbons. For her next few appearances, she would have braids with beads attached. I'd already pitched an awesome idea about the sounds of her beads and music, which would include a history lesson regarding the styling.

"Why are you hiding out in here?" Phoebe Knowlton, our lead costume designer, asked.

"I'm not hiding."

"Well, you're not with the others enjoying day-old donuts in honor of the new guy, so something must be wrong." Phoebe's voice was coated and thick from a pack-a-day habit. Her style was Afrocentric. She wore long dresses in colorful Ankara fabric also known as African wax print. Mixed metal bangles ran up the length of both arms. She always rocked an ornate cowrie shell necklace, and on must days, her butt-length locs were piled on top of her head in a regal bun.

"Not really hungry." I'd already snagged two donuts before everyone else arrived.

"So does this mean the new guy is a dud?"

"No. Quite the opposite. Honestly, I just wasn't in the mood to hear everybody fawning over him."

"Whoa. Little Miss Optimistic woke up on the wrong side of the bed this morning."

"I didn't. It just takes me longer to process change."

"You think something fishy is going on?"

I crawled out from my hiding spot among piles of fabric and boxes, which created the perfect alcove. "I mean…" Scanning the room to confirm it was only me and Phoebe, I lowered my voice. "*Junction*'s budget is tight, and someone like Rustin isn't cheap."

"Kiddo, I've been in this business for quite some time, and I hate to say it, but I think the writing is on the wall."

"What do you mean?"

"People have protested all kinds of things, but never in my sixty-odd years has there been such a push to pull the plug on NCN. It's an educational network, for fuck's sake."

"Yeah, but that's all talk. Brea says everything is fine."

"She has to say that. If she told us the truth, most people would jump ship looking for a new gig. But not me. I'm going down with the cruiser." Her gold bangles made music when she waved her arms.

"Phoebe, the ship isn't sinking. My feet are completely dry."

She scanned my outfit, pointing to my bright yellow galoshes. "That's because you're wearing rain boots in ninety-degree weather."

"The weather app said there was a twenty percent chance of rain," I defended myself. "Plus, if the show was in jeopardy, Rustin would've passed. Who wants the albatross of a failed show on their résumé?"

"Rustin is our Obi Wan Kenobi—a last-ditch effort to turn things around before we hit an iceberg."

"How do you know these things?"

"Because I'm old. When you're tiptoeing toward the grave, you'll know things too."

My eyes glazed over. Phoebe was guessing at best. This job was all I'd ever wanted to do, and the specialty was so niche that if we all lost our jobs, we'd have to fight to the death for potential openings. Sure, I'd come across news that claimed *Jellybean Junction* was too progressive and trying to push inclusive agendas on children—which was silly, because it was just a kids' show about respecting our differences and learning your ABCs. The only agenda was helping kids to feel seen and accepted.

Benny Buttons encouraged curiosity by teaching us how to fix things. And Tilly Twiddle was a monster with an infectious giggle who adored word searches and puzzles. It was about learning. Why would anyone what to squash that? *Jellybean Junction* was woven into the fabric of our culture and society. It was an institution.

"We need to write to our local officials, or I could make some flyers. They can't take this away from me…and all the kids too." My breathing was shaky, and goosebumps pebbled my arms. "Did I mention I just bought an apartment?"

Phoebe bounced a nonchalant shoulder. "Or maybe I'm wrong. If Brea says everything is okay, then I'm sure she's right."

"It's a studio, six hundred square feet. It's small but the price tag wasn't."

"When can we expect the housewarming party?"

"The way shit is going, it's more likely to be a grand opening followed by a swift grand closing."

Phoebe grabbed my hand. "*Jellybean Junction* has been around for fifty years, and we ain't going nowhere." She picked through scraps of fabric, pulling out swaths she deemed worthy. "And if we do—"

"No, no. We aren't going anywhere, hard stop."

"Letitia?" Brea called.

"Back here."

Brea's head popped out from behind one of the racks. "Where were you this morning? You missed the welcome breakfast for Rustin."

"I wouldn't call old donuts and unfiltered coffee a welcome." Phoebe rolled her eyes.

"I'll have you know I brought in fresh coffee from Bean There Done That, thank you very much."

"So, Rustin gets a coffee budget?" Everything in the breakroom was community funded. The cast and crew had pooled their money to get a sixty-dollar microwave. We brought in condiments to share. I stole creamer from my local coffee shop to replenish dwindling stock. Everyone did their part to keep costs as low as possible. The less waste, the more money could be rolled into production and paying the cast and crew. "On my first day, there were half-eaten bagels and over-pulped orange juice."

"The juice with the extra pulp is cheaper."

"I bet you wouldn't force Rustin to drink excessively pulped OJ."

"Letitia Vincent, are you jealous?"

"No, I'm not. I'm hungry, house poor, and I have a stubborn patch of eczema on my forearm, but jealous? Don't be ridiculous."

"Yep. She's jealous," Phoebe confirmed while Brea nodded in agreement.

"I looked it up," I continued. "Guys like Rustin can get paid anywhere from eighty to one hundred and fifty thousand dollars—that's per episode, by the way."

"If you think we're paying Rustin over one hundred thousand, you're wildin' out."

I'm not saying I deserved to get paid more, but if we were financially strapped, hiring someone as experienced as Rustin Hayes wasn't adding up. No one knew this more than Brea. She was the queen of making something out of nothing. So, the inclusion of a puppeteer with more than two hundred and seventy thousand followers on HypeLoop was a big deal. Maybe I was a little salty because I'd only just cracked ten thousand, but…I wasn't a hater. It was just that the more I thought about it, the weirder it all seemed. Why would a man with an indie studio and a Broadway musical need *Jellybean Junction*? I loved this show, and I'd be damned if some random from Brooklyn crashed the party trying to change shit.

Junction was a well-oiled machine, and the kids loved our shows because they were relatable and included real people from the neighboring community, like the locksmith from the East Village, the beekeeper from upstate, and the dancers from the Alvin Ailey Dance Company. Rustin was all flash, and if he thought our puppets were going to be dropping F-bombs and singing about S-E-X like they did in his musical, he had another think coming.

Granted, I'd seen the musical three times, and what he was doing on the stage and for the puppeteering community was amazing. *He* was amazing. Maybe I was a little jealous because if *Junction* had someone like Rustin, then why would they need me? I was good at my job and had fresh and innovative ideas, but I wasn't fully confident I could compete.

"Did you get a chance to review the script changes?" Brea asked.

"Yes. I was up past my bedtime trying to memorize them. You know I don't do well with impromptu changes."

"I know, and I apologize, but Rustin had some last-minute thoughts."

"Rustin? So now we're deferring to him?"

"We hired him to make improvements."

"Did you tell him script edits should be submitted in timely fashion—not just as a courtesy but because Letitia succeeds when she has the proper time to prepare?"

"No, because I didn't think it was my place to share that you're dyslexic."

"When I look unprepared, I want him to know it's not a knock on my work ethic," I said.

"Noted. Rustin's first table read is in fifteen minutes, and I expect you to be there."

"Have I ever missed a table read?"

"No. Listen, this episode will be the first time viewers meet his character," Brea said. "For that, I chose to indulge him a bit. Is that okay?"

"It's fine. His changes were fine."

"All right. You've got five more minutes to pout, and then you need to head down."

"I'm not pouting," I shouted, my bottom lip poking out as Brea walked away.

Why was I nervous? It wasn't my first day, but this week's episode had been completely reworked to introduce Rustin Hayes's characters.

And this would be the first table read. I liked to be prepared. My scripts were color coded. Each character was assigned a color. Aaliyah was purple. After reading the script in its entirety, I would add notes to the margins about the tone of each scene, which would help to inform my line delivery.

Next, I'd memorize the entire script. When it was time to rehearse, I knew my lines and the dialogue for my scene partner, which was why diverting from the script caused me anxiety. I wasn't quick on my feet, not with everyone watching and expecting me to perform. Don't get me wrong, I was capable of improvisation. I just needed a heads-up so I could plan my on-screen spontaneity.

The show was made up of prerecorded material that could've been filmed several weeks prior to the official taping. These segments focused on people and places in the community. *Jellybean Junction*'s studio was located in New York, so much of our real-life segments featured the city and the people who lived in it.

The puppet portions of each episode were filmed in studio and tied into the real-world segments. This week's episode was about Harlem's green spaces, including Marcus Garvey Park and a community garden. To tie it all together, the puppets would be starting their very own vegetable garden and talking about food deserts. All of this was exciting and useful information, and Aaliyah would play a prominent role alongside Rustin's puppet, whom I hadn't even met.

Yes, it was important to meet the puppet I'd be acting with. Based on their vibe, the recitation of my lines could vary. And I kind of wanted to make a good impression on Rustin's first day. He was a power player in this very exclusive club, of which I wanted to remain a member.

In the conference room reserved for table reads, potlucks, and group venting sessions, I pulled Brea aside. "Have you seen Rustin's new characters?"

"No, but I trust they'll be on brand. You wouldn't ask Bisa Butler to preview her work, would you?"

Bisa Butler was an extremely talented fabric artist who incorporated quilting into her portraits. "No."

"Exactly. He's a genius, and he's going to create puppets that fit our aesthetic while offering something unique, just like you did with Aaliyah."

Brea knew I was a compliment whore, and on cue, the corners of my mouth curved. "Why do I have all the scenes with him?" Rustin and I were slated to appear on screen together for all the in-studio scenes.

"He requested it."

"Excuse me?"

"It makes sense. His puppet is the same age as yours. Why wouldn't the two hang out together?"

"But Aaliyah doesn't like boys—she thinks they're yucky and infected with cooties."

"Maybe Rustin's character will change her mind. Speaking of…" In walked Rustin with a large bag. "Welcome to our humble conference room."

"Thank you," he said. "It's good to be here. I read through the script, and I'm really excited."

"Read and made changes," I noted aloud.

Rustin chuckled. "Read and made minor changes."

"Hmm. And yet every page was filled with red-lined notes."

"That's kind of how I work. I like things to be polished."

"I wrote the first scene. It was *sparkling*."

Brea yanked on my sleeve.

"Consider it a collaboration. Your initial ideas and my refined hand," he said.

Bitch. I recognized a subtle dig when it was presented. I'd heard a lot of things about Rustin Hayes—he was an ego monster, a perfectionist, and a control freak. Now that I was getting a firsthand experience of him, I could swear under oath that all the rumors were true.

Brea pinched me, stalling my objection. "Since the man of the hour is here, I say we start."

I secretly rolled my eyes. *Rustin this, Rustin that. He's a genius.* Yes, I was coming down with a minor infection of hateration. Mary J. Blige would be so disappointed. In most instances, I was mild. I wasn't a hater by nature, but I was very competitive. One time during Bunco, I'd punched someone in the face. What made it especially heinous was the setting, a senior living facility. Needless to say, my volunteering days were cut short and I was kicked out, but that old biddy deserved it.

"Let's start with an icebreaker," Brea said with a big smile that didn't falter due to the lackluster response. Even the new guy appeared to be annoyed, flinching as if he'd gotten a whiff of something foul. "If you had a teleportation machine in your house that could go to one location, where would that location be?"

"That's easy," Stanley called out. "Atlantic City to test my hot hand."

"Really?" Rustin's brow furrowed. "What's your game of choice?"

Before Stanley could answer, I spoke up. "This man would bet on a guinea pig race if he thought the odds were in his favor."

"What's that saying, you have to play to win?" Stanley coughed out.

"Yeah, but the way you play, winning is few and far between," Diego teased.

"You joke now, but when I win at the craps table, don't ask me to comp you at the buffet. You know, I'm thinking we should do a very special episode of *Jellybean Junction* and take a trip to Atlantic City—show the kids what the real world is like."

Rustin was the only one to laugh.

"He's actually serious," I said.

"Then that's a hard pass."

"I'm shocked." I said. "Aren't you the guy who has puppets saying the F-word and humping on stage?"

"It's an adult show, and there's no humping on stage."

"Uhm, I've seen the show three times. There's *some* humping," I corrected him.

Brea audibly breathed through her nose. "Can we please stop talking about humping and gambling and get back on track? Rustin, where are you teleporting to?"

"My grandmother's kitchen. She's the best storyteller, and her stories come with a warm plate." My eyes performed a three-hundred-and-sixty-degree roll. "Leigh Hayes is my favorite person in the whole world."

For much of this meeting, he'd looked like he was constipated, constantly bouncing his leg and eyeing the exit. But talk of his grandmother seemed to temporarily soothe his nerves. I mean, I get it; some grandmothers were cool—mine wasn't, but not everyone was as unfortunate as me.

Any time there was a new hire, the social stratum shifted. Alliances were tested and new friendships formed. And all of a sudden, Phoebe, the costume designer, was skipping lunch to hang with the new guy and my supply of cute ribbons ran dry. Ribbons that I relied on for Aaliyah's hair and mine. I'd been able to strategically wedge myself in with the cool cast members. Last summer, I'd had a knock-down, drag-out silent feud with Stanley, who for some reason was among the cool puppeteer ranks. And yes, he was an icon and a legend, but I needed the social cred. So, I may have let it slip that Stanley was the refrigerator bandit. He'd been secretly stealing other people's food for months. He'd taken an entire slice of apple pie from me. Who does that? A social deviant, that's who.

That bit of intel garnered me a coveted spot at the popular lunch table. But with Rustin's appearance, my hold was tenuous.

Pulling my puppet from my bag, I took a seat at the long oak table. This table had been here forever. Phoebe said it was the original one from when the show started fifty years ago. Could you imagine the gossip this table could share if it had a mouth? I mean, it would also be terrifying sitting here while the table cleared its throat.

"Letty, you're up." Brea pulled me from my thoughts.

"I'd set my teleporter to Glazed Over so I could roll out of bed and get donuts fresh out of the oven at five in the morning."

Rustin's gaze settled on me. He was the type of individual who could wear a mask at will, so it was difficult to determine what he was thinking. His effect was neutral—he wasn't amused or perplexed, but his eyes were curious, searching my face for an answer to a question only he had knowledge of. I was the complete opposite; my face was representative of exactly how I felt at any given moment. As you can imagine, it made things very difficult at table reads and pitch meetings.

"Let's start with the first scene. Letitia, whenever you're ready." Brea nodded in my direction at the same time Rustin removed his puppet from his bag.

"Whoa, is that your puppet?" Valerie, who voiced Lulu Lark, asked.

"Yeah. This is Jabari." Rustin raised his arms high so everyone could get a good look. Jabari was similar to Aaliyah but slightly better. His clothes were more vibrant, and his hair was styled in a curly, tapered fade.

"Nice. A dude puppet, very original. Did you say his name was Jabari?" I asked.

"Yes."

I could see right through him. So, he'd just *happened* to create a kindergarten-aged puppet with an Afrocentric name. I'm not saying he was stealing my intellectual property, but Aaliyah was the first Black puppet to appear on *Jellybean Junction*, if you could believe that. In the early days, there were just monster puppets and live-action actors, then they introduced puppets that were supposed to represent humans. Those puppets were orange, green, blue, or some other vibrant color. But now we were including puppets that were undeniably specific. Aaliyah was obviously Black with her rich brown color and hair.

While I welcomed the inclusion of more Black characters… No, that was the full statement. Inclusion of additional Black characters was welcomed. One of my deep-seated beliefs was that people were out to get me. I was adopted at the age of three, and although I barely remembered the first few years of my life, it was clear those experiences had left a lasting impression. Rustin didn't know me, so why would he be gunning for me?

"Should we start?" Brea asked.

"I, for one, am very excited to embark on this journey." My voice had a cheery demeanor. Brea flashed a glance in my direction, which told me I had too much dip on my chip. "Reasonably excited. Not excited to an excessive degree," I added, trying to course-correct.

"I'll read the action line. This first scene includes Letitia and Rustin. After each action line, you'll pick up where your characters speak. Rustin, we keep things pretty casual here, but I do like to read each scene all the way through and ask everyone at the table to be supportive and respectful."

"I like it, and I can use all the support I can get, so thank you," Rustin replied.

How did he always know the right thing to say? Outside the bar at happy hour, I got the sense he was shy, but now he was smiling, cracking jokes, and being self-deprecating. The saying *fake it until you make it* came to mind. Maybe he was pretending to be confident and chill, but inside his skin was crawling and brain racing. New people didn't make me nervous, but I often overextended myself in an attempt to fit in.

And I had a desperate longing to be liked, which I was actively trying to rid myself of. Not everyone clicked or got my sense of humor, and that was okay. Also, I was intimately familiar with the taste of my foot because I was constantly putting it in my mouth.

Brea read through the opening paragraph, which set the scene, and then turned to me for the first line.

"Whatcha doing, Jabari?" I said in a high-pitched voice.

"My dad and I are going to start a community vegetable garden."

"What's that?

"It's a place we can plant seeds that grow into food we can eat."

"Like the tomatoes my mom gets from the grocery store?"

"Yep. Wanna help?"

"Excuse me?" Stanley interrupted. "Is it just me, or is this scene missing something? Perhaps we could add a grumpy monster for comic relief."

Rustin pretended he was seriously considering the suggestion. "I see where you're coming from, but I think we're already introducing some new concepts to the kids, and we don't want to overwhelm them with theatrics."

Take that, Stanley.

Brea chimed in, "This is what these table reads are for, brainstorming. Rustin, I'm loving this. Now for the next scene, Jabari's dad is going to explain the concept of food deserts?"

Rustin nodded. "Yes. He'll explain, and Jabari and Aaliyah will each ask questions."

"Great. I love it." Normally, Brea had more notes than just *I love it*. It was clear she didn't want to ruffle Rustin's feathers on his first day, which was cool overall. It was a great scene.

We dove into several other scenes, and it appeared that everyone, with the exception of Stanley, was on their best behavior. It was too early to let it slip that the cast was a dysfunctional band of rabble rousers. If we revealed that fact too soon, it might scare Rustin off. But we could only hold the mask up for so long. I think when I joined the team, it was rainbows and lollipops for a total of three days before two former cast members got into a fistfight with their puppets still on their hands.

Brea thanked us for our time and ended the table read. I collected my things and was prepared to make a quick exit so I could finish Aaliyah's hair.

"Hey. Can I have a word?" Rustin asked.

"Sure." I followed him to a less-populated corner of the room.

"First, I want to say I'm really excited to work with you. And I think Jabari and Aaliyah are going to have some fun adventures."

"Aaliyah and Jabari...but go on."

"I was hoping...if you were up to it...maybe we could set up a brainstorming session and write together."

My posture softened. Rustin Hayes wanted to be my writing partner. To put it in terms you'd understand, this was like Stevie

Wonder asking me to cowrite a song. Stevie didn't need my help—he was a musical powerhouse. What sentence could I suggest that would make "Ribbon in the Sky" any better? Rustin wasn't Stevie, but he was definitely being mentioned with the likes of Jim Henson and Kevin Clash.

While I was flattered, my creative process was a bit unconventional, and I preferred working alone. "I'm used to pitching my own ideas." Each week, we pitched stories in the hopes that they would make it onto a show. Cast members were allowed to submit up to three scenes. To qualify, the scene had to match that week's theme, and be educational and engaging. Occasionally one or more of us would team up to pitch something together.

"Two heads are better than one," he said.

"You're not going to do some felonious backstabbing shit, are you?"

"I wasn't planning on it, but I like to play things by ear."

"That's funny. You're funny, handsome, and talented."

"Handsome?"

"No, not to me, but I've heard others say it."

"So, in your opinion, I'm unattractive?"

"It's the ears. They're almost as big as your puppet Jabari's."

"That's why I wear beanies."

"I thought that was because of your big head," I joked.

"Are you talking about the actual circumference of my head or my ego?"

"Why not both?"

"How about a test-run writing session? I'll even buy the food."

I brightened. I was on a fixed income, and food that wasn't from a microwave was a hot commodity. "Can I pick the place?"

"Oh, I was just going get us hot dogs and two cans of soda from the guy on the corner, but I could swing a proper meal."

I moved from side to side, kicking my feet and waving my arms.

"What is this? What are you doing?" he asked.

"Food is my love language, so the thought of eating something hot and spicy gets me going."

"Let's make sure to get the wiggles out here, because I don't want you doing whatever the hell that is at the restaurant."

"You're looking at the three-time Irish dance competition winner."

"How the hell did you get into Irish dance?"

"Well—"

"You know what? Save it for lunch."

"I love an agenda. Second topic. Do you have supersonic hearing, or do you process sounds like everyone else?"

"Because of my big ears? Very funny. A little mean, but mostly funny."

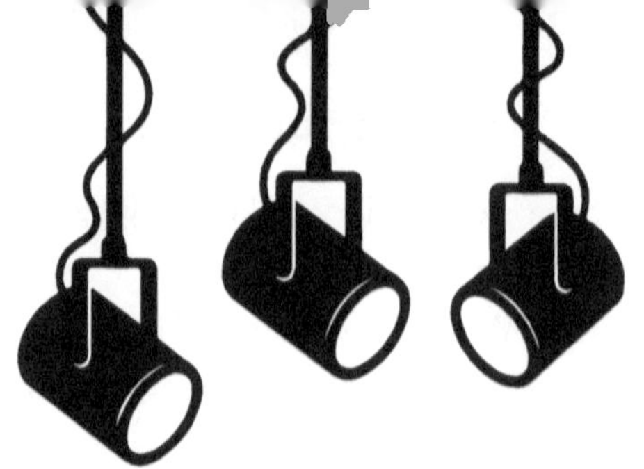

CHAPTER 4

Rustin

THE FIRST DAY was a blur. My second day was unremarkable, but the third day at *Jellybean Junction* was when I realized I should be receiving hazard pay. Viewers only saw the polished final product. What they didn't know was that shows on the National Community Network did not have the same budget, access, or support as shows on traditional network television. After reviewing the budget and profits, it was obvious we were constantly robbing Peter to pay Paul.

In the breakroom, I ventured to have a cup of coffee. The *Jellybean Junction* studio didn't seem to have two things that went together. Coffee but no sugar. Fans but no AC. Soap but no paper towels. I had to perform the shake-and-wipe on my pants in the bathroom. And before you start, I'm talking about my hands, you pervert.

Taking a slug of the bitter brew, I could feel my organs corrode.

"Do we have coffee on the premises that isn't a biohazard?" I asked.

"Yeah. Three blocks down and around the corner," Stanley joked.

"Shit. I don't even need the fancy pods. I'll take the canned stuff."

"That *is* the canned stuff. It's just generic from the dollar spot. Welcome to *Jellybean Junction*."

Was I spoiled? Yes. At my studio, there was an in-house coffee shop with the best drip brew for miles, warm, flaky pastries, and hearty sandwiches. Our staff worked hard and deserved to be rewarded with free food and sushi parties, minus the food poisoning. Everything about *Junction*'s facilities seemed neglected. In the bathroom, the laminate floors were peeling. The paint was chipped and probably lead based. And there was this smell that was impossible to shake. It left me checking my underarms, the fridge, or the person next to me to determine the source.

"Good morning." Letitia breezed into the breakroom, and the fluorescent lighting seemed to shine brighter. She had an aura about her that drew people in. Maybe I shouldn't speak for others, but she certainly had that effect on me. Her personal style was colorful and expressive, which made it hard for me to remain in a bad mood. Today she was rocking striped pants, a graphic T-shirt, a long-fringed sweater jacket, and ballet flats split at the toe, resembling animal hooves.

"Morning. How was the commute?" a crew member asked. I was still working on learning everybody's names.

"It was lovely. Being within walking distance of the studio is a real plus, because even when I'm running late, I can still be on time."

"You live in the neighborhood?" I ventured to ask.

"Yeah."

"She just brought her first place," Stanley said.

"It's only a studio apartment—nothing fancy, but the building is located on a really pretty block," she added.

"Congratulations. That's a big deal," I said.

"Rustin was just asking about the coffee," Stanley interjected.

"Ah, trust me, eventually it'll grow on you," she replied. "The coffee, the heat, the windows that are painted shut… All a part of working at this legendary studio."

"If you ask me, they should condemn it," Stanley said.

"No," Letitia and I said in unison.

"I just mean that this place is a landmark. Just think of all the amazing creatives who've walked these halls," I said.

"Exactly. It may be old and in need of a little TLC, but it has so much character and charm," Letitia added. "You can't get that from a modern studio."

"At this point, I'd opt for working AC," Stanley grumbled. The others left the breakroom, leaving Letitia and me alone.

"So, tell me the truth—is there a hidden breakroom where the coffee is actually potable?" I asked.

"What fun would that be…telling you. You need to discover these gems on your own. The secret coffee stash, the best bathroom for privacy, if you're in need of a good cry or a good shit. My favorite spot on the roof with spectacular views."

"Wow. Sounds like I have a lot to learn."

"Oh, and don't ever get into the freight elevator, because it may be haunted."

"By?"

"I don't know, an angry former employee or a possessed puppet who likes practical jokes."

"Take the stairs, noted."

Letitia unscrewed her coffee tumbler and poured a hearty serving. Taking a sip, she screwed her face up, and her next words were raspy. "Just needs some creamer and tons of sugar. The creamer helps to cut the bitterness."

"Is that the secret recipe?"

"At *Jellybean Junction*, we have to make do. When it comes to supplies, we either have too little or none at all. I interned at one of the big movie studios in college, and they had everything—catered food with coffee made by baristas and not a timer. And if you needed a button or bobbin, they had you covered."

"And then you came to public television."

"Talk about a reality check." Her big brown eyes landed on my features as if she were taking me in for the first time. "So, how's your first week going?"

"Good. Everyone's been really helpful."

"If you don't mind my asking, what made you join our little public TV powerhouse?"

"Honestly, because it's *Jellybean Junction*. It was kind of a no-brainer."

Her eyes narrowed as if she were running each of my words through a lie detector. "I agree, but you'd be surprised with the number of people who think the show is outdated."

"ABCs and one, two, threes never go out of style."

"This show is important to me and many others, and anyone who tries to jeopardize that will have to answer to me." Her normally soft features hardened, signaling she was prepared to fuck me up if the need arose.

Being the new guy wasn't only scary for me, but it was also anxiety inducing for the existing cast. It was understandable that the cast and crew would have questions about what role I intended to play. Not only was I introducing new characters, I was also the producer. Usually, a new producer meant change—often radical changes. "Message received."

"That wasn't a threat, by the way," Letitia said.

"No? 'Cause it felt threatening."

"Brea always tells me I have problems with my tone."

"I'll keep that in mind the next time you suggest fitting me with concrete shoes."

"I'll never be accused of being eloquent, but I hope you understand people's whole lives are wrapped up in this show. We're not here for money or fame. We're here because we love what we do. And this show gives us the opportunity to be creative and collaborative while giving back. *Jellybean Junction* is about making education fun. There's no need to tinker with that."

"That was pretty succinct to me," I said. "Sounds like you're putting me on notice."

"Consider *Jellybean Junction* my daughter and you the eager, pimple-faced, hormone-fueled teen boy accompanying her to the prom. I expect her to return home unbesmirched."

"Is that how prom night worked out for you?"

Her mouth fell open, and she served an incredulous stare. "Wow. You haven't even been here three days, and you're vying for a conversation with HR."

"Me? You were the one who was all like 'have my daughter back by midnight.'"

"And not a minute after." I thought she was joking but couldn't be certain.

"I understand you and the others are far more invested than I am, but I'm here because I want this to work, and I'm open to passionate discussions regarding how we accomplish that." I inched toward the door.

"I just might take you up on that, because I have *many* thoughts."

"And I'm excited to hear every last one."

Letitia's eyes grew wide, and her plump lips curved upward.

"Places, everyone," Diego called.

I was surprised to see Letitia heading to the soundstage with the Wendy Whimsy puppet in hand. She flashed a smile, taking her place next to me. "Wendy Whimsy is your creation?" Disbelief was clearly etched across my face. I'd spent most nights leading up to my first day reviewing employee files, and if that bit of intel was in there, I'd missed it.

"No, but Rhodes is retiring in a few months, and I'm adding the role to my roster, so we're just sort of alternating as a soft transition."

"Cool."

Wendy Whimsy was a monster puppet with blue fur and purple hair. Known as the show's storyteller, she'd share folklore from around the globe and invite viewers to join in on the magical adventures. It wasn't unusual for a puppeteer to voice several characters in one production. Experienced professionals were hard to come by, and on a show like *Jellybean Junction* you needed to be a jack-of-all-trades.

"Quiet on the set," an intern yelled out, and a reverent hush fell over the crew.

"Action," Diego half shouted and half whispered.

That was my cue for Jabari to speak. "Are the sun and moon friends?"

"You ask a complicated question. To answer it, I must first tell you why the sun and the moon live in the sky." Letitia's voice was now grounded and wizened, nothing like the puppet Aaliyah, whose cadence was bubbly and infectious, almost like a song. As she dove into the folklore about the sun and moon, the set remained hushed. Everyone on the soundstage was mesmerized by Letitia's performance. Her voice was expressive and deep, and if you closed your eyes, you'd think you were sitting with an ancestor while they shared their wisdom.

This was what made *Jellybean Junction* special. Storytelling was a tradition, and in some cases, a lost art form. This show introduced new concepts to viewers while breathing life into the past, through song, poetry, dance, and storytelling. Our cast was stacked, and Letitia was one of its brightest stars.

"Rustin, do you need me to feed you the next line?" Diego whispered.

I'd been so enthralled by Letitia's performance that I hadn't realized it was my turn to advance the conversation. After clearing my throat, I said, "My bad. I was lost in the folklore. I hope we got all that."

After the scene was completed, I followed Letitia to the meager craft table in the corner of the set. The table looked like a buffet ten minutes before closing, scattered with bruised bananas, sugar-free apple juice boxes, and Peppermint Patties, which in my opinion was an assault on the taste buds. Money was tight, but this was an insult. The staff was expected to do their best work, but resources were thin.

Letitia selected one of the minty chocolates, and I cringed. "Do you want one?" she asked.

Recoiling, I rebuked her offer. "Hell no."

"Do you have something against chocolate?"

"Chocolate I love, but mint and chocolate don't mix."

Unwrapping the mini-sized round, she popped it into her mouth. "Clearly it does," she said around her mouthful.

"Wow. Here I was thinking you were cool and interesting, and now I find out you're a mint-chocolate eater."

"All the trendy kids love minty freshness." She deliberately blew her fresh breath in my face.

I scanned the table, searching for words to say to keep her talking to me. "This is the saddest craft table I've ever seen."

"It's not usually this sparse. The team brings in homemade items all the time. Last week we had tamales."

"I don't eat other people's food."

"What do you do at restaurants?"

"That's different. There are laws and inspections that govern how they operate. But with office potlucks, you don't know if someone washed the greens in the bathtub or has a cat they allow to hang out on the kitchen counter. Or maybe they let their kid help make the cupcakes."

"You can't work at *Jellybean Junction* and hate kids."

"I don't hate kids. I hate their lack of hygiene. Just walking germ factories."

"That's why I send up a prayer before ingesting anything. After that, it's in God's hands."

"God and the nurse who's going to have to pump your stomach."

"I've never had a problem. It's been over ten years since I last vomited. It was due to late-night tacos after the club."

She was conveniently ignoring the office food poisoning. "What about the tainted sushi?"

"I was sick, but I didn't vomit, and let's just leave it at that."

"Let's hope your streak remains intact."

"I have a grandmother who puts raisins in the potato salad, so I think I'll be fine."

"No shit. What does that taste like, exactly?"

"You know—"

"Don't. Please don't." If she said anything other than *disgusting*, I was canceling her.

"—it's actually not that bad."

I groaned, and Letitia reached out, grabbed my arm, and gave it a soft squeeze. Her nose crinkled as her sweet giggle rang out. *Hmm.* At the same moment, my heart went into erratic pitter-patters. I wasn't anxious—quite the opposite. I was enjoying my conversation with Letitia. She was so full of life, and her presence was almost whimsical. My glass was half empty while hers seemed to always be overflowing.

"I'll make it for you, and I bet I'll change your mind," she said.

"And I will respectfully place the untouched paper plate in the trash face down."

A sudden loud boom pulled me from my starry-eyed state. The sharp crack was so intense it reverberated across the set. Cries and hurried footsteps activated my protector mode. Wrapping my arm around Letitia's waist, I pulled her toward me, trying my best to protect her from the cascading shards of glass raining down all around us, hitting the floor of the soundstage. Her screams of fear made me hold her tighter. Letitia buried her face into the crook of my neck, and the warmth of her breath momentarily distracted me from the fear of being electrocuted. After the falling glass settled, in the rafters there was a lingering low humming, and the studio was partially dark.

"Are you okay?" I stepped back so I could examine her for any cuts or scrapes.

"What the hell was that?" she asked while shaking glass from her hair.

"I think all the light bulbs just blew out." Squinting in the darkness, I tried to locate our director. "Diego?"

"Yeah, boss," a voice called from across the room.

"Are we good?"

"I think so. I'm going to check the circuit breaker."

"Has this happened before?" I removed my beanie, shaking out loose pieces of glass.

"No. Not since I've been here."

Claiming Letitia's hand, I walked over to the nearest exit, opening the door. "The lights are still on in the hall, which is a good thing. Looks like only the studio was affected."

"This building is a landmark," she said.

"Yeah, a landmark with bad wiring. Are you sure you weren't hurt?"

"More scared than anything else."

I glanced at our hands, still entwined. Her hand was the perfect fit, and part of me didn't want to let go. "I should give you back your hand." Reluctantly I allowed her digits to slip from mine.

"Thank you for looking out for me. One time, there was a small toaster fire in the breakroom, and Stanley pushed me aside on the way to the door."

"Fired. He's immediately off the payroll," I joked.

Her carefree giggle returned. "I'm gonna go find a dustpan and broom so we can clean this all up."

Did I watch her walk away, her hips swaying from side to side, until she was out of view? Yes. There was just something about her I couldn't quantify or express in words. How do you describe that tingly sensation at the bottom of your stomach or the tickle in your brain making room for your next all-consuming fixation?

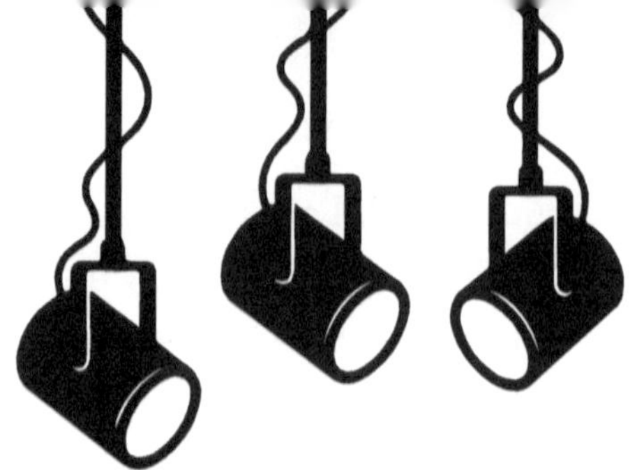

CHAPTER 5
Letitia

BREA WAS AT my place opening boxes I'd neglected for far too long.

"What is this?" She held up a sardine baking dish I'd promised to donate when I was packing for the move.

"In my defense, it's a really cute dish."

"Yes, but you said you wanted a grown-woman apartment, and all I'm seeing are cupcake stools and these kitschy ceramic tomatoes."

"Are you here to help or attack my design choices?"

"Is that what you're calling this? I lost the battle over how you dress—"

"Hey, my style is thrift-store chic."

Brea scanned the length of my body, a disapproving tilt to her mouth. "All I'm saying is maybe you're still single because you wear shit like that." She pointed to my wide-collared ruffled shirt that was very much giving *Little House on the Prairie*.

"Wow. You sound like my mother: 'Letty, you're such a pretty girl. You should wear clothes that demonstrate that.'" I performed a perfect imitation of my mother's mild New England accent.

"Eloise makes a good point."

I took pride in my unique sense of style. Growing up in a predominantly white suburb in Connecticut, I'd spent most of my life trying to fit in. I was a dark-skinned Black girl with type 4C hair. Those two traits alone drew attention. So, as a teenager I'd dressed like everybody else and pretended to like Hayden from the popular group Boys Tyme. Moonstruck Hollow was the trending angsty series, and I read every book, even though both of the male love interests were toxic fuckboys. And I became a cheerleader to cancel out the fact that I was vice president of the puppet and animatronic club.

When I was accepted into Langston Blythe University, an HBCU, it was the first time I'd felt safe enough to explore what being Black actually meant. According to my mother, my family didn't see color—which was crazy, because everyone else did. Four years in college taught me to embrace all the things that made me unique and vow never to conform for the purpose of making others feel comfortable.

"How do you think the first week with Rustin went?" I asked.

"Uhm, I like him."

"But? I can hear a but." My tone was giddy from the prospect of fresh gossip.

"It's just that some of his ideas are too lofty for our meager budget."

"Part of what makes the show so special is our ingenuity." I unwrapped salt and pepper shakers in the shape of a shell and a pearl and placed them on the kitchen counter.

"Ingenuity is great; cash flow would be better."

"We've always operated on a shoestring budget and managed."

"That's the thing—Rustin had his accounting firm review the books."

"And?"

"Based on donation trends and growing inflation, *Jellybean Junction* has six months—maybe a year, tops."

My head jerked back, and I blinked rapidly in an attempt to process the news. "So, we find more donors."

"I've been trying. Puppet shows are a dying art form." Brea lifted a red crab figurine and motioned to the trash.

Snatching Mort the Crab from her hands, I dusted it off. "That's not true. Kids and adults love puppets. They hold a sense of whimsy and magic. And they allow us to tell stories we wouldn't be able to practically."

"You're preaching to the choir."

"Two weeks ago, you told me *Jellybean Junction* was good."

"I didn't want to stress you out for no reason. I was hoping Rustin's review of the books would reveal something different."

"Is this final?"

"It's not final, but it's a real possibility. Rustin's going to make an announcement next week, and then he'll implement a stopgap plan."

"Okay," I said. "Do you remember that episode of *My Brother Damarcus*? The one where the kids are trying to save the community center and they sell lemonade." *My Brother Damarcus* had been a popular sitcom when I was growing up.

"You want to open a lemonade stand?"

"I mean the lemonade could be spiked, and then we could charge more."

"We'd need to sell a shit-ton of lemonade for that to work."

"You can't just give up."

"I'm not giving up, but we also have to be realistic," she said.

"Realistic? If *Jellybean Junction* ends, you'll just go back to your penthouse on the Upper West Side, replacing your nine-to-five for ladies-who-lunch events. But for me and many others in the cast and crew, this could uproot our entire lives."

"Are you suggesting I don't care?"

"No. I'm just saying the stakes are higher for some, and I think every option should be considered. I could operate a RideX on nights and weekends."

"You don't have a car," Brea pointed out.

"Technicality."

"This is why I didn't want to tell you. You're like Evilene."

"Nobody likes receiving bad news," I yelled, my chest tight. Buying this apartment was the scariest thing I'd ever done, and now I was about to be unemployed. My skills were not transferable. Maybe I could audition to become Elle the Elephant, mascot for the New York Liberty.

Who was I kidding? I didn't have her coordination or swag.

"I think it's time for wine," Brea said.

"Yes, I agree, but all I have is probiotic soda pop. And looking back on it now, who the fuck did I think I was buying name-brand pop? My bank account is generic pop at best."

"I tell you what… If you change that ugly-ass shirt, we can get some drinks, my treat."

I pulled the top over my head without undoing a single button. "Done."

After we hit up a local bar, Brea wanted to check out a lounge in Midtown, and since she was still generously paying, I was down for the trek. We stalked the bar until we got seats and were now enjoying the fruits of our labor—Brea with a gimlet, which was what I considered a grown-up drink. Old Fashioneds, Manhattans, and gimlets were all drinks people ordered when it was still acceptable to smoke indoors and men wore suits to the club. I, on the other hand, ordered a mai tai because I like my drinks to feel like I am on vacation.

"What are you going to do if the show ends?" I asked.

"I don't know. Maybe adopt a baby. Sandra and I have been talking about it, but it never seemed like the right time." Brea leaned in closer, speaking louder over the crowd. "I'd been meaning to ask you about your thoughts on the whole process, seeing how you have firsthand knowledge."

I shrugged. "I can only speak about it from an adoptee perspective."

"That's exactly what I want to know about."

"Honestly, looking back on it, I was just grateful for a home. No one wants to be alone in this world. And at least I have...*family*."

Brea examined my features. "Why'd you say it like that?"

"Like what? I mean, if I had any advice to give, it would be to make sure you really want to nurture and love a child. Most people just want a kid but don't take into consideration all the extra responsibilities that come along with it. It's more than just really wanting a baby...so much more."

I'd been adopted at the age of three by a white couple from Connecticut who really wanted a baby. After trying for years with no success, they'd settled on adoption. My mother read every adoption book and watched all the family-planning videos. My dad toddler-proofed the house with socket covers and childproof locks. They created a beautiful princess-themed bedroom with curtains and a tiara-shaped headboard. Bookshelves were stocked with books and dolls that looked nothing like the little girl they desperately wanted. My social calendar was filled with playdates with neighborhood families and kids named BeccaLynn and Artemis. They thought of everything but me.

"Yeah, that makes sense. I think that's why we've waited so long," Brea said. "We both work long hours, and that wouldn't be fair to a child, seeing the nanny more than they see their parents."

"Don't get me wrong, when everyone understands what they're getting into, it can be a beautiful thing," I said. "Giving a kid a supportive and safe home is the kindest thing a person can do."

"We're still thinking about it. There are other options we're considering, like IVF."

"I'm here to support you and Sandy no matter what you decide. You two would be the coolest moms ever—as long as the baby doesn't take my guest room. I really love that room."

Brea's eyes grew wide. "Rustin."

"What about him?"

"Isn't that him over there?"

Turning, I scanned the direction Brea was pointing in. It was indeed Rustin with a group of friends. He had one of those bougie beers and a smirk on his face. I'd thought he hated socializing, but there he was in the middle of some story that had everyone busting a seam. Rustin, the comedian—was there no circle he couldn't charm? He was rocking jeans that were cuffed at the bottom, with well-loved classic Converses. This man was textbook New York bohemian naturalist.

If he drove, it was a hybrid. If he read, it was a dog-eared copy of Richard Wright's *Native Son*. And his taste in music was Kendrick, J. Cole, and Common. He was unique in a cookie-cutter kind of way. Passing him on the street, you wouldn't assume he was famous, but there would be signs of his silent wealth if you bothered to really look.

"I'm going to call him over," Brea said.

"No. Don't do that."

She didn't even let my objection sink in. "Rustin!" Brea called, standing and waving her arms in the crowded bar. "Rustin!"

Somehow, he managed to hear her calling his name and waved back. Brea motioned for him to come over, and, excusing himself from his group, he headed our way. When his eyes landed on me, his face lit up, and he began fidgeting with his beanie and shirt. In that moment, I was so glad I'd ditched the Laura Ingalls blouse for a more flattering one.

"Hey. What are you two doing here?" he asked.

"Drinking the pain away," Brea said.

"What about you?" I asked. His gaze settled on me, warm and inviting. FYI: I'd had several drinks and was notorious for misreading cues.

"A work obligation. You're far from home."

"Luckily, my deal with the government allows me to travel freely between all five boroughs."

"That's a sweetheart deal."

"Yeah. Upstate New York is off-limits, though."

Brea's eyes pinged from Rustin to me. "Oh shit, look at the time."

I pried my gaze from Rustin. "What time is it?"

"Time for me to make my exit."

"Oh, okay. I'll head out with you." I grabbed my crossbody purse from my chair.

"No. Don't be silly. You should stay."

"By myself?" I asked.

"I could keep you company, if you don't mind being seen with a big-eared nerd," Rustin interjected.

"No. It's actually a good look. People will think I'm benevolent and doing charity work."

He smirked at me, and familiar butterfly wings tickled the lining of my stomach.

Brea pulled me into a rushed hug, whispering, "I think he likes you." So it wasn't just me and the mai tais. "Rustin, see you Monday."

We watched her leave, and he quickly claimed her vacant seat. "You and Brea are close?"

"Yes. She's my best friend. When I moved here, I knew, like, two people, so I attached myself to Brea, and she's been kind enough not to shake me off."

"That's nice. She's good people—someone you want in your corner."

"Yes. She's helped me dislodge my feet from my mouth on more than one occasion."

"You? But you're so thoughtful with your words," he teased.

"Now we both know that's a bald-faced lie. I've always said what pops into my head. I like to keep things spicy."

"I appreciate people who can speak before thinking."

"*Ouch,* I think, and then I just say it anyway."

"I didn't mean it as a dig. I tend to think too much. Makes for tons of missed opportunities."

"You should stop doing that." Rustin bit down on his bottom lip. "See, right there," I said. "It's obvious you're holding something back."

"If I said what I was thinking, this would morph into a *very* different conversation."

"I'm down for conversations that veer off the beaten path."

"Unfortunately, I'm not inebriated enough to venture into uncharted territory."

"What's up with the pretentious beer?" I asked.

"Pretentious in what way?"

"It's the minimalistic orange label. Like it's trying to be a secret."

"You got all that from a label?"

"I'm a poor man's Inspector Gadget."

"You do know he was horrible at his job."

"But somehow, all the cases got solved."

"Somehow? It was his niece."

"No."

Rustin smiled—I'm talking all thirty-two teeth. "That's your answer, just no?"

"I will not be falling for the propaganda."

He leaned in, his breath against my ear making my insides feel like fizzy soda. "You're so weird."

"Thank you."

Rustin's eyes dipped to my lips, dropping to my tits, which were nicely perched in a V-neck top, before making the trip back to the lips. If he kissed me right now, I would kiss back. Tongue-down-throat, public-spectacle kissing. Unfortunately, Mr. Overthinker reset, taking the final sips of his beer.

Pointing to his hat, I asked, "Do you mind?"

"Knock yourself out."

I removed his beanie to reveal a perfectly shaped head with a freshly tapered fade. Squinting, I looked for something to scrutinize. His bourbon-brown eyes were flawless and seemed to hold several secrets. Rustin's lips were full, and I was still imagining them overtaking mine, which was a silly thought because, technically, he was my boss. And generally, men, while good in theory, were fuckboys in practice. Men who wanted to text you, *Good morning, beautiful,* until you were blue in the face. Always asking you to hang out but never actually making plans. And when plans were made, they kept it noncommittal, demanding you pay half.

God forbid a man admit he liked you or thought you were pretty. Don't get me wrong, I hadn't sworn off men, but I was done with accepting the bare minimum. Love wasn't dull; it was loud and shiny. It wasn't filled with empty promises but overflowing with action. At the end of the day, most men were operating from the same playbook, and I refused to lace up my cleats.

"Can I get you another drink?" Rustin asked.

A little harmless flirting was fine, but with a few more drinks, we could cross the line, and I still had to work with him. "No. I think I'm gonna head out."

"Are you sure?" He almost sounded disappointed.

"Yeah. It's getting late."

"I'll walk you out."

On the street, the slight breeze was a refreshing change from the at-capacity bar.

"Can I call you a RideX?" he asked.

"I'm good. I'm totally good. I was just gonna walk home."

"To Harlem? That's a long walk."

"I like walking. Plus, it's a nice night, and seeing how I spend most of my days cooped up in the studio, it'll be good to get some fresh air."

"I'll walk with you."

"What about your friends?" I asked.

"Not my friends. It was a work thing."

"You don't have to do that. Plus, you live in the opposite direction."

"Like you said, it's a nice night."

I knew how shit was going to go. A walk home turned into *can I come upstairs*, which transitioned into a horny make-out session, followed by sex. And then come Monday morning, I'd have to avoid him, especially if the sex was bad.

But what if the sex was good?

"All right, but keep up."

"Yes, ma'am." We headed up the block, his pace matching mine.

"So, are you a transplant or native?" I asked.

"Born and raised in Brooklyn."

"So you never left home."

"Never leaving Brooklyn isn't like never leaving Duluth. My hometown just hits different. What about you?"

"I'm from Duluth and high-key offended."

"No…really?"

"I'm kidding. I'm from Midford, Connecticut."

He chuckled, which he did a lot around me. Perhaps I was the next Eddie Murphy. "That sounds expensive."

"It's middle class."

"I didn't take you for a Connecticut girl."

"Looks can be deceiving."

"Siblings?"

"Yeah. I have a younger brother and sister. They're twins. My parents couldn't get pregnant, so they adopted me, and then, surprise surprise…twins."

"I imagine that was sort of weird."

"Yeah…for sure. What about you?"

"Only child. I think after me, my parents were just like, *hell no.*"

"So, you wrecked the parenting experience for them?"

"I was a difficult kid. I was afraid of everything, severely shy, and into arts and crafts."

"Why were you afraid?" I asked.

"I don't know. Usually kids are fearless, but I lost my grandpa when I was six, and I remember the horrible realization that everyone we love and everything we care about would eventually die."

"Shit. That's a tough pill to swallow at six."

"Yeah," he said. "It kind of freaked me out. It still does, if I'm being honest."

"Personally, I like to focus on the middle parts—not the end or the beginning, but all that happens in the middle. Life is like a cream-filled donut—the best shit is in the middle."

He stopped in his tracks and stared at me.

"What?" I asked.

"I think that you may have just rewired my brain."

"So you grew up in Brooklyn. How about college?"

"Columbia. They had an amazing creative arts program."

"Is that when you started writing your musical?"

"Yeah. Sophomore year."

"How do you do that, exactly?" I asked. "I mean, I can write short stories, poems, five-minutes skits, but an entire musical with songs seems a little daunting."

"And that's why I only have the one musical on Broadway," he teased.

"Well, that's one more than me."

"Is that something you're interested in?"

"I don't know. At twenty-seven, I should probably have my career goals figured out, but I haven't. I like television and film and would probably want to continue to do more of that. For a few years I was thinking about..." I peered up at him. "You know what? It's silly."

"I thought you weren't scared to speak your mind."

Normally, I wasn't, but in some areas I was private—like my relationship with my mom or my big, audacious goals for the future. But Rustin was in the business, and he'd accomplished something I bet no one thought he could. A dream was just a dream if you never spoke it into existence.

"I considered opening up a puppet theater, teaching kids about the art form, allowing them to create their own puppets, write their own stories, and eventually perform them." I was big on ideas but short on funding, time, and a cohesive business plan.

"I think that's amazing," Rustin said. "We need more spaces and opportunities for kids to express their creative sides. Most schools are axing music, art, and after-care programs due to funding."

"Why does it always come down to money?"

"Because we live in a capitalistic society. If it doesn't make dollars, it doesn't make sense."

"You know what I find wild?"

"Hmm?"

"Humans could have created any society we wanted," I said. "We could have lived in a utopia, but no, our forefathers decided on endless hours of work and nothing for free, not even the water, fruits, and vegetables that come from the earth. Did you know there's a couple who owns sixty percent of all the water resources in California? Water, owned by some random white couple. So we have to work for everything, and housing prices are sky high. If you wanna eat healthy, fucking forget about it. Everything is taxed. In some places, you have to pay to physically view the deceased body of your loved one. We could be chilling in a field filled with wildflowers, eating berries, and singing songs, but instead we're on this monotonous hamster wheel called life."

"Yeah, it's fucked for sure, but we do have some glimpses of beauty, sunrises, waterfalls, your smile, and *Songs in the Key of Life*, which sonically is a wonder."

Did he just casually compliment me on my smile? "'Knock Me Off My Feet'"—I placed my hand over my heart—"is a masterpiece."

Rustin swayed side to side as if dancing to the memory of the melody of Stevie Wonder's song in his head. I couldn't help but sing aloud, and Rustin didn't hesitate to join me. His voice was strong and confident and a bit lighter than his speaking voice. We belted out the song while spinning around passersby and jumping over potholes as we strutted down the street. He was a good dancer. And for a kid who apparently grew up shy, he had no qualms about making a fool of himself alongside me.

Like Sandy said, too many people took themselves too seriously—afraid to look silly or be uncomfortable. With most people I met, I found myself dimming my light, fearing they'd eventually tell me I was too much to handle or too difficult to love—but in this moment, the shy kid from Brooklyn was matching my vibe, allowing me to shine bright.

At the end of our sixty-block scenic walk, we made it to my apartment building.

"Thank you for keeping me company," I said. "It made the time fly by."

"For sure. Anytime you're in need of a walking buddy, just let me know. Good cardiovascular."

I stared up at him in anticipation, waiting for him to ask permission to kiss me or just bend down and take it. If he asked, I would let him come up for a nightcap.

He teetered, leaning close and then backing away. "I'll see you at work on Monday?"

His salutation snapped me back to reality. "Yep. I will be there, so there's a high probability we'll cross paths."

"I'd like that."

"Cool. So have a good night." I headed toward the entrance, turning around to find Rustin waiting for me to make it inside. "I'm sorry, but were you going to kiss me?"

He plunged his hands into his pockets. "I was thinking about it."

"Next time…don't think."

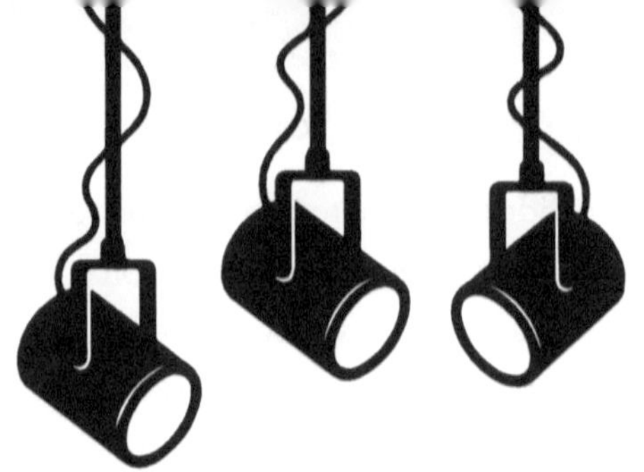

CHAPTER 6
Rustin

I'd been at *Jellybean Junction* for two weeks, and somehow, it had fallen on me to deliver this distressing news. The show was underwater. Our budget relied on donations, and as times got hard economically, charitable donations were one of the first things to go. If you were worried about the cost of eggs, you weren't going to write a check for fifty dollars to a public television kids' show. Surprisingly, the vast majority of our money came from small donations. I'm talking as little as five dollars.

On a show like this, fundraising never ended. Management probably spent more time making calls and going to events in hopes of finding willing donors. We needed an infusion of cash ASAP or *Jellybean Junction*, despite all our good intentions and hard work, would cease production.

Brea had asked the cast and crew to gather in the studio for a quick meeting. As individuals filed in, I gritted my teeth, rehearsing what I planned to say. Make no mistake, shit was dire, but I planned to offer a ray of hope. Because it wasn't over until all the cards were played.

"Gather around, guys. Thank you," Brea shouted. "I know we all have a busy day, but our producer has an announcement."

She'd offered to make the announcement, which I appreciated and seriously considered, thinking maybe hearing this news from one of their own would be less jarring. But I was willing to be the bad guy and the punching bag they took their feelings out on. Brea didn't deserve that.

"Thank you, Brea, and thanks to all of you. First, I want to start by saying in the two weeks I've been here, I've recognized how hard each and every one of you work to make this show happen. I'm convinced in this room are some of the most talented and dedicated professionals in this craft. When I took on the job as producer, one thing I vowed was transparency—"

"Oh my God, we're being fired," Stanley called out. He was living up to his puppet alter ego Grumpy Gus.

"No one is being fired. However, after a thorough review of our financials by Brea, a team of accountants, and me, *Jellybean Junction* is not where we would like to see it. As you all know, we have a tight budget, and we rely on donations. The budget has only gotten tighter, and the donations have been down year over year."

"Well, maybe if we hadn't hired a fancy Hollywood producer, there'd be more money in the coffers," Stanley spoke up, and others in the crowd grumbled in agreement.

"Now wait a minute, that's not fair," Letitia countered. "Rustin joined the production to help, so let's hear him out."

My heart had been acting funny lately, and today was no different. The beat seemed to be all chopped and screwed at the sound of Letitia's supportive words. "Thank you. I'm not going to lie: we are in desperate need of a cash infusion, and if we don't see a change, *Jellybean Junction* has six to nine months before we have to close our doors. I'm going to do everything in my power to make sure that doesn't happen."

"Hogwash," Rhodes said. "I've been here since the dinosaurs, and every year somebody puts us on death watch, and every time we make a full recovery. This shit is circular. We just need to put our heads down and continue the good work."

"We also need money. Make no mistake, we can't just sit back and expect a blessing. We are going to have to work harder than ever to get donations. I'm talking all hands on deck—after-hours mixers, weekend fundraiser events, kids' parties. Whatever we need to do to draw attention and money."

"We could do a bake sale?" Letitia offered, and was met with laughter.

"You laugh, but Letitia isn't far off. We are not too good for any forms of outreach. We need to keep open minds. I know this is a lot of information, and I also understand I'm an imperfect messenger, but if we don't increase our ratings and secure funding, this passion project that started over fifty years ago may be ripe for the chopping block."

"Thank you, Rustin," Brea chimed in. "If you have any questions or ideas, please feel free to come to Rustin or me. As always, we will keep you posted as things develop. We hope to share a more substantial plan in the coming days. Have a great morning, everybody."

The crowd broke off into smaller groups with Stanley recruiting the largest one. I didn't need negative Nellys spreading fear and apathy. Right now, we needed to focus on solutions. Anyone not on board with this plan could miss me with any and all bullshit.

I needed a Letitia pick-me-up. My weekend had been consumed with thoughts of her and how I blew my shot to kiss her. She was right there looking up at me with her curious eyes, and I'd choked. On the ride home, I'd called myself every name in the book, but I landed on *bitch made*. All the signs were pointing to yes, but my head was riddled with all the reasons why I shouldn't open that door.

Dating someone you worked with was always a bad idea, but I'd never worked with someone like Letitia Vincent. I'd told her she was weird, and I meant it in the best possible way. She was avant-garde, punk rock, and underground hip-hop all rolled into one. If given a second opportunity, I wouldn't hesitate.

Letitia was alone in the breakroom when I walked in. "On a scale of one to ten, how bad was it?" I asked.

"Luckily Brea gave me a heads-up, because if she hadn't, I'd be in the secret bathroom stall crying."

"That bad?"

"We've talking about people losing their jobs and the possibility of *Jellybean Junction* becoming a *Jeopardy!* question, so… kind of bad."

"Fuck. Do you think I should've been more optimistic? That's not really my strong point. I tend to focus on the worst-case scenario because nine times out of ten, it's the most likely outcome."

Letitia's jaw dropped, and a look of panic danced in her eyes.

"By no means is the show going to be shuttered, leaving us to auction off parts of the studio right down to the Ralph Chessé Studios sign outside, leaving us to hit the pavement looking for new ways to pay our bills."

"I'm glad you didn't say that at the meeting." She swallowed hard. "I can't help but think about the inevitable reality of my having to sell my apartment and move back to Connecticut. The local library could use a puppet show. I used to volunteer. Maybe I could convince them to create a full-time position."

"You've not going to have to move back to Connecticut."

"You know, in school, they tell doctors and lawyers never to make promises you can't keep. I think it's a good rule of thumb for all aspects of life."

"Well, don't start looking for a new place of employment just yet."

"I'm like Phoebe from costuming; I prefer going down with the ship. Just consider me the musician on the *Titanic*. 'Gentlemen, it has been a privilege.'" She said that last part in a bad English accent.

My memory sparked. "I know what will cheer you up." Circling her, I picked up a box I'd tucked away in the corner earlier.

"Is it in the box?"

"Yeah. Open it."

Letitia skipped to a nearby drawer, pulling out a pair of scissors, breaking the seal on the packaging. She flung Styrofoam and plastic to the ground. When she finally made out the slightly smaller box inside, she squealed. "Is this a coffeemaker?"

"Yep. I figured the world may be crumbling, but at least you'll have good coffee to get you through it."

"Can I tell you a secret?"

"Please."

She erased the space between us, tugging on the tail of my shirt. "I hated the coffee. I just pretended it was decent because I couldn't afford the five dollars required for a real cup."

"Well, you mentioned food was your love language, and I hoped drinks were included in that."

Her face warped, the corners of her eyes crinkling, her nose twitching, and her mouth slightly agape. "You bought this coffeemaker just for me?"

Yes, *duh*. Why else would I purchase a top-of-the-line coffeemaker with a three-month supply of various-flavored coffee pods if not for her? "Uhm…it's for everybody. Hoping to soften the blow of this morning's news."

"Well, I'm sure *everybody* will be very appreciative."

"Do you like it?"

"I love it, but I'm easy to please." She tapped her fingernails over top of the box. "When the studio goes dark, I'm claiming dibs on the coffeemaker. You're my witness. That is, of course, it you don't want it."

"No, it's fine. You called dibs. I'll back you up with anyone who asks."

"Thank you for this." She nodded in the direction of the box. "And for being my witness in what's bound to be a highly contested custody battle over a gently used machine."

"Rus, where you at?"

"Up here," I called from my bedroom.

"Whoa. What's happening? Omar scanned my bed with discarded articles of clothing.

"I have a meeting."

"What type of meeting has you emptying out your closet?"

The type that involved Letitia Vincent. I'd suggested we work on material together, and today was the day she'd decided to take me up on my offer. So now I was in the middle of picking an outfit that said, *I care about my appearance, but I in no way wore something special for you.* I wanted my attire to be a subtle flex.

"Who's the girl?"

"What makes you think there's a woman involved?"

"Because you're usually meticulous, but this is bordering on obsessive."

"Not obsessive, just want the right fit." I tossed a pair of painter jeans into a growing pile.

Omar shoved the mound of clothes aside, taking a seat. "Give me the deets. Name, weight, height, eye color."

Who was I kidding? I was dying to talk about her and possibly get a different perspective. "Her name's Letitia. She's slim thick, about yea high, brown eyes."

"She's Black?"

"Why are you acting surprised?"

"Because you dress like a dude who doesn't see color, but who constantly dates outside his race."

"I've only dated a non-Black woman once."

"True. It just felt like you were on the precipice of a crossover episode," he joked.

"Shut up."

"Where'd you meet her?"

"At *Jellybean Junction*. She's a puppeteer."

"A talented female puppeteer who kinda sorta likes you."

I tossed a hanger on my bed. What had he gleaned from this conversation that I hadn't? "Why do you say that?"

"Typically, women only say yes to dates when they're interested or hungry."

"Never said this was a date."

"Then what is it?"

"A working lunch. I picked lunch because it was less romantic."

"So if it's not a date, why all the fuss?"

"Because this could determine her consideration of a date."

"Like you're going to ask."

"If the vibes are right, I might."

"You are the worst at reading vibes. Last year, Marcy was into you hard, and you fumbled."

"It wasn't a fumble."

"She invited you back to her place, and you said you had to go home and floss," Omar said.

"In my defense, I was just coming off my first-ever cavity. The doctor said I needed to floss twice a day."

"Let me think: gingivitis or sex." He shifted his hands like a scale. "I'm picking sex every time. Fuck the plaque buildup."

"Why are you here?"

"I'm dropping off the extension contracts for the run of *U-Turn* for another five years."

"You could have just emailed them to me."

"I did, but I also wanted to pitch the idea of taking the show on the road for a limited time. The demand is there. People travel to New York from all over the country to see your show. We've never done a tour, and I think we're leaving money on the table."

"How many shows, which cities, and with what cast? We can't shut down our Broadway show to jet-set."

"I knew you'd say that. We can work out the logistics, but I think this deserves real consideration."

"I really can't think about this right now," I said. "I'm already up to my neck in *Jellybean Junction* funding."

"Why? What's up?"

"We're running out of money. No money, no show."

"We? Are you speaking French now?"

"I'm the producer."

"You just got this gig. I didn't realize you were so invested."

"I wouldn't have taken the job if I weren't."

Omar rolled a blasé shoulder. "You'll figure something out. You always do."

"Maybe." I held up two shirts, hoping to settle on one.

"Go with the green shirt. It complements your eyes."

"Gee, thanks." I tossed the other shirt aside.

I got to the restaurant earlier because I didn't want Letitia to have to wait, and I needed buffering time to get acclimated to the space and shake off some of my nerves. Liking Letitia was a given—she was outspoken and full of life—but I'd never expected to like her as much as I did. Silly of me to think a woman like her would have me anything but head over heels.

Upon arrival, she spotted me quickly in the same café. Letitia wore patterns that in theory should not be paired together, but on her, they just seemed to work. She was wearing a bright blue polka-dot blouse and silk green skirt with black tiger stripes.

I stood as she made her way to the table. "Hey."

"Hi," she said. We were both frozen, uncertain if we should shake hands or hug. Letitia presented a closed hand, and I bumped my fist into hers. She made an explosion sound, flicking her fingers open. Waiting until she sat, I claimed my seat.

"Did you find the place okay?"

"Yeah. It was right where you said it would be." She started removing her laptop from her bag.

I was in no rush to talk shop. "Maybe we could order first."

"Sure. I already know what I want."

"I thought you hadn't been here before?"

"I haven't, but last night, I perused the menu while in bed. I like knowing what I'm going to order before I get to the restaurant, that way I have something to look forward to. I do it all the time when I go on a date." She paused. "Not that this is a date, but on dates, I like to have my meal planned out so if the man is a dud at least I'll be able to rave about the paella."

"Smart. I actually do the same, but only because I don't like surprises and I'm a picky eater."

"Don't tell me I'm sitting across from the chicken finger brigade?"

"No. I'm not picky in *that* way. I'll eat almost anything, but I'm a bit of a food snob."

"A connoisseur?" she asked.

"I'm the type of guy who explains the spice mixture, tongue feel, and says shit like 'the juices are exploding in my mouth.'"

"Don't we all like things that explode in our mouth?" Letitia's demeanor was innocent, but her words were laced with amusement.

Leaning in slightly, I debated whether to say the thing tickling my brain.

As if she possessed the ability to read minds, Letitia said, "Say it."

"Excuse me?"

"The thought tumbling around in your head. Say it."

"I was just thinking sometimes…people prefer a heads-up before you just explode."

Her nose crinkled, and even though she was shorter than me, it felt like she was looking down on me. "Hmm. I stand corrected. Maybe we don't need to say *everything*."

If not for the rich hue to my skin, my face would shine beet red. "Do you get sick pleasure out of embarrassing me?"

"I don't know that it's sick, but it's definitely pleasurable. I think it's the way you squirm."

"Let the record show you're the one who brought up things exploding in mouths."

"No. That was all you, and you said the words *tongue feel*."

"It's used to describe the way food sits on the palate."

"I know what it means," she said. "I just never want to hear those words again. It's like when people say the word *moist* or men refer to their member as cock-a-doodle-doo."

"Can we just order?"

"Yes, as long as you promise not to give me a play-by-play of the food entering your moist mouth."

We placed our order, and when our food arrived, Letitia wasted no time steering the direction of the conversation. "What are your intentions for this working lunch?"

"I hoped to get to know you a little better—figure out what makes you and your characters tick."

"That's easy. For me, it's all about representation and making learning fun and interactive. Growing up in Milford, I was often the only one—the only Black girl in swim class, the only Black girl at the sleepover, the only Black girl on the cheerleading squad—so television was my escape to see people who looked like me living normal lives."

"I remember all the afternoon kid shows featured the outgoing, spunky Black best friend."

Letitia grimaced. "Yeah, and I hated it. We were always relegated to the role of sidekick, never the main character. Representation matters, and not just seeing ourselves in print and film but the characters we play."

"Agreed. The Black experience is nuanced. Fun fact about me: I had a bit of an acting bug when I was younger. After classes, I'd run to auditions, thinking I'd get my big break."

"You wanted to be an actor?"

"Honestly, at the time, I just wanted to be famous," I replied.

"With all due respect, you're a little too reserved to be a film actor."

"That's why they call it acting. Do you think Eddie Murphy is always walking around laughing?"

"Yeah, I kind of do."

"Anyway, back to you. Representation is important to you."

"Yeah, not just for me, but for all marginalized groups," she said. "Puppeteering is a niche market, but having Black and brown puppets matters, and I would be as bold to say it's revolutionary."

Most people didn't get to do what they loved every day. It was clear Letitia was passionate about her craft, and it explained why

I'd felt a strange connection to her from the start. I could talk about the history of puppets and their creators until I was blue in the face. Thread and Thespian allowed me to live my dreams, and *Jellybean Junction* was the reason I was able to dream so big.

"Most people just see it as entertainment, but it really is so much more. I agree there's nothing like being seen and having that image reflected back," I said.

"Working on *Jellybean Junction* is a thankless job, and sometimes I think people see us as relics of the past. Digital graphics and AI are the wave right now, and practical art forms are feeling the pinch. Why hire a puppeteer when you could just create a puppet by typing a prompt and pressing enter?"

"Exactly, exactly that. I think people expect AI to revolutionize the way we do things. And don't get me wrong, it one hundred percent will. And I personally embrace it and welcome it."

"You do?"

"I think it has a place."

"I find it utterly terrifying, devoid of passion, and cold," she said.

"Listen, I agree with you. And as AI art, music, and movies take off, I believe there will be a not-so-quiet resistance and yearning for human-generated art."

"I'll be right smack dab in the middle of it, because I prefer my art not be created with code. Art is a love language—the artist is conversing with the audience. You can't enter a bunch of whosits and whatits and expect it to resonate in the same way. The fact that our hands-on job could be replaced by machines is wild. Enough about our future techno overlords—what's your deal? You write this amazing musical; people start calling you a prodigy. That had to be exciting."

"You'd think," I replied. "I was on several 'thirty under thirty' lists, posing for magazine covers, doing all kinds of interviews. I told you I was a failed actor because, at the end of the day, I'm an introvert and prefer to be behind the camera. When the play came out, it just took off. No one expected that. But it's kind of like lightning rarely strikes twice."

"When you're as talented as you are, you can create your own lightning—fuck Mother Nature," Letitia said.

"While kind, I'm not so sure that's true."

"Rustin, you created *U-Turn*. It's innovative and smart, and it changed the way I view the art form."

Ducking my head, I said, "Thank you."

"Do you not like compliments?"

"Does anyone?"

Letitia raised her hand. "Me. I *love* them."

"Oh. Well, let me take this opportunity to say you look pretty… today. Actually, you look pretty every day, and I'd probably mention it more if I weren't directly in your chain of command."

"Thank you." Letitia beamed. No self-deprecation, no deflections, just absolute agreement, which I found refreshing. I could learn a thing or two from her about recognizing my worth. "So, what made you decide to sign on to the show?"

"I took a blind meeting. I thought they were going to ask me to be a guest."

"And when they suggested producer, you…"

"I jumped at the chance. I mean, it's *Jellybean Junction*."

"Hopefully you're not regretting your decision."

"I knew there would be trials."

"That's putting it mildly," she said.

"I like a challenge."

"Well, you'll get a lot of that at the helm of the show."

"I invited you here because I'm a fan."

"Of the show? So am I."

"No. I'm a fan of your work."

Her head jerked back. "Me?"

"Yeah. I've been watching you. I know that sounds weird. I mean, I've been following your professional journey."

"Do I have a journey?"

"After college, you were hired at the Brooklyn library and had a popular puppet story time. You were like Shari Lewis and Lambchop, just in a cooler font. What ever happened to Wags?"

Her eyes sparked at the mention of the name. "He's still around. Not many people remember Story Time with Letty and Wags the Fox."

"I do. It's kind of good business to keep an eye on up-and-coming puppeteers. Based on that and your stint on *Jellybean Junction*, I was eager to work with you. Aaliyah and Jabari complement each other. That wasn't an accident—it was by design. I think we should lean into the kindergarten angle. There're opportunities for great storytelling there."

"And you want to create those stories with me?"

"I know everyone thinks I'm territorial and possessive…"

"You're not?"

"No, I am, but I understand the value of collaboration, and we both bring unique perspectives."

"Your pitch is giving car salesman," she said.

"Is it really that hard to believe I think you're amazingly talented and I'm excited for the chance to work with you?" I asked.

"It's not hard to believe someone would want to work with me. But the thought that *you* do is giving me pause."

"Because I'm Rustin Hayes?"

"Yeah. People are probably blowing up your phone for a chance to work with you. Why me?"

"Maybe I just see myself in you—before the industry made me jaded."

"So, you want to mentor me?"

"I want to partner with you. But I'm sure we'll both learn things along the way."

Letitia, who never appeared at a loss for words, was speechless. Her eyes pinged from my face to our empty plates as she slowly processed my request. "Do I have to answer now?"

"No. You can give it some time to marinate."

"Thank you for lunch."

"I mean, you demanded I feed you, so just doing my part. What do you have planned later?"

"Laundry."

As she packed up her bag, my mind raced, trying to think of a way to extend this meeting. I sucked at cool pickup lines and flirting. "Do you… Is it okay if I show you something?"

"Uhm…"

"It sounds like a no, and that's okay. I get it."

"I don't think that you do. It's not a no. I'm just sort of realizing you're my boss's boss, so technically my boss, and honestly, I'm not one hundred percent sure what's happening."

"That's fair. Full transparency: I like talking to you."

"They say it's a bad idea to mix business with pleasure."

"Agreed," I said. "Always a bad idea. But there are the exceptions."

"You think I'm the exception?"

"I mean, you're a beautiful woman who tolerates my jokes and doesn't roll her eyes when I talk about puppets, so yeah."

Her eyes landed on me soft. "All right. Take me to the undisclosed second location."

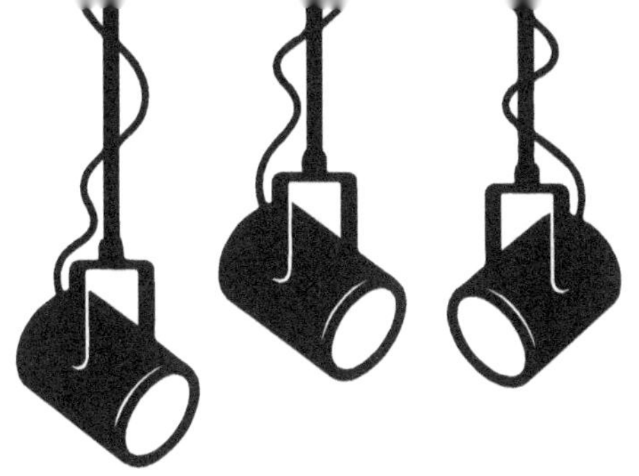

CHAPTER 7
Letitia

WE HOPPED ON the subway, getting off at Fourteenth Street, and walked west toward the Hudson River. At Pier 57, we entered the marketplace. Inside, we took the elevator located all the way in the back to the top floor, and when we exited, my jaw dropped.

"What is this place?"

"It's a rooftop park."

I surveyed the space. There were views of New York Harbor, Hudson River, and the New York skyline. I'd never seen anything like this. It was a clear summer day, and the views were breathtaking. "This is stunning. I didn't even know this place existed."

"Another perk to New York living. It may be congested, and everything costs an arm and a leg, but the city is also filled with secrets. You just have to know where to look."

"See, I think that's my problem. I'm always looking down so as not to make direct eye contact."

"Try looking up instead. The view's better."

Taking his advice, I looked up toward the sky, and the glass-and-iron skyscraper stretched to the heavens. New York was nothing like Milford. There was always a new experience or a unique place to explore. After five years in the city, I'd probably only witnessed five percent of what it had to offer.

On the weekends, I'd take the subway to a random neighborhood and just walk around, dipping in and out of boutiques and craft shops—treat myself to a new restaurant or coffee spot. It was a cheap and interesting way to spend the day, and I always felt so accomplished afterward.

"Thank you for sharing this." We were practically all alone. "Your secret is safe with me."

"Do you want to sit for a while?"

"Yeah. That would be nice." We selected a bench with the best vantage point.

"I come here all the time," he said. "It's a great place to think. I'm not a fan of crowds, so this place is perfect."

"I'm the exact opposite. The hum of a crowd or utensils scraping against plates is the best background noise."

"I prefer the sound of the city over people."

"You're not a people person. I'm getting a strong don't-talk-to-me vibe."

"I thought I was doing a good job hiding it."

"Nope. You're not," I said. We shared a laugh. "Can I ask? Why did you downplay your success earlier?"

"Did I?"

"Yeah. You tried to make it sound like your fifteen minutes were up."

"I've come to find not everybody celebrates you. It's easier to just water it down a bit."

"You shouldn't have to dim your light," she said. "Let bitches squint or get fucking sunglasses."

"Trust, if you get to know me better, you will learn I'm the least humble person on the planet. I'm really fucking good at what I do, and in the future when people mention puppeteers, they are going to name Jim Henson, immediately followed by Rustin Hayes."

"Okay, I take it back. You're not at all humble."

"No. I'm a menace. My business partner Omar hates me. So, what's your braggadocious flex?"

"Uhm."

"Not *you* catching a case of the humbles."

"It's not that," she said. "I just haven't really accomplished anything yet."

"What do you mean?"

"I'm still trying to figure out my place."

"Letitia, you single-handedly increased visits to the Brooklyn Public Library with Story Time with Letty and Wags the Fox. They had to create a reservations list for story time. Do you know how wild that is?"

"How do you know all that?" she asked.

"I read your feature in the *Fifth Borough* a few years ago, so don't pretend you don't have anything to shit on me with."

"Well, I did get the first lady Clover Elmsworth to host one of my story times. The White House and the library partnered to host an event. That was pretty special, and I got to meet the president."

"See, I've never met the president or first lady."

"People always ask me what she smells like, and I can confirm she smells amazing."

Hearing Rustin's praise made me swell with pride. It took me by surprise that he knew so much about me. I'd made some small waves, but in comparison to Rustin's career and impact, I was still very much a newbie. My mother thought I had tons of potential, just not in the career path I'd chosen. She wanted me to be a pharmacist.

"It's a reliable job that will always be in demand," she would say. I had no desire to count pills and drop them into a bottle. For the record, I knew pharmacists did more than that, but none of it interested me.

Oftentimes, I felt like I was in the wrong seat on the bus, or maybe the wrong bus altogether. I loved what I did, but now, with the potential closure of *Junction*, I wasn't so sure. When I told people I was a puppeteer, they were interested for all of fifteen minutes, but over time when comparing their corporate jobs to mine, theirs were always more important, stressful, and time consuming. Don't get me wrong, I was blessed to be able to do what I loved, but don't let the puppet voice fool you. It was a job with expectations and stressors, just like any other occupation.

"What do your parents think about what you do?" I asked.

"At first they didn't get it," Rustin replied. "'What do you mean you want to play with puppets?' But as things started taking off, they backed down."

"I can't wait until my family's perspective shifts."

"They don't see the vision?"

"Honestly, I think they're just waiting for me to fail so I can get a real job," I said.

"I get the added stress to prove them wrong."

"I just want to make them proud and not give them any more reasons to regret adopting me."

"I don't think they regret having you."

"You haven't met my mother. I'll just leave it at that."

Rustin raised his hands, gesturing that he was backing away from the subject. "If anyone understands having a strained relationship with parents, it's me."

"I think my mother's idea of me has never matched up with who I really am, which is why most of my true friends are all in creative careers—artists, musicians, crafters, and street performers. They just get me."

"Can I ask you a question?"

"Yeah."

"If you could do anything to improve *Jellybean Junction*, what would you do?" he asked.

"In a perfect world where money wasn't an object?"

"Yeah. Perfect-world scenario."

"Everything is falling apart. The lights, the equipment. It's a hundred-year-old soundstage, and the seams are coming undone—puppets being held together with hot glue and a prayer. It would be nice not to have to scrounge for scraps."

Since joining the show, I'd filled in as the boom operator, the cleaning crew. I'd manually entered scripts into the teleprompter, which was now broken, so I'd also had to act as the cue-card person. During scenes, I'd hold up backgrounds because they kept falling on the cast. If we needed a tree, I'd volunteer to dress up as one. And it wasn't just me—it was the entire cast and crew going above and beyond to make the show work.

I continued, "Phoebe, our lead costume designer, has to sew scraps of fabric together. The cast and crew are spread thin trying to meet the demands of a twenty-two-episode season. Our lack of a budget is killing the creative process, and I think it's starting to show in our end product."

Rustin nodded thoughtfully. "Money solves, like, ninety-nine percent of the world's problems, and anyone who says differently is lying."

"What about you—what would you change?" I asked.

"You know, I've been seriously thinking about that since I was offered this job. The powers that be definitely want to see change."

"That's a lot of weight on your shoulders."

"Yeah, and I fully expect there will be some resistance."

"As long as you don't do anything like change the name or the theme song, I think we'll be fine."

Rustin offered a crooked smile. I didn't envy the position he was in. Being enlisted to implement a plan to save the show was a lot to expect from one man. I would support him in any way I could, but I had my own interests to look after. Did I mention I'd just purchased a studio apartment? That apartment was the most expensive purchase of my life. My savings were a joke, and I still needed to furnish my place. All I owned was a futon I'd found on the street several years back and beanbags for chairs. I didn't even have a trash can, because when I went shopping I was shocked to find I would have to pay upward of one hundred dollars to hide my garbage.

"Let's get you home," Rustin said. "It's laundry day, and I don't want to keep you from it."

Despite my mild protest, he rode with me to Harlem. The entire way there, he let me dominate the conversation. I talked about music, the best street food, and my fear of falling into one of those subway grates.

Back at my place, I made an indecent proposal. "Do you want to come upstairs?"

"Yeah, I do."

We shared a knowing smile. I was going to ride him like my name was Trixie Buckshot. Homes needed to be christened, and what better way than with loud afternoon sex?

Inside, I couldn't help but make excuses. "It's small."

"Should I take my shoes off?"

"Yes, please. Don't mind the boxes. I haven't actually unpacked yet. I'm still living out of a suitcase."

"No, this is nice. Good layout, great windows." He admired the view. "Love the street below."

"The windows really sold me on the place. And the original hardwood."

"I like it, and once you finish decorating, I'm sure it will mimic your over-the-top personality."

"Thanks. I'm really proud of it. My first grown-up purchase."

"I get it. I felt the same way." He scanned my space. "Do you have speakers? You mentioned music, and I want to play something for you, if that's okay."

"Sure." I unlocked my phone, pulled up the music app, and handed it to him. "Just find the song you want. My phone's already connected to the speakers."

Music filled the air as Rustin claimed a seat on the futon. I followed his lead toward the couch, but before I could sit, he reached out, guiding me to straddle his lap.

Strong hands moved along my body like the sultry saxophone-led jazz song. His fingers coasted over my lips. I parted them slightly, and his thumb lingered, slowly inching inside. We both observed in awe as he worked his digit in and out of my mouth, each swipe making me eager for more. I was unable to contain the moan that tripped up my chest and spilled from my lips.

Circling my tongue over his thumb, I could tell from the look in his eyes we both wished this was a different part of his anatomy. Was a non-first date too soon to offer up my throat to him? Rules were made to be broken, and the stiffening of his dick let me know that if I dropped to my knees, I would be pleasantly surprised.

"Can I take your shirt off?" he asked.

His voice startled me, I was so deep in my imaginings. "Yes." My voice was breathy.

He slowly undid each button until my sheer neon-green bra was on display. I shrugged out of the shirt as Rustin performed an inventory. His hand swept over my pierced nipples through my bra. "Did it hurt?" he asked.

"A little bit, but I have an affinity toward pain."

The intensity with which he searched my gaze, looking for the truth in my words, was unexpected. Unhooking my bra, he swirled his tongue over my breast, sucking the nipple and stainless-steel clamp into his mouth. My head lolled back as the ravenous suckling of my nipples relayed the message to my pussy that it was about to be fucked, which caused my kitty to contract and pool with moisture at the prospect.

Rustin scooped up both my breasts, alternating his attention between the two, and I rewarded him by whispering in his ear, "Your mouth feels so good. I love how wet and soft your tongue is." This man paid attention to the finer details. He was in no rush, apparently content to languish over my modest mounds. I was torn, wanting just this and so much more.

"Your breasts are perfect," he mumbled between mouthfuls.

"One's actually smaller than the other."

"Imperfection is what makes us human. It sets us apart from others."

"What about you, what are your flaws?"

"Most of my flaws are internal."

"Like?"

"Like professionally, I'm an advocate, but personally, I don't always ask for what I want."

"What do you want?" I asked.

"I kind of want to eat you out until your legs tremble and you push my head away because you can't handle any more pleasure."

"Oh my God, I want that for me too."

He chuckled. "I like it—you're a taker."

"I'm a giver too, but I'm very interested in taking all you have to offer."

"You could start with taking your clothes off."

"Yes…okay. God, I'm loving your ideas right now." I tugged at my skirt, my hands trembling. Had I been planning on having sex today? No. Did I always stay ready? Yes! Rustin's quirky, understated confidence was really doing a number on me. Maybe I was drawn to him because self-assurance was a quality I lacked.

Just as I was about to slip my skirt over my hips, the doorbell rang. We both froze, the unexpected buzzing puncturing our hazy, lust-filled bubble.

"Are you expecting company?" Rustin whispered.

"No. No one knows where I live except Brea and you."

The buzzer rang again, followed by knocking.

"They're pretty insistent."

"Whoever it is will go away."

We waited in silence for the person to leave, me clutching my skirt with my tits on display. From the hallway, I could make out heavy footfalls followed by screams.

"That's not normal. It's a pretty quiet building." I zipped up my skirt, my spider-senses tingling.

"Maybe I should check it out," Rustin offered.

"Yeah."

He headed to the door while I searched for my shirt.

"It's smoky out here," he called out. "Hey, what's going on?" I assumed he was speaking to someone passing by. "Fire!" Rustin shouted.

"Fire! Where? In the building?" There was a ton of commotion but no definitive response.

Rustin came rushing back. "I think we should evacuate. People are running down the stairs."

"Did you see a fire?"

"The hallway is filled with smoke, so—"

"Where there's smoke, there's fire."

"Bingo."

I ran around the apartment in a momentary state of shock, not knowing what to do.

Rustin interrupted my spiral. "We need to leave."

"Sure, yeah, that makes sense." After I grabbed my keys and an *Ebony* magazine from 1979 with Diahann Carroll on the cover in a stunning white dress, we headed for the door. I followed the growing crowd toward the first floor. Rustin had a tight grip on my hand so we didn't get separated. Outside, the fire department was already on the scene, and the residents were directed across the street. We both stared in horror at a window several doors down from my apartment engulfed in flames.

"Do you think they're going to be able to contain it?" I asked.

"Yeah, of course. They're professionals. This is what they do."

"'Cause that's a big fire. Do you think everyone got out in time?"

"I sure hope so."

"I do too. But also, what if they can't contain it and it spreads? Everything I own is in my apartment. Not to make it about me, but…"

"That's not going to happen."

My heart dropped. "I forgot to get Aaliyah. She's still in there." I advanced forward, but Rustin quickly grabbed my arm. "I have to go get her."

"I know you're upset right now, but you are exactly where you need to be. Aaliyah will be fine."

"You don't know that."

He pointed to the building. "The firefighters are on site, and the flames are not spreading. I bet you they already have it contained."

I counted the windows to confirm the distance between the fire and my apartment. If my numbers were right, the fire was in Miss Burke's place. She was an older woman who'd never been married and affirmed it was the best decision she'd ever made. When I moved in, she was one of the first people I met. Her apartment was a treasure trove of Black art and vintage pieces.

Searching the crowd, I was unable to locate her. The older I got, the more I recognized just how precarious life was. All the material things we held dear—photographs of your grandparents, keepsakes from your firstborn child, diaries spanning years of reflection, your favorite mug—could all be taken in an instant.

"I'm glad you're here," I said, squeezing Rustin's hand.

"Me too."

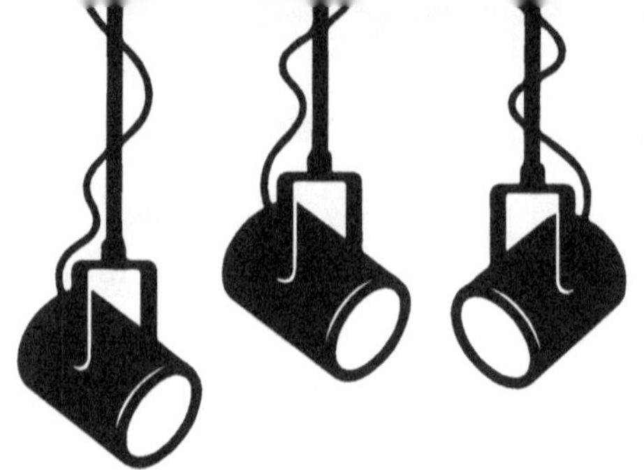

CHAPTER 8
Rustin

I'D NEVER BEEN more eager to return to work. Seeing Letitia was the highlight of my day. As I traversed the busy sidewalk, I glanced at one of the social media pages for the show. For it to survive, everything needed to be reviewed. *Jellybean Junction*, the branding and social media presence, would need a complete overhaul.

My brisk pace stalled when I came across a comment saying, *God, this show is still on the air? I thought Lulu Lark died of bird flu years ago.* Do you know how big of a loser you needed to be to shit on a kids' show?

"Why the long face?"

I looked up to find Letitia standing in front of me with a bright smile. My heart constricted in my chest as I registered her effortless beauty. Her thick, fluffy hair was piled on top of her head in a messy bun, and she was wearing a long orange dress, which popped against her rich brown skin.

"Have you checked out our social media pages?" I asked.

"Not really. I think Brea handles that."

"It would probably be best to hire someone with communication experience."

"You know how it is at *Junction*. If you're not wearing at least three hats, you're not pulling your weight."

"If we can raise enough money, we won't *have* to be jacks-of-all-trades and masters of none."

"I'll have you know I've become really good at fixing leaky faucets."

"So, I should add junior plumber to your long list of responsibilities?" I asked.

"When I interviewed for the job, they asked if I was a team player who was willing to step up when needed. Naturally I said yes, claiming to be a team player who was more than ready to offer a lending hand. Little did I know that hand would be holding the boom mic and adjusting the focus on the studio cameras."

I tossed my phone into my pocket. Why talk about work when I could flirt with Letitia? "How's your neighbor's place?"

"The fire started in her kitchen. Luckily, it didn't spread. Of course, there's some smoke and water damage, but it could have been so much worse."

"That's good to hear. And are you doing better?"

"Yeah. Sorry for the mini freak-out. I just saw my life flash before my eyes. It's a classic case of not realizing how important something is until you almost lose it, and it's not just the apartment, but the life I've created for myself. Growing up in Milford and being able to make it in this city and carve out a place for myself means a lot."

"I get it," I said. "I think people tend to gravitate toward big cities like New York because you can be who you truly are—something many small towns don't always encourage."

"What about you? How was your weekend?"

"I was with you for part of it, so you tell me."

"If you were with me, then you had a great weekend."

"True, but I think I could make next weekend even better if given the opportunity," I said.

"And how would you do that?"

Licking my lips, I scanned the length of her body. "I could show you better than I could tell you."

"Are you flirting with me at eight in the morning?"

"I gotta get it in early. Making you smile is now mandatory. Shower, brush my teeth, say my prayers, and try to make Letitia laugh. So, when do I get to see you again?"

"You're seeing me now." She brushed a wayward strand of hair from her eyes.

"I like after-hours Letitia. She's a better kisser."

She tossed a glance over her shoulder to ensure there were no cast or crew members passing by. "I liked kissing you too."

"My singular focus is kissing you again," I said. A smile tickled the corners of her mouth. "I'm not usually this forward, but I'm also not one to play games. I like you."

Letitia's head jerked back, and her eyes widened at my words. I'd only known her for a almost a month, but she was one of a kind. The characters she created were witty, vulnerable, and real. Yes, Aaliyah was a puppet, but she reminded me of the little girls in my family who were inquisitive, brave, and filled with so much promise. That was all Letitia, bringing Aaliyah to life and connecting with our target audience. Being seen and represented was affirming. And even as a twenty-nine-year-old man, I found a familiar comfort in both Letitia and Aaliyah.

Added bonus—she was passionate about her craft, and seeing how I could talk ad nauseum about all things puppeteering and the practical effects industry, we were a perfect match. Her sense of humor kept me on my toes, and it didn't hurt that she was the most beautiful woman I'd ever met. It was her smile, which practically took up half her face, the way her arms flitted around excitedly when she told a story. The wrinkle that would crinkle her nose when she was ready to disagree with you.

"I tend to avoid workplace dalliances," she said.

"Really? Is that before or after you grind on their lap and let them suck your nipples?"

Letitia gasped. "Okay, you've got me there, but I want to be smart about this. I'm excited to come to work every day, and I'd hate for this relationship, for lack of a better word, to sour, turning my joy into dread."

"So you don't wanna kiss me again?" I teasingly pouted.

"I never said that."

"I've dated a coworker before."

"And how did that go?"

"Horrible."

"You're helping to build my case."

"You're right. I'll just quit."

"What?" Her tone was marked with alarm.

"If you don't wanna date a coworker, then I'll quit. Fuck this job."

"Can you be serious?"

"I am being serious." I inched toward the entrance. "I'll go in there right now and give my notice, effective immediately."

Letitia grabbed my arm, pulling me back. "Slow down, No Limit soldier. Are you that hard up for ass you'd quit your day job?"

"This isn't my day job; this is my side hustle. And I'm interested in seeing where we can go, and I'd prefer to do that while still employed, but if I have to jump on a grenade to get next to you, then so be it."

"I can't take you seriously," she said.

"You should, because I don't joke about matters of the heart. Do you need character references? Because I can provide you three right now."

"One date?"

"A first date."

"That implies there will be subsequent dates."

"Trust me, there *will* be additional dates."

"I'll think about it."

"That's all I ask."

I was ready to be obnoxiously romantic with this woman. I'm talking text messages filled with heart-eyed emojis, sharing food from each other's plates, and kissing on the sidewalk during rush-hour foot traffic. People would scream at us, suggesting we "get a room."

Her face lit up, and she said, "I heard we have a meeting this afternoon, and I'm really excited to hear your game plan for Save the Junction, Keep the Function."

"What's that?"

"It's our working slogan. I made it up in the shower this morning."

"Uhm, we might want to continue to workshop that."

"I have others. How about 'Don't pull the plug, show *Jellybean Junction* some love'?"

"That's better. But do we need a slogan?"

"Yeah. Every movement has a slogan. We can put it on shirts and sell them to help replenish our coffers."

I loved her optimism, but it was going to take way more than a cotton T-shirt to get us back in the game. We could raise all the money we wanted, but if the viewership wasn't there, we'd still get chopped. Television and film was a ruthless business, and it always came down to profit. If you weren't making the studios money, it didn't matter how beloved you were, how many big-name celebrities made guest appearances, or how worthy and important the work you were doing was. Do you remember *The Electric Company*, *Reading Rainbow*, or *Gullah Gullah Island*? All were amazing shows centered around education, and they were all gone.

"I mean, every little bit helps, right?" She looked to me for approval, and I didn't have the heart to disagree.

"Yeah, it does. Heads-up: in the meeting, I'm going to mention some production changes."

"Great. I'll be ready to ask follow-up questions to keep the meeting exciting."

"I'm more concerned with how the message will be received."

Letitia stepped closer, eliminating the distance between us. I was tempted to kiss her, but we were outside the studio with cast and crew coming and going. The last thing I needed was talk of favoritism or the inappropriateness of our relationship. For the record, I didn't see anything wrong with the idea of Letitia and me dating. We were both grown, and what we did after hours was our own business.

Letitia reached for my hand, giving it a squeeze. "Just tell them all the things you said to me."

"I don't think I should mention how perfect I think your breasts are in mixed company."

Letitia bit her lip. "Okay. Don't tell them that. But if you let them know how much this show means to you, then it will help to relieve anxiety."

"Thanks."

"And remember, I've got your back."

Hearing those words made my heart swell. With Letitia in my corner, I was convinced I could do anything.

After our table read, I headed to the set to rehearse some of the scenes. Our sets were built to resemble a New York neighborhood, with the focus being a brownstone. The scene included Letitia and me hanging out on the stoop when Grumpy Gus showed up and challenged us to a game of dozens.

"Let's hit our marks so we can begin," one of the interns called out.

Grabbing my puppet, I made my way to the recessed frame built into the set. Letitia made it to the spot at the same time as I did. "Ladies first," I said, extending my hand so she would have stability while navigating into the hole.

"Thank you." She slipped her hand into mine, and my brain immediately started planning the rest of our lives together. Silly, I know, but I hadn't felt this in a long time. The "catching my breath, butterflies overtaking my stomach, goofy smiling while swinging my legs" feeling. For the most part, life was comprised of mundane moments, but crushing on Letitia had made every day less uneventful. In fact, each day was filled with surprise, because I wasn't used to being overtaken by these starry-eyed emotions.

Climbing in, I settled into a seated position. "Could they make these things any tighter?" After the words left my mouth, my face warmed with a blush. We were at the point in my crush where I said stupid shit and felt forced to fill even the minutest of silences.

"Days I'm on set, I use men's deodorant because it's definitely close quarters."

"Comfy cozy. Like peas in a pod." *God, Rustin, shut the fuck up.*

"Make room," Stanley shouted while he practically stepped on us to get to his place by my side.

"Mind your coffee." I raised Jabari overhead so he didn't get splashed by a wayward coffee droplet.

Stanley slid next to me with a huff.

I cast an irritated eye in his direction. On my set, food wasn't allowed for this exact reason.

Letitia nudged me in my arm, and when I turned, I was rewarded with her bright smile. "Ignore him," she whispered.

"I liked it better when it was just you and me."

Stanley, who was a tall man, attempted to carve out additional space for himself by pushing me closer to Letitia.

"Mind those elbows," I said.

"I'm gonna need you to scooch over." Stanley spread his elbows like they were wings.

"If I move any further, Letitia will end up in my lap."

"Like you wouldn't love that." Stanley sipped and spilled his coffee at the same time.

"What's that supposed to mean?"

"That *means*, I peep everything." He pointed his finger at Letitia and me.

"With those bifocals, I would hope so." He smelled like day-old burnt coffee and newspapers, and he wore big, brown, chunky glasses, which hung from his neck. At table reads and rehearsals, he'd put those glasses into sports mode, tightening the adjustable strap so his frames were affixed to his head almost like goggles.

"Boys, don't fight," Letitia whispered in hopes only I could hear. "He's just trying to assert his dominance. He wants you to know there's a pecking order." The thing about Letitia was she didn't know how to whisper. The set was already loud, with crew buzzing about, so she overcompensated by talking louder.

Stanley shouted back, "Gotdamn right there's a pecking order. I've been a part of this show since before you two were born. That should count for something."

"Thank you for your service." I rolled my eyes, not hiding my sarcasm. Don't get me wrong, Stanley was a working puppeteer.

His film, television, and stage credits stretched to over a hundred different projects. Showing him respect as a forefather in the field was a given, but he was also annoying, and he'd shoved me so far left you'd think I was a contortionist.

"Are you guys ready?" Diego asked.

"Yes. Let's just get done," Letitia said, groaning. "I have, like, ten minutes before I turn into a melted heap."

The air conditioning in the building was nonexistent. It was on but incapable of cooling down this hundred-year-old structure. Even if you stood directly underneath a vent, the flow of air was more of a trickle than full blast. Not only did we need money to continue operating, we needed money for building improvements.

"Got it. Stanley, start when you're ready," Diego called.

Stanley cleared this throat. "Hey, do you want to play a game?" His naturally monotone voice was now filled with expression. He'd trained his voice, which was unremarkable when not on set, to be rough while still affable. As a grumpy monster, there needed to be irritation mixed with levity in his tone.

"What kind of game?" I said in the childlike voice of Jabari.

"It's called dozens."

"Is it a matching game? Those are my favorite." Letitia's voice was high and bubbly.

"Nope."

"That's a relief," Jabari said. "Aaliyah is really good at matching games and always beats me."

"With the game of dozens, we take turns making fun of one another," Gus said.

"My mom says if you don't have something nice to say, you shouldn't say anything," Aaliyah said.

"That's what makes the game so fun, because you get to break the rules."

Aaliyah and Jabari looked at each other and shrugged. "Okay."

"I'll go first." Gus's words were followed by a delighted laugh. "You're so young, you think naptime is a punishment."

"It is. I'm not tired, and you can't make me go to sleep," Jabari protested.

"No one likes naps. You miss all the good stuff," Aaliyah said.

Letitia was a great counterpart because she was well prepared, and when she delivered the lines, the crew could be heard chuckling. There was a hop in her voice, and the intonation to her words brought Aaliyah's curious, upbeat nature to life. Crouched in the small space, I had no choice but to look in Letitia's direction. I didn't know how I didn't miss a line, because I was mesmerized by her performance and the way she beamed, her whole face glowing with joy. This was her happy place, and I could relate, because I also felt euphoric when I performed. Letitia was a star. I don't think she realized it, but for me it was undeniable.

"Now you have to insult me back," Gus said.

"Why?" Jabari asked.

"Because that's how this game works."

Jabari shook his head. "This doesn't sound like a fun game."

"I think I've got one," Aaliyah said. "Your apartment is so messy, I can't tell if it's a room or the lost-and-found for the entire neighborhood."

"That was a good one, Aaliyah," Jabari replied.

"Now, wait a minute. I don't like this game," Gus grumbled.

"But it was your idea," Aaliyah said.

"As neighbors, we should be kind to one another," Gus said.

"I think you hurt his feelings," Jabari said.

"I'm sorry, Gus. I agree, friends should be nice to one another."

"You consider me a friend?" Gus asked.

"Yeah. You were the first person to say hi to me when I moved to the neighborhood. Sure, it was to tell me I was too short and needed to move out of the way before I got stepped on…"

"I was just joshing."

"Who's Josh?" Jabari asked.

"I think it's his imaginary friend," Aaliyah whispered.

The surrounding crew chuckled at Letitia's delivery. "That was great, team. Let's break and prep for the next scene. Can we get Lulu Lark on set?" Diego barked out orders.

Stanley took that as his cue to leave, which freed up a ton of space. I slid over, giving Letitia room. "That was good. You were great."

"It's just rehearsal," she said.

"But you're consistently good…every time, every take, which I appreciate."

Letitia's eyes softened and settled on me. "You make it easy for me to be at my best."

Her big mink eyes had a warming effect, pulling me in. I was ready to be wrapped around her finger, to fulfill her every wish, to extend my hand and feel the softness of her palm connecting with mine.

Jellybean Junction was a full-time job on top of my other full-time jobs. I didn't have time to fall in love, but for Letitia, I was ready to clear my calendar.

An afternoon meeting was placed on the cast's and crews' calendar to continue to discuss plans to save the show. We didn't even have a year. We needed to hit the ground hard and fast and never let up. I'd created an aggressive plan that would touch every area of production, and I'd need everyone's help to make it happen.

Luckily Brea was firmly onboard, and Letitia seemed to be down for creative ways to get the show off life support. As the room gradually filled, I organized my thoughts. Normally, I preferred to hang back in the cut and watch things unfold. But as I was producer, *Jellybean Junction* was now my baby, a responsibility I took very seriously. Failure was an experience I was unfamiliar with, and the next few months would test my resolve.

"I want to thank you all for joining this meeting after a long day of production. But I wanted to share my thoughts on the direction of the show going forward."

"What does that mean?" Stanley asked.

"Viewership is down. We're going against thirty-second shorts and programs that overstimulate to capture attention. We need to compete."

"How do you propose we do that?" Letitia's eyes smiled at me, offering support.

"I think we need a refresh. Some of our puppets haven't been reimagined since the seventies." I surveyed the room, pointing at Stanley. "Take Grumpy Gus: his fur is shedding, and his coloring is a burnt mustard."

"Gus's fur is a rich Dijon yellow, thank you very much." Stanley scowled.

"Yeah, and it plays horribly on high-definition televisions."

Letitia raised her hand, anxiously waving as if there was a possibility I'd miss her.

"Yes, Letitia."

"Grumpy Gus has been mustard yellow forever. It makes him who he is." Her usual cheery, relaxed tone had an edge to it.

"What played in the eighties doesn't work now. We can't keep doing the same things when it's clear they're no longer benefiting us. Lulu Lark could benefit from a remake. Right now, she's a dingy white bird. What if we made her a vibrant blue jay or red robin?"

The crowd grumbled. I'd expected my ideas to be met with resistance. We only had a few months to make major changes that would engage our evolving audience. The show was iconic, but it was stuck in the past. If we didn't make adjustments, we'd be obsolete in a year's time.

"So you want to change everything that makes *Jellybean Junction* great?" Letitia asked.

I liked Letitia a lot, and I hoped to spend more time with her in the future, but this was business. My decisions were in no way personal, and I was hopeful she could distinguish between the two. As the producer of the show, it was my responsibility to provide the best product. And after reviewing previous episodes and each cast member's file, I'd come up with a comprehensive plan of improvements that could put us in a better position to succeed. Truthfully, these changes might not move the needle, but doing nothing would definitely seal our fate.

"If it was great, I wouldn't be here. If the show was doing great, we wouldn't be seriously considering putting a for-sale sign on the building."

Brea cleared her throat and spoke up. "I think we should be open to the possibility of some changes. It doesn't have to be a negative thing. Change can bring forth a rebirth, which we desperately need."

Forging ahead, I continued, "I also think the show should focus less on the monsters and more on the human puppets."

An audible gasp overtook the room. I'd anticipated resistance, which was why I was ripping the Band-Aid off and laying out my plans. Despite what Brea had said, these weren't suggestions.

"Let me get this straight—you're evicting puppets from *Jellybean Junction?*" Letitia said.

"Are we talking layoffs?" a gruff voice in the crowd asked.

"No. The goal has always been to avoid layoffs, and that hasn't changed," I replied.

Letitia raised her hand again, but this time she didn't wait for me to call on her. "I'm all for minor tweaks, but this seems like a knee-jerk reaction. You haven't even been here a month. You don't know what this show needs."

"Maybe that's true, but if the ratings from the past few months are any indication, neither do any of you."

Daggers. Letitia was shooting daggers in my direction.

"I'll be meeting with the costume department and puppeteers individually to provide details and direction on our revamp. Are there any general questions I can answer?"

"Was the coffeemaker your way of buttering us all up?" Rhodes asked.

"No. An office should have a working coffeemaker."

"I have a question," Letitia said.

"Go for it."

"Was all that stuff you said from the other day bullshit?"

I could only guess she was referring to our private conversation over lunch. "That's not a general question."

"Wow…*wow*."

"I think this is a good stopping point," Brea said.

The screeching of chairs and hushed whispers filled the room as the cast and crew made their way out of the conference room. Letitia was in a heated exchange with Stanley as I approached.

"I've got your back," she reassured him, and I could only assume she'd be protecting him from me.

"Pardon the interruption. Letitia, can we talk?"

Stanley eyeballed me. "I should have known. Any time we've hired a new producer, they always bring their big ideas, and I've seen them all come and go."

"Well, if we don't get it right this time, we'll both be out of a job." I wasn't going to let a man with a matted and funky-smelling puppet try to put me in my place. Stanley walked away, and I continued, "I just wanted to check in, make sure you were okay."

"*Jellybean Junction* is important to me," Letitia said. "It's an institution and needs to be protected. Those were *your* words."

"And I meant them. Change isn't inherently a bad thing."

"Neither is tradition. The show works because it's predictable. That predictability creates comfort and safety. Not everything needs a rebrand."

"I agree with you. But our declining viewership says otherwise."

"You're new here, so I don't know why you're so intent on rocking the boat."

"I'm attempting to patch the holes so we don't sink," I said.

"Grumpy Gus doesn't need an extreme makeover, and Lulu Lark is a fucking dove, not a blue jay or a red robin."

"Tell me how you really feel," I joked, hoping to lighten the mood. The last thing I wanted was for work to get in the way of the friendship we were building. For the first time in a long while, I'd found someone I felt comfortable talking to for hours, and when the words ran dry, I still had a warm contentment in my belly because silence with Letitia was just as magical.

"I loathe each and every one of your ideas."

Okay...I needed to fix this. I didn't want to be at odds with her, not for something as cut and dry as this. *Junction* was failing and required an intervention. "You weren't opposed to my suggestions this weekend of the increased airtime for Aaliyah."

"Don't even get me started. You don't think I know what that was?"

"What do you mean?"

"You said all the right things, complimented me, talked about my work at the library. You are good. *Wow.* I stand corrected—you'd make a great actor, because you fooled me with your lies."

"Lies? I said all those things because I meant them. You're extremely talented."

Letitia covered her ears. "*La, la, la, la…* I can't hear you. Compliment bombing isn't going to work on me again."

"Do you really think that little of me?"

Her brow furrowed, and for a second, I thought her tone would soften. "I don't know you."

"Letitia, I would never use you. I genuinely wanted to get to know you better creatively. What happened after that was a pleasant surprise, but in no way was it my plan. I like you, and I want to see you again."

"I'm just finding it hard to get past the feeling I was played. You know what this show means to me. *Jellybean Junction* is like a beautiful brownstone, and you want to take a sledgehammer to it and build a contemporary box. I'm sorry, but I can't get past that." Letitia didn't give me a chance to persuade her-she walked away, leaving me to try to pinpoint where we'd gone wrong.

CHAPTER 9
Letitia

"**WHAT WAS THAT** in there?" Brea asked as I entered her office.

"I came here to ask you the same damn thing."

"Why were you attacking Rustin? He's here to help us."

"Fuck Rustin. We don't need his help."

"Well, my boss thinks differently. He believes having Rustin's name attached to the new season of *Junction* will pull in viewers. And Rustin has been given authority to make any and all changes he deems necessary."

"And you're okay with this?"

"I didn't have a choice. But I happen to agree with him."

"You're in a small camp, because most of us hate this. All of it. Consider this *the resistance*," I shouted.

"You're ill-prepared to lead a resistance. You cut the crusts off your sandwiches."

"I like my bread to have one consistency. The crust is an unwelcome surprise."

"Yeah, you'll make a great leader."

"Hey, hey, ho, ho, Rustin Hayes has got to go," I yelled.

Brea circled her desk, shutting her office door. "*Junction* is in danger. Anything Rustin can do to fix that is invited. He'll bring eyes to our show."

"We don't want Rustin Hayes fans. We want *Junction* fans."

"Why are you so mad?"

"Because his ideas will ruin everything."

"Okay, but seriously, why are *you* so upset?"

The list was long. Rustin was trying to change everything that made the show great. I now realized our working lunch had been some sort of fishing expedition to gauge my temperature. But chiefly, it was his almost sending me to the upper room when we made out at my apartment, only to reveal himself as Judas. "Because I made out with him," I blurted.

"With whom?"

"Rustin."

"When did this happen?"

"On Saturday."

"And you didn't call me the next morning?"

"I was still processing everything. And honestly, I'm feeling a little played."

"How so?"

"Because there is a very real possibility the only reason he was cozying up to me was so he could gain an ally."

"An ally?" she asked.

"Yeah. I watch shows like *Ultimate Gameplan* and *Outlast Island.* The sole purpose of which is to gain alliances so in the end you can just stab them in the back."

"And you think Rustin has his knife at the ready?"

"He played me like a fiddle," I said.

"Details. I want *thorough* details. You know when you tell a story, and I usually ask for the abbreviated version?"

"Yeah."

"Not this time. I want blow by blow." Brea rubbed her hands together. "First, was he a good kisser?"

"Yes. He was very good. So good, in fact, I was prepared to go all the way. And I would have gotten away with it too, if it weren't for the fire."

"What?"

"Someone in the building had a minor kitchen fire, and we had to evacuate."

"How far did you go?"

"It was a fairly adult make-out session."

"Wait. Make-out? Were you naked?"

My ears and cheeks grew hot. I wasn't interested in sharing the finer points. "It doesn't matter because it's never happening again."

"Why not?"

"Because he is enemy numero uno."

"Please stop acting like you're bilingual."

"I can count to ten in Spanish. And you know where I learned that? Watching *Jellybean Junction*." I pretended to drop an imaginary mic.

"He doesn't have to be the enemy. Maybe if you work with him and push some of your ideas, he'll listen."

"So, if I suggested he quit and go kick rocks, you think he'd agree to it?"

"I suggest you figure out how to move past this, because Rustin isn't going anywhere," Brea said.

"Don't be so sure," I whispered.

"Hmm. What was that?"

"Nothing."

"Good. That's what I thought." Her phone rang. Before answering, she reminded me, "After work, I want a full report."

Over a cheese and meat board, Brea grilled me about Rustin. I had to choose my words carefully because I didn't want to mention just how far we'd gone. Mostly because this was Classic Letitia. I moved way too fast, fell way too hard, and often ended up having to pick my broken heart up off the floor. Who was I? Flirting with the new hire who was technically my boss and then eagerly participating in sexual activities, only for him to be the complete opposite of who he claimed he was.

And my willingly offering up my support and pussy with no discernment. Rustin wasn't even my type.

Okay, that was a lie. He was exactly my type, right down to the painted fingernails. In every iteration of this life, that man would be my perfect physical match. Why were the men I was attracted to never attracted to me—or worse, attracted but morally gray? *Jellybean Junction* wasn't the problem; everyone else was.

Back at home, I surveyed the room filled with half-empty boxes and clothes in plastic bags. Unpacking should be my focus, not reminiscing on Rustin's big dick. I didn't even get to touch it. There had to be a correlation between dick size and fuckboy activity, because men with small dicks understood they had one time to fuck up because the dick wasn't keeping her. Rustin, on the other hand, had a dick that would have a bitch extending grace. But not this bitch, because I was standing on business.

My phone rang, pulling me from my thoughts. The face of my mother was displayed on my screen. Rolling my eyes, I called up a quick prayer that the conversation would be brief and non-hostile.

"Hello?"

"Hello, Letitia. Can you hear me?"

"Yes. Hi, Mom."

"Wait… Hello?"

"Can you not hear me?" Maybe I should lean into this bad connection and just end the call.

"Ah, there you are. How are you?"

"I'm good."

"And the new place?"

"I'm still settling in. I have a lot of boxes left to unpack."

"How much unpacking could there be? Your place is the size of a closet."

Brace for takeoff. "Yeah…but, like, a really *nice* walk-in closet."

"I don't know why you opted for a studio in Harlem, of all places."

"I like Harlem. It's close to work, with great restaurants and friendly people."

"It's not the safest environment."

"That's not true," I said. "It's just as safe as any other place in New York. Safer than Connecticut. I saw online this rich lawyer guy and his wife just got murdered, killed in their home, so not very safe."

"Incidents like that are few and far between. But in Harlem, well, they don't even report it because of the frequency of occurrences."

"You need to lay off the Facebook."

"Work's going well?" she asked.

"Yeah…you know. How's Dad?"

"I think his eyes are getting worse. He may need bifocals, which is sending him into a spiral. First his hair, and now his sight."

"Bifocals are cool now. Tell him all the trendy kids are rocking them in Soho and Tribeca."

"Is that so?"

That was a lie, but I would say anything to make my dad feel better. And if I had to pretend his new bug-eyed lenses made him look good, I was prepared to do it.

"So, I'm calling with some news," Mom said.

"You're pregnant."

"Letitia, don't be rude."

"What? Women are having children well into their fifties."

"Can I please finish?" Her voice was laced with irritation, which was all a part of my plan. If our sparse interactions were unpleasant, she wouldn't want to seek them out.

"Sure, but fair warning, I'm only accepting good news at this time."

"Then this will brighten your day. Your sister and I are coming to New York."

"Do you mean North Yorkshire in England?" I asked hopefully.

"No, silly, the Big Apple. The city that never sleeps. The melting pot."

"Why? I mean…why?"

"We have a pageant in New Jersey, and I thought, why not extend our stay and visit my eldest?"

"Madison's doing pageants again?" I asked.

"She got a job with the organization."

"Doing what, exactly?"

"Registration."

"Why didn't she get a cool summer job, like polishing the pole at a strip club?"

"Your jokes are unsettling. It's just busywork. After college, she'll focus on the wedding."

"She's really going through with that?"

"Why wouldn't she?"

"I don't know, Mom, maybe because she's far too young and inexperienced to settle down," I replied. "Maybe because Jared is a man-child who will expect her to cater to his every whim. You don't marry your high school sweetheart."

"Not everyone needs to kiss a line of frogs to find the right one."

"I'm not kissing frogs, and I'm not looking for the right one. I'm young, and I live in New York. Your twenties are about having fun."

"And your thirties are all about regrets."

"When are you planning on coming? Because I don't know… Work's hectic. We got a new boss, and I'm still getting situated in the apartment."

"You live in a shoebox and work for nonprofit television. It can't be that overwhelming. If you'd stayed in Milford, you could've bought a four-bedroom home for the same price."

"Yeah, but that means I'd have to live in Milford."

"I don't like the thought of you in a strange city all alone."

"It's not strange, and I'm not alone. I have tons of friends."

"When we get in, I plan on staying with you," Mom said.

My hearing went wonky, and I couldn't make out any other words. She sounded like the teachers from Charlie Brown. Why would she stay with me? I said my prayers at night. I ate vegetables. I tried to get up at a reasonable time on the weekends. What did I do to deserve this? "Excuse me?"

"I said, I hope that's okay. Madison keeps hinting at wanting adventure and a possible move to Manhattan."

"I live in a shoebox…remember?"

"Exactly. She needs to see the realities of city living."

"So you're going to use my place to scare her straight?"

"Something like that. You won't even know we're there. We're going to be at the MoMA and visit that huge candy store, and we have an appointment at Kleinfeld."

"I thought your plan was to discourage Maddie from moving here," I said. "I can guarantee the Museum of Modern Art and a sugar rush isn't going to help your cause."

"We're also going to take the subway, which is essentially an underground death trap."

"Okay. Good to hear you've thought this through."

"Maybe you could take a few days off to hang with us."

"Is Dad coming?"

"No. He has to work," she said.

"The show is in a really big transition, and I don't know if I'll be able to get away, but maybe. Send me the dates."

"I'm so excited to see you, Letitia."

My mother was the type of woman who meant well, but often got in her own way. She'd meant well when she opted to adopt a Black child. She'd meant well when she relaxed my hair at eight because it made it more manageable. She'd meant well when she said she refused to see color, even though everyone else made a point to let me know I didn't quite belong. I loved my mother, but I'd be lying if I said I did not resent some of her choices.

"Yeah. Tell Dad I said hi."

Tossing my phone aside, I face-planted onto my futon. Could this day get any worse? The last thing I needed was my mother picking apart my unfinished apartment, all while I tried to save *Jellybean Junction* and deep-dive into why I always picked the wrong guy.

For the next few days, there were closed-door meetings I wasn't invited to involving Brea, Rustin, and Harold DiMaggio, the studio head. Harold only showed up in person to deliver bad news—when our season was reduced from twenty-eight episodes to twenty-two, Harold was there. When they fired some of our senior crew members because of union concerns and replaced them with kids fresh out of college, Harold was there, claiming it was a good thing and would free up additional funds for the show. Ask me if we ever saw a dime of those funds. No, we didn't, because Harold DiMaggio was a fucking liar.

And now he, Rustin, and Brea announced yet another meeting of the full cast and crew in the small auditorium we used to host live shows in. The tickets were reasonably priced, and on the third Saturday of each month, kids were free with a paying adult. I loved those shows because the energy was different when you performed live, and the payoff was seeing the faces of the little ones light up. I would have done that shit for free.

But Harold put the kibosh on the event after crunching some numbers and determining we were losing money with the added electricity costs and free refreshments. So, Saturdays at *Jellybean Junction* were canceled. No discussion. We all just received an email telling us the shows would end, effective immediately.

And this was what happened when television executives weren't artists or creatives. They didn't appreciate the craft, and if something wasn't making money, then it didn't make sense for the bottom line. Don't get me wrong, of course we needed to make money to keep the lights on and the staff paid, but being in the black wasn't always the most important thing.

"This room smells like mothballs." Phoebe took a seat next to me. The once-decent theater space was now a storage room with boxes of cleaning supplies and mop heads.

"Did you know that the detailed moldings are real gold? Technically, it's gold leaf they brushed on, but gold all the same," I said.

The theater was small, but the attention to detail was top notch. Back in the day, people took pride in majestic spaces, and this place was a jewel and one of my favorite hiding spots, even if after spending time in it, I suffered a contact high from the fumes.

The ceiling was painted a deep twilight blue to mimic the sky, designed to make the audience feel like they were witnessing the constellations at work. The ornamentation was elaborate, with columns and chubby-cheeked cherubs. Front and center, the stage was framed by a golden curtain, which was slightly tattered from disuse, but you could still imagine the majesty this space once offered.

Beautiful buildings shouldn't be allowed to turn into wastelands. We could thank Harold and his cronies for this. This studio was neglected and in need of a massive overhaul. It was also located in a prime location in Harlem, which, at the moment, was experiencing a resurgence. If Harold had his way, he'd tear this place down and turn it into a Whole Foods. I swear to God, I would chain myself to the building if it ever came to that.

"How many times are they going to tell us to start working on our résumés?" Phoebe said. "This is why I stay my ass in the costume department, because all management wants to do is talk. I bet they'll suggest we take a pay cut or try to push out the old folks at the top of the pay scale."

"They can't do that, can they?"

"When you hold all the cards, you can do whatever you want."

"But we have the union. They'll step in and protect us."

"Everyone has their own motivations." She pointed to Rustin, who was making his way to the stage. "Take him, for instance. What is a whiz kid like him doing at an aging show like this? I did some Googles, and he is being touted as the future of virtual effects and puppetry. He was the head puppeteer on several Celestial Divide projects. Celestial Divide, that shit is like the holy grail for people like us."

"You think he's got an ulterior motive?" I asked.

"You don't come down from your perch unless you see something shiny you want to claim as your own."

The gears in my head were spinning. Rustin being here had never made sense to me. He claimed to be trying to save a beloved show, but what was his real angle?

"Come on in, don't be shy. There're still some seats in the front," Brea shouted, ignoring the microphone Rustin was attempting to hand her. "We want to jump right into things and not take up any more of your time then we have to. Yep, Stanley, we have a seat front and center just for you."

"Why does it feel like we're sheep being corralled to our slaughter?" Phoebe was a classic pessimist. Everything was horrible and getting worse with each passing minute.

Brea continued to shout. Her calm and collected demeanor seemed slightly off kilter. No doubt because of Harold, whom we all hated. He didn't get it, and he never would, and he was content with allowing this show to fail. You didn't want to be the guy who canceled a venerable show, but if you made it impossible to operate, harder to produce quality episodes, then we'd eventually implode for him. Harold worked for public television, but he wasn't in this position out of the kindness of his heart. He was like the pastor who drove a top-of-the-line luxury vehicle while his parishioners had to stand in food lines and work second jobs to make ends meet.

"As some of you may have noticed, Harold from National Community Network is here today. Big thank you to him for making time in his busy schedule."

Harold waved, and a discontented grumble rolled through the crowd. Maybe we were on the precipice of a revolt. Down with executive control who only want to stifle us! Creatives didn't thrive in cages. We needed to be allowed to roam free to be inspired. Studio heads wanted ten versions of the same thing. If it worked at NBC, it should work here.

"Glad to be here. I'm just looking forward to lending my support during this challenging time." If support was a final twist of the knife Rustin had lodged in our backs, then he was in the right place.

Brea continued, "The other day, Rustin mentioned necessary changes that could potentially revamp the show."

I released an audible huff, pinning my arms across my chest. Brea flashed a warning glare in my direction. She was going to make a great mom, because she had the expression most mothers made when their child was doing too much down pat.

"We thought it be best to have a conversation that was structured and allowed Rustin to fully articulate the reason for the shifting focus. Rustin, the stage is yours," she said.

"Thanks, Brea, and thanks again to Harold for being in attendance." His tone did not align with his words. Rustin's back was rigid and his jawline tight. He was not happy to be on this stage with this group. "I love this show. I distinctly remember singing along to the numbers song, the jazzy beat helping me remember that nine came before ten. I remember Grumpy Gus and wondering, why is he always so mad? Beyond that, I wondered how did they do it. Even at six, I knew the puppets weren't real, but the magic was undeniable."

For some odd reason, I was holding my breath, hanging on to his every word. He sounded like the man I'd had lunch with who was in love with the show as much as I was. Maybe he was having second thoughts. Perhaps this meeting was about a change of heart and not a change in circumstance.

"Time changes everything. Take this theater, for instance. I'm sure at one point this place was bustling with positive energy and possibilities, and now it's a storage room that until today I didn't even know existed. You don't see craftsmanship like this nowadays, and it's been covered in painter plastic and hidden behind boxes."

"It's a fucking shame," I whispered under my breath.

"*Jellybean Junction* is going to end up just like this space…frozen in time, only appreciated by a select few, and eventually forgotten."

The crowd grumbled at the thought. Phoebe shouted, "We've heard this song and dance before. Guys like you making threats, cutting talent, asking us to do more with less."

"We won't make it to the next twelve months, let alone fifty more years, if we don't do something," Rustin said.

"We bust our asses every day to put on a great show," Valerie called out.

"I believe you. I've seen it with my own eyes. But no one cares because no one is watching."

I spoke up, having heard enough. "That's not true. Our ratings are decent, and we are in the news and all over social media. People love this show."

"People love nostalgia. People used to love listening to stories on the radio, and then, *poof*, the era was over. And cut to forty years later, and now people are flocking to podcasts—storytelling for the twenty-first century. It's a pivot and evolution. It's about transmutation, a metamorphosis. Consider the transformation from a caterpillar to a butterfly—the process is hidden, but we know it's a painful one. The caterpillar's cells are dying and regrowing into something new. In the end, after the growing pains, you are presented with something unique, something beautiful. *Junction* can be beautiful again, innovative, interesting. We have good bones—a strong, talented cast."

Surveying the room, I tried to determine if others were buying what Rustin was selling. Many were leaning forward in their seats, just like me. Some were nodding. He was a good speaker, and he almost had me convinced. I wasn't opposed to change; I just wasn't willing to lose the essence of the show. And Harold being here wasn't a ringing endorsement for our embracing these sweeping changes.

"And you think changing Grumpy Gus's fur is the radical change we need to get five-year-olds to tune back in?" I asked.

"There are cosmetic changes and then there are foundational changes."

"*Ding, ding, ding.* Foundational changes. I know what that's code for. Last time we made foundational changes, we lost a crop of talented engineers, camera operators, and stagehands," Phoebe shouted.

"Yeah, I remember that. The bigwigs said some shit about streamlining," Stanley chimed in.

Phoebe continued, "And we all know how that turned out. We were left with crew in their twenties with no practical experience, using our show as a stepping stone to bigger studios like Nickelodeon or Cinevault. Two seasons ago, Valerie and I were filling in as camera operators because we were so severely understaffed."

"And no one paid us extra for that," Valerie added.

Rustin cleared his throat. "Can I speak to some of your points?"

"Be my guest," Phoebe said.

"I wasn't here for a lot of that, but I've witnessed the need for the cast and crew to know a little bit of everything to keep this show running. And while I appreciate the ingenuity, aren't you tired? Don't you deserve state-of-the-art equipment and AC that doesn't feel like someone's just blowing warm air in your face? Don't we deserve quality fabrics and embellishments?"

Fuck, his delivery was similar to a preacher's, with the obligatory excited hop between sentences. *Are you tired?* Ha. *Do you think you deserve better?* Ha. *You can do it alone, but why should you have to?* Ha. *Jesus,* ha, *can save you. Put your trust in the Lordt. Can I get an amen?* Ha. *Can I get a witnesssssss? Let the congregation shout hallelujah.* Insert spontaneous praise dance here.

"The only way we get those things is through course correction—aggressive, full force, all hands on deck to change the trajectory of our future."

"What about an increase in pay? When do we see that?" Stanley asked.

"Listen, none of us are here because of the pay. We show up every day because we love what we do. But if we're successful and funds are available, I'm sure Harold would be agreeable to pay increase discussions on a case-by-case basis."

Harold's head jerked backward, and his eyes slammed into Rustin. This had *not* been agreed upon. Rustin was off script, making promises he could never keep.

"We've had our fair share of empty promises," Stanley said.

"Well, right now, all I have is promises, or you can opt for the unemployment line if you prefer."

Fuck him. I wasn't going to let him control me. "I'm not afraid to start over." I was terrified, but I always managed to land on my feet.

Rustin's eyes narrowed, and his features were marred with concern. "I don't want to lose you. Uhm…any of you. But I understand we all have tough decisions to make. Anyway, I've brought on a social media manager from my studio to help increase our engagement and tailor our message for a target audience. The social media password has been changed, so no more clutter posts from the crew. I appreciate the enthusiasm, but our page is scattered and lacks professionalism. This is a business, not a recreational improv troupe."

"So you're cracking the whip," Phoebe said.

"I'm not cracking any whips. I just think we'd benefit from some new processes and—"

"Say it…streamlining." I knew that word was a trigger for many in the room, and my aim was to rile them up.

"—procedures. I was going to say procedures."

Brea clapped. "What lively discussion. I was going to open it up for questions…" She eyed Rustin to gauge his temperature. "But I think we've been very vocal, which is a good thing. Remember our open-door policy if you ever need to talk to Rustin or me."

Phoebe leaned in and whispered, "This was an epic waste of time."

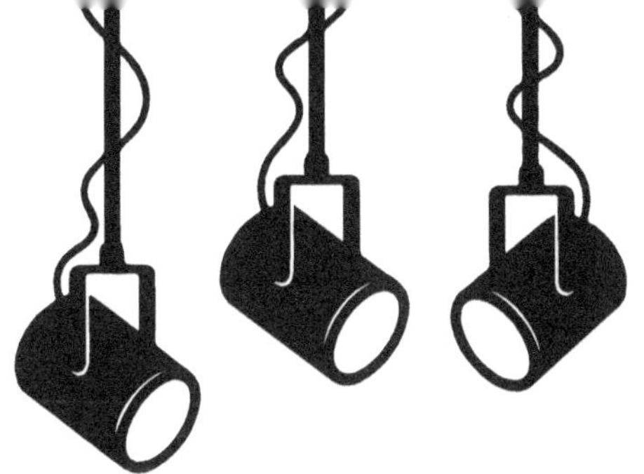

CHAPTER 10
Rustin

THE DAY-TO-DAY OPERATIONS of my musical *U-Turn* were no longer managed by me. For the longest time, I was territorial when it came to the show, and could you blame me? I'd written it and composed all the songs. *U-Turn* was my baby. I was like a protective parent—my newborn could only be cared for by me. But over time, the concept of controlling every aspect of the show burnt me out. I'd had to step all the way back and trust the people I hired were capable of keeping the wheels on the bus.

Outside the Ewing Theatre was a huge poster behind glass with the human and puppet cast. Fans of the musical would line up before the show to take pictures with the poster in the background. Opening night seven years ago, the first show was sold out. The next morning, the reviews were glowing. All of a sudden, I was getting calls from various morning shows asking me to be a guest. I didn't even have a manager and just checked my calendar to confirm my availability.

Being a one-man show, I'd quickly learned instafame demanded a lot. It was like being tossed into the middle of the ocean with no floaties and an immense fear of water. I felt most comfortable behind the scenes or on the stage. Center stage was far less intimate than sitting next to Kelly Ripa and fielding questions about my personal life. *Where are you from? How long have you been a playwright? What was your inspiration for* U-Turn*?* The secret answer to that last question was weed.

One night after a smoke session, I thought it would be funny to create a world in which humans and puppets coexisted in a not-so-ordinary neighborhood, navigating the absurdities of adulthood with wide-eyed optimism…and occasional existential dread. I played Malik Buttons, a bright-eyed puppet fresh out of college, who moves to a big city with dreams of becoming a famous author. But reality hits hard when he's stuck working at a questionable theme restaurant, struggling to pay rent, and realizing life doesn't come with a script like his favorite childhood shows. I guess others resonated with the idea, because the show became a hit.

The question I was asked most often was: "What's next?" After *U-Turn* premiered on Broadway, when I opened Thread and Thespian, when I was named to *Forbes'* 30 under 30, it was always, "What's next?" Never "great job" or "amazing work." For some reason, I wasn't allowed to rest on my laurels. If I wasn't working on the next big thing, I was wasting my talents. The what's-next of it all stalled my creative ambition because it was clear that whatever was next wouldn't be enough.

"Hey. You made it." Omar and I exchanged a dap.

"What am I looking at?" I asked.

"I wanted to show you some of the set changes we have planned. I know you saw the sketches, but they're nothing like the real thing."

"I'm still wondering why we need to make a change. If it ain't broke, don't fix it." I know…the irony wasn't lost on me. While I was making big changes at *Jellybean Junction*, I was resisting changes to my own show. *U-Turn* was different because what we were doing was working, and the proof was in the sold-out shows and months-long waiting list. *Junction*, on the other hand, was hemorrhaging viewers. The way with which children consumed content was shifting, and *Jellybean Junction* needed to pivot or get left behind.

"I knew you were going to say that," Omar said. "Didn't we discuss keeping an open mind?"

"My mind is open. I'm just hoping that it's blown."

Omar pointed to the stage. "What you're seeing right now is our revamped neighborhood. We've just made things a little bit brighter. When the story starts to get dark, we're going to rely on lighting to give it that ominous feel. But I think you'll agree the vibrant background will play well with the costuming and puppets."

I surveyed the stage dressing, which was supposed to look like my childhood neighborhood in Brooklyn before gentrification took over. There were brownstones and an apartment building with a fire escape. The changes were slight, but I had to admit they popped from the audience.

"You know I hate it when you go quiet. Say something."

"I like it," I said. "It's subtle but impactful."

"That's what I like to hear. I know you better than most, and I worked hard to ensure this would impress your critical eye."

"Show me the rest."

Omar ran through the other changes, with me signing off on all but one.

"See, that wasn't so bad," he said. "Now you can go home and be cranky somewhere else."

"I'm not cranky."

"Yes, you are. You've been in a mood the past week or so. Do you want to talk about it?"

"There's nothing to talk about."

"Okay."

If he was going to twist my arm, I'd talk. "It's just Letitia."

"The puppeteer at *Jellybean Junction* you're trying to fuck?"

"Why are you talking so loud? I'm not trying to do anything. And at this point, it doesn't matter because she hates me."

"Did you show her your Tony Award?" he asked.

"Shut up."

"My bad. What did you do?"

"I did my job and gave the team the cold, stark reality of the future of the show."

Omar cringed. "You suck at delivering bad news."

He was right. I preferred to get to the point with no filler. "Is there any good way to do that? People should know they could be unemployed in six months. I'd want to know."

"Shit, not me. Ignorance is bliss. I'd rather come in one day and get shitcanned than obsess over it for months."

"I needed to explain the reason for the rapid changes."

"You're the show's new producer. Of course there would be changes."

"Well, Letitia isn't happy about any of it," I said.

"You know as well as anybody that being the boss can be hard, and there will always be individuals who'll try to test your authority."

"I get that, but I think she's building a mini rebellion. They're making signs."

"What do the signs say?"

"*Rustin is busted. Hayes's days are numbered.*"

"That second one sounds like a threat."

"I know I have to give them time to process their emotions, but shit's getting old, especially with Letitia at the helm, and it sucks because we hit it off early on."

"I hate to say I told you so, but you had no business taking on this job when we already have other important projects in the works," Omar said.

"*Jellybean Junction* deserves a chance."

"Maybe it does, but that doesn't mean you have to come riding in on your white horse to save the day. That show has gotten a ton of second chances."

"And each time, it was pronounced dead, it managed to find a way to inhale fresh air."

"It's gonna suck when it takes its last gasp for breath on your watch." Omar patted my back sympathetically.

My welcome at *Jellybean Junction* had shifted. Normal getting-to-know-you conversations were replaced by people trying to suck up to me, thinking it would garner favor when the ax dropped. Crew members stood in corners and excluded me from joining but were almost certainly talking about me. And Letitia was leading the charge. She rolled her eyes at the sound of my voice, audibly huffing to note her disdain. Any idea I presented was met with her counter-opinion.

If I stated the sky was blue, she'd disagree and rally the cast to agree with her. She was a disrupter, and everything I did, she took as a reason to push back. I thought she'd created a hit list just so she could scribble my name in permanent marker in the number one position. She reserved all her smoke for me and only me.

Maybe I deserved it. Who did I think I was coming to this production and moving shit around? That was a rhetorical question, because if anyone could save this show, it was me.

In my office, I reviewed our analytics, which showed year-over-year viewership was slipping. There was an abundance of content to consume, and *Junction* wasn't breaking through the noise. Loss of viewers meant loss of revenue, which would ultimately result in terminations, followed closely by cancellation. I'd never backed down from a challenge when people said a musical with puppets wasn't marketable; I proved them wrong. When I was told I should stick to Broadway, I chose to create a production studio. At first we were small potatoes operating out of my apartment, but things quickly picked up. I was a Black man in the entertainment industry, where talent was a dime a dozen. What really separated one from the pack was perseverance and patience.

A knock on my open door pulled my attention from my laptop. It was Letitia, the last person I'd expected to pay me a visit.

"Hi. Come on in."

"Don't mean to bother you," she said.

"No, it's not… You're never a bother. How can I help you?" The fact that we were at odds didn't sit right with me. Not trying to be Captain Obvious, but I liked Letitia…a lot. And I was hoping to get to know her better, but now I was unsure.

"Brea said you had an open-door policy. Is that true?"

For her, yes. "Yeah… I mean…anything you need, I got you."

Letitia took a seat, scanning the room, landing on the framed posters stacked against the wall. "If *Junction* is on its last legs, why bring in office décor?"

"Because I plan to be here for a while."

"Are you gonna put them up?"

"Yeah. I just need to bring a level from home," I said. But she hadn't come in here to trade décor tips.

"At the staff meeting, it felt like you were saying a whole lot of nothing. If you have a plan, why not share it in full?"

"Because every time I spoke, you were looking to cut me off at the knees."

"I just want the truth."

I banged my hand on the desk and yelled, "You can't handle the truth!" Letitia appeared alarmed, and she fidgeted in her chair. "Sorry. Force of habit. Any time someone says they want the truth, I'm compelled to deliver that line."

"Is that a movie you're quoting?"

"*A Few Good Men.* You can't handle the truth," I said again, hoping it sparked recognition.

"Never heard of it."

"You can ask me anything."

"And you won't gaslight me or try to distract me with the possibilities of bonuses and pay increases?"

"I never guaranteed that."

"No, but you did casually drop it into your speech so ears would perk up."

She had me there. I'd known exactly what I was doing when I hinted at compensation, but I had to do something—I was losing the crowd. Letitia and others were shouting and questioning my claims. To get the staff on board, you had to make them believe there was something in it for them. They needed to feel invested. And if we managed to save this show, I'd strongly advocate for bonuses. Most people didn't call me on my bullshit because they either didn't notice or didn't care, as long as they were happy with the end result.

"I'm not the bad guy," I said.

"If you're not, then why are you using their playbook?"

"I found it in the trash and thought it might be useful." My quip didn't land.

"You know, I thought you were one of us. Imagination over profit. Connecting with your audience. Feeling something every time you step on the stage."

"Everyone wants honey, but no one wants to pay for a jar. Television, films, and educational programs can't run on awards, attaboys, or that buzzy feeling you get when you step in front of a camera. We need money to keep creating. And if you think otherwise, you're just being naïve."

"We already have something great."

"I'm not disagreeing with you, but no one is watching, so it doesn't matter."

Letitia rummaged in her extra-large tote bag, pulling out stacks of envelopes. "Janiyah is watching and learned her ABCs." She tossed the letter on my desk. "Carlos watches every day with his *abuela*." She chucked another letter on my desk. Her voice was tight and trembling, each word pushed out like it weighed too much to carry. It wavered at the edges, cracking mid-sentence, as if emotion were squeezing her throat closed. "An-ming tunes in after school. Grumpy Gus is her favorite monster." She added that letter and a pile of twenty or so others to my desk. "People are watching. You just don't fucking care." There was a fragile quality to her words, soft but strained.

I narrowed my eyes and homed in on her face, noting the way her eyes glistened under the harsh office lights. Letitia was blinking too fast, like she was trying to will the tears away. The muscles in her jaw ruminated tense and tight; her normally plump lips were pressed together in a line so firm it looked painful. Her arms were crossed like a barrier, shoulders drawn in as if she could shrink away from whatever had cut her so deeply.

Was it me? Was I the cause of all this pain? I wanted to help, but it felt like at every turn, I was making shit worse. There was a tremble in her fingers that she didn't seem to notice, and though she hadn't said a word since slamming the fan letters on my desk, the tension in her body spoke volumes. One more nudge, one wrong word, and she'd unravel right there.

Reaching for one of the letters, I searched for my next words. I wasn't good with emotions—mine or others'—but I wanted to round the desk and just rock her in my arms until she was in a better place. "I, uhm, I don't know what to say."

The energy in the room shifted like the first drop on the Steel Vengeance roller coaster. Letitia's gaze smashed into me, sucking the air from my lungs.

My mouth was dry, but I managed to eke out, "I'm not good with words."

"You had a whole lot of words on that stage."

"I wrote that—prepared, planning for every possible question."

"Playing the role of the concerned citizen to a T."

"Why do you insist that the only right way is your way?"

"Funny, I was going to ask you the same fucking thing." Her chair squeaked as she stood. "I want you to know I see you. You're not this phenom power player. You're a fucking phony, and it's just a matter of time before everyone knows it."

Letitia left my office, leaving me thunderstruck—because she was right.

CHAPTER 11
Letitia

SOME WEEKENDS I'D take the train to Connecticut to visit my family. Often my trips coincided with days my mother would be away from home. She was a kiddie pageant judge, so on weekends, she was usually somewhere in Middle America objectifying toddlers. Eloise Vincent was a premier competition judge. As a former Miss America contestant, what she thought mattered in the pageant world. I would like to note here that she never won and actually never ranked higher than third place during her run.

The sleepy coastal town of Milford was everything you'd expect a place named Milford to be, with quintessential small-town vibes, charming homes, and tons of white people. It had been named one of the best small towns ten years in a row per the City Scope Rankings.

"Hello?" I called after using my key to enter my childhood home. "Dad?"

As if on cue, my father rounded the corner with his World's Best Dad mug in hand. "Hey, kiddo. What are you doing here?" He pulled me into a hug that, even while he was trying not to spill his coffee, was soul affirming.

"Needed a change of scenery."

"Well, you missed your mother. She left last night for Overland Park."

"Where's that?" I dropped my weekender bag on the tile in the entryway.

"Some place in Kansas."

The pageant circuit had an app, which I checked regularly. When competitions were held in the city, which was surprisingly rare, I was either conveniently out of town or swamped by work, making a meet-up impossible. "So sad I missed her."

"You hungry? I have some leftover bacon from breakfast, and I can whip up some eggs."

"Yes, please." My dad was… Imagine Tom Hanks and then amplify the awesomeness meter by one hundred.

My childhood home was a bright two-story colonial. Every nook and cranny felt lived in, in a good way. Family photos decorated the walls, putting our "perfect" family on display. The space smelled of spring water, Lysol, and bacon. My memories of this place were initially fond, but the longer I stayed, the more the reality of growing up with Momma Vincent bled through.

"Nice to have a free weekend?" I took a seat at the kitchen table.

"It is, but don't tell your mother." My dad handed me a glass of his newest smoothie creation.

I know they claim opposites attract, but my mom and dad were *so* dissimilar. He'd let us put Dawn soap on the hardwood floors in the long entry hall and use it as a slip-and-slide. My mother's idea of fun was table etiquette drills.

"Where do you place the salad fork?" she'd ask us kids on a Sunday afternoon when I just wanted to watch *Bring It On* for the millionth time.

"Your secret is safe with me," I said to Dad.

"How's work treating you?"

"Uhm." I took a long sip from my smoothie. "Busy—some major changes. We got a new producer."

"Is she cool?"

"He. And *he* is Rustin Hayes."

My dad snapped around, facing me. "The puppet guy? I just watched a TED Talk with him. He seemed kinda arrogant, but there was no doubting he's smart as a whip."

He has a TED Talk? "He's all that and more."

"So, you like him?"

"What?" Heat whooshed up my neck, settling on to my cheeks.

"Your new boss—you like him. I bet you're learning a lot. I hope he knows how talented you are."

"He definitely knows my name." I was never one to cause a fuss, but *Junction* deserved better than a man-child's attempt to rip power from the people who stood by the show. I wanted brand-new 4K cameras and a bigger costume budget, not monster makeovers. I suspected there was more to this rally for change than Rustin and crew were letting on. And if he wouldn't talk, I'd have to go to the next best option, Brea.

"You're the best thing on that show," Dad said. "I only watch for you."

"That would make sense, seeing how you're sixty—not exactly our target audience."

"I'm fifty-nine."

"My bad." I instinctually scanned my phone screen. Nothing new, just friends trying to coordinate bar-hopping locations for tonight. A notification from DoorDash trying to tempt me to order a sweet treat.

A text message from Rustin Hayes.

Rustin

Hey. I don't like how we left
things. Can we talk?

Why was he texting me, and why did my heart skip when I saw his name? At least we agreed on one thing—our last conversation had left a sour taste in my mouth. I'd damn near poured my heart out to him, and his response was essentially, "Cool story, bro." For a genius, he was terrible with people. I don't even know what I wanted him to say—that he heard me? That *Junction* was his number one priority? That he'd treat this property with care? Maybe that he'd rethink some of his changes?

At our lunch, he'd seemed to agree that the claims that our show was a fossil of yesteryear were wrong. And now he was leading the charge to splice and manipulate the DNA of the show to create a facsimile of what it was—a watered-down carbon copy that did not measure up to the original.

"Hey, space cadet. You okay?" Dad asked.

"Sorry. It's nothing, just a work email. How are the twins?"

"Good, but you'd know that if you called them."

"The phone works both ways."

My father set a plate in front of me before taking a seat across from me with a fresh cup of coffee. "Curly Q, you know I wish you kids were closer."

"The twins are close." Same friends. Same mannerisms. *Twin powers, activate!* When they shouted that, it was usually right before they ratted on me for things I didn't do.

"We're family. You don't have to navigate this world alone. Everyone needs someone. I worry about you."

"I'm fine, and I love Madison and Mason."

"But?"

"No but. Why would there be a but?"

"I know we're not perfect, but I hope we did right by you."

When they adopted me, they didn't know anything about raising a child, let alone a Black one. I was three, and I remember very little from those first few years. But I distinctly remembered the moment I knew I was different. It was when the twins came home from the hospital and the doting look in my mother's eyes told me I was second tier. Who wanted a Black girl with developmental delays when you had the dynamic duo of M&M?

"Trust me, I recognize how lucky I am," I said dryly.

"Letty, I didn't mean it that way."

"No, I know." I tore off a piece of bacon and popped it into my mouth.

He patted my hand. "Are you spending the night?"

"Yeah, if it's okay."

"Great. You can come to bingo with me tonight."

"At twenty-seven, I thought I'd be spending my Saturdays bar-hopping and making out with cute guys, but this is good too," I joked.

"You know David is the bingo announcer."

"David?"

"Your prom date."

"Oh, *that* David. Eww."

"You used to like him."

"I was a teenager, and he looked like a modern-day Jason Priestley." I truly believe I was born in the wrong decade, because if I was an adult in Priestley's heyday, I'd have let him fuck me 90210 times.

"So what else is going on with you? Any boyfriends I need to know about?"

"Daddy."

"Not trying to pry, but I want to know if I should start saving for another wedding."

"If and when that day comes, I'm going to the courthouse."

"You'll have to run that one by your mother."

"She is not the boss of me."

"Says the kid who only visits when her mother is out of town."

Wow, he'd clocked me.

"Here. Have another drink. My treat," I said, pulling Brea to the bar.

"What has gotten into you?"

"Can't a girl just show her bestie some love?"

"Not when that girl's a cheapskate."

"I'm not cheap, I'm house poor." My plan was to ply Brea with drinks until she became loose-lipped. I wanted to know what Rustin was scheming so I could put plans in motion to stop it. Our Friday team happy hours were the perfect setting—drinks were half price, and everyone was trying to let loose after a long week.

"I think we have a good show in the can," she said. "Love the whole thrift-shopping angle—shows kids you can find cool threads if you're willing to search."

Cool threads? Yeah, she was tipsy. "Totally agree. Let's find a table." I carried the three glasses to our table like a pro. Sliding into a booth, I scanned the room for Rustin, who was in a corner nursing a beer while talking to Phoebe. More like she was talking his ears off. I'd paid her twenty dollars to keep him occupied. So, twenty dollars and the forty I'd already paid for drinks… If I were lucky, I could get out of this for under one hundred dollars.

"Sandy asked about you," Brea said. "She's convinced you're wasting away because you haven't been over for dinner in a while."

"You can assure her I'm not malnourished."

"Are you going to flake next week too? We were going to try that new restaurant everyone's raving about in Brooklyn."

"No, I'll be there. Last thing I need is allegations of being a bad friend."

"I was thinking of inviting Rustin."

"Why would you do that?" I asked.

"I feel bad for him. You and the others haven't been very nice."

"That's because he's a capitalist douchebag."

"He's not. He actually has some pretty good ideas."

Like manna from the heavens. I didn't even need to direct the conversation—Brea was ready to open the vault.

"Really, like what?" I hoisted a casual shoulder to indicate I wasn't all *that* interested.

Brea checked behind her to confirm no one was eavesdropping. "He wants to appeal to a modern audience."

"What the fuck does that mean? Our target audience is comprised of two- to five-year-olds. How do we get more modern than that?"

"I think he's meaning the parents who determine what their children watch. He believes if you hook in a fresh crop of parents, increased viewership will follow."

"How's he going to do that?" I was no longer playing it cool. Just call me Lois Lane, because I was fishing for a story.

"That's why he brought on a social media manager."

"I liked our social media arrangement."

"It was like the wild, wild west. And some of the content Stanley posted was overly political and polarizing. This new manager has a bona-fide degree in communication and social media analytics."

"Whoopty-fucking-doo."

"Be nice."

"What else?" I plastered a smile on my face.

"I don't know—edgier topics; shorter, punchier segments."

My face turned sour, and I had to briefly conceal it with my glass. He wanted a kids' show to be *edgier*. What were we supposed to become, the *South Park* of children's television? I didn't recall Mr. Rogers getting a sleeve of tattoos and smoking whacky tobaccy.

"What's wrong?" Brea asked.

"I'm fine."

"No, you're not. You have that strained smirk, and your eyes are so wide it looks like you took a hit of LSD."

"None of this concerns you?"

"No. I trust Rustin."

"You barely know him, and you're inviting him to family dinner. What's next, asking him to be your future child's godfather?"

"Stanley is going to be the godfather."

"Eww. What? I will not raise a child with Stanley."

"Good, because I don't plan on dying anytime soon." Brea pushed her drink aside and reached for the water. "Can I say something?"

"Can I stop you?"

"You've been in a mood lately."

"Gee, I wonder why."

"Rustin—"

"Ugh."

"Rustin is smart, and he's actually tracked the trends and watched hours of programming geared toward kids—both traditional and online. He is not just pulling shit out of his ass."

"He's just the smartest motherfucker in the room." I rolled my eyes.

"He's a child prodigy. Did you know he can play the piano like Herbie Hancock?"

"I can't say I'm familiar with Mr. Hancock's Wikipedia page."

"He was part of the Miles Davis Quintet."

"Okay. I'll add Herbie to my playlist. Now, can we stop talking about him and Rustin?"

"Final piece of advice: you need to have sex. Not just any old type of sex, but the kind that when it's over, you have trouble recalling your name." She downed the last of her drink. "Now I have to take a piss."

Sex was the last thing on my mind.

Okay, it was on my mind a little. Sure, I could stuff my own fanny pack, but sometimes it was nice to hold other people's stuff. It had been a while for me. The last guy I'd kissed was Rustin. I'd also rocked against his lap and felt the girth and firmness of his dick. But things had dissolved quickly, and he was now public enemy number one instead of a viable suitor, which, if I were being honest, pissed me off. Rustin ticked off all of my boxes—smart, passionate about his career, someone you could talk to for hours about everything and nothing. He was a good kisser; he had immaculate fingernails.

And I know that's kind of frivolous, but most guys did not pay attention to hand hygiene. Because who wanted to worry about a UTI while being finger-banged?

Did I mention his dick was big? Because it was, and I'd hoped to ride it hard and often. But then he'd had to go and be an asshole.

You know what? *Bump this shit.* I didn't have a chill button, and right now, I was in heat-seeking mode, fittin' to light Rustin's ass up.

Weaving through the crowd, I made a beeline for the man of the hour. "We need to talk."

"You owe me twenty dollars," Phoebe said.

"I already paid you," I responded through gritted teeth.

"I was talking to Rustin. I bet him you'd be storming over here in less than fifteen minutes, and I was right."

Rustin pulled out his wallet and handed her a fifty-dollar bill. "Do you have change?"

"No, I do not." Phoebe tucked the money in her bra. "Good doing business with y'all. I hope you two figure it out."

"Really? You're placing bets with an old woman?" I said.

"What was your money for?"

"Nunya."

"As in none of my business?"

"Yep."

"What are you, eight?"

"Well, I do work on a kids' show."

"What do you want?"

Phoebe had taken a bit of the steam out of my sail, but I was a theater kid. I could improv while the rage reignited. "I'm onto you."

"Okay." His smile was the most irritating thing about him. It was aloof, like we were playing a game of chess, and he already had me in check.

"I know all about your plans to gut *Jellybean Junction* and turn it into a neighborhood with a Bean There Done That and smoke shops."

"What?"

"Edgier, punchier, hmm. What's that code for?"

"Pretty self-explanatory."

"You want to gentrify the *Junction* with puppets who wear beanies and have gauge piercings."

"And that's a bad thing?"

"Yeah, because this isn't one of your fucking plays. How is a parent supposed to explain the addition of Inky the monster with body modifications and a split tongue?"

Rustin grabbed my arm and pulled me down the hall, which was lined with patrons waiting to use the restrooms. Brea was among them and flashed me a concerned look. Through an exit-only door, we found ourselves on the loading dock in the back of the building. No doubt he was trying to avoid being cussed out in front of a crowd. From the dock, the music was still loud, but at least I didn't have to shout to be heard.

"What the fuck is your problem?" he asked.

"You. You're my problem."

"And you're a pesky thorn in my side."

"I hope it leaves a bruise," I snarled.

"Who have you been talking to?"

"Wouldn't you like to know?"

"Brea?"

My head retracted at the quick guess. "No…not Brea. Not Brea."

"You're a bad liar."

"Well, we can't all be an expert at it like you who, lies any time his mouth is moving."

Rustin's crooked little smirk re-emerged, and he licked his lips while scanning the length of my body. The weight of his glare had the desired effect. Butterflies circled my stomach, and I swallowed hard to regain my composure. "You look nice tonight. Did you go home and change before you got here?"

"Liar. I do not. Wait. What?" I was ripping him a new one, and he was doling out compliments?

"You clearly went home and put on fuck-me jeans, and I'm just trying to figure out why."

Running my finger over the denim, I objected, "These are *not* fuck-me jeans."

"Then why's your ass sitting like that?"

"That's just my ass."

"I'm just trying to figure out who you got all dressed up for."

I may have run home, taken a just-the-essentials shower, and selected this specific pair of faded wide-legged jeans because I liked the way my butt and thighs looked in them. But it was not for him… Do you hear me? If you take his side, I swear to God, I will never talk to you again.

"News flash, Buster Brown: not everything is about you."

In response, he just bit his lip.

"You changed the subject because that's what guilty people do."

"I have a clear conscience about most things. Did you get my text message?" he asked.

"Do you ever get tired of poking your pudgy fingers into everything? You have the musical, your studio, and film projects lined up five years out. You don't need *Junction* too."

"I would have difficulty sleeping at night knowing *Jellybean Junction* was set for the trash heap."

"I would save it, duh, obviously."

"Okay. How?" He stepped back, crossed his arms over his chest, and waited for me to reveal my plan.

"What?"

"How. Are. *You*. Going. To. Do. That?"

"Quality content."

"We already have that. No one's watching. What's next?"

"I'd personally reach out to past and potential donors."

"How does that fix the ratings problem?"

Know-it-alls were the worst. They always had so many fucking *questions*. I wasn't a planner; I was a doer. And if I had to strap explosives to my chest and bum-rush the fancy corporate offices to get the studio execs to change their minds, then so be it.

"We'd advertise."

"With what money?" he asked.

"You don't think I see what you're trying to do? You're confusing me. I may not have a twenty-five-page slideshow, but I can fix this."

"Letitia, I think you're brilliant, and you light up a stage…"

Totally, absolutely unrelated, but can we just talk about the fact that he thought I was smart and talented and my ass was phat?

I was angry, but can we just have a moment for his appreciating my finer assets? Truthfully, if the show wasn't going under and Rustin wasn't a maniacal evil genius, this could be something. When we kissed, it was like I already knew him. Like we'd lived a lifetime together. But then he'd ruined it all with his shenanigans.

Rustin's shoulders relaxed, his gaze softened, and for the first time tonight, I was momentarily at ease. "If I'm being honest with you, I'm not even certain my changes will move the needle," he said.

And just like that, I felt like I was drowning. *Jellybean Junction* was so much more than a paycheck to me. This show had saved my life and fostered my passion. It also had given me a family in a city where friends were difficult to make. Yes, we squabbled and disagreed, but at the end of the day, I'd do anything for them—even Stanley, who was, in fact, an amazing puppeteer.

If you tell him I said that, I'll deny it. His head is already big enough.

"How can they do this?" I said.

"Because not enough people give a fuck about this show. It's just us. We're all we've got."

I knew why *I* rode so hard for this show, but Rustin's reasons always seemed a little thin. A man who had everything didn't have to go so hard to save a fledgling public television show. "You're not telling me something. I don't know what it is, but there is no way in hell you joined this show just to watch it fail."

"I just need to get these changes pushed through," he said. "I'm working on new script requirements and taking meetings with celebrities for possible guest voices."

"Voicing our puppets?"

"Nope. New puppets that the design team is already working on."

"So stunts and fanfare. That's your plan?"

"My plan is based on numbers and data. Your plan is based on throwing spaghetti at the wall and hoping it sticks."

"Who's your first guest voice? The Rock voicing a rock? Super fucking original."

"It's a fresh take."

"It's a gimmick." I gasped, my eyes growing big. "I get it now. Your ego wouldn't let you say no to this. Only the great and powerful Rustin Hayes and his band of celebrity friends can fix it."

"Nope. That's not it at all."

"While you're looking for your viral moment, I'll continue to do what I've always done, look out for the best interests of these kids." My voice was shaky because I wanted to pummel him. "Look at me," I snapped. "I'm going to be on your ass like white on rice. No sleep. No peace. From this moment on, it's my mission to make your life a living fucking hell."

"The conversation started out bad, then it took a slight turn in the positive direction, but you swung it around, turning it into a complete dumpster fire."

Rustin was walking toward me. Why was he doing that? Was he going to make the first move and push me off the loading dock? As he advanced, I slowly retreated into a wall, leaving me nowhere to go. He was inches from my face.

"We can disagree, but we don't have to be disagreeable, so stop acting like a Mafia boss and be all the way fucking for real." Rustin tilted his head, his eyes narrowing. "I'm going to touch you now."

"What?" I managed to eke out. It was hard to be mad when he was this close, looking so good and smelling like warm spices and damp lumber. This was his after-hours go-to scent. At work, he smelled like the forest with a hint of floral.

"There's a bug in your hair."

I screamed bloody murder, running around in circles on the dock while shaking my hair incessantly. "No. Help me. Please get it." Rustin grabbed my arm, and I screamed louder. "I don't like bugs." He ran his fingers through my hair, and for a second, I forgot I was in distress.

"It's gone."

"Is it on me?" I spun around several times.

"It's gone."

"I don't like bugs. Are you laughing at me?"

"I mean, one minute you're threatening to break my legs, and the next you're crying and screaming like a baby."

I pouted in response.

"Are you okay?" he asked.

"Yeah. I don't like bugs; I never have. My brother was always bringing things home in jars and shoeboxes." I shivered at the memory.

"It's a rational fear. I hate rats."

"You live in New York."

"Yeah, and I'm in a constant state of terror."

I tried desperately to hide the smile that was tugging at the corners of my lips.

"Is that a smile? I haven't been able to get a smile out of you in god knows how long."

"Not a smile, it's…gas."

"I've been cussed out by a lot of people, but I like your insults the best. And that's saying a lot, because you know that one guy who reviews food online in his car? He once told me to fuck off, and he's cool with *everybody*."

This time I couldn't quash my laughter. "What did you do to piss Keith Lee off?"

Rustin's jaw went slack, and he released a deep exhale. "I don't…I don't know. I guess I just bring out the worst in people."

"I should go. Brea saw us leaving, and it's just a matter of time before she comes checking to make sure you're still alive."

"Got it."

"Oh, speaking of… Brea's going to invite you to dinner."

His face brightened. "Oh."

"Say no."

He paused for a moment, and I readied my rebuttal to an objection that never came. "Okay."

Static-filled music played overhead like someone was scratching a turntable with no specific rhythm in mind. "What the *fuck* is this?" I yelled, feeling pressure building behind my eyes.

"It's Herbie Hancock's 'Rockit.'"

"Why is everybody talking about fucking Herbie Hancock?"

CHAPTER 12

Rustin

"JACKIE, SO GLAD you could make it." I stood, pulling her into a hug. Jacqueline Bernard was my financial advisor, a trusted friend, and the mother of Omar's daughter.

"Rustin, how did you get a reservation at Salt and Smoke? I've been on the waitlist for months."

"I said I was Rustin Hayes, and it kind of fell into place from there."

Jackie sat, and then I returned to the seat across from her. This place was family-style seating, with long wooden tables partially set with a bread plate, wine and water glasses, and silverware. In this instance, the silverware was black and gold. Since day one, this place was a must-try for residents, with a Black chef who'd attended the prestigious Culinary Institute of America.

"I knew taking you on as a client would come with perks but I was thinking free Broadway tickets. Not dinners at Michelin-star restaurants."

"Only the best for the woman who manages my money. You drinking?"

"I'm always drinking." Jackie was a powerhouse with her own firm. All of my friends were college-educated overachievers who thought they were going to change the world—next in line to becoming the next Steve Jobs, Shonda Rhimes, or Jay-Z.

We ordered drinks while we waited for our table to fill up. If I'd known it was family style, I would've passed on this restaurant. I wasn't interested in awkward small talk with a middle-aged couple who'd flown in from Wisconsin just to try this restaurant because it was one of Oprah's favorite things.

"So, let's get the business out of the way so we can just enjoy the night." Jackie swirled her glass of wine.

This was why I kept Jackie on the payroll. She was smart, efficient, and knew I didn't like filler conversations.

"Agreed. I asked you here because I need a clear picture of my spending power."

"Are you buying another place?" she asked.

"No. Nothing like that, but I am interested in the possibility of a big purchase of the TV show variety."

Her head pitched back. "How big are we talking?"

Leaning in, I whispered, "*Jellybean Junction*."

"The kids' show? Oona used to love that show."

"Yeah, well, now she thinks it's a show for babies."

Jackie chuckled. "Did she tell you that?"

"Yeah. I asked your child if she wanted to be a part of my focus group, and she told me she was now into the *Yippee* show and something called *You've Been Served*, which I thought was the Omarion movie, but apparently, it's something entirely different."

"It's on YouTube. It involves kids playing pranks on each other."

"Very highbrow."

"*Jellybean Junction* may be out of favor, but securing the rights isn't going to be cheap."

"I just need to know if I can swing it alone or if I need to wrangle some investors."

"If you go the investor route, I'd imagine you'd want a controlling stake."

"You would imagine correctly," I said.

"I'd have to officially crunch some numbers, but you could swing it, leverage the studio, cash out some stocks. Can I ask why *Jellybean Junction*?"

"Because it's a gold mine, and I want all of it."

"I didn't realize it was for sale."

"Technically, it's not, and it may never be, but if it does go up for sale, I want to get my ducks in a row so I can scoop it up. I don't want some fucking bidding war."

"Are you sure it's a sound investment?" she asked. "I mean, Oona says it's lame, and she's on the pulse of what's cool."

"Shit is circular—everything comes back. What's considered uncool now is touted as a refreshing, nostalgic spin on a classic in five years."

"When did you become an optimist?"

"When I'm betting on myself, I'm always a glass-is-half-full type of guy." I winked.

"I'll work up some potential scenarios for acquisition."

"I want all the intellectual properties, the show, the catalog, the merchandising."

"Whoa. The price just went up considerably. Have you and Omar talked about this?"

"Not directly."

"Rus, I do not want to get in the middle of you two."

"Do you work for me or Omar?"

"I work for you, but Omar and I are in a really good space, parenting-wise."

"And I'd never do anything to jeopardize that," I said. "I'm not swiping my Amex just yet. I just want to know my options so when I have to present it to Omar, I'm coming with facts and not hypotheticals."

"What's this about?"

"Saving an institution, building generational—"

"Rustin?" a very familiar voice called my name, and I turned to find Brea at the hostess stand waving at me. I offered a timid wave back and froze when I caught sight of Letitia in a blue floral milkmaid dress that cinched at the waist. The fact she was walking around the city looking this fucking hot… You couldn't tell me men weren't approaching her left, right, and center, and I hated that for me.

"Who's that?"

Shit. I'd almost forgotten I was here with Jackie. I snatched the tasting menu from her hand. "Hey, do me a favor, and don't tell them who you are."

"What?"

I glanced at Brea, Letitia, and another woman I didn't recognize, making their way over to my table. "Don't tell them you're my financial advisor."

"Why?"

"No time to explain."

"Are we on a date? Should I say this is a date?"

"Hey! Small world." Brea was now right up on me with arms outstretched. Standing, I gave her a hug. "Rustin, this is my wife, Sandra."

"It's so nice to finally meet you." I sounded like I'd just finished running around the block.

"This night just gets better and better—first dinner at Salt and Smoke and now meeting the infamous Rustin Hayes," Sandra said.

"Letitia's here too." Brea stepped aside so Letitia was in full view. "Such a small world."

"Actually, there's eight million people in New York city, so this is like a *Twilight Zone*–level coincidence," Letitia said. "And you are?" She shoved her hand in Jackie's direction.

"Uhm, Jackie Bernard… Uh, Rustin's—"

"Jackie, this is Brea, her wife Sandy, and Letitia," I interjected. All three took seats, and in a stroke of luck, Letitia ended up next to me. "I work with Brea and Letitia."

"At Thread and Thespian?" Jackie asked.

"No, at *Jellybean Junction*."

Jackie's face was one of shock. "When did that happen?"

"Feels like fourteen years." Letitia sighed.

"Let's get you ladies some drinks." I waved over the waiter.

Brea mentioned Sandra was a doctor, and for the next few minutes, I listened politely as she discussed her profession. While the ladies asked questions, I snuck peeks at Letitia. Seeing her outside of the dusty, overheated studio was similar to catching a zebra walking down Fifth Avenue. She was one of a kind, and being in her presence was something you'd recall fondly for years. The thin straps revealed a tan line a shade lighter than her current complexion. Her focus was trained on the menu, and she appeared to be deep in thought, contemplating whether to order the fish or duck.

Letitia set her menu on her bread plate. "So, this is a date?" She pointed at me and Jackie.

"Erm, well, uhm—"

"Yeah," Jackie blurted.

Letitia's eyes met mine, and they were laced with an emotion I was unfamiliar with from her. "You're on a date?"

"Uhm."

"Great. The salad's here!" Brea's reaction to a tossed pear salad was over the top, if you asked me.

"How'd you two meet?" Letitia asked.

"We go way back. We've known each other for years," Jackie said.

"And you're dating now?"

"Can we talk about something else, anything else?" I asked.

"We can talk about where the prices are." Letitia flipped the menu over.

"Places like this don't have prices. If you have to ask, it's out of your budget," Sandra said.

"Next dinner is on me," Letitia replied. "We're going to McDonald's, and you can each have a Happy Meal."

"Life is about experiences," Sandra said. "Work hard, play hard. Don't you agree, Rustin?"

"That's one of my favorite mottos," I said.

"I play hard," Letitia chimed in.

"Sitting in an unfurnished apartment saving pins to a décor vision board is not playing hard." Brea selected a dinner roll from the bread basket.

"Wow. Your idea of fun is blowing wads of cash, and my idea of fun is aspirational thinking. Eventually, I'm gonna hit add to cart on that couch I've been eyeing, and you'll all be jealous."

"I doubt that."

"What's that supposed to mean?"

"It means you have decision paralysis, babe," Brea said.

"I do not."

Brea and Sandra exchanged glances. "Then I dare you to buy something—anything—from your wish list," Brea said.

"The fuck? You invite a girl to dinner and then chew her ass out? Enough about me, let's talk about Jackie. What do you do?"

Jackie deferred to me. "She's a hair…celebrity…hairdresser to the stars," I said.

Brea's eyes lit up. "Yeah? Like who?"

Jackie was in the hot seat. "Sam."

"Pop princess Sammie?"

"No, uhm, Sam Jackson. Samuel L. Jackson."

"He doesn't have any hair," Letitia said.

"That's right, because I cut it all." Jackie smiled at me apologetically. She was a whiz at numbers and decimal points, but it was clear lying wasn't her strong point—which, when you think about it, was actually a good thing. Who wanted an accountant who could lie without breaking a sweat?

"Rustin, I snuck a peek at the new guest puppets. Very nice," Brea said.

"Thank you."

"Letitia saw them too."

I turned to look at Letitia. "What did you think?" Yes, I was fishing for a compliment.

She shrugged my question off. "You've seen one puppet, you've seen 'em all."

"They're not really finished yet so…erm…"

Brea frowned in my direction. If I didn't know better, I'd think she was an ally in the Rustin Hayes Isn't That Bad Club.

"I don't think I've ever seen you at a loss for words." Jackie was quicky putting the puzzle pieces together and realizing Letitia was the Joanne Woodward to my Paul Newman, the June Carter to my Johnny Cash, the Pauletta to my Denzel.

"Sometimes words fail me," I said.

"Not true. You always have hot air to spew." Letitia took a sip of water.

Brea jerked her arm and whispered, "Be nice."

"I *am* being nice. I could have called him a thimble-headed dullard, but I didn't."

I leaned in, encroaching on her space, sparking a shocked expression. "Now you and I both know that's a lie. I'm a lot of things, but dumb ain't one of 'em."

"This is an A and B conversation."

"You're acting like a child." I dropped my voice so only she could hear.

"This is how I always act."

"If you're jealous, just say so."

"Of what, exactly?"

The waiter arrived with the next course—wild mushroom soup. I scanned Letitia's barely touched plate. It would be a shame to let good food go to waste. Nudging her with my shoulder, I asked, "Are you going to eat your pears?"

"No. Knock yourself out."

I stole each pear one by one. "You know these slices are, like, fifty dollars apiece?"

"I'd be much happier at home in my PJs with a bowl of clean-out-the-fridge ramen."

"Mmmh. That sounds good."

Jackie was in a heated conversation with Sandra about a reality dating show in which the participants married total strangers.

Letitia dropped her voice lower. "Do you like her?"

"Would it bother you if I did?"

"No, eww."

"If the circumstances were reversed and you were at this restaurant with some dude, I'd be crashing out right now."

"Ah, I didn't know you cared." Sarcasm was dripping from each word.

"I do care—very much so—even though you constantly abuse me."

"You're an easy target."

"This was so much fun." Brea rapped a hand against my back. "We must do this again."

"The food was amazing," Jackie agreed.

Letitia hurriedly hugged Brea and Sandy, whose car was waiting, and after a second round of hugs, the two were off. *Awkward* did not adequately describe the energy as we remained on the sidewalk. Me, my fake date, and the woman I wanted to be my girlfriend.

"It was so nice meeting you, Jackie," Letitia said.

"You too, Letitia. I hope we meet again. Maybe you and Rus could come over to my place for dinner sometime."

Letitia's eyes widened, horror-struck, like Jackie had suggested a threesome. "Mmm…maybe. You two get home safe." She headed in the direction of the subway.

"Hey. Wait up," I called before turning back to Jackie for a rushed goodbye. "Thanks for coming out." I hugged her.

"Anything, even lying, for my favorite client."

I opened the door to her RideX. "I definitely owe you one for that."

Jackie pointed down the block. "Your dream girl is getting away."

"Text me when you get home."

I jogged to catch up to Letitia.

"Hey, I asked you to hold up," I called.

"You're not the boss of me."

"Technically, I am."

"Don't remind me."

"I called a car…and, erm, it's… I'm going uptown. I could add a stop and drop you home."

"I'm fine." Her brisk steps didn't falter.

"It's late."

"I'm a big girl."

"The train from Brooklyn to Harlem would take forever. A car would cut your time in half, and you could be in footie pajamas with a bowl of ramen in no time."

Finally, she stopped hoofing it like an eighties businesswoman navigating rush-hour traffic. "Okay."

"Okay." I smacked my hands together, and my features finally relaxed into a smile. When the car arrived four minutes later, I opened the door, and we both slid in. Our driver pulled away from the curb, and we were off.

The city always had a humming, pulsating energy just underneath the surface, cloaked in neon from signs promoting a new movie, lip gloss, or a music project. I preferred RideX over the subway, in spite of the cost differential, because careening through a tunnel didn't feed my imagination. As a visual creature, I enjoyed watching the streets blur past in streaks of red and gold.

Headlights pooled like liquid stars against the slick black asphalt. Steam rose from manholes covers like ghosts exiled from the underworld. Every stoplight was a heartbeat. As we passed, you'd catch a glimpse of a couple arguing under a flickering bodega sign, a group of friends laughing at a crosswalk, or zooming by a food cart sizzling on the corner, perfuming the block with the roasted peanuts of halal spice.

"Do you really think your foreign puppet troupe is going to make the show better?" Letitia asked.

I released a sigh from the depths of my soul. The last thing I wanted to talk about was work. I'd offered Letitia a ride because I just wanted to be in her presence for a bit longer. "Can we just be nice to each other for the next hundred blocks?"

"We could just sit in silence."

I turned back to my window, resolving myself on a silent ride to Harlem, which normally I appreciated and often requested. I didn't want to make small talk with my driver. Of all the forms of conversation, small talk was my least favorite. But I wanted a chance to talk to Letitia to get another shot of getting her to like me. Or at the very least, not snarl when I entered a room. Right now, I was 0 for 273. But I was determined to keep trying.

Letitia inhaled as if she were going to speak, then stopped short. She was probably distracted by the bass thumps from a car beside us bumping some drill track that rattled its trunk and our windows. When our car finally turned left, she said, "I love riding in cars at night. There's something about watching the city go by and the sound of jazz music softly playing in the background."

"It has a calming effect, I'll give you that. Omar thinks I should listen to more jazz and less electronica."

"You like electronica?"

"I do."

"I took you for a neo-soul type of guy."

"I like that too." The switch-up was a mindfuck. One minute she was claws and teeth, and the next she was blinking lashes and bright smiles. For just a moment, she forgot she hated me. "Favorite electronica artist?"

"That's easy, Jayda G," she said. "We both bounced back and forth as we called up the song in our heads. "What about you?"

"Prodigy."

"Really? They're so intense."

"Their music is what my head sounds like at any given time."

"All breakbeats, distorted synths, and snarling vocals?"

"Exactly. Just like that."

"They're rebellious, high energy, and chaotic."

"Three words that do *not* describe me."

"No. Your descriptive words are *asshole, mega asshole,* and *more asshole.*"

"I thought we were being nice?"

"Just keeping you on your toes," she said.

"On my toes and walking on eggshells."

"Do I make you—"

"Horny?"

"Nervous. Who the fuck still says horny?" If I could have any superpower, it would be opening portals so I could easily disappear. Back to the window I'd go, watching the world pass me by. I was twenty-nine and often felt like I was falling behind. Crazy, I know, having accomplished so much in a short period of time. But success was difficult to maintain, and I'd often obsessed over my next move. After graduation, I thought by the time I was thirty I'd have *two* Broadway musicals, an off-Broadway play, and several movie options. By most measures, I was a success story, but for me, something was missing.

"Is Jackie going to get a second date?" Letitia asked.

"It wasn't a date."

"She seemed to think so."

"Jackie's a compulsive liar. You didn't know that, did you?"

"She was giving you eyes all night."

That had never happened, but I was touched she thought Jackie was interested in me. Jackie was my best friend's ex. There were no intimate feelings there.

"Jackie is like a sister to me. Like she said, we've known one another for a long time. What you saw was two friends catching up."

"You don't have to explain your love life to me."

"It's not like that." I snuck a glance at Letitia from the corner of my eye. "There is this woman at work, but the signs are kinda wonky."

"You have a workplace crush?"

"She's brash."

"Of course."

"Opinionated."

"What woman isn't?"

"And she smells like White Diamonds."

"What?"

"Phoebe. I have the hots for Phoebe," I joked.

"Hate to break it to you, but you don't stand a chance with her."

"Story of my life."

"Are your parents still in Brooklyn?" she asked, changing the subject.

"Yep. They live in a brownstone in Crown Heights. They talk about moving to Florida when they retire. But it's just talk; they'd hate it there. It's nice having them close, you know?"

"Yeah, the first chance I got, I moved away from home. I didn't want my parents—more specifically, my mother—to be all up in my business."

"Is she a micro-mom?"

"Micro-mom, helicopter mother, whatever you call it, she was the conductor, and we were the musicians following her lead. I didn't really know who I was until my senior year of college. Everything about me—all my likes and dislikes—were formulated by my mother."

"Was she a stay-at-home mom?"

"No. She's a judge for kids' pageants."

"Like *Toddlers & Tiaras*?"

"Exactly like that."

"Did you ever…?"

"Once or twice."

"Whoa. I'd like to see pictures."

"Never, ever. Those are in the vault, and when she dies, I'm going to burn them."

"Did you win?" I asked.

"Yes. I was *very* good. I wore a wig, fake teeth, and everything."

"Hold up. How old were you?"

"Six."

"Talent?"

"Ventriloquism."

"Shut the fuck up."

"Hand to Bible," she said.

My face brightened with excitement. "That explains Wags."

"I can drink a glass of water and sing at the same time."

"I don't really have any secret talents, but I can pick things up with my toes."

"Weird flex."

Letitia smiled at me and casually twirled strands of her hair. I enjoyed the comfortable ease of being together knowing we didn't need to put on airs or pretend to be someone we weren't. I loved her fire and the soft edges she'd accidentally revealed. How dumb did you have to be to fall in love with someone who hated you?

The car slowed to a stop in front of Letitia's place. "Thank you for the ride." Opening her door, she slid out.

"I'm going to get out for a second. Please don't drive off. I'll be right back," I told the driver before exiting the vehicle. "Letitia, hold up." She stopped at the entrance and turned to face me. "It was nice seeing you… Being able to see you…" I dropped my head in frustration. Why was my tongue betraying me in this moment? "I was hoping, erm, maybe, erm… It was nice seeing you."

"Good night."

I needed to not be here. I hurried back to the car with my tail tucked between my legs.

"Rustin?" Letitia called, and I stopped short of the door handle. "It was nice seeing you too."

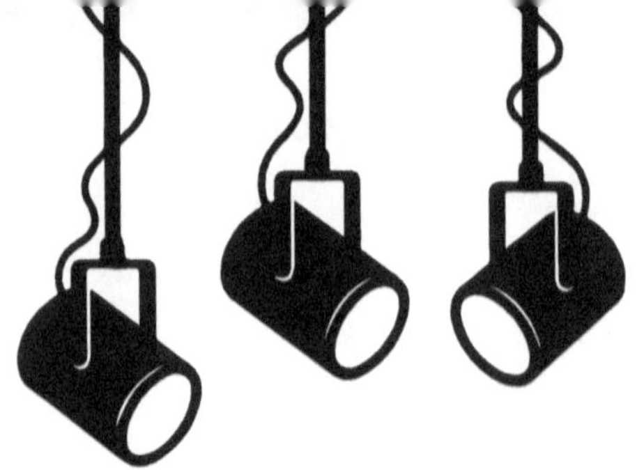

CHAPTER 13

Letitia

SEVERAL CAST MEMBERS were on set today to film a musical sequence. There were solos and choir parts that required everyone to hit their correct marks. Everything was going as planned until the end. When the song ended, Rustin fell back into his Jabari voice, which was light and childlike, a stark difference from his deeper speaking voice.

"And that's why working together makes everything better! Right, friends?"

The silence was longer than we'd practiced in rehearsal as the puppets glanced at each other suspiciously. I cleared my throat. "Ahem. Yes, about that… We, the puppets, have a few…demands."

"What are you talking about?" Rustin whispered.

"We feel unheard and overworked."

"The puppets or you?"

"Both."

"This isn't funny. Can we just finish the scene like we rehearsed?"

"You'd just love that, wouldn't you—a bunch of mindless minions who do what you say, when you say?"

Rustin cast a glance at the camera, laughing nervously. The one thing he hated more than anything was when people caused a scene. I was tired of debating. It was time for a revolt. If Rustin and Co. wouldn't listen, then they'd have to learn. "Oh, come on, guys, we're all a team! There's no need for a—"

My puppet Aaliyah interrupted him, raising a tiny megaphone. "Rustin Hayes, this is a *puppet rebellion*, and we want you to listen to our demands."

"Demands? What type of demands?"

Stanley shouted, "I never get to push the button."

"What button?"

"To the bubble machine. I never get to push the button because I'm the Grump. News flash—Grumps like bubbles too."

That was *not* one of our demands. We'd talked about this— only serious inquiries would be considered, and the bubble machine wasn't one of them.

"No. That's not a part of the plan," I protested.

"Okay… What if I let you press the button next time?" Rustin said.

"Shake on it?" Stanley walked over to Rustin with his hand extended, forcing me to intercept by wedging myself in between them.

"No deal. We talked about this, Stan. If you want bubbles, I'll buy you a fucking wand from the dollar store."

"Is that all I'm worth?"

"Hold on now. What about better snacks in the vending machines?" Valerie chimed in.

"Better snacks? How is that gonna help you when you're replaced by a celebrity puppet?" My mini revolt was not going as planned. I'd drafted a full script and everything. Stanley wasn't even supposed to speak. I knew I should have just chained myself to the front door.

Valerie elbowed her way to the front. "If we're asking for shit, I want more than just bubbles. I want name-brand chips and candy bars. No more of that knockoff shit."

"Can you please cut?" Rustin asked the camera operators.

"No. This needs to be documented," I said.

"What exactly, the mutiny you have on your hands?"

"We want a restoration of order and tradition. We have a list of well-thought-out demands."

He surveyed the crowd. It was clear their hearts weren't in this exercise. Everyone was all rah-rah an hour ago, but now when it really mattered, it was crickets. "Bubbles and quality snacks for everyone who puts down the mini picket signs, and next happy hour drinks are on me."

"Deal." Stanley pushed me aside to shake Rustin's hand. Turning to me, he patted my shoulder. "Tough break, kiddo."

"Tough break? You folded like origami."

"Let's quit for lunch."

On Rustin's cue, the cast and crew dispersed, leaving me with miniature signs and an unopened box of silly string.

"You can bribe the entire team, but that doesn't change the fact you just want to Rustify this show," I said to Rustin.

"Rustify?"

"You know exactly what I mean."

"Nope. Gotta say I'm lost."

"This isn't *U-Turn*, and we don't need the Rustin Hayes treatment."

"What you *need* to do is touch grass."

"And you need to choke." His eyes grew wide in response to my own venom. "That...was probably too far."

"You think?"

"I'm not the best with quick comebacks because I don't usually have to deal with unagreeable people, so no, I don't want you to choke, but if you suffered from a stye in your eye I wouldn't mourn."

"Letitia, you do know I'm trying to do what's best for the show, right?" he asked.

"I think the success or failure of this show is secondary to your own personal motives."

"And what are those?"

"I haven't figured that part out yet, but I Googled Jackie— full name Jacqueline Bernard—and she owns Parkline Wealth Management."

My intent had been to learn more about Rustin's mystery date. She was pretty and smart, and she and Rustin appeared comfortable with each other. First dates were usually awkward—at least, mine were. Those two were practically finishing each other's sentences.

"So you're a stalker?" he asked.

"Concerned citizen. So, I had to ask myself, why would Rustin be on a date with a financial advisor?"

"It wasn't a date. But what did you come up with?" His eyes pinged from my face to the floor.

"Wouldn't *you* like to know." I currently had nothing, but I was on the right path. "You should probably change your name to Rockwell, because wherever you go, I'm gonna be *watching you*."

"That was actually a very good tie-in."

My body language shifted, and my shoulders retreated from my ears, a slight smile taking over my face. "Thank you. I just kind of thought of it on the spot. Luckily, you got the reference."

Shit, I'd let my guard slip. Do you know how difficult it was staying mad at a man whose face you wanted to sit on? I quickly shut down my giddy emotions and returned to my harshest tone. "Watch your back, because at any second it could all go BOOM!" I exploded my hand in his face before walking away.

"You sound like an old-timey mobster," he called after me.

Thank goodness my back was turned, because I couldn't help but crack up.

"Give me one good reason why I shouldn't put you on a PIP?" Brea asked.

"What's that?" I said.

"A performance improvement plan."

"I don't have performance issues."

"You coordinated a puppet revolt…onset."

"It wasn't a puppet revolt. It was a human revolt—the puppets were just symbolic."

"Letitia, what the fuck?" she said. "Call it what you want, but it was totally out of line."

"So free speech is dead?"

"You're lucky we're at work, because if we weren't, I would pummel you. Rustin told me you suggested he choke."

"So, he's a traitor *and* a snitch. It tracks; it's so on brand."

I knew I'd get my hand spanked for my stunt earlier, but Brea was not correcting me as a friend. This was Boss Brea, my least favorite of all the Brea variants. *She* was all about business.

"*Jellybean Junction* landed Rustin Hayes, and what do you do? You bully him," Boss Brea said.

"Whoa. Calm down. Let's not throw out words like *bullying*. I was just voicing my opinion."

"That no one asked for. You have done some dumb shit, but this…this takes the cake."

"Everything I do is well thought out and planned."

"What about the time you went home with your RideX driver because he told you he was going to grill some lamb?"

"It was delicious, by the way, and his wife and kids were delightful."

"You could've been killed."

"I could've missed out on the best lamb ever. So juicy, so tender. We still keep in touch."

"You are going to apologize to Rustin."

"Did he cry like a baby and demand a mea culpa?" I asked.

"No. He asked me to drop it, but I can't because it was all caught on video."

"Can't I just send him a text message with a thumbs-up emoji?"

"No. I'm going to need a full-throated apology."

"I can't take you seriously when you say things like *full-throated*."

"Apologize or get written up for insubordination."

Brea knew the last thing I wanted was a write-up besmirching my permanent record. In school, I'd worked hard to avoid the principal and looked forward to my perfect attendance award each year. I caused trouble but hated being in trouble.

"Okay. I'll apologize."

"And then maybe you can work on mending your relationship," Brea said.

"There is no relationship."

"You made out with him, so that's not entirely true."

"That was before I knew he was a power-hungry capitalist."

"Well, it's a shame, because I think he really likes you."

"What do you mean? Did he say something?" I asked.

"I'm good at reading people."

"So no, he didn't mention me at all." Rolling my eyes, I leaned back in my chair.

"He mentions you all the time."

"Details."

"Just the other day, he asked me why you were such a weirdo."

"Very funny." Not that I cared what he thought of me.

Well, maybe I had at first.

"I just think you shouldn't be so hard on him."

"This isn't about him, it's about *Jellybean Junction*."

"And he wants to save the show as much as you do. So maybe you should work with him instead of against him."

"Boo."

"I'm serious," Brea said.

"Okay, apology loading."

I loved the studio at night because it was quiet and allowed me to actually hear my thoughts. During the day, my brain was going a thousand miles a minute, trying to remember lines, making sure I was on my mark, and pivoting when someone decided to improvise. Unexpected changes to the script proved challenging for me because I spent all week memorizing my lines along with all the others. I needed to know exactly what Milo Muddle was going to say to understand why Aaliyah was saying what she did.

I had an approved, reasonable accommodation for extra time and cue cards, but things moved fast on set, and I often felt left behind. Currently, I was walking around the building aimlessly reciting my lines. "My favorite part about the neighborhood is the trees. They're big. In the summer, they provide shade, and in the winter, they give us large piles of leaves to jump into." I dropped my voice several octaves to mimic Grumpy Gus. "I hate leaves. They have bugs all over them, and they get into my fur."

Hiking up the stairs, I entered the second floor. After several loops of the first floor, I needed a change of scenery. This area of ice building was where we re-recorded songs any lines that needed to be fixed in post-production. These individual recording rooms would be a rapper's dream. *Note to self: Maybe we can start a side hustle in which we rent out these rooms for singers and rappers to lay down their tracks.* What were recording studios going for? Five or six hundred a pop, and more for bigger spaces.

"Hey, Lumi, how much does a standard recording studio charge per hour?" I asked my phone.

"Recording studio sessions can cost anywhere from thirty to a hundred dollars per hour."

My estimate was a little off, but that was okay. "What about the bigger studio spaces?"

"Larger studios can cost one hundred to three hundred per hour. Of course, cost will vary based on location and studio type."

"Do you think if I opened a recording studio, I could get top dollar?"

"The return on interest is unlikely. Would you like me to provide a cost analysis?"

I needed a variation of Lumi that was delusional like me. My business plan was still viable, even if Lumi was pessimistic. Even if we got a hundred dollars an hour, we could make… *Eight p.m. to, like, five in the morning, that's…* I had to count it out on my fingers. *One, two, three, four, five…* Fuck it, it was a lot of hours, which would translate to tons of money.

Returning to my script, I jumped back into my line. "What do you like about the neighborhood, Jabari?"

This time I kept my voice high, but made it a smidge deeper. "I like my friends—playing hide-and-seek and chasing after the ice cream truck."

The sound of music coming from down the hall distracted me. It couldn't be the cleaners, because they were in the administrative offices vacuuming. I'd thought I was the only one burning the midnight oil. Rolling up my script, I headed to investigate. As I rounded the corner, the music grew louder. It sounded like a piano. The door from which the sound emitted was propped open by a trash bin. Peeking through the opening, I scanned the room and found Rustin in the middle of it standing over a keyboard he'd placed on a desk, hesitantly tapping the keys as if trying to find the correct chord. Once he decided on a combination, his fingers floated over the keys. He wasn't even looking at them.

He cleared his throat, and his next words were a melody.

"Now I'm stuck in these days that don't feel like mine
Trying to find some meaning in a crooked line
Trying to find meaning in a crooked line. Crooked liiiiiine."

He hummed the last two words. He appeared to know the lyrics but wasn't comfortable with them yet.

"I lost my way somewhere I forget
Now I'm drifting
I lost my way somewhere I forget
Somewhere between your goodbye
Now I'm drifting…"

His voice caught me, soft and warm, like sunlight spilling through a half-open door. There he was, completely unaware of my presence, playing slow and low, as if he were tiptoeing through the lyrics. Something in me held my breath. There was a different level of intimacy in witnessing someone sing when they thought no one was listening. No mask, no performance. Just…truth. I couldn't help but feel like I was eavesdropping on something sacred, something not meant for my ears. Every note made my chest ache.

His voice was now more assured, as if he'd found his footing; he hit the high note with furrowed brow, his fingers plucking the keys. This wasn't about the melody; it was about the words. He'd repeat lyrics over and over again in an attempt to perfect their delivery. And suddenly I wanted things—to know the story behind the song and who or what had broken his heart, and to sit beside him and unabashedly drink him in as he serenaded me.

I could ignore all sorts of things. My dwindling bank account and need for a couch, bed, and proper dishes. The need to have an honest conversation with my mother. Or the fact I actually hated being called a strong Black woman, because in truth, I didn't know what I was doing, and the reality that I was allowed to just move through the world with no guardrails was terrifying.

But one thing I couldn't ignore was the gravitational pull this man had on my heart. I just stood there, quietly, stupidly, hopelessly pressing farther through the crack in the door. Too close, I kicked over the metal trash can, and Rustin's head swiveled. Ducking out of sight, I held my breath.

"Letitia?"

I popped up, trying to act nonchalant. "I was just checking the trash cans. Cleanliness is next to godliness, so no trash left behind."

"I think snooping is considered a sin."

"I went to church religiously for years, and they never mentioned snooping. Plus, church folks are the nosiest people ever."

"What are you still doing here?" he asked.

"Working. What about you?"

"Same."

"It seemed dark—the song, I mean. Who hurt you?"

"Everybody."

My eyes grew wide as I invited myself in.

"Sorry, I think that's something people just say," he added. "You can't be a brooding artist without some scars. Truthfully, I've been luckier than most. All my wounds are self-inflicted. What about you? What's your damage?"

"You know about the bugs."

"Why'd you ignore my text about wanting to talk?"

"Why do you keep asking me that?"

"Because it's rude. And then a few days later, you chewed my head off, accusing me of atrocities against God and man."

"Well, Metro PCS is my provider, so it probably got lost in the 5G."

His eyes were lazy and hooded. "How long are we going to do this?"

"We fundamentally disagree on important issues, so forever."

Rustin held up his finger like he was testing the strength of the wind. "Do you feel that?"

"What?"

"Undeniable sexual chemistry."

"It's probably static building up in the carpet."

The corners of his mouth twitched upward. "I really wanna kiss you again."

"Have we kissed? I don't remember." I was too sarcastic for my own good, because truthfully, same.

"You fucking remember, and at night you hump your pillow wishing it was me."

"Are you drunk?" Normally he was calculated in his word choices.

"No, no, I'm not. I may be a little high."

"You're at work."

"It's ten o'clock, well after hours."

"This is a children's show. The studio shouldn't smell of ganja." I flipped through the notebook next to the keyboard. It was filled with lyrics, doodles, and random quotes.

Rustin smacked my hand away and quickly closed it. "You sound like a snitch. Are you a snitch?"

The thought had crossed my mind. I could report him to HR and get him terminated. "No." And honestly, I could really go for a hit to soothe the aching in my lady parts.

"So, when you hump your pillow at night, do you say my name or just think it?"

"I don't hump pillows, and I never think of you." *I scream your name out loud each night.*

"Interesting. What type of driver are you, manual or electric?"

"You're asking a lot of questions but answering none."

"I'm manual. And I think about you all the time, but at night it's so persistent I think someone cast a spell on me."

I could attest that I'd been afflicted by the same spell. Every day, all day, without end, this man stayed on my mind. "I think in the morning when the witch's brew fades, you're going to regret this conversation."

"I doubt it. I don't remember shit when I'm high. That's kind of the point."

I remembered everything from when I was high. I'm talking repressed memories sparking like olden-days motion pictures in my head. I would recall a woman who was not my adopted mother telling me everything was going to be okay. There was crying—I think it was from me—shouting from a man, and the sound of dishes tumbling to the ground.

Then there were the other memories, like me saying "You too," when the waiter told me to enjoy my meal. The time I walked around an art gallery with my skirt tucked into my panties, and nobody told me anything. Or the first guy I kissed telling everyone I tasted like fried chicken and watermelon. I didn't even like watermelon.

Considering Rustin's words, I decided to be bold. "If that's true, then I'll share this."

"Secrets… I love secrets." He rubbed his hands together, and I was tempted to open my mouth and allow him to drive his fingers in and out while I sucked each one. Yes, I had a hand fetish, and I wasn't afraid to admit it.

"If you weren't such an asshole, I'd be on my knees right now sucking the meat off the bone."

The lackadaisical look in his eyes shifted. It was as if he'd drunk a pot of coffee in a split second, the sudden lucidity in his cognac eyes was so startling. "I have a secret too. Smoking is therapeutic and provides me with clarity. And I don't forget shit." His laugh was wicked. "Isn't this more fun than scowling at each other across the room?"

"I dislike you." I stomped the floor to drive my word home. "I mean, I can usually find the good in anyone, except my mom, but you're just *unlikeable*. My dad is right—you are arrogant."

"You told your dad about me? Aww, heart eyes."

"Is it the weed that's making you insufferable or is this just your true nature?"

"It's the weed for sure. I wouldn't have said half this shit without it," he said.

I turned on my heels to rid myself of this conversation.

"Wait. How are you getting home?" His face was in his phone.

"Walking, like I always do."

"No. Nope. It's too late for walking. I ordered you a car. It should be here in four minutes. Your driver's name is Mateo." He tossed his phone on the table.

"Thank you," I said without a shred of gratitude.

Rustin's response: his hands in the form of a heart that he held up to his face.

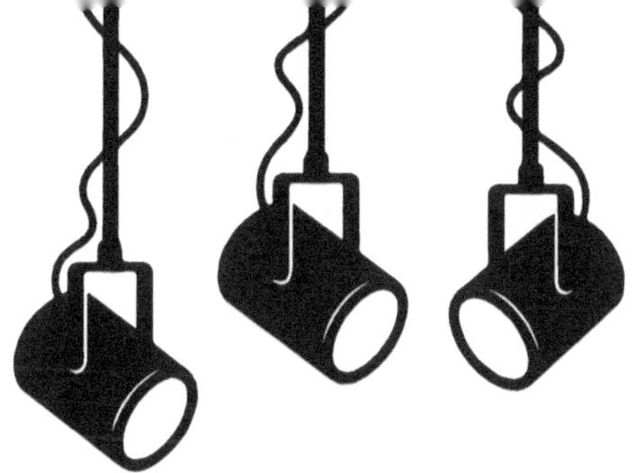

CHAPTER 14

Rustin

DESPITE MY AGREEING to a bounty of new and plentiful vending machine snacks, everyone still hated me, which I was actually fine with. Letitia Vincent hating me, however, was something that caused me to lose sleep at night. Granted, my little stunt with Jackie the other night hadn't helped. I wasn't a betting man, but on this I was willing to bet three to one that Letitia secretly liked me.

You wouldn't know it by the way she acted. For most of the week, Letitia avoided me, and when she couldn't do that, she chose to ignore me instead. She refused to acknowledge my presence or make eye contact when I was nearby. If I entered a room, the smile faded from her face, and any conversation would shift to hushed tones.

Were they talking about me? Probably. Letitia and some of the others in the cast identified me as an op. This was not how I'd imagined my first few months as the show's producer playing out. It was like being in high school all over again and getting teased by the "cool" kids because I had a puppet head sticking out of my backpack.

Growing up is realizing adulthood is just high school with less acne and more expendable funds.

Just like that, I was the nerd with thick glasses and off-brand shoes who loved sci-fi, musicals, and animatronics. And Letitia was the out-of-my-league girl who was also a nerd but way cooler than I could ever be. I was drawn to her immediately, so much so I'd almost fucked her under the metaphorical bleachers. My week had started on a high, and now it was Friday and Stanley called out, "Dead man walking," any time I passed by. I was thinking of rescinding my offer allowing him to work the fucking bubble machine.

Brea knocked on the door of my office, which was more like a storage closet. "Hey. How's your day going?"

"Uhm. Someone just whistled 'Taps' on my way back from the bathroom, but other than that, it's going great."

"Are you coming to happy hour?"

"No. I've got a thing."

"What thing?"

"A thing that doesn't involve subjecting myself to twisted stares and smart remarks."

"You just need to give everyone some time to adjust. This is all really scary."

"No, I appreciate that, and I want the employees to feel safe enough to voice their concerns. I've been here a hot second, and I still need to build the trust."

Brea plopped down in one of the visitor seats and stuck her hand in my opened bag of gummy bears, fishing out a few. "You're doing a great job, and I'm excited about your vision for *Junction*."

"I wish everyone was."

"Who isn't?"

"Every-damn-body."

"Granted, I've only known you for a few months, but we both know you don't give a fuck what anyone here thinks, except maybe one."

"You mean Letitia?" I asked.

"Letty wears her heart on her sleeve, and she's not the greatest with change. She prefers routine and knowing what comes next. I think practical conventions help foster her creativity."

"You and she are pretty close, right?"

"Yeah. She's like a little sister or niece to me."

"Does she tell you everything?"

"She tells me most things."

I surveyed Brea's face, trying to decide if I should drop the subject or go out on a limb. "Did she tell you we kissed?"

"She might have mentioned it."

"It's so fucked up, because that kiss seemed like a lifetime ago," I said.

Brea opened her mouth to speak, but quickly shut it.

"I'm not trying to get you to betray the girl code. I just wish I could understand or get the fuck over it. I'm too presumptuous, too cold, or too jokey-jokey."

"Jokey-jokey?"

"It's scientific terminology. It just feels like I've ruined any chance with her."

Brea exhaled a thoughtful breath. "Letitia is passionate about her craft and this job. It's what I love the most about her. You two have a lot in common. Maybe you should talk to her."

"I've tried. Funny Rus, sweet Rus…" I lowered my voice and added, "Sexual Rus. She's made it clear she's not interested in any variation of me. And I respect that. The last thing I want to do is make our working environment more stressful."

"She just needs time to process."

"It's been months."

"Letty's late. Late to work. Late to social functions. Late to admit she might be wrong. Maybe you should try again."

If I thought my words could actually make a difference, I would. Yes, I'd been high the other night, but I distinctly remembered her saying she disliked me. *Dislike* was the polite way of saying *hate*, and if she hated me, then professing my love wouldn't change that. I'd joined *Junction* because of Letitia—her enthusiasm and excitement about this place and kids resonated with me. She'd been doing this since her library days, showing up for children and providing them with a safe place. I wanted people like her on my team and in my corner.

At the first happy hour, I'd just knew she and I would be fast friends, and, I hoped, potentially more. Fast forward to today, and she wasn't even speaking to me. Right now, nothing was going my way—not saving this show, not the new musical I couldn't get beyond page twenty-seven on, and not any kind of meaningful connection with Letitia. I needed a win. One fucking positive outcome.

"I appreciate the advice."

"That's what I'm here for," Brea said. "The first session is free, but after that you have to pay."

"Good to know."

"Why are you always early?" Omar chided me at the front door of his brownstone.

"Force of habit."

"I should make you stand outside until the agreed-upon time."

"Fool, if you don't move out of my way…" I pushed past him, heading up the stairs to the third floor. Omar's brownstone had three separate units. His former mother-in-law lived on the first floor, his ex-wife Jackie, lived on the second, and he occupied the top floor. Fiscally responsible, for sure, but it was still weird as fuck. I had an ex or two I was still cordial with, but I couldn't imagine having to run into them every day. Omar and Jackie shared a daughter who floated between their units. She had a fully decorated bedroom on each floor.

Upstairs, I took my favorite seat in a brown leather chair.

"Beer?" Omar asked.

"Please."

He returned from the kitchen with two bottles, handing me one. "How you been? I feel like all our conversations have been over text."

"You ain't lying. I've been good."

"How's the writing going?"

I knocked back half my beer. I should be almost finished writing this new musical, but I didn't have the heart to tell him I wasn't even close. "You know it's good. It's coming along."

"I can't wait to read it. Can you imagine two shows on Broadway at the same time? That's real boss shit."

"Yeah. Thanks."

"I gotta give you your tens," he continued. "You spoke all this shit into existence. In college, when you said you were going to submit your play for query, no agent, just following stuff you read online, *Shit,* I thought, *this Negro ain't got no sense.* I didn't know much about Broadway, but I was fairly certain it was a whites-only club like every-fucking-thing else. But somehow you managed to break through. And you continue to hit home runs over and over again."

The way you see yourself doesn't necessarily align with how others see you. Take me, for instance—I was at my lowest point mentally. Suffering from writer's block. The state of *Jellybean Junction* was keeping me up at night. I barely slept as it was, so missing any additional hours was detrimental to my health. And then there was Letitia.

"I've been luckier than most, I guess," I said.

"Don't be modest now. It doesn't suit you."

"What about you? How are things?"

"You know I'm always trying to get shit to shake," Omar said. "I hired the understudy we talked about. The Broadway League reached out. It's time to raise money for charity, and they wanted to know if we wanted to participate."

"How does that work again?"

"Various productions commit to donating a portion of their proceeds from a full week of shows."

"What's the percentage?"

"Ten."

"Do they already have a charity lined up to receive the donations?"

"I think they're in the process of making a decision."

"Do you think I have time to make a recommendation?" I asked.

"For?"

"*Jellybean Junction*. It aligns with the league's mission, programming on public television is important, and the benefit is it's available to everybody."

"You could try, but decisions like that are usually made months in advance. And voting is more performative than anything else."

"If you could just get a slot on the ballot card, I could do the rest."

"You and the impossible," Omar said.

"It only seems impossible until it's not. Get *Jellybean Junction* on the ballot." Money from this charity event wouldn't save us, but it would make a hefty dent in the funds needed. I was willing to do anything—make promises, grant access to my personal space, trade favors.

"I'll add it to my to-do list," Omar said.

"Top of the list."

"Got it. That reminds me, a box of merchandise is coming to your place. I need it signed and returned ASAP."

"Will do."

"I'm serious, Rus. I don't want to have to chase you down. Sign and give it to your assistant."

"You have my word."

"One last thing."

"Is it bad news? 'Cause if it is, we can just put a pin in it."

"No, quite the opposite," Omar said. "It's big news…huge."

"What?" I was scrolling through my phone, reviewing the content posted on *Junction*'s social media pages. Hiring the manager was the smartest decision I'd made. The content was well received, and page engagement had increased by twenty-nine percent in just a few weeks.

"I'm gonna need your undivided attention for this one."

With a huff, I dropped my phone. "Do you want me to look deeply into your eyes while we hold hands and syncopate our breath?"

"Don't be an ass."

"My interest is piqued. Lay it on me."

Omar cleared his throat, and his tone was one of reverence. "We got the Imaginex movie."

"Quit playing."

"I'm dead fucking serious."

"Why are you just telling me this?" I asked.

"Because I wanted to tell you in person so I could witness that goofy smile of yours."

"Do you know what this means?"

"Yes. We're about to be making Imaginex money, and that shit is long."

"We are so fucking paid." I clapped my hands together. Imaginex was a massive entertainment conglomerate. We're talking films, television, and theme parks. "Way to go, Omar. That's what the fuck I'm talking about."

"Are we hugging? What are we doing, because I feel like this deserves a hug."

"For Imaginex money, I'd do all types of things to you," I joked.

We both jumped out of our seats, dapped each other up, and reveled in a bro hug, hands locked in a pound between us with vigorous pats to the back and affirming words.

"We're about to make stupid money," I said.

"I'm buying a Lamborghini; I don't care if it's impractical," Omar shouted.

"Am I interrupting?" Jackie called out from the front door.

"No," we said in unison, pushing each other away.

"What are we celebrating?" she said.

"I told him about the Imaginex deal," Omar replied.

"Congratulations."

"Do you need a new pair of red bottoms? Because I'm feeling generous," I joked.

"I'll email you my size."

"Don't buy my ex-wife footwear. That's disrespectful," Omar teased.

"I came up here to tell you dinner's ready," she added.

Jackie's apartment was a stark contrast to Omar's. His was all leather and dark wood. And Jackie's was something out of a Pinterest board. Perfectly chopped pillows. Strategically placed art to make up a gallery wall. Wallpaper exhibiting that she wasn't afraid to take a risk. Omar and Jackie were two sides of the same coin, and even though they were no longer together, the lines were often blurry—like with Sunday dinners for which they all pitched in to prepare a dish.

"Uncle Rus, are you coming to my kumite?" little Oona asked me when we were seated at the table.

"When is it?"

"Not for another month, but Oona's afraid people will forget," Jackie said.

I handed her my phone. "Put it in my calendar, and I'll get a reminder." I booped the tip of her nose.

"So tell me what the Imaginex movie is about." Jackie casually sipped from her fancy wineglass.

"It's essentially a modern-day *E.T.* A group of kids happen upon a furry alien creature. Imaginex wants the alien to be practical puppetry—no CGI or AI. And that's where Thread and Thespian shines. I have Omar to thank for closing the deal."

Omar smiled bright and said, "It was easy once I dropped your name."

"Getting in with Imaginex, if it all goes well—this could be a collaboration for a lifetime."

"Who's Lettuce?" Oona asked.

"Hmm?"

"Lettuce is calling." She held my phone in my face.

Reclaiming the phone, I answered, "Please hold." I quickly placed the call on mute.

"Who is it?" Jackie asked.

"It's, erm, Letitia." I clumsily pushed back from the table, spilling my water glass. "My bad."

"You good, son?" Omar asked.

"No! It's Letitia." As if that was all the response needed to explain my weird reaction. *She doesn't call me. Why is she calling me? What the fuck have I done now?* Had she figured out Jackie wasn't just *a* financial advisor but *my* financial advisor?

Heading out of the room, I wandered into Oona's bedroom with large, squishy plushies, posters on the wall, and pink everywhere you turned.

"Hello?" I said into the phone.

"Uhm…why are you answering your phone?"

"Because that's what people do when they have an incoming call."

"I don't. I just stare at the screen until it goes to voicemail."

"I guess that's one way to skin a cat." I paced the area rug with a big, dramatic flower print.

"What does that even mean? Why would anyone be skinning cats?"

I chuckled. "I think it's referring to catfish."

"No shit. Wow, learn something new every day."

"Because skinning actual cats would be—"

"Cruel, but humans are cruel, so I wouldn't put anything past them." There was silence from her end. Maybe she'd butt-dialed by accident and hadn't intended to be in conversation with me on a Sunday evening.

"Are you still there?"

"Yeah. I hope I wasn't interrupting anything."

"Just in the middle of dinner."

"Then why'd you answer?"

"Because you were on the other end."

Letitia cleared her throat. "I'll keep this brief, then."

Bump that. I could listen to her speak all night. "How's your night going?"

"I spent most of the evening looking at paint swatches."

"Any top contenders?"

"Honestly, no. I can't decide if I want to lean into my feminine energy or go the total opposite direction with a bohemian vibe."

"I'm drawn to boho for sure. I love the color palette."

"Pink princess it is," she said.

"Glad I could help you come to a swift resolution."

"I don't want your TV dinner getting cold, so let me get to the point."

"Nah, I'm good. Jackie cooked—"

"Jackie? So, she did get a second date."

"No, wait—"

"I was just calling to say sorry." Her tone was cold. "For the stuff at the office. The public resistance and the on-set revolt."

"Did Brea put you up to this?"

"She did."

"I didn't ask for that."

"Well, you got it. Enjoy your dinner. Tell Jackie I said hi, and don't choke on a chicken bone."

"Letitia…" The line went dead. I scanned the room, trying to make it all make sense. "Fuck!"

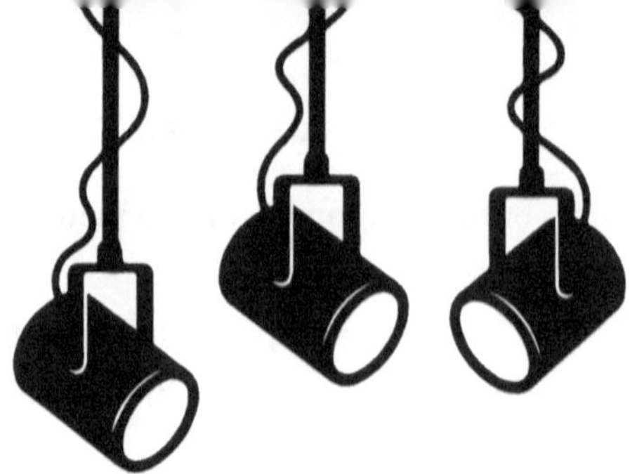

CHAPTER 15
Letitia

BREA HAD SAID I had to apologize to Rustin, which I'd done last night. Now I could just go back to ignoring him and plotting ways to sabotage his plans to gut the essence of what made the show great. I might be operating in silence going forward, but I would not be silenced. Impact could be made with no words at all.

I was an expert grudge holder. My mother and I had been in an ongoing beef for damn near twenty years. When I cared about something, I didn't let shit slide. And the future of *Junction* was in my top-three priorities. Number one was getting my apartment in order and number three was learning that new line dance—I would not fall behind like I had with the Wobble. In college I'd attended a party, and when that song came on, I was not prepared. At the time, the only line dance I knew was the Electric Slide, and white people performed it differently.

"Hey, Letitia, hold up," Rustin called from behind me.

I swiveled my head to find him a few feet away. He was the last person I wanted to see right now. In an attempt to evade him, I hastily hopped in the freight elevator, furiously jabbing the close-door button, hoping the elevator would take me to safety. No matter how hard I pressed, the doors didn't budge.

Rustin stepped inside as I was still pressing the button. "Going somewhere?

"Not anymore." I moved toward the door, which shut in my face. The dimly lit freight elevator lurched, descending the shaft.

"Can we talk?"

"Can't talk. I was just heading to the costume department."

"You're going in the wrong direction."

The elevator reached the basement, which was creepy as hell. I'd only visited it once, and it acted like an extended storage room. It was a puppet cemetery down here, with retired puppets, set pieces, and various boxes with random felt limbs hanging out. I went to the control panel and pressed the button for the third floor. The elevator whined and creaked but didn't move.

"I think we should at least move to a cordial place—not asking you to like me or forget everything you know," Rustin said. "We can have varying opinions, but we don't have to be adversaries every time we cross paths."

I scanned the basement through the small rectangle window in the elevator door, waiting for a slow-moving ghost to round the corner. "Why isn't the elevator moving?"

"Maybe you should press the button again."

I did, and once again the elevator released a lazy, creaking groan.

"We'll just get off and take the stairs." Rustin pushed the open-door button, but it appeared stuck. "Didn't you say this elevator was a death trap?"

"No. I never said that. I said it was temperamental."

"The button isn't working," he said. I pushed him out of the way and mashed all the buttons. "You're definitely not supposed to do that."

"So now you're an elevator technician?"

"It's common sense. Pressing all the buttons makes the machinery go boom. You know if you'd just talk to me instead of running away, we wouldn't be here right now."

"I wasn't running; I was strategically avoiding. Big difference."

"Right, because avoiding me is your number one mission of late."

"Maybe I just don't enjoy your company." The elevator lurched suddenly, then nothing. The dim lights flickered, and a deep silence filled the space. "You have got to be kidding me." I returned to pressing each button frantically.

"Insanity is doing the same thing over and over and expecting the result to be different. Kind of like your not wanting to change anything about the show when it's on the chopping block."

"I never said I wasn't open to change. I just think your ideas are stupid," I said. Rustin approached the doors again and tried to pry them open with his bare hands. "That's not going to work. They're too heavy."

"It shows B for basement, so I don't get why the doors aren't opening." He pulled out his phone, tapping the screen. "Do you have any bars?"

"You wanna start a rap battle right now?"

He looked at me deadpan. "I'm talking about bars on your phone. What the fuck is wrong with you?"

"I skipped breakfast, I'm lightheaded, and don't yell at me."

"Why did you skip breakfast?"

"I had first breakfast, which was avocado toast. I just didn't have my second breakfast yet."

"Second breakfast. Are you a fucking Hobbit?" Rustin asked as he walked around the small space in search of a signal.

"Yeah. Costuming usually has breakfast sandwiches or burritos, and that bit of intel needs to stay between you me and Imogen."

"Who?" he asked.

"The elevator ghost. Don't worry, she's friendly for the most part."

"I'm gonna need you to stop talking."

"Why are you scared?" Maybe I could get him to quit with my retellings of creepy ghost sightings.

"No. I'm Ray Parker Jr."

I did my best to suppress a smile. "Because he's not afraid of ghosts. Good one," I mumbled.

"Still no signal. I think we need to press the emergency button."

My eyes grew wide, and my breathing increased.

"Don't do that," Rustin said.

"Do what?"

"Freak out."

"We're stuck in an elevator. The *appropriate* response is to freak out. At any fucking moment, we could plummet to our deaths."

"We're in the basement."

"Just sitting ducks for the ghost and ghouls. Have you been in the basement? It's a horror movie down here. Hooks and contraptions and tight spaces." Sweat pebbled my forehead and upper lip. "Is it hot? I'm so hot."

Rustin swept past me, aggressively pressing the red emergency button, which immediately set off flashing lights and a shrill alarm. "At least we know *that* button works."

"What if we're just trapped in here forever? What if when they find us, it's just bones, clothes, and the lingering, unflinching stench of your cologne?"

"Ouch."

"I mean, it's pretty intense, don't you think?"

Static crackled, and a voice called out, "He-hello?"

"Hi. Can you hear me?" Rustin shouted.

"Hello?"

"Yeah, hi."

"Who is this?"

"It's Rustin. We're stuck in the elevator."

"How'd that happen?"

"The hell if I know. Can you just get us out?"

"No. I don't know shit about elevators."

"Well, maybe you could call somebody who does."

I pushed Rustin aside. "Yes, hello, hi. Could you just find Brea Sinclair? She's my boss."

"Is she an elevator tech?"

"No, but she'll know what to do. Brea Sinclair."

"I'm gonna turn off this alarm, if that's okay with you."

"It's fine," Rustin called from behind me.

"All right. Don't go anywhere. I'll be right back."

"Where would we go?" Rustin whispered.

"Maybe up through the shaft, like in the movies," I said.

"Or maybe we could shrink ourselves and escape through the cracks like in *Honey, I Shrunk the Kids*."

"That's one of my dad's favorite movies. You don't realize how hostile the world is until you're only inches tall."

Rustin paced the cramped space. It would appear he'd hit his limit, and he was no longer able to conceal his aggravation. I didn't know why he was mad. It was his fault we got stuck. If he hadn't chased me down, I'd be on the third floor enjoying a burrito dipped in salsa.

God, I was so hungry. My stomach growled, announcing the fact.

"Was that your stomach?" he asked.

"Yes. I'm wasting away in here."

He huffed out a long sigh, scrubbing his face with his hand.

"Hello?" Brea's voice broke in.

"We're trapped," I shouted.

"Letitia, is that you?"

"Yes."

"Who's we?"

"Rustin and me."

"Rustin's in the elevator?"

"Yeah."

"I'm gonna need proof of life."

"I'm good," Rustin said. "She hasn't murdered me yet."

"So what happened?"

"Rustin barged onto the elevator, and then it went down to the basement when I clearly pressed the third floor, and then it got stuck," I replied.

Rustin pushed his way closer to the speaker. "We got stuck because brain trust over here mashed all the buttons."

"I was trying to get it to move."

"It didn't work."

I knelt so I was eye level with the speaker. "Can you get me out of here?"

"The last time someone got stuck, we had to call the fire department," Brea replied.

"We're running out of oxygen!"

"That's not how this works," Rustin attempted to correct me. "How long do you think this is going to take?"

"First, we'll try calling the elevator from each floor to see if it starts moving," Brea said. "If that doesn't work, I'm afraid we'll have to get fire rescue involved. Give us a few minutes." The speaker crackled and then fell silent.

"So, you're just going to blame this all on me?" he asked.

I turned to him, stumbling backward upon realizing just how close he was. "This was probably all a part of your plan. Get me alone so you could berate me into another apology. You're probably enjoying this."

Rustin's voice dipped slightly, teasing. "What, being stuck in a tiny metal box with you? What's not to love?"

"You know, it was pretty shitty of you to rat me out to Brea."

"I didn't rat you out. She came to me after your little stunt."

"And you were all too eager to give her the play-by-play."

"She watched the video."

"Which you provided."

"Whoa. It always comes back to me."

"And then demanding an apology. Really?"

"I never asked for an apology," he said.

"Well, Brea made it sound like my continued employment was dependent on it."

"Then take it up with her. I told her the entire thing was no harm, no foul. And I just wanted to drop it."

Knocking could be heard from beyond the elevator doors. "Hello. Can you guys hear me?" Brea called.

"Yes," Rustin and I shouted in unison.

I pressed my face against the small window and mouthed, *Help me,* in the hopes Brea could read lips.

"We've tried calling the elevator from every floor. I think you guys are stuck."

"So, it's on to plan B?" Rustin asked.

"Afraid so. I'll make the call. Do you two need anything?"

I didn't know why she asked, because if we couldn't get out, she couldn't get in. "Yeah. I'll take a slice of pepperoni," I said in jest.

"Make that two, and throw in some orange sodas," Rustin joined in.

"Just hold tight, guys. Help is on the way."

Footsteps receded, leaving Rustin and me alone again.

"And now we wait." He lowered himself to the floor. Rustin's eyes followed me while I fidgeted with my clothes, jewelry, and shoelaces. Anything to stop thinking about the walls closing in on me. "You know, for someone who acts like the glass is half full, you're really bad at hiding when you're nervous."

"I'm not nervous. I just…hate small spaces."

"You might as well make yourself comfortable. We could be here for a while."

"You think so?"

"It's New York. Two people stuck on the bottom floor of a building doesn't really rise to the level of an emergency."

"What if one of those people has to pee?" I released a resigned sigh, sliding down beside him. Our shoulders brushed, just barely, but enough to send an unexpected jolt of heat through me.

The corners of his mouth curved as he noticed the way I stiffened at the contact. "So why do you hate small spaces?"

"Who doesn't?"

"Small can also be cozy. Take your apartment, for instance."

"My place is way bigger than this freight elevator."

"Not by much."

I chose to ignore the apartment slander. "If there was a proper window or a ray of natural sunlight, it would be different. But it's just a sterile, cold box moonlighting as a death trap." I clutched my chest. "I think we're running out of air."

"We're not."

"Then why is it so hard to breathe?"

"Can I tell you a story?"

"What?"

"A story. I want to share something with you."

"Okay." I inhaled a deep breath, hoping to slow my heart rate.

"When I was younger, I used to draw on the walls of our apartment. As you can guess, that made my parents unhappy. They'd punish me and repaint the walls, but I swear, once the paint was dry, I'd take out my colored pencils and get to work on another masterpiece. We went back and forth like that for months. My parents would put me in timeout, take away my TV time, no dessert after dinner, but none of their punishments worked."

"How'd they finally get you to stop?"

"They didn't. One day I came home, and they'd painted one of the walls in chalkboard paint. My dad said this was now my own personal mural wall. They went all out. There was chalk, stencils, and sketchbooks."

"Parents who support their kid's creativity are the MVPs."

"Yeah. They really are. My parents didn't always get me, but they did always try to support me."

My breathing leveled, and my skin was no longer damp with sweat. "Were you good?"

"I was great. When I got older, I started tagging walls in the neighborhood. I got caught by a business owner, but instead of calling the cops, he gave me a job. He offered me three hundred dollars to paint a mural of Marcus Garvey on the side of his building. I'm embarrassed to admit that at the time I didn't know who that was. But that's when I realized I could make money off this shit."

"Did you just tell me that random story to stop me from spiraling?" I asked.

"Yeah. Did it work?"

"It did. I read somewhere that your musical is getting honored with a Miffy award."

Receiving an Alfred H. Miffy award was a theater kid's dream. Miffy only recognized the best work in the creative space. Art, mixed media, and performance were popular categories, and winners were usually admired and revered by this very special group of peers. I'd been to the award ceremony once as a seat filler and had the best time.

"I'm still pinching myself about that one," Rustin said. "Art is so subjective, and it's a singular feeling when other people get what you're trying to convey."

"Have you started working on your speech?"

"I hate public speaking, so no. I'll probably save that for the absolute last minute."

"You know Stanley has a Miffy?"

"Really?"

"He was part of an improv group when he was younger."

"That would explain why he's constantly going off script."

"Apparently, they were pretty big back in the day," I explained. "The whole troupe received Miffys in the eighties or something."

"Sounds like I'm in good company."

"I saw the redesign of Grumpy Gus. He doesn't smell, so that's an improvement."

"That was the most important change of them all."

"Stanley never washed it. He refused," I said. "That was over thirty years of dirt and grime. So maybe you were onto something with that transformation."

Rustin's eyebrows creeped upward. "Are you saying I was right?"

"No. I'm saying it was an okay move. Personally, I liked the smell of burnt coffee and pipe smoke in Gus's fur."

"Liar." He playfully nudged his shoulder into my arm. Suddenly, the air felt different…charged, crackling. His gaze flickered, just for a second, to my lips before snapping back up. My breath hitched in my chest. I hated that he had this effect on me.

"It reminded me of home. My grandfather is a huge pipe smoker," I said.

"The pungent scent of Gus always stuck in the back of my throat. When I walked away, it felt like the odor was following me."

"We should take bets on how long it takes to return. My guess would be four months."

"And you would be wrong, because I've written into the contract that all puppets need to be professionally cleaned at least once a month—at the show's expense."

"If we're losing money, how can we afford that?"

"Cuts to the budget need to make sense," he said. "The puppets are integral to the show, and they should be clean and cared for as such."

"No bullshit, just reality. Do you think all your sweeping changes are going to make a difference?"

"I hope so, but I can't make promises."

"People threaten to cancel funding, like, every other year," I said. "Maybe this is just that—all talk, no action."

"I've been in the business for a long time, and this feels different. People say they appreciate art, but they don't value the craft and the time it takes. The landscape of what we do has changed. In a few years, we'll be watching movies and listening to music made by AI-generated personalities. We see it every day—the parasocial relationships fans have with celebrities. Imagine a star who could be exactly what the fans wanted. Always perfectly put together, never tired, never mean, always ready to engage with fans. They could digitally create the next Basquiat or Beethoven, and most people won't be able to clock the difference."

"Like The Sims on crack."

"If they can do that with real actors and singers, it's going to be ten times easier to erase us. *Jellybean Junction* could be replaced with an AI-generated cartoon for a fraction of what it costs to put together one of our shows."

"But this show is so much more than puppets and songs," I protested. "It's a feeling, it's an affirmation. I felt seen because of *Jellybean Junction.* That feeling can't be easily replaced. Art isn't copy-paste, it's tangled with emotion, desire, and time. Quality can't be rushed or reduced to a code. Sure, you can call up a heartwarming educational program for kids, but Skynet is always going to spit out a product that is off and uncanny valley-ish." My eyes were misty, and I was tempted to curl into a ball and rock while humming the theme song.

"Everyone is waiting for us to fail, including the studio executives," Rustin replied. "I'm here because there is one bleeding heart who truly sees the value we provide. We need to get a whole lot more people on board so we can gain some traction. And those viral moments you're opposed to are a critical part of our success. If people aren't talking about the show, it'll die in silence."

"People genuinely love this show. There would be protests and petitions."

"I remember hearing this show was getting canceled five years ago, and I donated fifty thousand off rip. But overtime fatigue sets in, and people just assume someone else will donate, lead the charge, call their representative. Somehow, with little to no effort on their part, things will all work out in the end."

"We're losing our supporters?" I asked.

"*Junction* has millions of supporters. Ask anybody, and they sing the show's praises. But times are hard, and people can't put their money where their mouth is. If you have to choose between paying your rent or sending a fifty-dollar check to NCC, which are you picking?"

"Maybe we need to remind people why they love the show."

"How do we do that?"

"I haven't figured that part out yet."

His voice dropped as he leaned in slightly—just enough that I could feel the warmth of him, his cologne mixing with the faint scent of metal and dust in the air. "I'm determined to save this show, but even I know I can't do it alone. I need you, Letitia."

I knew he was talking about the show, but hearing my name in that combination of words sounded amazing. "I'm in." Maybe the lack of sustenance was speaking, but I would follow this man anywhere.

Rustin's features appeared to smooth out, as if weights had been removed from his shoulders. "You and I are gonna save this show."

His voice held a confident finality that made me believe him.

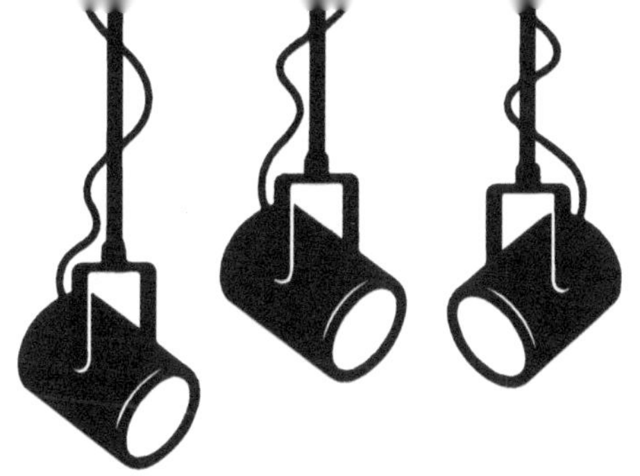

CHAPTER 16
Rustin

IT WAS SIX o'clock on a Friday, and our standing happy hour was canceled because the current state of the cast and crew was conducive to anything *but* "cheers to the weekend." Tooling around the building, I stopped to admire the new vending machines with brand-name snacks, just like I'd promised. At least I'd been able to deliver on the vending machines. Everything else at *Junction* seemed out of my control. My changes were slowly being implemented, but it would take months to determine success. I needed to consider the real possibility that there was nothing I could do to save this show, and its ultimate demise would rest solely on my shoulders. I didn't need this type of stress in my life, but I'd taken it on because *Jellybean Junction* was important to me, and I planned to exhaust every option in an attempt to save it.

On my way back to my office, I noticed a light from the partially opened door to the conference room. Maybe I wasn't the only one without a social life. Pushing the door wider, I found Letitia hunched over her laptop, bopping her head to the music from her headphones.

"Hey?"

There was no response. She was so lost in her world that she didn't notice I was there. I reached for the light switch next to the door and flicked it off then back on to announce my presence.

Letitia's head jerked upward as she scanned the room. When her gaze landed on me, her surprised expression turned something adjacent to pleasant.

"You're still here?" I called out.

Pulling the headphones around her neck, she asked, "What?"

"You're still here."

"Yeah. I prefer this place after hours. It's easier to concentrate. What about you?"

"Trying to avoid rush-hour traffic. I find giving it an hour or two helps."

"Do you take the subway?"

"No."

"Nothing but premium RideX for you, I guess."

"I don't like being that close to other people."

"Isn't riding the subway a part of being a New Yorker?"

"I was born here. It doesn't get more New York than that. Can I?" I pointed to the seat next to her.

"That seat's taken, by Imogen."

I scanned the empty conference room. "You need to stop tempting the spiritual realm before they mess back."

"I'm always very respectful."

"That's great. Hopefully they respectfully murk your ass."

"It's murder," she said in a pretend deep, raspy voice.

"So, your brain is just filled with Murder Inc. lyrics and ghost stories."

"Pretty much any form of entertainment media. Sixty-five percent of my responses are references to movies, TV shows, or songs."

"I can dig that. I watched a lot of television when I was a kid. I can recite entire episodes of *Martin*."

"An African American classic."

"High key, I think he was secretly in love with Pam the whole time," he said.

"Excuse you? Gina and Martin were *iconic*."

"Nobody goes that hard on someone they don't care about. I think maturing is realizing Martin wanted to fuck Pam, and who could blame him?"

Letitia pushed her fluffy, lightly curled hair from her face. Her hair always looked like she'd spent time styling it and then she stepped outside, and the summer humidity got to it, making it twice as big. I loved her hair and imagined burying my face into her curls and breathing deeply.

My desire to bury my face in something didn't just stop at her hair. If I could open her thick thighs wide and make them my new resting place, I surely would. And don't even get me started on her ass, breasts, and the crook of her neck.

"My eyes are up here."

"My bad. What was I looking at?" I said.

"My feet." She wiggled her bare toes.

"Promise I don't have a fetish."

"That's a shame." She said it so fast that I thought I'd misheard the words.

"What are you working on?"

"So, not only are we dismantling fifty years of tradition, you're also micromanaging me."

"Actually, I've been accused of that once or twice." I plopped down in the seat, scanning the outline on her laptop. "A field trip. What's that about?"

Her face came alive, her brown eyes big and animated, her hands flinging around in tandem with her words. She leaned in close, as if this were a secret between just her and me. "You want to focus more on the school element, Aaliyah and Jabari. I've been workshopping storylines that would mesh with that, and I thought, what was your favorite part of school?"

"Naptime."

"Wrong, field trips. So, I'm proposing Aaliyah and Jabari go on a class field trip." She positioned her laptop so I could fully view the screen.

I scooted closer, reading through the concept. "I like this."

"Why do you sound surprised?"

"Because you've been admiral of the resistance and then wrote this."

"I'm an agitator, not a quitter."

"So we'll need to craft a set for the field trip location."

"No, because I think we should take an actual field trip to a real-life location," she said. "It's definitely outside the box. It's exciting. We could even host a meet-and-greet after, get some of that buzz you're looking for."

The thing about Letitia was that I didn't think she was afraid of change so much as she was afraid of failure. When you worked in a creative, collaborative space, eight times out of ten your ideas would be pushed aside because *everyone* was pitching a concept. I was drawn to Letitia because even though she heard no often, she didn't allow that to stop her from taking a shot from half court.

"What do you have in mind?" I asked.

Squinting, she sized me up. I didn't know if she was going to tell me to go fuck myself or share her thoughts. "I was thinking of someplace unconventional. I jotted down a few ideas, like a car wash or hardware store, but they didn't seem special enough."

"What about a fabric shop?" I paused, waiting for her to shoot me down.

"Yeah?"

"There's this place called Fab Scraps in Brooklyn."

"I've been there before. The warehouse space is cool as fuck and would be great on camera."

"And bonus points because it's a sustainable nonprofit shop, and they accept volunteers."

"We could film there, get awe-inspiring footage for the show, and promote the shop on our socials. It's a win-win for all involved." She scribbled notes in her dog-eared journal.

"How do you see the scenes playing out in a place like that?"

"It's an interesting space—it's creative based, and it can spark imagination. We could introduce shorts of our two characters playing make-believe using some of the fabrics from the shop." There was an excited hop to her voice. "We'd need to reach out to Fab Scraps to see if they'd be interested."

"I know a guy who knows a girl who could help make the introduction."

"Cool. I'll start working on the script."

"My offer still stands," I said. "I'd love to collaborate with you."

Letitia had a way with pregnant pauses that made me second-guess my words. "If we're going to work on this together, there's something you should know."

"Okay."

"I don't really know how to say this, so I'm just going to: I'm dyslexic."

"Okay."

"Do you understand what that means?"

"Difficulty reading, confusion of words."

"Yes. Reading, writing, and memorization can be a challenge for me, and when it comes to organizing my ideas, I often need more time. It doesn't mean I don't know what I want the story to look like; I just need time to process and work through several outlines. So normally I work by myself, because working in a team or group setting can be frustrating for me and everyone involved."

"So, you'd prefer to write alone?" I asked.

"I don't *prefer* it. I'd love to collaborate with others, but it can be difficult, and I don't expect my coworkers to switch up their writing processes to accommodate me. So I keep my mouth shut and try to follow along the best way I can."

"And when you do that, it feels like…"

"It feels like I'm being dragged or pushed through a scene, and it's hard to contribute when you don't fully grasp how you got there."

Leaning back in my chair, I considered her words. I didn't want to hinder her process, but I thought we could learn a lot from each other, and I was willing to try if she was. "What if I follow your lead—allow you to take the reins and guide me through it?"

"Why would you do that?"

"Because I think you're clever, and I want to collaborate with you. I've wanted that from day one."

"For this to work, you have to really mean it. I have a method, and it's sort of unconventional, but it works for me. We can't co-write if you're just going to make fun or poke holes in it."

"I would never do that. Let's find common ground in the places we can."

"Oh, you'd make a great politician," she said.

"So what do you say?"

"If we're going to work late, we'll need food." She looked at me expectantly.

"I can handle that."

With food delivered, we got to work drafting the field trip episode. Letitia let me know she processed information better when it was visual. She used index cards to rough sketch each scene. We each had a card and were drafting different parts of the skit between mouthfuls of Chinese food.

I pushed a fork in her direction. "Here."

"I'm good," she said while repositioning her chopsticks.

"I think in the time you've been eating, you've only gotten one good bite."

"I'm still trying to figure out how to use chopsticks, but I'm determined to get it."

"How long have you been practicing?"

"Months…almost a year." She dipped her head. "I get the concept, but I think there's just a disconnect when it comes to actual implementation."

Raising my hand, I positioned my chopsticks. "First, you should hold them like this."

"Yeah, I am." She raised her hand and awkwardly animated her chopsticks.

"Why are you holding them like that? It should be an extension of your hand." She tried to reposition her fingers, but ended up holding them the same way in the end. "May I?" I asked.

"Sure."

"Are you left-handed or right-handed?"

"Left-handed."

Reaching for one of the sticks, I positioned it under her thumb. Her hand was soft and petite, and I imagined it would fit perfectly in the palm of my own. "Let it rest against your palm. Don't move it. Next, the second stick rests between your thumb and index finger."

"Like this?"

"Yep. You don't need a strong grip, but it should be stable." I tucked her ring and pinky fingers behind the chopsticks, and Letitia's eyes rested on my face. Her gaze was squishy, as if she were looking beyond my pencil mustache and bushy brows. "Now your middle finger is going to act like a guide. Try it out."

Letitia's big eyes finally moved from my face, and I immediately missed the scrutiny. Scanning her container, she made several attempts to claim a spear of broccoli from the box. When she was able to capture it, she lifted a shaky hand, beaming with pride.

"Good girl. That was great."

It was brief, but her expression was reminiscent of the day I was in her apartment rolling my tongue over her nipples. She popped the green into her mouth, chewing thoughtfully.

I glanced at the clock on the wall, realizing we'd been at it for hours. "Nothing more pathetic than working late on a Friday."

"Gee, thanks."

"The dig was intended for me. You just got hit by a stray bullet."

"I'll admit, my Friday nights have been uneventful lately," she said.

"You spend a lot of after-hours time here. Everything okay at home?"

"You sound like a guidance counselor. Home is fine. It just doesn't feel like home."

"Why's that?"

"Probably the boxes," she replied. "I'm still living out of them, and I cannot for the life of me muster the energy to remedy that. At this rate, I'll be fully moved in just in time to put it back on the market in a few months when I'm jobless."

"You're like a cat; you'll always land on your feet."

"You don't know that. You barely know me."

"I know without fail every Monday you wear a graphic T-shirt with a saying from the eighties—*What's your damage?; Totally tubular.* My favorite is the *More you know* shirt from NBC."

"Mondays are the worst for me. I always want to sleep in, so I usually throw on a T-shirt."

"I know that you're a pageant queen," I said.

"*Princess.*"

"My bad, a pageant princess. And that's where your love for puppets was first put on display. I know your nipples are pierced, and I like the way they feel in my mouth."

"Is it hot in here? Do you feel hot?"

"I feel fine." I inched closer. I was seconds away from getting on my knees and begging for the pussy.

"We should call it. It's late, and you have to go all the way back to Brooklyn."

"Not without walking you home first, if that's okay."

"Rustin, I think you're great."

"Oh my God, are you about to friend-zone me?"

"I just think the window of opportunity has passed…for us. Plus, a sexual dalliance with my boss isn't the smartest career move, and uhm…" Letitia bit down on her full bottom lip. "We've both been very busy with the show and other obligations."

"Letitia, I like you more than I've liked anyone in a really long time. Now that we're at a ceasefire, I want to get to know everything about you. Plus, dating is like a death match right now. My finger is numb from all the swiping."

"I hate those apps."

"And it's kind of hard to ignore that we make sense together— like a fork and spoon, peanut butter and jelly, Martin and Pam."

"Listen, you're making excellent points. And…and, just spitballing here. We're attractive people with biological needs."

"We're adults, and if we both want you to ride my face, why deny it?" I asked.

Her eyes became hooded, dropping to my lips. "It's just unnatural to *not* want that."

"So can I take you home?"

Letitia slammed her laptop shut. "Yes, Luther Vandross, you can."

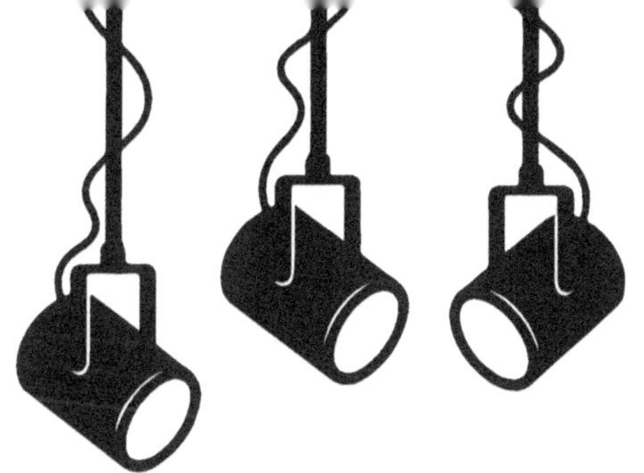

CHAPTER 17

Letitia

I **UNDERSTOOD THIS** was giving sleeping-with-the-enemy vibes, but the enemy was so damn fine. My apartment was short on fuck-worthy surfaces, but luckily Rustin was strong and determined. We eagerly shed articles of clothing, and when he dropped his pants, my theory was confirmed. Rustin was five feet eight inches, but the dick… If you take nothing else away from me, remember this: short men be packing. My pussy and mouth watered with the thoughts of all the ways I could make that dick disappear.

He fumbled for his jeans next to his feet, pulling out a condom. While he slid the latex over his length, I stepped out of my panties. His eyes tripped down my frame, and I basked in his adoring glow. Rustin grabbed my hand, pulling me close. "You're so damn fine."

When his lips met mine, it was just kinetic, with his hand stroking my neck before plunging into my hair. Our tongues played a game of slip-and-slide, circling each other. If my lady parts could talk, she'd beg for the dick. I'm talking whimpering, breathy pleas for him to dive in dick first. Did I ever want anything more than

I wanted him? I was drawing a blank…maybe world peace. Yeah, world peace was a close second.

Rustin pulled my leg upward, slowly inching his dick inside. I braced my back against the wall for support. His girth knocked the wind out of me as I gasped for breath.

"Are you okay?" His voice was soft with concern.

"Yeah. Just getting accustomed to it. It's been a while."

"You're really tight, but hopefully, I can help stretch you out a bit."

I was ready for him to demolish this pussy. Once he was snugly inside, he tapped my thigh, lifting me off my feet. Wrapping my thighs around his waist, I draped an arm over his shoulder. He wasted no time making good on his promise, sliding in and out nice and easy. Rustin's tongue found my breast, and he teased the metal bar before planting kisses and love bites against my skin.

"What a sweet little treat you are," he whispered into me.

"Take every last bit. I want you to make a mess of me."

Rustin scanned my face to determine the veracity of my words. I wanted to be wrecked from pleasure, and the spark in my eye communicated that. He slid out and hoisted me higher so my pussy was inches from his mouth. Hooking my legs over his shoulders, I sent up a prayer of gratitude. The first sweep of his tongue sent a shock wave through my body, and I reached for the wall, fearful I would fall. But Rustin was in full control; I could shudder and squeal, but I wasn't going anywhere. He suckled my clit, and I cried out.

"That feels good, doesn't it?"

"Yes," I moaned.

"Who deserves this?"

"Me?"

"Do you deserve to come?"

"I think so."

One minute, I was in my apartment, and the next I was drifting beyond the weight of my skin. I rose like a breath, exhaled into the ether, light as a whispered promise. The world below softened, edges blurred as if painted in watercolors, as I floated between the beats in time itself. My body wasn't my own, like my spirit was reaching for something more, something infinite.

And then my soul found his, a familiarity in the way stars recognize each other across galaxies—an understanding, a pull, a belonging written in the fabric of all that is unseen. I let Rustin drink me in and howled to the moon, untamed and free. His voice brought me back. "Don't hold back. Tell me how good it feels."

I did as instructed, praising him with a mixture of coarse words and giddy laughter. When my feet touched the ground, I immediately sank to my knees, pulled off his condom, and offered a proper thank you, planting kisses against his sensitive skin while his hand massaged my neck. My eyes were bigger than my mouth, but I was determined to take as much of him in as possible. And Rustin rewarded my attempt with gentle compliments. "You're so beautiful when you struggle to take it all. Drop your hands. I just want to feel your mouth."

Why I was so set on pleasing this man, I couldn't tell you, but if he asked me to balance on my head and twerk with his dick in my mouth, I would. You couldn't be judged on the choices you made during consensual sex, especially when the dick was this good. Rustin gathered my hair at the base of my neck and helped to guide me over his length.

"Look at me. Stick out your tongue." When I did, his body tensed, and cum squirted down my throat. Sucking his tip, I ensured I got every last drop, eagerly opening my mouth to confirm the fact. Rustin bent down, and our lips met like sparks catching a flame— hungry, urgent, and inevitable. Time folded in on itself as our mouths moved in perfect, fevered rhythm. His hands cradled my face, fingers tracing the curve of my jaw as if he were memorizing the shape of my desire.

My breathing hitched as he deepened the kiss, our tongues tangling in a slow, sensual dance. In that moment, I surrendered my senses—all that mattered was us and the way he made my body come alive. I reached for his dick, thinking I would have to bring it back to life, but he was still hard. "You know, I get tested regularly, and I'm on birth control." Yes, I wanted to be fucked deep, hard, and raw by this man.

"I got tested two months ago. All green lights."

"Don't move." I hopped up and rummaged in a box. Returning with several blankets, I spread them on the floor. Dropping into the cozy love nest, I opened my legs, licked my fingers, and worked my pussy, my sticky fingers gliding in and out. Rustin dropped to his knees and slapped my slit with his shaft, sending electric currents coursing through my body. When he slid inside, I held my breath, clutching the pile of blankets.

My only mission was to be deeply fucked by this man. Sure, I ran the chance of his ruining me for all other men, but it was one I was willing to take, because his body sparked something hidden within mine. I wanted to hear him tell me how good I made him feel and how wet and deep it was. I wanted him to beg for me like I was the cure to what ailed him.

Burying my face into the crook of his neck, I inhaled. I wanted him to possess every part—my pussy, my nostrils, my line of sight. Sex with Rustin was an immersive experience, his hands caressing my skin while digging me out.

"I needed this so badly," I whined.

"And I like being needed." He dusted my lips with his, and we exchanged air.

My core was tight and pulsing, and I knew I was minutes away from unraveling. "I'm gonna come. Are you close?"

"Yes, but ladies first." His words were like holding a door open for me, standing when I entered a room, and offering me his seat on a crowded train all wrapped up in one. The consideration and the tip of his dick hitting my spot was the final tug of a thread that swaddled me in a wash of flushed cheeks and soundless moans. Rustin shivered over top of me, his groans in my ear primeval.

"I like the way you moan for me," I said, and he enveloped my neck with measured pressure. We danced in unison, words escaping us. We were tethered by an unspoken longing of souls that once loved deeply in another lifetime. The moment stretched eternal yet fleeting, and I left a piece of myself behind, woven in the space between us. As my body settled once more, my soul carried echoes of him that reverberated through me long after the leg quakes, goose pimples, and calls to the heavens ceased.

Rustin collapsed next to me, pulling one of the blankets over us. "We need to go mattress shopping so next time I can put your ass through it." His tone was stern but casual, like he already knew there would be a next time.

"Okay." Because who was I to protest? As our breathing patterns returned to normal, we listened to the sound of apartment living—doors slamming, muted voices, a gumbo of music and television sounds. Rustin intertwined his fingers with mine, gently rubbing my palm. I loved the sex, and this was nice too. The ease of just being. Knowing we'd each satisfied a much-needed itch. "You're still wearing your hat," I said.

"You never took it off. Besides, I fuck better with it on."

"I'd like to test that theory."

"Two months and no bed? Where do you sleep?"

"The couch is a futon."

"That can't be comfortable." He turned on his side, facing me, propping his head in his hand.

"It's free, and free trumps comfort."

"So you just fuck everyone you meet on the floor?"

"I don't meet a lot of guys. In fact, you're the first guy I've slept with in my new place."

"Shut up. I'm the inaugural lay? I'm honored, truly."

"You're welcome," I said. "Brea was supposed to help me unpack, but most of the time she comes over, we end up gossiping and drinking. Blame her. My mom and sister are coming to visit, and if it looks like this when my mother gets here, she'll tell everyone back home that her oldest daughter is poor and probably has to suck rando peen for money."

"I think it's in parents' DNA to find something to pick at."

My mother's DNA must have been laced with criticism. Complaints when given were often backhanded, and nothing I did was correct or good enough. The twins could do no wrong, but I was scrutinized for every misstep. "Let's change the subject."

"Okay." He planted delicate love bites to my neck. "Tell me your one really useless but impressive skill."

"What?"

"Everyone has a talent or ability that, while impressive, is completely useless. Some people can even transition it into a full-fledged career, but for the most part, it's just useless."

I sat up, crossing my legs. "I'll play. I can speak fluent Simlish."

"What's that?"

"You know the video game The Sims?"

"Yeah."

"I'm fluent in that language."

"Again, what? How would you know that?"

"I used to love the game, and it started with me saying random phrases, and before long, I could say sentences, and it just took off from there. It's gotten to the point where I can sing whole songs in Simlish."

"I'm going to need an example."

"*Sha blarb womp me chah?*"

"And that's supposed to mean something?"

"*What do you want me to say?* For someone who asked me to share my hidden talent, you sure are neeblo."

"Neeblo?"

"Judgmental."

"Okay. I need to hear you sing."

Without hesitation, I broke into song. "*Ma morkshap brigs aba doys taba larb. Indee blight, eesh beega dem blars. Dorb night, eesh beega dem blars. Aka tweesha barvalaffa larve.*"

"Is that 'Milkshake' by Kelis?"

"Yes, yes it is." I beamed.

"Wow. I don't know if I'm impressed or horrified. I'm gonna go out on a limb and guess you didn't have a ton of friends growing up."

"Wrong. I was actually very popular," I said. Rustin eyeballed me thoughtfully. "What about you?"

"I'm double jointed in my hands, arms, and shoulders."

"Prove it."

Rustin held up his hands, and the top of his thumbs bent outward instead of the normal direction.

"That doesn't hurt?"

"Nope."

"It looks painful."

"It's not."

"How did you learn you could do that?"

"As a kid, we do all kinds of weird shit. I quickly learned my limbs bent farther than others. My friends would beg me to do the trick. I was a one-man circus."

"You would make a pretty penny if you took your act to the streets or subway," I said.

"I don't like crowds or attention."

"But you work on the stage and in film."

"I was in my play for a few years. The minute I could pass the role on to someone else, I jumped at the chance."

"Do you miss it—the stage?"

"Sometimes, but what I really enjoy is creating and then the process of birthing my art into the world. After it's born, I step back like a proud parent."

"I'm the complete opposite. I find it hard to let go, which in turn makes it difficult to focus on new projects."

"Letting go is freeing. You should really try it sometime. I think the best lesson I learned was to find beauty in the imperfect. I'm a recovering perfectionist who found it hard to accept that impeccable, pristine art doesn't exist. Art is human at its core, and that is what makes it so amazing. A painter, musician, or photographer is sharing a piece of their soul with each project."

Rustin placed his hand between my breasts. "This is art, the rise and fall of your chest as you intake air. The freckles dotting your neck. The subtle lines around your eyes when you smile. The feel of your soft, wet pussy as it surrounds me."

He used his index finger to pry my mouth open before sliding several digits inside, and I practically levitated. For a girl with a hand fetish and an oral fixation, this was the dream. His eyes were intently fixated on me like he was cataloging my reaction for future reference. When he finally pulled out, his hand slipped to my sweet spot.

My head rolled back as I cried out, "Oh, fuck."

"You are… How do I say *masterpiece* in Simlish?"

"*Blorptastic,*" I moaned.

"You are a *blorptastic.*"

His fingers caressed the deepest parts of me, pulling desire from my core like a spindle of honey.

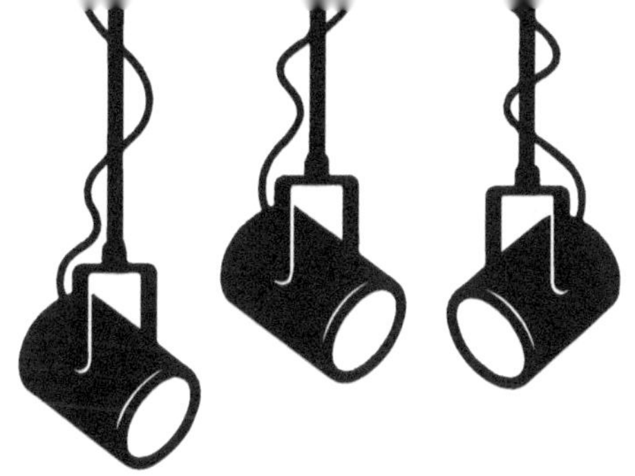

CHAPTER 18

Rustin

"HI," I SAID.

"Hi."

She was prettiest in the morning. Fresh-faced, she looked like she could still be in college. We'd both drifted off to sleep, and I hoped she wasn't regretting seeing my ugly mug first thing in the morning. Maybe I should've snuck out before the sun came up to avoid the anxiety seizing my gut.

"I should probably head out."

"Why?"

That was a good question, because the last thing I wanted was to leave our cozy sex fort. "I don't wanna overstay my welcome."

"But I like having you here. Waking up to you was such a pleasant surprise."

"I don't have to leave."

"Good."

She nuzzled my neck, and a fire crackled underneath my skin. Many a night, I'd imagined what it would feel like to hold her in my arms, and now I didn't have to wonder. It felt right and ordinary in the best way, as if her resting in the crook of my neck was natural.

"Do you have plans today?" I asked.

"There's probably a dozen things I need to do today, but right now, I can't think of one."

"I'm sure you already know this, but God, you're beautiful."

"I don't know if that's a universal belief, but I'm glad you think so. What do you have planned?"

"It would be a great day if I could spend it with you."

"Doing what?"

"Nothing and everything—the most important things."

"It's crazy to think I was ever mad at you. I mean, look at your face." She traced the outline of my lips with her finger.

"Don't worry. I'm sure I'll give you a fresh reason for vengeance eventually." The sunlight danced across her skin. "This place gets really good light."

"That's why I bought it."

"Give me your phone."

Letitia sat up, patting the blankets in search of her cell phone. When she finally found it, she swiped away notifications before handing it over. I pulled up her music app, quickly scanning her eclectic taste in music—Mary J. Blige, Robert Glasper, and Guns N' Roses. In the search bar, I typed in Roberta Flack's "The First Time Ever I Saw Your Face," the song encapsulating the moment, the way the sun bounced off her skin as if God himself was signaling that Letitia was the one.

"I wanna give you a proper good morning," I said.

I pulled her on top of my lap, and she eased over my erect dick.

"Good fucking morning," she said over my lips.

"I've got two objectives right now. The first is to sweat out your edges, and two is making sure every time you touch yourself, you think of me."

Letitia released a nervous giggle.

Flipping her under me, I thrusted deep. "I'm not joking."

Her response was defiant. "You can try."

And I did just that for the next thirty minutes, fucking and suckling her within an inch of her life. After our morning activities, I tagged along while Letitia ran some much-needed errands. I got the sense her life was a sequence of pushing the can down the road when it came to responsibility. Her trash bag was filled to the brim, as if she were attempting to break the world record for the tallest garbage pile. Almost every item she owned was still in a box or plastic storage bin, even though she'd moved in months ago.

Right now, we were at the laundromat because clean underwear was scarce. Who goes to the laundromat on a date? Me, I do. Shit, if Letitia had a root canal scheduled, I'd pull up a chair and hold her hand. Anything for one more conversation, one more kiss, another smile.

"Favorite puppet of all time?" she asked.

I zoned in on her clothes circling the washing machine. "I don't think I've ever been asked that question."

"Did I stump you?"

"No. I got an answer. Collectively, the Fraggle Rock crew."

"You can't pick them all."

"I can't just pick one. They're a team. Do you know the theme song?"

"Of course I do."

"Do you know it in Simlish?"

"No."

"Red Fraggle and dem, final answer. What about you?"

"Since we're shouting out entire crews, the Muppets, but specifically Statler and Waldorf, the two little old white men."

"They aren't half bad," I said, quoting a joke from the show.

"No, they're all bad," she finished, imitating the old men's laughter. "I think having a washer and dryer is the real wealth divide." Letitia offered me some of her hot Cheetos.

"You think?"

"Do you have a washer and dryer in your place?"

"Yes."

"See, rich."

"Don't act like you're poor. You just bought a place." I popped a Cheeto into my mouth.

"And now I'm house poor. Before buying, I was just regular poor, which was better because I didn't have any obligations."

"You don't seem to be a happy homeowner."

"Of course I am. I love my place, but I'm also terrified I'll miss a payment and be tossed on the street."

"It would take several missed payments and court dates before something like that happened." A guy walked in with a portable speaker, his music turned up to full volume. "Plus, if you had a washer, you'd miss this."

"What? A strange man blasting DMX at ten in the morning?"

"I mean, it's DMX." I growled like a dog. "Is the reason you haven't made your place a home because you're afraid of getting attached to it?"

"No. Brea thinks I have slight decision paralysis."

There was a loud bang at the Plexiglas service window. The man with the speaker was fussing with the clerk. "Five dollars for a mini box of Tide? That's why I don't fuck with you. The Dominicans would never. Give me my fucking change. I gave you a twenty."

I turned my attention back to Letitia. "Maybe you just need to focus on one thing at a time. Baby steps."

"We can't all have our shit together like you."

"I'm just faking my way to the top," I said. Letitia picked a Devil Dog from our vending machine smorgasbord, filled with items a ten-year-old would eat. "Tell me about your sister."

"Random as fuck."

"I'm just making my way through the obligatory getting-to-know you questions."

"Uhm…hmm. She's in college and recently engaged."

"Kind of young for I-dos."

"I agree. He's her high school sweetheart, which makes it even more unsettling."

"You don't believe in one true loves?" I asked.

"Honestly, this is going to sound terrible, but I think you don't marry the only guy you've ever fucked."

"So you want your sister to fuck more guys? That's new."

"Guys, girls, herself. Just someone—anyone—who isn't him."

"Does she work?"

"She sort of works but mostly parties," she replied. "I could never. The expectations for me and my twin siblings are night and day. I had to follow all the rules, and Madison got to break them. I'm not bitter—maybe a little tart, though. Don't get it twisted, my sister is also smart, funny, and I love her to bits."

"Does she have an animated personality like her big sis?"

"I mean, I'm pretty obnoxious—it's hard to compete. My mother always said I needed to share the spotlight."

"Sometimes the spotlight just finds you, no matter how hard you try to dodge it."

"Being funny was my thing. If I was known as the funny girl, then that meant they weren't calling me the stupid girl or the Black girl."

"You're not stupid—you're far from that," I said.

"I was a slow reader who stumbled over simple words, and I'd break out into a cold sweat anytime a teacher called on me."

"When did you find out you were dyslexic?"

"I was twelve," she replied. "My doctors ran me through a series of cognitive and reading assessments. They tested my memory, reading comprehension, and writing skills. I guess I failed. Going through all that was scary, but knowing why keeping up in school and at home was so difficult was a relief. For the longest time, I just thought I was dumb, so being diagnosed helped to shift my perspective. And having the tools and resources to navigate it was a godsend. Don't get me wrong, it was still a struggle, and I was terribly self-conscious, but a least I had a why."

"Did it make school less daunting?"

"Not really. I think I just got better at hiding it, and I tried to excel in other areas in the hopes people would focus on my backflips and not on my sounding out words when asked to read aloud."

"You couldn't pay me a million dollars to go back to high school."

"Did you hate it too?" she asked.

"High schoolers are vicious. I learned to just take the insults on the chin. I went to a performing arts school where everyone thought they were going to be the next big star."

"And now you're probably the most famous person to come out of that school."

"Not even close. Probably don't even crack the top ten."

"I think that's the best type of fame."

"The type where no one knows you?"

"Yeah, niche famous. It allows you to still be a normal person."

"Like you?" I said.

"I'm not famous."

"Uhm, I think you kinda are."

"New York is so funny—one minute you're hosting an event with the first lady, and the next you're getting yelled at by some random dude on a subway."

"And that's why I love this city. It doesn't give a fuck about who you are, what you do, and who you know."

Letitia hopped up, switching her damp towels and bedding to a nearby dryer. And I shamelessly stared at her ass in her shorts while she did so. I hadn't checked my phone since last night. When I did, there would be dozens of missed calls and text messages waiting for me. But all that shit could wait, because Letitia demanded and deserved my full attention.

"Hey, you're that one lady." The DMX aficionado pointed at Letitia.

"Excuse me?"

"The lady with the fox at the library. Whatever happened to you?"

"You know…budget cuts."

"I fucking hate the mayor. My kid was obsessed with Wags. I need you to do the thing."

"What thing?"

"What thing? Would you listen to her?" The guy gestured in my direction. "The song. At first, I hated it 'cause my kid would sing it over and over, but not gonna lie, it grew on me."

"You don't want to hear that." She fidgeted with her tank top.

"I do." I stood, enthusiastically nodding.

The man pulled out his phone. "Can I?"

"Yeah, sure," she said.

"Any time you're ready, sweetheart."

Letitia's voice took on an airy quality as she sang.

"Come on in, it's time to play,

Let's read a story—hip-hip hooray!

Turn the page, let's start the fun,

With Wags the Fox and everyone!"

"That's what I'm talking about. I love it. You're a New York icon, right up there with that guy who plays guitar in his underwear. My kid's gonna love this." He rummaged through his pockets. "Here's twenty dollars. Your next wash is on me."

"I can't take your money."

"I will not be insulted. Take the money." He was yelling in that affectionate way New Yorkers do.

Letitia looked at me for help.

"You heard the man. Take the money."

Letitia flounced and rocked next to me. "Is it too firm?"

"It depends on what you're looking for." We were in a department store test-driving various mattresses. This was the ninth we'd rolled around on.

"Do mattresses usually cost this much?"

"In a store, yes. I think a mattress is the one thing you should splurge on, seeing how it supports your entire body."

"Since getting my own place, I've realized everything is so expensive," she said. "My last apartment was furnished with items I salvaged from the sidewalk or thrift store."

"Thrifting a mattress off the street is diabolical."

"The mattress was from a secondhand store, and it served me well."

I stood, eyeing the store clerks who had resigned themselves to the fact that we were lookie-loos and not cash-in-hand buyers. "Which one would you get if money weren't an object?"

Letitia hopped up and headed through the maze of beds. "That's easy. I'd get this one." She grabbed the tag and squinted. It was clear she was working hard to decipher the words.

Leaning in, I read the title. "The Caspian."

Her face lit up. "Yes, the Caspian. It's firm but not rock hard, and I like the way it feels on my skin. I know it'll have sheets on it, but it's nice knowing even when bare, it's still inviting." She surveyed the space. "So now we just have to find a cheapo version of the Caspian, because I can't bring myself to spend five thousand dollars."

I waved the store clerk over. "Hi. We'll take this in a queen."

"No, we won't," Letitia added. "But if you have a slightly less pricey mattress with similar specs—maybe something refurbished?"

"Absolutely not," I said. "You want this, and you shouldn't have to settle. Consider it my treat."

"A treat is ice cream, popcorn at the movies, maybe even a fancy dinner. Not a mattress more expensive than my monthly mortgage payment."

"It'll double as my housewarming gift."

The store clerk's eyes pinged back and forth between us.

"Rustin, I couldn't accept something like that. Trust me, I want to, but I just can't."

"Why not?"

"Because it's rude to accept something like that."

"Says who?"

"My mother. I can hear her now: 'People don't extend themselves out of the kindness of their heart. There is always a price to pay.'"

"Damn, your mother is kind of bleak."

"She's definitely a sky-is-falling type of personality."

"Well, she's right. I do want something."

She nodded, indicating she knew there was a catch. "What?"

"I wanna make you happy."

Letitia circled me, tilting her head up and down.

"What are you looking for?" I asked.

"The strings."

"Zero strings attached. The bed is yours, free and clear."

Letitia turned to the clerk. "Can you just give us a second?" She waited until the clerk was a respectable distance before she turned back to me. "Rustin, I know."

"Know what?"

"I know my pussy is amazing, like sunshine, or nibs of chocolate, but I can't let you do this."

"Who told you that?"

"Several gentleman callers." She stuck out her tongue and tucked her hair behind her ear.

"Are these gentlemen still calling, like right now? Because long term that could be a problem."

"Why don't we go half and half?"

"Absolutely not. I could do this all day, because we are leaving here with something."

"Damn, the pussy bandit strikes again. Stealing men's hearts and money."

"Is that a yes?"

"Yes," she said.

"And just so you know, your box is mid at best." We stared at each other in silence, and I was the first to crack, bursting out in a belly laugh. "I really tried to keep a straight face."

Letitia tossed her arms over my shoulders. "It's the best you've ever had."

"It's five-star, Michelin-rated, award-winning, slap-your-momma, top-tier pussy."

"Don't you ever forget it."

The clerk released a heavy sigh from across the room, signifying he was sick of our shit. "So do you want me to ring you up or what?"

"Yes, please." Letitia smiled sheepishly. Turning to me, she said, "Thank you, really."

"Of course. I do have one request."

Her eyes creased in the corners. "And what's that?"

"That you let me help you break in the mattress."

"If you weren't hanging out with me, what would you be doing today?" Letitia licked strawberry ice cream from her cone.

"I'd be on my third cup of coffee with an open laptop, staring at the cursor blinking incessantly, waiting for me to fill the page." I pointed to outdoor seating sandwiched between two buildings.

"What are you working on?"

"A new play."

"That's exciting." We sat, and she tried to keep up with the melting rate of the ice cream.

This random Saturday with Letitia was the most fun I'd had in a long while. I guess you could call me a workaholic. Saturdays were usually reserved for working on my next musical. It was less a work-in-progress and more a work-in-limbo. I'd been nursing the project for years. I had a plot and a thorough outline. Given the opportunity, I could talk for hours about character motivation and beats of the story. Despite all that, I was having a difficult time getting the vision in my head onto the page.

Letitia noticed the uncertain expression on my face. "Or not?"

"I'm just in the middle, and that's when things get sticky for me."

"How so?"

"I just start questioning every choice I've made and have to fight the urge to delete everything and start from scratch."

"That's weird. You seem like the type of guy who never struggles and things just come easy. I mean, look at *U-Turn*. It's a masterpiece, and a puppet cast was revolutionary at the time. You spawned a ton of copycats, none of which could touch the high bar you set."

It was the thought of being a one-hit wonder that haunted me the most. No one was saying it, but I felt it slowly inching closer, boxing me in to forever be known as the guy who made *U-Turn*. Sure. I had my studio, and we were partnering on all types of productions, but those stories weren't mine. I loved creating puppets for movies and TV because that was where the money was, but I still had this unyielding desire for more.

"Expectations can be a creative person's kryptonite. When I wrote *U-Turn*, I was an unknown college student. I never expected for it to take off in the way it did."

"And now you're Rustin Hayes." She said my name with exaggerated reverence.

"Yeah, exactly."

"I get it. When Story Time with Letty and Wags took off, I started to feel the pressure. I was just mostly riffing, and I'd say these off-the-wall things that the kids loved. But with more eyes comes more scrutiny, and every event needed to be bigger than the last."

"I never thought the thing I loved would cause me so many sleepless nights."

"Why do you have to write another play?"

"What?"

"Who's asking for that?"

"Wow. Thanks."

"I didn't mean it like that. I just meant, what's driving this?" she asked.

"I'm driving this, one hundred percent because I'm a masochist."

"You already have tons of balls in the air. Why are you so eager to toss up another one?"

"Because it's kind of what you do. In the entertainment space, you're only as good as your last project, and *U-Turn* is almost a decade old. There has to be something else."

"I hear you, but maybe there doesn't have to be. Maybe you just sit back on your laurels. I find I'm always the least productive when I implement a forced deadline or unrealistic due date. When I was sixteen, I thought future me would have a job in fashion. I applied to be a contestant on *In the Cut*, like, four times."

"*In the Cut?*"

"Yeah. It's a show where designers compete in various events making clothes. The winner gets a bunch of money and a big-name agent." She tugged on her outfit she'd changed into after the laundromat. "This dress I'm wearing… I made it myself."

"Seriously? That's pretty impressive."

"Yeah, thanks. Why did I bring any of this up?" She scratched her forehead, her face blooming into a smile once she remembered. "I'm just saying, we all have ideas about where we should be and what we should've accomplished, and I think we can be too hard on ourselves. Everyone I know is chasing the next big thing. Have you noticed when you ask somebody what they do, they'll rattle off a primary job and two or three side hustles? Fuck all that. Why isn't existing enough?"

"Because we only have one life to live, and the thought of wasting the time you have is criminal."

"Who's to say painting the Sistine Chapel is more important than enjoying a sunrise?"

"I think everyone would say that."

"Then they'd all be wrong."

I studied Letitia, trying to determine if she actually believed the words she was saying. The thought of being okay with life as is was *unfathomable* to me. My parents didn't get a chance to chase their dreams because they were too busy raising me. Have you ever met someone who stopped dreaming, stopped believing there was more, a person who slowly, over time, had their light dimmed because reality knocked them down too much? My parents had poured all their hopes and dreams into me, and I'd be damned if I squandered their sacrifices.

If I could block out the fans and haters and turn off my overactive brain, then maybe I'd know some peace. But I was destined to obsess over this project until it was right. This was only my first draft, which meant I'd be stuck in the trenches for a long time. While I appreciated the advice, I knew it would go in one ear and out the other. I was my toughest critic, and I wouldn't give up until my libretto was as polished as possible.

Nudging her shoulder with mine, I said, "I could watch a hundred sunrises with you."

"Yeah?" Letitia cupped my face, slowly planting kisses on my lips. "I just don't want you to beat yourself up. You're more than your work. And I know that's hard to hear for people like us. But your worth isn't tied to your success or failures. This, eating ice cream on a bench in the middle of the day, is just as important as any play. Because this is real life, and I can touch you and listen to your heartbeat and know this moment is different than any other."

It was funny the way life worked—one minute you were just hurtling through space, and the next you were sitting on a bench with the woman who was no doubt going to be your wife. "I like you so fucking much."

"You do?"

"I do. Prepare to be sick of me." I kissed her like I was laying claim.

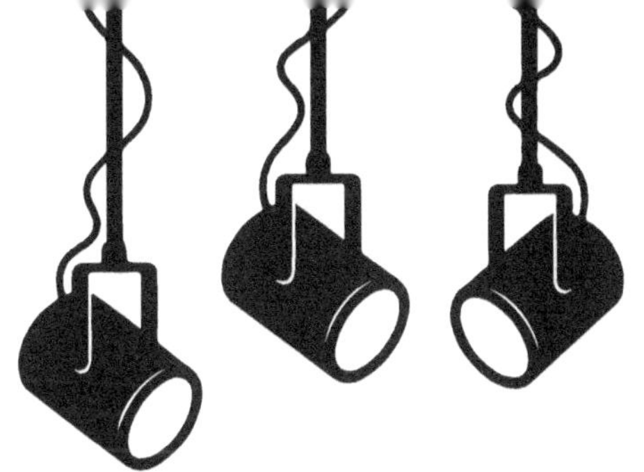

CHAPTER 19
Letitia

"TELL ME, WHAT'S the vibe for the fundraising event?" I asked Brea while flipping through dresses on a rack.

"It's just like every other year. Rich people and us working the room with our hands out."

"It's all so horrible."

"We're entertainers. We have to beg for cash if we want our art to survive."

"I hate that part, walking around with my hat out in search of spare change."

"Agreed. It's the least fun part about what we do." Brea already had four dresses she'd picked out for me draped over her arm. None of my outfits at home were suitable for this black-tie fundraising event. When I told Brea I was going to wear what I'd worn last year, she'd planned this impromptu shopping trip.

"I just want to write skits and produce quality television."

"And to do that, you'll need to perform a quick tap dance." She held up a pink silk dress, and I fake gagged.

"A four-hour event is far from quick."

"I expect you to mind your P's and Q's."

"Of course."

"I'm serious, Letty. I don't want any of your shenanigans."

"Got it."

"And you better contain the smoke you have for Rustin. Nobody is interested in your imaginary feud. *Jellybean Junction* needs to raise money to fund next season, so be nice to him."

The corners of my mouth twitched upward.

"What was that?" Brea asked.

"What?"

"Your face when I said Rustin's name."

My features betrayed me once more.

"There it is again." Brea pointed at me.

"I mean, when you think about it, Rustin is such a weird name. Who names their kid after something that tarnishes?"

"Now you're babbling. What are you not telling me?"

"Don't be ridiculous." I circled the rack, picking out a dress two sizes too big. I just needed to get to a dressing room.

Brea wasn't far behind. She grabbed my arm, looked me dead in the eye, and said, "Rustin."

I dissolved into a fit of giggles.

Brea tossed the dresses on a cushy bench right outside the dressing rooms. "Letitia Vincent, are you and Rustin sleeping together?"

My eyes grew wide. "You know the ancient Egyptians use to believe—"

"Stop it. Answer the question."

"Kinda."

"What is that supposed to mean?"

"All the time. We're fucking *all the time*." I exhaled a breath, relieved to be freed of this secret.

"All the time?"

"He's always ready—like, I could breathe on him, and his dick would get hard."

"Oh my God." Brea yanked me down to sit on the bench. Every detail, every last one."

"I'm not giving you every detail."

"Okay. Tell me this: is it big?"

My words complemented the blush that overtook my cheeks. "Yes…uh-huh."

"Bitch, how long has this been going on?"

"A week."

"A week, and I'm just now hearing about it?"

"Because you rush things and start planning weddings and couples' trips."

She gasped. "Do you think he'd be down for a couples' trip?"

"I don't know, because we're not a couple."

"Have you two not had the talk?"

"Let me remind you, it's been a week."

"Does he provide all the services?"

"He provides the ones that are most important—the *vital* services."

Brea dropped her voice to a whisper. "Is he a happy eater?"

"Like it's his fucking job."

"I'm happy for you. Does Hallmark have a card for moments like this—you know, like, 'congratulations on getting your carpet munched'?"

"It's probably in the LGBTQ section."

"True. I'll check." We both chuckled at the thought. "On a serious note, I like him."

"I like him too."

"I know you hate when I do that thing where I'm two steps ahead, but I think Rustin could be the one."

"You're right," I said. "I do hate it. Let's just stay in the present."

"I'll do my best, but I'm going to Google engagement party locations tonight."

"Yeah. That's totally normal."

"Have you told your parents?"

"What exactly? 'Hey, Mom and Dad, I met a guy, and he sucks my clit every morning. He claims eating pussy is the most important meal of the day.' Do you see how that would be awkward?"

"Rustin's a freak. I wouldn't have guessed, because he's kind of uptight."

I didn't want to talk about this topic anymore. It was anxiety inducing. Rustin and I were having fun and enjoying each other's company—no need to read any more into it. I was only thinking about tomorrow, not where we'd be months for now. Casual was good. Casual was low stakes—no pressure, just fun.

"Did I tell you Madison and my mom are coming for a visit?" I said, changing the subject.

"Wait. What? Are you okay with that?"

"There's a pageant in New Jersey, and my mom decided it would be the perfect time to hop on the turnpike and head my way."

"I thought you were checking the events on the app."

"I did, but I've been a bit distracted with work and the apartment."

"And being fucked," Brea said.

"She caught me off guard, and I couldn't come up with a good excuse to get out of it. But I've been thinking it'll be good to see them again. The last time was Christmas."

"Yeah. I remember you telling me about that. She pulled out her measuring tape because she thought you were getting fat."

"Mmm, and she suggested we take before pictures so I could track my progress," I added.

"Letty, you can't fool me."

"I've already made peace with the fact that nothing will be good enough for my mom. She'll hate the apartment, the neighborhood, the noise."

"You have to know it's not personal—it's just her."

"No, no, it's definitely personal."

After college, I didn't return home for a reason—my mother and her expectations. She had a plan for my life and never bothered to ask me if I was okay with it. My mother wasn't a bad person, and my childhood was picturesque—a hardworking father, an ever-present, super-involved mom who made sure fresh-baked cookies were waiting for me when I came home from school. Summers were filled with pool parties and sleepovers, and winters were cozy with hot cocoa and fluffy blankets. My boo-boos were always met with a kiss, and my bed was dressed in clean pink bedding with Black ballerinas all over it.

We weren't lacking in love, but underneath, there were expectations. My mother was constantly trying to fit my square peg into a star-shaped hole. And after being told you're not enough for years, you start to believe it. When I went off to college, the fissures became more pronounced. I was living on my own for the first time at an HBCU, and it felt like I was finally free.

For most of my life, my mother had tried to control me—what I wore, whom I was friends with, what activities I participated in. I wanted to be in the robotics club, but she demanded I try out for the cheer squad. I wanted to hone my artistic skills, but my mother was of the opinion that creative endeavors rarely paid the bills. And I was grown enough to admit on that specific point, she was kind of right. But I would work at *Jellybean Junction* for free because it was my dream job.

Granted, I mean that in theory and not in practice, because these bills were very real.

"How long are they staying?" Brea asked.

"A few days."

"Well, at least they'll be at a hotel."

"Actually, my mom wants to stay with me."

"Letitia, you don't have a bed or a set of dishes."

"Correction, I *do* have a bed. Well, a mattress. I got it last weekend."

"What made you finally pull the trigger?"

Rustin's kind offer to purchase it and the idea of his fucking me through it. "My mother's going to hate my place, so I need to put in work to mitigate the damage, and a bed is a great start. Because if she comes to town and finds out I'm sleeping on a futon, she may take up a collection at church."

"You know this is my time to shine. Just give me a weekend, and I'll have your place decorated for maximum mommy approval. We'll go thrifting and find items in your budget."

"Thanks. I'm definitely taking you up on your offer."

Brea examined the tangerine dress I'd pulled from the racks. "Put that shit back."

I complied, returning with two new options. "Enough about me. How are things going with you?"

"Sandra thinks I should quit."

My head jerked back at her unexpected words. "No. I forbid it. I wouldn't make it a day without you. You're the one who told me to give Rustin a chance to cook, and then you're thinking about leaving during meal prep? Not cool."

"I think the writing's on the wall, and *Jellybean Junction* will soon be a fond memory."

"Nope. I'm not accepting that. The show is like a cat with nine lives."

"Letitia, we are on our ninth life."

"Rustin's supposed to fix all that."

"Now you're betting on Rustin?"

My stomach flipped at the knowledge that maybe I wasn't seeing things clearly. If I weren't sleeping with Rustin, I would be less inclined to hail him as our savior, but I believed him when he said the show was a priority and he planned to fight to save it.

"I love your optimism, but I've been at galas like this before, and it's getting harder and harder to get the guests to attend, let alone open their wallets," Brea continued.

"Well then, we have to do something to grab their attention."

"Like what?"

"Leave it up to me."

"Letitia?"

"I give you my word, I'll stay in between the guardrails, and I'll even run it past Rustin."

When Rustin opened his front door, he looked surprised to see me. "What?" I asked.

"It's just weird seeing you in my doorway."

"Good weird, like 'I can't wait to kiss her'? Or bad weird, like 'get your shit and go'?"

"The first one." His voice was deeper than normal, like I was the first person he'd spoken to today.

"Well, you're in luck. I'm accepting kisses at any time."

He eagerly accepted my invitation, leaning in for a kiss that made waking up at five in the morning, standing in line at the newest trendy bakery, and riding the subway all the way to Brooklyn worth it. My free hand slid over his naked chest. Grabbing at the waist of his shorts, I pulled him closer.

"I prefer waking up next to you, but this isn't bad either," he said.

"And I brought pastries." I held up the pink bag.

Rustin stepped aside, and I entered his loft-style apartment with jaw-dropping views of the Brooklyn Bridge. The large windows made the space feel massive. Like a moth to a flame, I was drawn to the windows, moving closer to get a better look.

"This view is…" Clearly it was stupefying, because I was at a loss for words.

"Like you, I enjoy a good view."

"The view from my apartment and this are not on the same level."

"I love apartments with views of the street below. Your neighborhood is so filled with life. You get to watch kids jumping rope outside, or a neighbor carting their laundry up the block, and when there's a fight, you have a front-row seat." He came up behind, enveloping me in his arms.

It was weird how quickly one could get used to someone's presence. Just a few months ago, Rustin was someone I'd only heard about, and now the idea of not being able to touch him, kiss him, fuck him, seemed unnatural.

"Some weekends, I'll make myself a coffee or have a glass of wine and just window-watch. I love making up stories about where people are headed and what the day holds for them. It's probably silly." I shrugged.

"Not at all. You're a storyteller, and people in this city have unique stories to tell."

"If I weren't at *Junction*, I'd love to go up to people for impromptu interviews on the street."

"Why not do both?"

"Because unlike you, I can't juggle fifty-eleven jobs."

"That's only because I can't sit still. If I'm not doing something, creating something—"

"There's beauty in silence. In just being and not producing."

"Teach me your way, sensei."

"First, you have to turn off your phone." I demonstrated on my own phone, placing it on *do not disturb*.

"What if someone calls me?"

"Fuck them."

"Just fuck work and responsibilities?"

"We work in entertainment—it's not life or death."

He reached for his phone on the kitchen counter. "Done. What's next?"

"Next, you turn your brain off and let me handle the rest." I extended my arm so he could retrieve the bag of pastries. Rustin got to work unbagging the items while I continued to tour his place. The walls were filled with bold art prints, and the décor comprised mid-century pieces I was certain he'd paid a pretty penny for.

"Are these your awards?" I asked.

"Yep." He glanced up before quickly returning to his work. "Coffee?"

"Already got you covered. It's in the bag." While he grabbed plates and napkins, I perused his shelf of accolades. Among them were several Tony Awards. I removed one from the shelf and was surprised by the weight. "I've never held a Tony before. What was it like winning your first one?"

"Surreal. I didn't expect to win, so when they called my name, I wanted to shit my pants, throw up, and retreat all at the same moment. When I got on stage, I couldn't even tell you what was said. It was like my brain and mouth weren't connected. I remember the crowd laughing, and I didn't know if it was with me or at me. I did thank my parents, I remember that."

Now that I knew him, I often forgot what a big deal he was, but the Emmy, Tonys, and Grammy were all reminders I wasn't fucking around with some random dude. This man was driven and creative, and people respected his craft. At the end of the day, he was *the* Rustin Hayes, and it would do me good to remember that.

"Are you expecting company?" He pointed to the counter with all the sweet treats.

"I like options." As I continued to explore, I stumbled on a wall that appeared to be a work-in-progress. "Is this you?"

"Yeah. I'm just messing around."

I pointed to the half-finished mural wall of graffiti art. "If this is you messing around, then what does your art look like when you're locked in?"

"I might just paint over it."

"That would be a shame." I made my way to the couch and took a seat.

Rustin joined me in the living room with pastries and coffee. Finding my thigh, he gave it a squeeze. "Thank you for coming to see me. It was a late night at the theater."

"It gave me a reason to wake up before ten, so it's actually a good thing. Plus, your place has room to spread out."

"Oh, I definitely plan on spreading you out."

My eyes danced across his face, and my only response was a goofy smile. "So how did last night go?"

"I took a meeting with the movie executives after the show, and they are very interested in adapting *U-Turn* into a film."

"Oh my God, that's major."

"Yep."

"You don't sound enthused."

"I just don't want to make some silly movie about puppets and people."

"It's your story, how could it be silly?"

"Some shit doesn't translate. And what works on stage may not connect when you're sitting in a movie theater."

"You sound like your mind's made up," I said.

"It's not. Trust me, Omar will work hard to persuade me."

"But…?"

"I'm just not interested in making mistakes. My next move needs to be better than what came before."

I stared at him in silence.

"What?"

"I think you're too hard on yourself. Life is about risk, and not every shot attempt converts into a basket. Look at Letty and Wags. That failed, but I learned a ton."

"That was not a failure. That was a stepping stone—an introduction to the great things you have in store."

God, I wish I could see myself the way he saw me. I couldn't resist the urge to mount him. Before I properly settled on his lap, he was already pulling my T-shirt over my head.

"Is this a safe space?" he asked.

"Yes."

"I like having you around." He unhooked my bra.

"Mutual."

Rustin leaned in slowly, his eyes flickering to my lips as if he were asking for permission with every breath. The space between us hummed with heat, and when his mouth finally met mine, it was soft but deliberate. Our lips moved in unison, like a whisper, tasting, exploring, lingering in the moment. Rustin cupped my jaw, tilting me slightly closer, and I melted into the contact. I clutched at his skin like it was the only thing keeping us grounded. With a teasing brush of tongues and a gentle pull, he left me breathless.

Our lips only parted for the seconds it took to undress. I repositioned on top of him, holding my breath as he slid inside. A tickle licked up my spine at the sensation of his skin against mine.

Words escaped me, but I hoped the moans and grunts expressed how much I appreciated him. Sinking my face into his neck, I suckled his skin. I wanted to brand him and mark my property, so if by chance another was in a similar position, they'd know I'd been there first.

"You feel so fucking good."The rich timbre of his voice caught me off guard. His eyes were hooded, almost as if he were intoxicated, and I recognized the expression because I was feeling it as well. Time and space were no longer tangible, and although there were over eight million people in this city, we now existed in a world where it was just us two, each thrust moving me further from reality.

Rustin's hands coasted down my back, landing on my ass. We were on the move. He stood, and I tightened my legs around his waist.

"You gotta let go, baby." He tapped me on my thigh.

"Nope." I was still rocking my hips.

"I promise I'll make it worth it."

Reluctantly, I released my hold, and he slipped out. Turning me around, he locked my arms so I couldn't shy away and reentered from behind. Immediately, my knees buckled. From this angle, the intensity of the strokes made my head want to pop. If Rustin's plan was to break me, it was working. Rustin one, Letty zero. Well, actually, there were no losers when his thick dick was hitting my button. When he went Matrix on my ass and slowed the stokes down, I almost collapsed.

"You okay?"

"I'm a gangsta," was all I could eke out.

"Oh, you think you're big and bad."

"Just call me Michael Jackson."

Rustin pulled out and stared at me.

"*Heh, hee.*"

"Cute. You think this is a game."

He tossed me on the couch face down and fucked me like he was on a quest to find pink hearts, green clovers, orange stars, and yellow moons. Rustin was Lucky, and I was his pot of gold. You ever been fucked so thoroughly all you can do is gasp for air and hope you make it out in one piece? Strokes rippled in my core and sent vibrations to my extremities.

I hate to admit it, but at this point, I wasn't even fucking back. How could I be expected to meet each thrust when I couldn't form complete sentences? But it didn't seem to matter, because Rustin was balls deep. My soul was gone. Edges snatched. Pussy dripping. When he dipped lower and wrapped his hand around my neck, I expired. Time of death: seven fifty-eight a.m. His mouth was pressed against my ear, and I was treated to each grunt and moan.

When he whispered, "You still with me, baby?"

I whimpered and uttered the first thing that popped into my head: "No, dead. Send flowers."

"Well, let me pay my respects."

What he did next was not respectful. He stole my senses—all I could do was give in to the throbbing pressure in my core. Luckily, he was kind enough to talk me through it as I called him every filthy name I could think of. At one point, I was ready to sign over custody of the pussy, granting him nights and weekends.

"Don't fight it. Don't you dare."

"What the fuck, Rustin?"

"I just want you to feel appreciated. Can you feel how grateful I am?"

"I feel everything."

"Letitia…"

"Yes?"

"I can't come until you do."

Nodding, I rallied my senses and leaned into each thrust until I exploded like a confetti bomb. Rustin wasn't far behind, trembling over top of me.

"Are you okay?" His voice had returned to normal, no longer thick and mischievous.

"You could've warned me."

He rubbed my back. I was still fused with the couch cushions. "I missed you."

"Rustin, I can no longer feel my legs," I half joked.

"I'm sorry." He bit down on his bottom lip while massaging my right leg.

When I finally attempted to stand, he had to grab my waist to brace me because my knees were like Jell-O. While I steadied my feet, he buried his face in between my ass cheeks. My freak-nasty ass could barely walk, but without hesitation, I bent over and opened wide so he could get a taste of our juices combined.

Relationships were funny, because a minute ago, I was writhing against Rustin's tongue, and the next we were enjoying scones and chocolate croissants. Not that this, what we were doing, could be classified as a relationship. Just two adults having fun.

"I went dress shopping with Brea yesterday," I said.

"Oh yeah?"

It was clear the idea of a lazy Sunday was growing on him as he slowly sipped his reheated coffee.

"Yeah, and we were talking about the fundraising event next weekend," I said around a huge bite of cinnamon roll.

"What about it?"

I was no longer talking to the guy who'd caused me to speak in tongues after a well-placed stroke, but to my boss. "The goal is to raise money, so maybe we put on a mini showcase."

"With less than a week before the event?"

"One thing the cast knows how to do is make shit move. Are you familiar with *The Sound of Music*?"

"The musical? Yes."

"And the scene where the kids sing goodbye to the guests while heading up to bed? I think we should do a spin on that. It could feature Aaliyah, Jabari, Gus, Lulu Lark, and a few others."

Rustin's mouth puckered, a habit when he was mulling information over. "That's not a bad idea. What did Brea say?"

"She's on board. We can start practicing tomorrow. I already have a draft of the song written."

Rustin clapped. "I love solutions. People usually come to me with problems, so solutions are greatly appreciated."

I beamed at the compliment.

Rustin scanned the pastries, selecting a raspberry-filled cronut. "Do you wanna go together?"

"To the fundraiser?" My eyebrow climbed my forehead.

"Yeah."

"*U*hm, how would that work?"

"I was thinking I'd pick you up and then we'd ride together."

"Ha-ha, I get the logistics, but I'm stuck on the optics."

"What do you mean?"

"You know exactly what I mean. If we go together, people will talk."

"Let them."

I wiped my mouth and licked my fingers clean. This was a serious conversation, and I couldn't have icing all over me. "I don't want people talking about me in that way."

"What way?"

"Could you stop doing that?"

"Doing what?"

I stared at him with daggers in my eyes. There was nothing I hated more than answering a question with another question.

Rustin slid off the couch, joining me on the floor. "You think the cast and crew would judge you?"

"Not all, but most. I was just screaming, 'Hey-ho, Rustin has to go,' and then I show up on your arm."

"I could see how that could be awkward."

"Plus, this is very new. I'm not ready to be asked questions I don't have answers to."

"I get it."

"Do you? It's not that I don't want to go with you, but—"

"Bad timing. I get it."

Office romances rarely worked. And if my coworkers knew I was sleeping with Rustin, I would never hear the end of it. I didn't want to be known as the boss's girl. We knew this had the potential to be more, but I didn't need the scrutiny of others' opinions shading this relationship. I wasn't ready to make this red-carpet official.

"Where's the bathroom?" I asked.

Rustin pointed. "Straight, then left."

I kissed his cheek before hopping up and heading in that direction. The heat of him caused me to blush. "Stop staring."

"But the view is so *divine*."

That was a first. No one had ever called my ass divine before—but he was right, this ass was spectacular.

In the bathroom, the walls were covered in a letterpress, vintage-news-type wallpaper. The cozy half bath was bright, with lights surrounding the circular mirror, perfect for ten-step facial routines.

Pulling down my panties, I took a seat.

There was a light knock on the door. "Yeah?"

"Can I come in?"

"Yes."

Rustin opened the door and stared at me for a second. "Uhm, I'm going to say something, and it has no connection to our conversation a minute ago."

"All right. Shoot."

"Erm, just so you know, you're my girlfriend now."

There was nothing to think about, no objection to be made, just joy. "Okay." I smiled at him from the toilet with my panties around my ankles.

Rustin fully entered the small space, towering over me, leaning closer. His lips dusted mine. "Yeah. That's what's up."

If this morning could be replicated a hundred times over, I'd die a happy woman. I wasn't big on finding Mr. Right because the dating apps and my general observations had confirmed that so many men were okay with being Mr. Bare Minimum or Mr. Not Ready to Commit. The last guy I'd dated claimed he wasn't ready to settle down. He was thirty-six with an aggressively receding hairline, but he still wanted to play it fast and loose.

Rustin was different. He liked me, and he wasn't afraid to show it, and honestly, that scared the fuck out of me. The thought of falling in love was more appealing than the actual act of falling in love. Because when you were in love, you could get your heart broken, and that was a feeling I wasn't eager to experience again. But like I said, Rustin was different, and he made me want to believe it could all be this simple.

After my *boyfriend* left, I freshened up and then rejoined him in the living room. Roy Ayers's "Searching" was playing, and Rustin was dancing like he was all alone. "What are you doing?" I asked.

"It's a beautiful Sunday in Brooklyn." He waggled his fingers, urging me to join him. Swaying slowly side to side, I let the music wash over me. Rustin wrapped me in his arms and spun me around, and I couldn't help but drink him in. I was in awe of this man. He gripped my waist as he practically swept me off my feet. When "Everybody Loves the Sunshine" played, he twirled us over to one of the windows. The rays of the sun beaming on our faces almost made our skin shimmer. I'd lost my balance the first time he'd kissed me, but now I was falling.

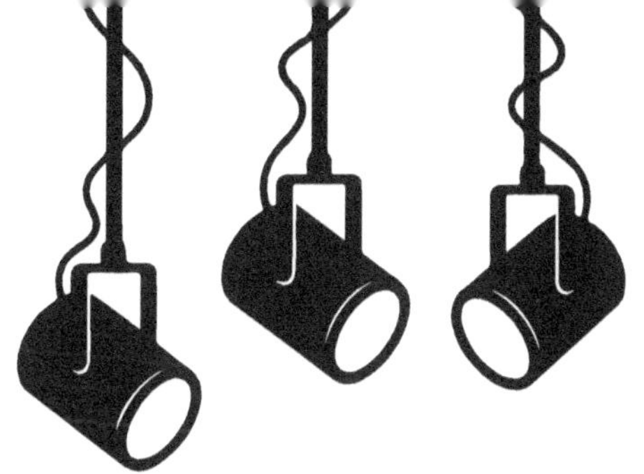

CHAPTER 20
Rustin

IF I HAD my way, I'd be spending my Saturday at home with a microbrew and some hot wings. But instead, I was in Midtown wearing a suit and trying to mentally prepare myself for the night to come. When you worked for public television, raising money was as important as the shows you created. Without donations and government funding, programs like *Junction* would not exist.

Tonight was one of many upcoming events that would require me to push aside my antisocial personality and convince people to cut the check. Usually, my reclusive demeanor worked to my benefit, but this evening, I would have to be gregarious and make sure my eyes didn't glaze over when someone recounted how *U-Turn* had changed their lives.

"I love being your plus-one." Omar was seated beside me in the back seat of a BMW. "You know how to make a guy feel special."

"The only reason you're here is for when I get overstimulated. We can pretend to be talking so people don't approach me."

"I understand my role. I'm your anxiety wingman. I'm going to work the room, give you space while also keeping a close eye out for your signal." My signal was patting the top of my head three times. We'd worked out this process early on in our friendship. At college parties, I'd tap my head, and Omar would come to the rescue with a joke to fill an awkward silence or make an excuse for why he had to pull me away. "Added bonus: I get to meet Letitia, so I'm pumped."

"If you embarrass me in front of her, you'll have to find your own way home."

"What do you take me for? I'm on my Clark Kent the entire night."

"Clark Kent?"

"You know, Mr. Perfect, can do no wrong. I'm eager to meet the woman who has you canceling plans and ignoring calls."

"She's teaching me work-life balance."

"I thought work *was* your life?"

When you're granted your fifteen minutes of fame, you hit the ground running, trying to take advantage of every opportunity. Branding and merchandising deals, consulting roles, commercial work. I was spreading myself thin trying to capitalize on the moment. A golden child era can be fleeting, and I wanted to ensure that when the excitement faded, I had something to show for it. But *U-Turn* had turned out to be the little engine that could, winning awards, with sold-out shows each night, and a growing fan base.

That sustained success had allowed me to become picky, only selecting projects that aligned with my overall brand. Thread and Thespian was dedicated to crafting bold, heartfelt, and innovative puppetry that educated, entertained, and empowered. Each fall, I taught a twelve-week course on voice and speech for performance at NYU. Our studio offered tours, and each school year, elementary students were treated to a behind-the-scenes look at film and TV production. Recently, we'd signed a first-look deal with the streaming service Cinevault, and they were patiently waiting for me to submit my first project, which was half written and scattered all over my loft. I had pages in my den, living room, and bedroom. I even had a notebook stashed in the bathroom in case inspiration struck.

"Maybe that's a mistake," I said. "Since graduation, it's been go, go, go. I don't remember the last time I had an unscheduled day."

"All by your design, my friend," Omar replied.

"Well, maybe I was wrong." Life couldn't be all work. There had to be more.

"Is Letitia a witch? Is her pussy a portal to serenity?"

"Please don't talk about my woman's vagina."

"*Your* woman? I didn't realize you two had made it official."

"Why am I being interrogated about my dating life?"

"I'm just making conversation."

"Letitia isn't up for discussion."

"Hmm."

"What?"

"It's just been a minute since you've been seriously into someone. It's been, what, over a year since Diane?"

My work was demanding, and dating often took a back seat. I'd also found that relationships with people not in the creative field made connection harder. For much of the last year, I'd chosen to focus on professional growth, but at some point, you look around at all you've accomplished and realize you have no one to share it with.

We pulled up to the venue, and I froze in my seat. "Could you just circle the block one last time for me?" I asked the driver, who, to my surprise, kindly obliged me.

"Why are you so nervous?" Omar asked.

"This show needs to raise a shit-ton of money. Even if we do get the funding, we're dead in the water if we can't manage to increase viewership."

"I love you, but I don't understand why you took on this project. We already have so many things percolating—you didn't need to add another."

"I don't need I-told-you-sos right now. I need positive energy."

"You are the chosen one. Everything you touch turns to gold, so why would this be any different? Is that cheery enough?"

"Failure is a real possibility here."

"If I know you, you have a backup plan for your backup plan."

We slowed to a stop once again. Closing my eyes, I said, "My thoughts are peaceful and calm. I'm ready for today's challenges. I'm filled with focus." I opened an eye and peeked at Omar.

"Cheers to that, brother." He took a swig out of a mini bottle of champagne.

Our event was at the Boathouse in Central Park. Brea's connections clearly ran deep, because securing this venue on a Saturday in the middle of wedding season was a feat. Sometimes you needed to spend money to make money, but *Junction* had very few dollars, so it was good to know people, especially when you were working on a passion project.

"So, who all's going to be in here?" Omar swiped a glass of champagne from a passing tray once we'd entered.

"The rich and philanthropic."

"Miles Graves…" He gasped before speaking the next name with reverence. "*Oprah?*"

"Maybe at the Chicago event."

"Maybe I can snag me a sugar momma."

"Why would you need one of those?"

"Because I'd rather spend someone else's money over my own."

"So, fuck the whole 'protector and provider' shit?"

"It's the twenty-first century, and I'm okay with being a stay-at-home dad," Omar said. "I will have dinner ready and my dick on hard when wifey gets home."

"For the next three to four hours, can you refrain from saying shit like that?"

"I have the talking points you texted me. Educational programming is more important than ever. The youth need to see what's possible in and beyond their community. Children are the future, and that's on Whitney."

"Great. I'm going to do a quick walk-through and make sure everything is set for tonight." I checked in with the sound guy and DJ. I confirmed Jabari, my puppet, was right where my assistant had said he would be after I dropped him off this afternoon. When I ran into Brea, we quickly rehearsed our lines for the introduction and mid-event presentations. These checks helped put my mind at ease, so in the moment, I could trust the process and at least appear to be enjoying myself.

I examined the space, making sure it was conducive to good vibes. The music needed to set the mood, and the open bar needed to be flowing. When people were happy, they felt better about parting with their money, and I was hoping to rob them blind tonight. TV screens had been set up throughout the space with images from over fifty years of *Jellybean Junction*. Mentally, I was rattling off facts about the show, cast, and crew so I could casually insert them into random conversations while working the room.

My nervous energy dissipated when I spotted Letitia in the crowd. She was wearing a chocolate silk dress that was molded to her curves. The skirt was several inches above her knees, elongating her miniature frame. Her skin was glowing with a hint of shimmer, making her the focal point as she navigated the room. Her hair, which was usually full of day-old curls, was sleek, no doubt Brea's doing.

Staring was my only option. Time seemed to freeze, and all I could do was wish she were on my arm.

We'd made things official, but showing up separately felt real undercover. Letitia was apprehensive about stepping out so soon, which I understood. Workplace romances could get messy, and the last thing I wanted was everyone in our business. But my desire to kiss and caress her whenever and wherever I wanted would have to be put in check for the night. I'd known of Letitia before we met from her YouTube channel and was immediately smitten, so I had a head start to this butterflies-in-stomach, heart-racing feeling.

"Gotdamn, I didn't realize there were going to be so may fine women here. Bad bitches love stuffed puppets." Omar handed me a drink. "I'm leaving with something. You hear me?" He scanned the room and seemed to home in on his next one-night stand. "Your nine o'clock."

I didn't have to turn my head because my eyes were already trained on the area where Letitia was talking with animated hands to a couple. "Which one?"

"Brown dress, legs for days, richly melanated shorty."

Wait a damn minute. He was describing Letitia. "Hey, check out your twelve o'clock," I said.

"That's the door."

"Exactly, and if you keep ogling my girl, you can step."

"Wait. That's Letitia?"

"Yeah."

"You normally like the hippie flower-child types. Chunky jewelry, wrist full of bangles, bell-bottom–wearing chicks."

"That's her, normally."

I couldn't help but smile as Omar described all the things that attracted me to Letitia.

"Now I understand why you're not responding to my text messages," he said.

"A woman like her requires undivided attention, quality time, joint bank accounts."

"Whoa. You got a little too much dip on your chip."

"I think she's the one."

Omar turned to face me, tugging on his chin, intensely examining my features. I'd probably only uttered those words once before, so declaring a woman as my future wifey was something Omar took *very* seriously. I didn't know if it was the sips of liquor I'd had in the car, my jittery nerves, or her champagne-hued silk dress, but I'd meant what I said. Omar was probably thinking our hot-boy summer was in jeopardy, and he was right. I didn't want to be in the streets, preferring instead to be booed up on my very expensive couch with Letitia. But to avoid the alarmed contortion of Omar's face, I allowed the corners of my mouth to twitch upward, a telltale sign I was bullshitting, and we both cracked into muted laughter.

"Fuck. You almost had me. You're too young, rich, and famous to settle down now. You still have an abundance of new pussy to conquer. Don't get me wrong, Ms. Legs for Days has some amazing attributes, but I'm not letting my boy go out like that in his prime."

I was ready to retire my membership to the players' club. Sure, I'd experienced my fair share of one-night stands and recurring booty calls, but fucking chicks whose names I barely remembered was a played-out pastime. I was a long-term lover who wanted to know everything about my new girlfriend. Like how Letitia got that scar on her knee. And her irrational hot takes and biggest dreams.

Letitia wasn't a fuck buddy…not for me.

CHAPTER 21
Letitia

THE MAN DIDN'T have a bad look. Dressed-up Rustin was just as fine as artist Rustin, but nothing could top naked Rustin with a stiff dick. Was I drooling? I was excited for tonight, but even more excited for the chance to fuck him again after. As boyfriends went, he was one of the best. His tongue never tired, and his penis was perpetually hard. And after sex, sometimes he'd let me be the big spoon, which made me feel in charge.

For an introvert, he was an open book—no question too personal, no area off-limits. If I asked, he'd answer. I was used to deception and lies, but it appeared Rustin was using an entirely different playbook, which made it hard for me to suss out his bullshit. Men liked to conquer things, so the more you played hard to get, the harder they'd pursue. But the minute you let down your guard and allowed them in, they would revert to destruction mode and wreak havoc.

Love was the only thing people willingly engaged in knowing statistically most relationships ended within the first year. And when they ended, they were oftentimes messy and complicated, and someone always ended up hurt. In the past, that someone had been me. So now I was trying to just enjoy the ride and not get attached too soon to the vehicle, despite the heated seats, leather interior, champagne chiller, and full sunroof.

The event was for *Jellybean Junction*, but Rustin was the main attraction. A line had formed like this was a superfan meet-and-greet. One guest after the other clasped his hands, or worse, pulled him into a hug, which I knew he hated. Rustin would return a warm smile and nod as grown men and women excitedly chatted him up. If you were close enough, you would overhear them gushing over *U-Turn* and probing about what was next for him.

For his part, Rustin seemed to take it in stride. Maybe he was so used to receiving flowers, he'd lost the ability to truly appreciate it. The compliments were all well deserved, but each seemed to just go over his head. His face was plastered with a smile, but genuine joy never reached his eyes. He spent more time scratching his neck and fidgeting with his suit jacket than engaging in the conversation, satisfied to let the crowd carry the load. Rustin would call out the occasional "Thank you," "I appreciate it," or "Tell your mother I said hello."

"This turnout is better than expected." Brea offered me a glass of champagne. "Typically, summer is the worst time for fundraising because everyone is in vacation mode."

I took a long sip. "That just goes to show how persuasive you can be."

"They're not here because of me. They're here for Rustin."

"Hence the large crowd gathered around him."

"He's a man shrouded in mystery, so when he makes an appearance, people get excited."

"Can you imagine having that level of fandom?"

"You have a fandom?" Brea said.

"Yeah, and they're all five years old and under."

"What about that one guy who writes you letters each week?"

"That's a stalker." I took another thoughtful sip. "Maybe bringing Rustin on wasn't such a bad idea."

Brea's eyes slammed into me. "Are you saying that because he's your lover, or are you admitting I was right?"

"No, never that. I'm just saying all these extra bodies have to translate into extra cash."

"Rustin is a lot of things—most of them negative. He's cocky, arrogant, and a know-it-all, but he is also fiercely dedicated to his art, and anything he touches is better because of it."

"Are you swinging back around to the opinion he can save the show?" I asked.

"Not even Jim Henson could save this show, but I trust that Rustin will give his last breath trying. Now if you'll excuse me, I have to wrangle the man of the hour, and you should head backstage for the opening number."

Brea and I parted ways, and my stomach churned as I made my way backstage. Was this all just destined to fail? *Junction* had survived for fifty years but could cease to exist six months from now.

The backstage area was just as hectic as the event.

"What's wrong, dear? You look like you've seen a ghost," Valerie said.

"Yeah, the ghost of our television past."

"Huh?" She was too busy fluffing Lulu Lark's wings to give me her full attention.

Shaking the thoughts from my head, I put on a brave face. "Okay, people, after Brea's speech, we're on. Remember your lines. Be cheerful. And enunciate like your job depends on it, because it probably does."

Rustin joined us in the holding area, and if he was nervous, I couldn't tell. He stripped out of his suit jacket and opened the bag housing his puppet. Absent-mindedly, I fixed Aaliyah's ponytails, but my eyes were trained on the flex of Rustin's arms under his perfectly fitted dress shirt.

"Should we be lining up?" Stanley asked.

"Yes. Please line up and wait for the cue," I said.

From just behind the set, which was crafted from an old letter L to look like a staircase, we waited in silence. Rustin fell in line behind me, giving my shoulder a reassuring squeeze.

From our vantage point, I could faintly hear Brea addressing the crowd. "It wouldn't be a *Jellybean Junction* event without alcohol. For a children's show, we sure do enjoy our drinks." There was laughter from the audience. "Thank you so much for joining us tonight at the Boathouse. *Jellybean Junction* has been on air for fifty years, providing fun and educational programming for children. I remember watching the show when I was a child, and I hope to one day witness my child singing the familiar theme song. We could not exist without the kind and generous donations from our friends. I will save my bleeding-heart speech for later in the night, but let's start the evening with a message from our *Junction* family. I think it's well past their bedtime, but they wanted to say goodnight."

The lights dimmed, and a spotlight was placed on our DIY staircase with the puppets lined up as if each was standing on one of the stairs. The others and I were concealed so all the attendees could see were our felt friends. The first line we all sang in unison.

"*See you, jellybeans. It's time to end the day,*
We sang, we laughed, and we learned a lot…hooray!"
First up was Lulu Lark with her farewell wishes.
"*I hopped and I clapped and shared my favorite rhyme,*
But now it's getting close to bedtime."

Lulu ascended the stairs and disappeared. Behind the scenes, she was just turning right, crouching out of sight, and walking away. While she exited, the remaining cast sang the chorus in unison once more.

"*See you, jellybeans. It's time to end the day,*
We sang, we laughed, and we learned a lot…hooray!"
Stanley's voice boomed as Grumpy Gus.
"*I told some jokes and played pretend with flair.*
But now it's time to brush my tangled hair."
The guests were laughing and clapping along to the catchy beat. I was next, delivering Aaliyah's lines.
"*I counted to ten and made a snack with cheese,*
Now I'm off to dream beneath the trees."
Rustin was the last to go.
"*So hug your teddy bear, and snuggle up just right,*
We'll meet again…good night, good night."
Our good-night song had the intended effect. Applause and cheers erupted from the crowd. We congratulated one another with huge smiles and hugs.

"They loved it." Stanley almost sounded surprised. "I'll be the first to admit I thought this song was lame, but—"

"Hey." I stamped my heel in protest.

"—I was wrong. I underestimated how corny the crowd would be, so your song was perfect."

"You can't burst my bubble. It was fun and a reminder to the guests about why they loved this show. *Jellybean Junction* is just getting started, and Stanley, you'll be around for another thirty years."

"I don't know if he's going to make it to another thirty. Twenty maybe," Rustin joked, nudging me with his shoulder. "I've seen what this man eats for lunch."

"We'll just designate a place of honor for his ashes."

"I'm not dead yet, and I'll have you know my grandfather ate bacon and smoked a pack a day and lived to be ninety-seven." Stanley grunted.

"Breakfast of champions." Rustin turned his attention solely on me. "Great job."

"Thank you." The smile on my face captured my giddy demeanor.

"Seriously, we need more wins like this. It gets the guests excited, and I'd like to think it sparks a sense of magic in them."

"When you're a kid, everything is magical. The troll in your closet, the puddles on a rainy day, the tip of your colored pencils."

"And then we grow up, and that magic morphs into witchcraft and becomes scary and something to avoid. Mind you, it's the same magic—it's just adulthood that makes us see it differently."

"That's why I love children," I said. "I think they're little pockets of magic and wonder."

"Omar has a daughter, and anytime I come over, we play pretend. I get to be a pirate, a treasure hunter, or an astronaut."

"I bet you make a very logical pirate."

"*Aye-aye.*" His voice became gravelly. "We must set a course for a reasonable amount of adventure." We shared a laugh, which seemed to propel our bodies closer. "I could dream up all sorts of adventures with you."

Shiver me timbers, or whatever the fuck pirates say.

My gaze settled on his face, so soft and dear. This was a bad time to fall in love. I had a job to save, an apartment to decorate, and a pending visit from my judgmental mother. I did not have time for carefree walks that led to nowhere in particular, or conversations that carried on into the wee hours of the night, both parties too enraptured to let the other go. Falling in love would complicate my already-complicated life. I rebuked it and Rustin's too-cool-for-school grin.

"There you two are." Brea's voice was sharp, and she took big gulps of air like she'd just lost a mini foot race. "I need you out and mingling. This show isn't going to fund itself." She grabbed Rustin by the hand and pulled him away. He was the purse whisperer, and he needed to be visible for the majority of the night. "You too, Letty. Get your ass out there, and do something strange for a bit of change."

I worked the crowd, introducing myself, answering questions, and recording voice notes for guests' kids as Aaliyah. If people were going to give you their money, you had to work for it. Fuck that—it was going to a good cause, and these people were rich. They wouldn't miss five thousand dollars—shit, most wouldn't break a sweat over fifty thousand. These were the type of people who lived on the Upper West Side, Tribeca, Riverside Parkway, and vacationed in the Maldives because Martha's Vineyard was no longer chic. The type of people who used the word *summer* as a verb and not a season.

"I've never been in a room with such bloated egos," a tall gentleman with a regional accent I couldn't put my finger on quipped next to me.

"I hope I'm not among those numbers."

"No. You seem down to earth." He extended his arm. "Omar Mendoza, Rustin's business partner."

"Nice to meet you. Letitia Vincent. I'm a puppeteer on *Jellybean Junction*."

"I'm familiar. Rus speaks highly of you."

Rus? I liked it. It suited him—much less formal than Rustin.

"Does he?" Nudging Omar with my shoulder, I asked, "What does he say?"

"That you're the future of puppeteering."

I couldn't stop myself from snorting out a laugh. "Shut up. He never said that."

"He did, and he was serious. You're the reason he signed on to the show as a producer."

"Excuse my French, but bullshit."

"Hand to God. The showrunner sent him some episodes to review, and he liked what you were doing with your character and saw an opportunity to expand on that."

"Wow."

"Yep. He was a fan before he met you."

"So, what do you do?"

"Everything Rus doesn't want to. He's the creative, and I handle the business side. Hiring, HR, paying the bills. It takes a village to support a genius."

"Well, I'm sure what you do is very important, because he hardly ever mentions you."

"*Ouch.*"

"I didn't mean it like that. It just means he trusts you, so you must be doing an amazing job."

"Rus is a bit of a control freak," Omar said. "He's only letting me manage what I do because he realized he could only be in two places at once."

"Two?"

"Yeah, in person and on the phone. Technically three if you count Zoom calls on his laptop."

"He doesn't."

"Yes. He'll put one group on hold while talking to another."

I loved being fed tidbits of Rustin's inner workings.

"So you're a puppeteer—what else do you do?" Omar asked.

"Why is it that everyone in this city has multiple streams of income? I'm so sick of people introducing themselves and saying, 'I'm a nurse, a DJ, and I cut hair on the side.'"

"Probably because most of us grew up broke, and we're not trying to go back."

"Well, I grew up middle class in a suburb of Connecticut, and I'll be damned if I ever go back, so maybe I should start working on that second gig."

Rustin approached and placed his hand on Omar's shoulder. "Don't believe anything he says."

"Really? Because he was just telling me how you were a genius," I said.

"Oh, okay, well that's true. I love this conversation."

"Omar also said when you're not micromanaging, he runs the day-to-day for *U-Turn*."

"Not too much," Rustin added. "I just have very strong opinions."

"Never a dull moment. Have you seen the musical?" Omar asked.

"Three times, but I didn't get to witness Rustin's performance," I replied. "By the time I saw it live, his role had already been recast."

"You missed out, but occasionally he'll reprise his role. When he does, I'll be sure you have front-row tickets."

"That's too kind. Thank you."

"Watching him perform on stage is like an unofficial wonder of the world."

Rustin rolled his eyes. "I said make me sound good, not like David the giant slayer."

"Too much?"

"I'd like to keep this one around."

My head jerked back. "Wow. Sounds like there's competition." I was only half joking. My neck and ears grew warm.

"He's a ladies' man," Omar teased.

Rustin's demeanor shifted, his cognac eyes focused on me. Any humor from moments before was gone. "Timeout. There is no competition. Zero, zilch, nada. There's just you and me."

Now I was hot and bothered for an entirely different reason.

I glanced at Omar, a bit flustered by the intense declaration. "How are you holding up with all this?" I asked Rustin. I'd hoped to change the subject, but the way he looked at me made me eager to touch him, feel his hand squeeze mine.

His features shifted once more, the fierce possession replaced with uncertainty. "I just feel trapped in a burning building, but it's fine."

"At least the night started off with a bang—the opening musical number was great," Omar said.

"That was all her. She wrote the song and made sure everyone memorized their parts."

My hand landed on his arm. "And you were very supportive, so that helped."

Rustin's eyes were hooded, and you couldn't tell me we weren't having a nonverbal conversation hidden beneath our spoken words. "I just love great ideas, so it was easy to support." *I can't wait to see you on your knees tonight.*

"The event's going well? Do you have a tally on the donations?" Omar asked.

"Brea's very optimistic," I said. *I can't wait to open up and say ahh.*

"We won't get an official number until Monday," Rustin added. *And I'm going to make sure you gag on it.*

"If the turnout is any indication, it should be a high number." *You should know I don't gag—I have amazing reflexes. Whole pickles, sausages, bananas…*

"This is the first of many nights like this one. I'm hoping we can start off with a bang to get the cast pumped." *You know I like it when you make a mess.*

"The messier the better," I breathed out.

"What?" Both Rustin and Omar flashed confused expressions.

"Huh?" *Did I say that last sentence out loud?*

"What do you like messy?" Rustin asked.

Okay, maybe the silent conversation was all in my head. Perhaps we weren't at the "finishing each other's sentences and reading the other's mind" stage of this relationship.

"Uhm…martinis. Most people like them neat, but I prefer messy."

"So, dirty?" Omar corrected me.

"Yep. Dirty martinis."

"Say no more. I'll get you one from the bar."

Rustin shoved Omar toward one of the two bars before I could object. I didn't know shit about martinis, preferring my drinks sweet. From now on, I needed to reserve my fantasies for moments I was alone. Crushes were great in theory—they fueled my wet dreams and brightened an uneventful day. But when you fucked your crush over and over again, you transitioned into something different.

Rustin returned alone, drink in hand. "Here you go."

"Thanks. Where's Omar?"

"Oh, he's looking for someone to go home with, so he may be gone for a while."

"I like him. He's nice and clearly rides for you." I took a sip of the drink and wanted to retch.

"Couldn't ask for a better friend." I handed him my drink. "What? Is it not good?"

"I don't like martinis."

"Then why'd you ask for one?"

"I didn't. Omar assumed I wanted one."

"You said you like dirty martinis."

"I say all kinds of things. I'm unreliable."

He downed the glass with a grimace. "I don't like them either." Rustin moved closer, sending an unexpected shiver up my spine. Leaning in until our foreheads almost touched, he said, "Can I show you something?"

Yes, whip it out and show me right now. "Uh-huh."

The Boathouse had an upper deck that was closed off from the party, but from this vantage point, you could see everything happening down below. When I first walked in, I'd failed to notice this space tucked away in the sky.

"How'd you know about this?" I asked.

"During the tour, I looked for spots I could escape to for a bit."

"Do you feel the need to do that often—escape, I mean?"

"I like maybe five people tops, and crowds only work for me in small doses."

"There's nothing wrong with a small circle," I said. "Look at me, I have a shit-ton of friends, but I can guarantee you only two people would return my call in an emergency. And one of those people is Brea."

"Sounds more like acquaintances to me. I'm not interested in giving my energy to half-baked relationships."

"Because you're an all-in type of guy." I turned to face him.

"Good people are hard to find, so when you come across one, you keep them close." Rustin pulled me in by the waist, pressing me against him.

"And you think I'm one of these good people?"

"You're one of the best because you're not afraid to look stupid."

"Why does everyone keep saying that?"

The corners of his eyes crinkled when he laughed. "It's a good thing. Everyone is so wrapped up in what others think of them, including me, but you don't care."

"I care. I just choose to do the weird shit anyway."

"I wish I could be more like you. I get caught up by the voices in my head telling me all the reasons I should stay in my comfort zone."

"Comfort zones get a bad rap. They're there to help us process the scary stuff. They can be a launching pad to your next evolution, and if you fail, they act as a sort of checkpoint."

"Like in video games."

"Just like that. You just have to be willing to step out of your zone for the possibility of something greater."

"I'm falling in love with you," Rustin blurted.

"That was a big fucking leap."

"I mean, if this fails, I can always return to the checkpoint where you didn't know I existed."

"That would be tragic. I honestly can't imagine a world in which you're not in it." In life, I was fearless, except when it came to my mother—then I was a twelve-year-old girl all over again. But love was a different beast. I'd been disappointed so many times, I'd stopped hoping.

Bitch, for once, just let yourself fall. If you end up stalking his socials and keying his car, c'est la vie.

Wait. What?

Tell him you feel the same.

"I'm right there with you," I said aloud. "Comfort zone vacated, just free-falling, hoping I make it to the next checkpoint in one piece." My heart was beating so fast, it threatened to crack my ribs.

Rustin grabbed hold of my face and devoured my lips. Our bodies melted into each other, making it clear we craved the same thing—each other. He slipped his hand under the skirt of my dress, fondling my thick thighs. Tracing my skin with his fingers, he moved upward, stopping at the seams of my panties. "Is this okay?" he asked.

In response, I pulled off my thong and tucked it into the breast pocket of his suit jacket. Rustin licked two of his fingers before swiping them across my slit. The first finger dipped into my pussy, instantly taking my breath away, and he was greeted with a warm, wet, soft center. My mind raced, trying to determine if I could fuck him quietly just feet away from the crowd below.

One of his arms hooked under my leg, and he positioned it wide as he finger-fucked me, reaching every conceivable angle. I gathered my dress around my waist so his path was unobstructed. Rustin inserted two fingers, working them back and forth while swiping his thumb over my clit. I made a mental note of his enjoyment, the undeniable lust in his eyes as he bit down on his bottom lip.

My growing moans echoed against the walls and floated in the air, mingling with the jazzy music. "I'm gonna need you to be a little quieter," he said.

"That's easy for you to say. You're not the one being fucked," I replied, grunting.

Rustin fed me his free thumb, and I sucked and licked it like it was nine inches long and ready to explode. Just put something in my mouth and watch me act a plumb fool. If I hadn't worn a silk dress, I'd have drooled all over him and me.

Leaning closer, he whispered in my ear, giving a play-by-play. "Your pussy is so damn wet. You like this, huh, being a naughty girl who gets finger-banged at work events? I can't wait to taste those fat lips." His words made me ready to risk it all, prepared to get butt-booty naked and spread out on the dusty concrete floor.

Undoing his belt, I gave up. Fuck this event, and fuck my better judgment. I needed every single inch of him rearranging my guts. He bent me over the railing, and when he entered, my eyes misted over from the intensity of each thrust. The crowd below was a blur of colors and shapes all moving and chatting, oblivious to what was transpiring overhead. Rustin's grip on my waist was the only thing preventing me from tumbling head over heels. Each thrust propelled me forward before his grip brought me back.

His large hands groped my thighs, the sensation of his palms fondling my sensitive skin causing me to giggle. My grip on the railing was tight as I did my best to return each stroke, igniting sparks underneath my skin. He toyed with my nipple ring through the silk fabric, and my body was all his. I wasn't the girl who had sex in public, but for Rustin, I was willing to break every rule. Dating a coworker…broken. Fucking in very public places…broken. Falling in love.

"Please, don't stop… Right there… Just like that."

"You don't have to beg. It's my pleasure to give you what you need—what you fucking deserve. Tell me you deserve it."

"I… Oh my God."

"Tell me."

"I deserve it."

"That's right, baby. Gotdamn right you do." He planted kisses to my neck and shoulders.

"Who are we?" I asked.

"The luckiest people in the world." The warmth of his breath tickled my skin. He slapped my ass, and I grunted loudly. "Glide that tight pussy over my dick." I met every thrust, slamming my ass into his crotch. His hand landed between my legs, and I was treated to a light show. Nothing made sense, but anything seemed possible. "Now come for me. Can you do that?"

"Yes." He picked up the tempo, and I focused on the delicious sounds our bodies made as Rustin moved inside me. "Rustin. Oh my God… Fuck."

"Say my name again."

"Rustin, I'm gonna come."

"Tell me how it feels."

My bottom lip trembled, and my eyes glazed over. All I was able to produce was a combination of words that made no sense. I hoped my soft moans and gasps for breath confirmed he was hitting the right spot. When my legs started to shake, his grip on my waist grew tighter, never letting up.

"Get every last drop. Mmm. That feels good. Yeah… Don't hold back." His voice was less controlled—it was clear he was also close. Rustin buried his face into my back and cried out, and I was right behind him; my body pulsated and my knees threatened to buckle. When our movements stalled, he removed his digits, licking them clean—the sight making my core throb. I tugged the bottom of my dress back in place while Rustin brushed my hair from my face.

"I'm really liking this boyfriend-girlfriend thing," I breathed out.

"Same."

I was still high, and Rustin's cum was dripping down my thigh.

"Has anyone seen Rustin?" Brea shouted over the mic. "Mr. Hayes, report to the stage, please."

Rustin pulled up his pants and attempted to make himself look presentable. "I'm sorry. I have to go." I helped him tuck in his shirt, and we temporarily got distracted by each other's lips, serving up long, drunken kisses that turned my thoughts to mush. He gripped my bare ass, my dress still askew. "I love your lips. I feel like they cradle mine just right."

My "Mmm" was my way of agreeing.

"Can someone check the men's room for Rustin?" Brea called.

"Shit. I gotta go." He pulled away, but then momentarily returned to cup my face and fondle my cheek with his thumb. "Are you okay?"

"Yes. Go before they send a search party."

He planted several quick pecks to my lips and neck before running down the hall.

Unexpected. He was unexpected. And to fully appreciate the beauty of life, you had to let the unexpected happen.

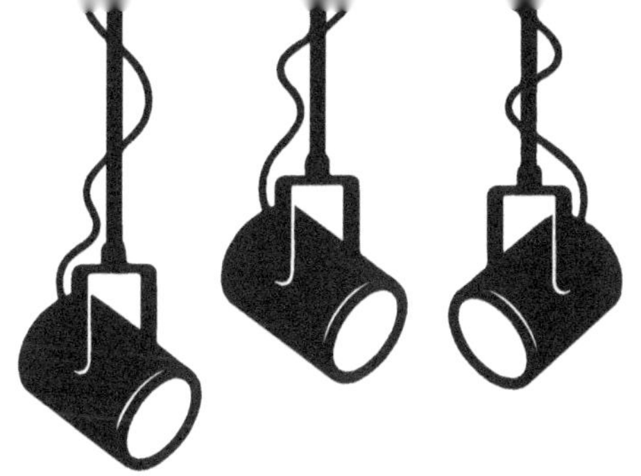

CHAPTER 22

Rustin

IT WAS ONE in the morning. Letitia and I were high as fuck and dancing way too hard to mid-tempo R&B music on the private rooftop of my apartment. That was when I realized she danced like a cheerleader—a cheerleader with no rhythm, but a cheerleader all the same.

"Why do you dance like that?"

"Like what?"

I mimicked her very sharp dance moves. "Like that."

"I was raised by white people," she said while performing an exaggerated body roll that transitioned into a hand clap that was borderline offbeat.

That made sense. Note to future me: *I'll have to teach our kids how to dance.*

I leaned in and scooped her up by her waist, and we floated side to side. Our feet were probably still on the ground, but I couldn't be certain. This was Letitia's playlist, and the song selection was questionable, but by the time "Walking on Sunshine" came on, I said fuck it and danced like I'd been transported to the eighties.

"I'm always gonna take care you because you're my Letty. Can I call you that? Is that okay?" I shouted.

"As long as I can call you Rus."

"Yes. My friends call me Rus."

"I'm your friend—your girlfriend."

"That was funny. You're so funny."

We were riding a much-deserved high. All the work, all the frustration and long nights, had just slipped away. The weed was just for razzle-dazzle to cap off the night. We still needed to count up the checks and cash donations, but Brea felt good about it based on the amount of checks in her hand alone. Funny way to measure success, but Brea had been doing this for a long time, so I trusted her judgment.

Letty, *my girlfriend*, swayed left then right. Taking another hit, I drank her in, the motion of her hips pulling me into a trance. I handed her the blunt, and she inhaled. "This is such good weed. Not the cheap stuff I usually buy. Hey, do you know who has good weed?"

"No. Who?"

"Stanley."

"He smokes?"

"He has arthritis."

"Fuck. Is he fun to smoke with?"

"No. He gets real somber and talks about his ex-wife." Her gaze was low, as if she weren't focused on anything in particular. Letitia's hair was slowly reverting, becoming puffy in the front. "How much money do you think we made tonight?"

"Billions," I exclaimed.

"Yeah, fuck yeah." She stamped her feet and pumped her fist in the air.

"Hey!" I reached for her hand.

"Yeah!"

"I love you," I shouted over the music.

"I'm loving you too."

"Okay, 'cause I'm getting kind of scared."

She stopped spinning. "Of me?"

"Of getting hurt."

"I'm not gonna hurt you. I'm just a girl."

"Yeah. Most of the people who've hurt me have actually been women."

"Oh."

I hadn't been in a relationship in some time, but Relationship Rustin was a lover boy. Assigning names to unborn children. Scouting the best spots to propose while running errands in the city. I hated that about myself because it was what always ended up getting me hurt. But no matter how many times my heart was broken, I was always prepared to give it a go with the same level of intense devotion.

Letty walked over to where I was seated, straddling me. "I think that's kind of the chance we take. I'm willing to be completely wrecked and irreparably damaged if you are." She took a long puff before leaning in and exhaling into my mouth with a kiss.

"Let's promise to always be real with each other. If something I do pisses you off, just tell me. We can fix anything."

"I believe in miracles, and love is a miracle." I think she was quoting Whitney.

"Promise?"

"I promise."

You can't fix problems when you never see them coming. I wanted a warning this time because I didn't want to wake up one morning to Letty's standing over me forlorn and proclaiming this wasn't working.

She ran her hands up and down my arms. "Everyone was all on your jock tonight. You're so popular."

"No. They just like the musical."

"You wrote that, so that's you. They like *you*."

"They don't know me. No one really does."

"Don't say that. I don't like it. I know you. I see you." She cupped my face.

"I appreciate that." Finding someone other than Omar who understood that my moods and hypercritical tendencies had nothing to do with them and everything to do with me would be nice.

I pulled off her T-shirt to reveal her body in all its splendor. Letty hovered over my lap so I could pull my pants and boxers off. When I dropped my hands to her ass, she took a seat on my dick. Drugs were great, but fucking Letitia was a whole other type of high. When we were connected, time stretched and bent, colors glowed with an otherworldly intensity, and the boundaries between her and me started to blur.

As she rode my dick, there was a rush of euphoria. The ground seemed to pulse, and objects like the side table and Letty's hair appeared to breathe. The city was still alive, and the street traffic and horns honking were a remix layered over our grunts and moans. There were no words, but we were engaged in a full conversation.

Letitia giggled when I pulled her closer, slipping her nipple in my mouth. With long swipes of my tongue, I suckled her breasts. They were perfect and had been my first introduction to how majestically beautiful she was. Pulling back, I witnessed her almost frantic movements as she rocked up and down. All the way in and back out. Our flesh was wet and sticky from the summer heat, and then Letitia opened up, exploding in colors so blinding I had to shield my eyes. Her breathing was ragged and choppy, and if we weren't fucking, I'd probably be calling 911 for fear of an overdose.

When she called my name soft and low, I ruptured into pieces—my earth-tone colors mixing with her pastels. It was beautiful, overwhelming, and deeply surreal.

On a good night, I typically slept four hours. This wasn't a good night. After putting Letitia to bed, I found myself unable to sleep. My brain was always running through three or four scenarios. Thinking back to the fundraiser, now I was no longer high, I questioned if it had been enough—which prompted me to send Brea a text message at a quarter past three asking if we had an estimate yet. There was no expectation for her to answer immediately, but sending the text helped to stop my obsessing. With the status of the fundraising in limbo, it allowed room for other thoughts to flood in—the deal with Imaginex, my overcrowded schedule, and studio commitments. We should probably hire some additional staff.

I pulled up my voice notes and riffed. "Omar, I've been thinking we need to hire some new employees for Thread—a couple of interns, a social media assistant to help Clara, since she's doing the job of two people. And I may have to request an extension from Cinevault. I'm not sure I can be ready to pitch next month. I was thinking our first project should be a documentary, but I'm still researching it. Hey, do you and Jackie wanna hang tomorrow? I was thinking karaoke.

"Also, I've been meaning to talk to you about a potential business venture. I'd really like your input. Oh, and did you see ole boy we went to college with is going to be in a movie with DiCaprio? Phillip couldn't act his way out of a paper bag, and now he's on the same call sheet as a legend. That's crazy work."

My nights were circular, always the same routine. I'd set up in the living room and hope inspiration hit so I could finish this play while I waited; I returned emails, sent voice notes at ridiculous hours of the night, and worked on my mural wall. There was tons to keep me busy. Sure, I was a wreck in the morning, but it wasn't anything a strong cup of coffee couldn't fix.

"What are you doing?" Letty's voice shattered the back-and-forth conversation I was having with myself.

"I'm writing."

"Rus, it's four in the morning. *What* are you doing?"

"I'm an early riser."

"If you're a vampire, just say it." She approached my working area with scattered notes, open mini bags of Takis, and cold coffee.

"Huh?" I said.

"You never sleep."

"Yes, I do."

"I've never seen it."

"That's because you're sleeping. Speaking of… Why are *you* up?"

"Dry mouth," she said. I handed her my tumbler of ice-cold water, and she gulped it down. "What are you worried about?"

"I just started watching *A Different World* for the first time, and I'm hoping Dwayne and Whitley get together."

"It's too early for jokes."

"Never too early for that."

"I was pretty high, but you said we'd always be honest or something to that effect."

"Ugh. I said so much dumb shit last night."

"You said my pussy was the Fountain of Youth." Her expression was appalled.

"It's great pussy, but I don't even know what that means."

"So you just lie when you're high?"

"I would commit murder—premeditated murder, second degree, all forms of homicide—over your phat box. Pussy lips thick, juicy."

"Thank you. That really means a lot. I needed that." She picked up a lined piece of paper with notes scribbled in every corner. "What's this?"

"It's my play."

Letty's eyes grew wide as she scanned the dining table with dozens of sheets all covered with my chicken scratch. "Is this your process?"

"It's *a* process."

"I always pictured you with pristine notebooks divided into sections with no writing outside of the margins." Letty sank into the seat next to me, giving me her full attention.

"You would be wrong." I was in the messy middle. I'd been here before and would no doubt be here again. The script for *U-turn* had come easy to me, but since then, I'd had to work for every line, every page. Right now, I had to trust the process—which was easier said than done when it was almost morning, you had a splitting headache, and the plot escaped you.

"What's it about?" she asked.

"It's about love, heartbreak. The fact that life can be funny and devasting at the same time. The little moments that inspire bigger ones."

"What's the protagonist's name?"

"Doesn't have one because I don't name my characters until I feel like I know them."

"My drama teacher in college would always ask, 'What feeling do you want your character to provoke?'"

"That's easy: satisfaction. I want everyone to be appeased and leave me the fuck alone."

"It sounds like you're not connecting with the art."

"Don't diagnose me," I said.

"I'm not. Just basing my conclusion on the things you've said. *U-Turn* was probably easy for you because at the time, there was no pressure."

"Duh."

"And this is why you need sleep. You're cranky."

I squeezed her thigh. "I'm sorry."

"It's okay."

"It's not."

"I'm not afraid of rough edges."

"My edges are precisely rounded. In truth, I'm a perfectionist who pushes everyone away. I work late, neglecting the people who are important to me, and I don't like admitting I'm wrong because I rarely am."

"Hi, Mr. Perfect. I'm Dazed and Confused. I have difficulty reading at a seventh-grade level. I don't know who I am or where I came from, and I probably never will. And I've spent most of my life feeling like I don't belong."

Letty's words hit me like a ton of bricks. We'd never really talked about her adoption beyond the initial facts. "Have you ever met or spoken to your birth mother?"

"No."

"Is that something you've thought about doing—reconnecting, I mean?"

"No." Letitia released a sharp exhale, her features darkened, as if the idea of even considering the question was painful. I thought it best not to push, but I was hurt on her behalf. The not knowing had to be the worst part. She could cross paths with her birth parents and never even know it. There was a whole group of people walking around with her face, and she'd missed it all. Aunties, uncles, cousins, years of family reunions. Adoption was a blessing, but it didn't erase the pain of what-if or why-me.

"I have writer's block," I blurted. Letty's harsh expression slowly softened. "It's pretty bad. I haven't captured anything worthwhile. Deadlines are fast approaching, and at night when it's quiet, I find it the hardest to breathe. So many people are counting on me, and I can't fuck this up. I have staff to pay and executives expecting the next *U-Turn*, and I have nada. I hate letting people down. It literally causes me to break out in hives…" I gasped, trying to remain composed. "Big red welts at just the thought of disappointing others. So no, I can't sleep. I don't *deserve* that shit. I'm up at four in the morning because I need to be fucking writing. I can sleep when I'm fucking dead."

"So next week? 'Cause if you keep going like this, you're going to hit the wall."

"I'm good. I have my coffee and… I have coffee."

"You're not doing anything else, are you?" she asked.

"Slow down on the intervention. I have ADHD, so I take Adderall—nothing that isn't medically prescribed."

"Tell me what you need."

I need the world to stop turning so I can get some much-needed rest. "I need you to trust I have this covered."

"Okay. Can you just come back to bed now? I can't sleep without you."

I stood with a stretch. What I really wanted to do was find an excuse or say, "I'll be in in a minute." In the past, shit like that caused fights, so I'd learned to acquiesce. "Big spoon reporting for duty."

Back in the bedroom, Letty rubbed my temples and rocked me to sleep while singing a stripped-down version of Ricky Martin's "Livin' la Vida Loca." Don't ask me why she picked that song, but it worked.

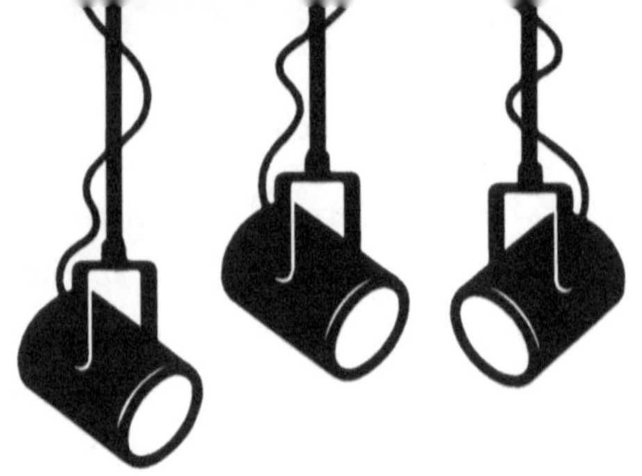

CHAPTER 23

Letitia

AS I WALKED into the main living area, my steps stalled. "Since when do you wear glasses?"

"Since I was ten," Rustin said.

"I've never seen you in glasses. Slow down on the surprise reveals. First it's astigmatism, and next it's a secret twin."

"Why would I have a secret twin?"

"Maybe you're a magician," I said. Rustin squinted at my pronunciation of that word, which sounded like *musician*. "And you and your twin use that to your advantage."

"So, *The Prestige,* you're referring to is the plot of a movie."

"Art imitates life."

"Do you want eggs? I'm making omelets."

"You're far-sighted, you have an undercover twin, and you can make omelets?"

"Are you still high?" he asked.

"No. My head is a little groggy." I wrapped my arms around him as he leaned in to kiss my forehead. "Did you sleep okay?"

"Mhm." He continued to whip the eggs, so I was taking that as a no.

I was a whore for this man. All I wanted to do was fuck him. While he was scrambling the eggs, I was trying to come up with the perfect segue. I could go with the forward approach and grab hold of his crotch. That was always a winner. Or maybe drop to my knees and wait to receive.

"Baby?" he said.

Pet names… I loved it. "Yes?"

"I was thinking, do you wanna go on a date tonight? Because I wanna show you off."

I could think of nothing I wanted more than to be on this man's arm and for the whole of New York to know he was taken by me. "I like the way you think. Date night sounds good."

"Cool. I'll text Omar and see if Jackie and him are free."

"Wait, Jackie, your date from Salt and Smoke?"

"Yes, Jackie, my friend—and Omar's ex-wife."

"You two were on a date. I mean, that has to violate some type of bro code."

"I never said that."

"She did."

Rustin opened the refrigerator, pulling out condiment bottles. "I don't think so. But I can assure you we've never been anything more than friends and business associates."

"So, it's a kinda-sorta double date?"

"Yeah they're still hecka cool with one another. Now, how do you like your eggs? We've got cheese, bell peppers, diced ham, some jalapeno if you can handle the spice."

"I like them to precede morning sex."

Rustin unhanded the bowl and released the whisk. "Listen to me. Lead with that shit next time. You got me over here scrambling fucking eggs when I could be scrambling your guts."

"I didn't know if you were up for it, with the glasses and the really strong nerd vibe."

"Do you want me to keep the glasses on or take them off?"

"On, because then it's like fucking somebody different," I answered. Rustin's mouth warped into a smile. "What? Why are you looking at me like that?"

"I'm just really happy I met you."

"Ahh, that's really sweet." I grabbed his face. "Now prove it."

Later that night, we met up with Rustin's friends. "Can I offer you an edible?" Omar held an open bag in front of me.

"No. I'm good." I could go hard some nights, but not every night.

"Okay. Your loss. Rus?"

"Nah, but thanks."

"We have two party poopers over here." Omar moved along to Jackie.

We were on a not-so-double date with Omar and Jackie, seeing how the two weren't an item. When Rustin said we were going to Pitch Please, a karaoke bar in Midtown, I was all in. I was a simple girl, and singing my favorite songs while buzzed was a great way to spend a Saturday night.

"You don't have to abstain on my account." I nudged Rustin.

"I'm fine. Plus, it's all bad when we're not both high. It can cause arguments and misunderstandings."

"Sounds like experience speaking."

"Omar and I got into one of our worst disagreements when I was high and he wasn't."

"What was it about?"

"I don't really remember, but I know he punched me."

"What?"

"Apparently I was saying some off-the-wall shit."

"And he punched you?"

"I punched him back, and that's when he called me a talentless hack."

"The nerve."

"And I said he was a dick rider."

"Ouch."

"Yeah. I was out of pocket for that one."

I spied Omar and Jackie talking in hushed tones, and my brow furrowed when she stuck out her tongue and Omar placed a gummy-bear–shaped weed edible on it. I wasn't this cozy with any of my exes, mostly because my past relationships had all ended on bad terms. Either I was madly in love with you or hated your guts—there was no in-between.

"What's the deal with Jackie and Omar?" I asked.

"They're exes who are cordially co-parenting." Rustin was already perusing the song menu, ticking off which ones he hoped to perform.

"And they live in the same brownstone?"

"Yep."

"And they're both single?"

"Uhm, I'm not sure about Jackie, but Omar is."

"You don't think that's weird?" I whispered.

"I think I'm just used to it."

It was weird.

Omar attacked the mic first and sang "Poison" by Bell Biv Devoe like he was the fourth member. Rustin cheered him on, and at the dance break, they both worked up a sweat.

"Get it, baby," I called out.

When the song ended, Rustin came bounding back to me, and he pulled me up so I could sit on his lap. "You were so good," I said.

Let's get this out the way now: I loved being in love, and Rustin had all my wonderment. Any man who could make me come three times in one afternoon had my respect.

"That was just the warm-up." He was so cute when he was excited.

"You have more in store?"

"I've got moves you've never seen." He planted kisses to my neckline. "Are you singing? Because we can't have Jackie go next."

"I can sing," Jackie protested

"No, you can't." Rustin looked at her with a straight face.

"Omar?" She looked to him to defend her vocal talents.

"Letitia, have you heard Jackie sing?" Omar asked.

"No."

He rubbed his hands together. "You're in for a treat."

Jackie got on the stage and sang Celine Dion's version of "All by Myself." She was off pitch and chasing a high note nowhere near her register. It wasn't the worst singing I'd heard, but it was damn near close. If I closed my eyes, I'd be convinced a cat had wandered in and started wailing. Omar kept feeding her the correct key like a vocal coach.

"To be fair, it's not about talent—it's about having fun," I said, trying to make sense of the sounds coming out of Jackie's mouth.

"Fuck that. It's absolutely about talent," Rustin corrected me.

"She works in finance. She doesn't have to know how to sing."

"I know UPS drivers who can croon like D'Angelo."

When Jackie was done, we all politely clapped, and Omar reassured her it wasn't as bad as last time.

"We need more rounds." He scanned the table, taking a tally. "We need shots, more beer, and for the ladies, fruity drinks. Rus, you coming?"

Rustin was comfortably entangled around me, and he shot Omar a look of irritation.

"I can't carry all that shit by myself."

Rustin planted soft kisses to my cheek and lips. "I'll be right back, okay?"

"Negro, she knows you'll be back. You're acting like you're going off to war."

I ignored Omar. "I'm gonna miss you every second you're gone," I said, and Rustin's smile turned goofy.

"Come the fuck on. She's gonna be fine."

With the men out of the way, Jackie slid over to my side of the couch. "I used to look at Omar like that."

"Like what?"

"Like he was the bringer of the moon and stars."

"What happened?"

"Life. We grew up and grew apart." Jackie shook her head. "Sorry. Not trying to be the love-sucks person."

"No. It's okay. Nine out of ten times, it does."

"I've known Rus for years, and he hasn't brought a woman around in forever. Omar and I are kind of an extension of his family, and he knows he can't just bring *any* old body around us. So the fact that he brought you means something."

"It's still really new."

"New is good—it's fun."

"Any advice as a longtime friend of Rustin's?"

"I'm the last person to give advice," Jackie said. "I'm still trying to figure my shit out. Rustin tries to pretend like nothing fazes him, but in truth, he feels everything, and he's the hardest on himself. He'll give everyone grace, sparing none for his own shortcomings. I should probably be regaling you with funny stories from Rustin's past. Let me think. He has ADHD, and when he doesn't take his meds, it's like he sees the world in 8K. Sorry. I'm not really good at being the backup wingman. What I'm trying to say is Rustin's a great guy—he's not perfect, but he's pretty close, and if you hurt him, I will beat you up."

I didn't know how to fight. I'd been in one fight in elementary school, and it lasted all of five seconds with me and Brielle Rogers swinging our arms and pulling each other's hair.

"Wow. Okay. Thanks for the warning," I said.

Rustin and Omar burst into the room laughing.

"Letitia, we ain't forgot about you. You're up next," Omar said.

After group shots, I hopped up on the small, raised platform and struck a pose. When En Vogue's "My Lovin' (You're Never Gonna Get It)" started, my body moved to the beat. At the first note, Omar flashed a thumbs-up in approval, and as the dance moves intensified, Rustin fanned himself like my performance was too hot to handle and he needed to cool down. At the bridge, we all joined in, letting whoever was in earshot know there was no way in hell they were getting any love from us.

When you put a bunch of theater kids and Jackie in a room together, this was the type of thing that happened—Grammy-worthy performances of classic songs. There was something so comforting seeing Rustin with his closest friends. You could learn a lot about a man from his friend group. And tonight, I'd learned that for Rustin, there was no distinction between family and friends. He was like the Dominic Toretto of New York.

Back at my place, we were sprawled out on the mattress because it was the most comfortable surface in the apartment. My mom and sister would be here before I knew it, and I kept acting like I had all the time in the world to get this place together. I didn't even have a headboard. Maybe I was in denial and hoped inaction on my part would stall the visit.

I just wasn't in a good headspace to be picked on. My clothes, my hair, my apartment, the neighborhood. Nothing was safe from critique. You know the saying, if you have nothing nice to say, don't say anything at all? My mother believed in the opposite: if you can't say something nice, say something *constructive*. Her idea of constructive was oftentimes rude, like when she'd smooth my hair and tell me it would look better straight. Or when she'd ask if I'd put on weight. Who asks that? When is that ever appropriate?

My thoughts were interrupted by a question. "Tell me about your last boyfriend." Rustin yawned.

"You don't want to hear about that."

"I do, and I want to know what he did to lose you so I don't make the same mistake."

"Ugh. He was an artist, but the nonworking kind."

"How'd you meet?"

"On the subway."

Rustin reached for my hand, paying close attention to each digit like he was auditing the nail art. "How'd that work?"

"He just approached and asked for my number."

"Strong game. Go on."

"He was fun to talk to. We had lots of fun."

"So, what happened?"

"It's stupid."

"Try me."

"There was a DIY art show, and a few of my ceramic pieces were part of the exhibition."

"I didn't know you sculpted."

"I don't, really. It's just a hobby."

"What do you make?"

"It was just colorful vases and flowerpots. This wasn't the MoMA; it was a small warehouse show with fun and funky handmade pieces."

"And he was jealous?" Rustin asked.

"Why would you assume that?"

"You said he was an artist, and I'm taking it that none of *his* shit was on display."

"I don't know if it was jealousy, but he wasn't excited—not in the way I'd been excited for him in the past. And it was just a stupid little show for my dumb vases."

"You are not allowed to do that." He entwined his fingers in mine.

"What?"

"Water shit down. Those vases were fucking amazing, and your ex was a loser."

"You don't know that. What if they were hideous?"

"Not possible."

"You're right. They were adorable, and I sold every last one. After the event, we just felt wrong. If you can't be happy for me for something so frivolous, then you won't be supportive during the big stuff. Love shouldn't be a competition. If you win, we both win because we're in it together. I dumped him a week later."

"Prison. He deserves prison."

"Right. Life without parole."

"Shit, I'll always be proud. I was like a proud parent at karaoke, so if you're selling ceramic wares anywhere in this city, I'm going to be front and center."

"Because you love me and can't live without me?"

"No, because I'm in desperate need of a new vase."

"Ha-ha." I rested my feet on the wall where a headboard should be. "On a different note, Esme called me."

"Who's that?"

"She was my boss at the library. She wants me to host a special Story Time with Letty and Wags."

"As a celebrity special guest?"

"I'm not a celebrity."

"That's exactly what you are, and I'm gonna need you to get cocky about that fact. What did you say?" he asked.

"I told her I'd think about it."

"What's there to think about?"

"If I want to do it."

"Why wouldn't you want to—"

"You know I hate when you do the twenty questions thing, *babe*."

He cocked an eyebrow. "That was a rough *babe*." He was right. I'd wanted to say *motherfucker* but stopped myself. "It sounds like a fun opportunity."

"It probably is, but it kind of feels like going backward."

"Or it could be like going home."

I'd never thought of it that way. "But what's the point? Where's the challenge?"

"Maybe it's just a chance to receive your well-deserved flowers."

"I was small potatoes."

"It was never that. It was a Black woman leading story time at one of the most influential libraries in the country. You made young

Black and brown kids feel seen, and we deserve that just as much as anyone else. I want that for all kids and my future children. I want them to know anything is possible. I don't want to just tell them they can be anything. I want then to see it reflected in the community around them."

"It's just story time."

Rustin dropped my hand and sat up. "Letitia, stop fucking doing that. Stop selling yourself short. You are fucking amazing. You have a knack for this stuff, and kids are drawn to you. You could leverage Letty and Wags into your own show if you wanted to. You need to start seeing yourself for who you really are, not who you pretend to be, and certainly not who your mother thinks you should be."

"Okay. You can let go of my edges now. It would be nice to see Esme again, and maybe if you're not too busy, you could come and support me."

"When is it? I want to lock it in on my calendar."

"Two Fridays from now, right before my mom comes to town," I replied.

"The twenty-seventh?"

"Yeah."

He sucked in air through his mouth. "Omar and I are in L.A. to finalize the Imaginex contract."

"Oh…"

"I can try to—"

"No, it's fine. We both have busy lives, and there's bound to be scheduling conflicts every now and then. I'll send you a picture."

"Preferably naked." He pressed his lips against my palm. "I'm sorry I have to miss it."

"You'll be in my heart." We both cringed at my words. "Seriously, I appreciate your defending me against me. Knowing you believe in me means a lot."

"I'm just a slutty fan wearing your jersey, giddily asking you to sign my pecs."

CHAPTER 24

Rustin

MY DAYS WERE starting to blur into one another. Wake up, fuck Letitia, work out, go to the office of one of my three jobs, after-work meeting, come home, have dinner, fuck Letitia, sleep, and repeat. Right now, I was in the middle of most important meal of the day, Letty's phat pussy. I think her pussy lips looked bee stung because my mouth was always attached to them. My perfect girl rocked her hips while I French-kissed her pussy. Letty looked on, eyes half open—she almost looked high, and I loved that my tongue was the thing making her intoxicated.

I whispered morning affirmations against her clit. "You are so perfect. Who's gonna have a great day?"

"Me," she moaned out.

"Damn right." I smacked her pussy before sinking back in. "You're gonna have the best day. Because you…deserve…it." My last three words were punctuated by focused, circular licks of her clit.

"Oh, Rus, please." She had one hand on the back of my neck, and the other was twisting her right nipple.

"I love you so fucking much." And that sent her over the edge. She boxed my head in between her thighs and took complete control, writhing and thrusting against my outstretched tongue until she convulsed into a content nirvana. Before collapsing, she licked and kissed her juices from my face. Pussy on demand was a feature of having a girlfriend I greatly appreciated. I was an eater, and Letty was wet and juicy, just like a peach.

"Do you want me to return the favor?" she asked.

"I would love that, but I can't. I have to get ready to go."

"Are you going to make the fundraising luncheon today?" she said. The deadpan look on my face let her know I wasn't following. "Private luncheon with Rustin Hayes and the cast of *Jellybean Junction* for ten grand a plate. Your being there is kind of important."

I stepped out of my boxers, and Letty's eyes homed in on Rustin Jr., who was still slightly erect and aching to be stroked. "If it's on my calendar, then I'll be there."

Her smile was serene, and I was jealous of her after-orgasm clarity. "Can you check your calendar to confirm?"

I tossed her my phone and then headed to the closet to select a fit for the day.

"We're good," she called out. When I returned to the bedroom, her expression told me she was plotting. "Come back to bed."

"Baby, if I'm not in the shower in the next ten minutes, I'll be late."

"I just need five." She dropped to her knees and stuck out her tongue.

So I was thirty minutes late for my first meeting.

"Not cool," Omar reprimanded me.

"I know. I'm sorry. Traffic was a beast."

"Rus, get your head in the fucking game."

"I'm here."

"This is Cinevault."

"Yep. You're right."

"That's why I built in a buffer on your calendar. The meeting doesn't start for another ten minutes."

Air whooshed from my lungs. On the ride over, my stomach had been in knots, but Omar, being Omar, had thought of everything. "Thank God. You know me so well. I'm locked in." And when I said that, I meant I had a loose pitch for our first project with the streamer. I knew what I wanted to do, but I was short on tangible documents to support it—armed with only a visual collage, a personal story, and an ability to bullshit.

After introductions and giddy assurances about how happy they were to work with me, how excited they were to witness all the amazing projects I was going to champion, the floor was mine.

"Thank you so much for taking a chance on a guy from Brooklyn. Growing up, I was a weird kid—or at least, that's what everyone in school told me. I wasn't popular, or tall, or particularly good looking..."

"Now I don't believe that for one minute." A thirty-something blonde batted her eyes at me.

"...but what I did have was an overactive imagination and the ability to tell a story. I loved putting on plays, and that's when I was introduced to puppetry. My mom bought me a puppet-making kit, and I was off and running from there. My first puppet was named Farley. He was orange with a red nose and those big eyes that wiggled." The executives in the room laughed. "My new hobby led me back to TV shows and movies featuring puppet work. I was watching anything—*Alf*, *E.T.*, *Cousin Skeeter*, and *Jellybean Junction*, just to name a few.

"I was obsessed, and from that obsession a career was birthed, and I think with anything, you need to know where you came from so you understand where you're going. I'm hoping our first project will be a documentary about puppetry in film, television, and stage. I want to capture these stories before we lose any more of the greats in this field."

"It's big, it's exciting, it a behind-the-curtains look at the entertainment world," Omar interjected. "We could interview some famous producers and storytellers, which would be the draw for people to watch. Right, Rus?"

"Yeah. I'm thinking *Jaws*, *Star Wars*, *Jurassic Park,* Labyrinth. And people love to be let in on a secret and see how the sausage is made. The visual aesthetic we shared is the vibe of the documentary we're going for."

The table went quiet as they reviewed the one-pager. I suppressed the urge to continue talking, not wanting to come off as desperate. Either you got it or you didn't.

"I love it," the director of programming announced.

The room erupted into applause.

In the hall, Omar stopped me. "How do you do that shit?"

"What?"

"Bullshit people into agreeing with you?"

"It's a gift. Plus, although my presentation was half-assed, the project is still an exciting one."

Omar moved closer so no one would overhear. "This is a feast year. We're pulling in new money hand over fist."

"It's only up from here, brother."

"You headed back to the office?"

"No. I'm having lunch in Tribeca with rich people."

"After what you pulled off in that conference room, lunch with the Richie Riches of this city is light work."

"Rustin, *U-Turn* is so raw and real. They're puppets, but they're speaking to the human condition."

The cast of *Jellybean Junction* was in a private room at Macao Trading Company in Tribeca. It was a dark and moody space, just how us artists liked it. We were hosting ten VIP guests at ten thousand a pop. One hundred grand wasn't bad for an hour and a half of work.

"Yeah, that was the goal. I think people hear *puppets* and expect shenanigans, but I wanted to tell a story with humor and heart."

"And that you did, young man."

I felt like a prize horse up for sale. I was just waiting for them to check my teeth.

"Why *Jellybean Junction?*"

The table fell silent, and ears perked up. "I wanted to be a part of something revolutionary. *Junction* has been breaking the rules for almost fifty years, and we have a cast of talented and dedicated puppeteers. Stanley Dinkle—Stanley, could you wave? Stanley is the OG of the *Junction.* He's been with the show for close to thirty years."

"It'll be thirty in December," Stanley said.

"Thirty years of thankless work just to put a smile on a kid's face. On my face. Grumpy Gus was one of my favorites as a kid. You have Valerie, who voices Lulu Lark. Valerie has decades in the game. I won't say your age—"

"And I appreciate that," Valerie interjected.

"Val brings musicality to the show, the likes of which I've never seen before. And then there's the crew you never see, like Phoebe in costumes. You could give her two mismatched pieces of fabric and a few inches of ribbon, and she will craft a masterpiece. We also have our newer puppeteers, like Letitia Vincent." Her name was a song on my tongue. "I joined this cast because of her. First Black female puppeteer in the history of *Junction*. What she is doing in this space is deeply important, not just to kids who look like me or her, but for all our kids. Diversity is what makes us special, and you can't convince me we're not better for it.

"I apologize. That was a long-winded answer, but I'm here because this is where the heart of puppetry resides, and I just think it would be a shame for this all to end. There are so many more stories to tell, and I want to be there with this group of extraordinary individuals."

"I don't know, but I think we should sing the theme song," Letitia said.

And to my surprise, there wasn't a single objection, not even from Stanley.

"*Jellybean Junction, come and play!*
Learn something new every day!
Friends are waiting, big and small!
Come on in, we welcome all."

After the luncheon, I found Letitia outside with Brea.

"There he is. Great job, Rustin," Brea congratulated me. "I have to run to a doctor's appointment, so hopefully, there are no fires while I'm gone. Letty, you're in charge for the afternoon, since Rustin and I are out of office."

"What?" Letty looked like she'd been caught in headlights.

"Don't burn the place down."

"Can I fire Stanley?" she joked.

"Don't care what you do, but don't do that." Brea hopped in her RideX and was off.

"You heard that too, right? I'm in charge," Letty said.

"Don't let the power go to your head."

"Too late." She giggled. "Thank you for speaking life into the cast and crew."

"I meant every word."

"Because at the end of the day, it's about the people and connections we make, and if this is the end, I'm going to miss every damn one of them."

"No, baby, we manifest over here. Sometimes the end is the start of a new beginning. We are strong, capable, and resilient."

"I love you, Rustin. I really do."

"I love you too. You give me a reason to stop and actually appreciate each moment and not just pivot from one assignment to the next."

"I really want to kiss you right now." Letty bit down on her lip.

"Why deny yourself pleasure?"

"Such good points." She leaned in softly, pressing her lips against mine.

I'd like to say the world faded away, but the shrill voices of Stanley and Valerie cut through. "I told you. All them googly eyes were leading to something."

"You were right. I stand corrected," Valerie said.

CHAPTER 25

Letitia

I WAS IN my most colorful, kid-friendliest ensemble. Being back at the Brooklyn Public Library really felt like home. I'd started here with a part-time job until I could land a full-time one. Initially, I'd just helped put books back on the shelves, but on my breaks, I always found myself in the children's area. It was bright and fun, with colorful rugs and miniature tables and chairs. I'd just hang out there and read one of the books.

Yes, an adult can still enjoy a kid's book—fun and imagination have no age limit. One day I was on a break reading *The Monster at the End of This Book*, a classic suspense read, when a little girl no more than four asked me what I was doing.

"Reading."

"You're too big to read that book."

"And you're too small."

"I can read."

"I doubt it." I handed the book over to the girl with gingham ribbons in her hair and deep-set dimples. And like I'd suspected, she couldn't read because, once again, she was four. "Do you want me to read this to you? It's really good and kind of scary, and I don't think I can read it alone."

"Okay."

I performed my best Grover impression, my voice all nervous and high-pitched. To my surprise, a small crowd of children gathered, and at the end of the book, we all found out there was no monster waiting to scare us, just Grover.

Parents thanked me. Someone handed me five dollars, and I received inquiries about when the next story time would take place. Esme Garvey, one of the librarians in the children's book section, took notice and offered me the gig. Eventually, I added Wags—he started out as an orange-and-white-striped sock with googly eyes before I put my limited sewing skills to use and created an actual fox puppet.

Being back here years later was flooding me with memories. I was crouched behind a bookcase, waiting for my cue. The place was packed—standing room only. So many people were in attendance that they'd rearranged the room so everyone could get a good view.

Esme tapped on the microphone. "Hello, hello, thank you all for coming. This week's storyteller needs no introduction. She is part of the Brooklyn Public Library family. She's also a puppeteer at *Jellybean Junction*, and if you have your listening ears on, you may get to meet Aaliyah. I consider her a good friend. It is my honor to introduce Letitia Vincent and Wags the Fox."

I jumped up with a big smile, waving at the crowd, who erupted into cheers and applause. Esme engulfed me in a deep hug. It had been a minute since we'd hung out, and it was clear I needed to fix that.

Sitting on one of the colorful mini chairs, I addressed the crowd. "Thank you. It's so great to be back, isn't it, Wags?"

"I've missed my friends." When Wags spoke, my lips remained still.

"Yeah, me too. It can be sad when friends move away."

"But getting to see them again is always the best."

"It's the bestest."

"Hey, Wags, it's been a while. Do you remember how this goes?"

"Well, first we say hello."

"Hello, friends." I looked to Wags for the next step.

"Then we sing a song."

"We do. Are you going to help me with the words?" I asked the crowd. "I'll sing it once, and then you repeat after me.

"Come on in, it's time to play,

Let's read a story, hip-hip hooray!

Turn the page, let's start the fun.

With Wags the Fox and everyone.

So grab a book, and sit by me.

Let's explore in…one, two, three."

Toddlers sitting crisscross applesauce scooched closer.

"That was Wag-tastic," I said. "So, what should we read today, Wags?"

"How about *Last Stop on Market Street*?"

"You mean this?" I pulled the book from behind me, but to the kids I was a magician, and they giggled at the surprise. "*Last Stop on Market Street* by Matt de la Peña, illustrated by Christian Robinson."

I'd read this book to Rustin every night for the past week to ensure I didn't get caught up on any words. As I read out loud, the audience filled with toddlers, elementary-age kids, and their parents would *ooh*, *ahh*, or break into laughter.

After each page, I'd pause so the kids could get a good look at the pictures. Scanning the audience, I spotted Rustin standing in the back with parents wearing baby slings and holding sippy cups. A wide grin lit up my face, and my pulse quickened. I'd thought he wasn't going to make it, but here he was with a reassuring smile on his face. Having a man other than my father show up for me was a game changer. You know the saying, *if he wanted to, he would?* Rustin was the embodiment of that because he didn't make excuses—he made a way.

"Should we keep reading?" I asked the kids.

"Yes," they shouted back in unison.

After the story, parents brought their kids over to meet Wags and me. Some kids had full-on, gibberish-filled conversations with Wags, which left me in awe.

When the crowd finally died down, I made my way over to Rustin. "You made it." I walked up to him with open arms.

"It was important to you, so I made it a priority for me."

This was a library filled with children, but when we got home, I was going to put his *bleep* in my mouth and let it melt. Pressing my forehead against his chest, I had to fight the urge to yell, *This is my boyfriend, and he's better than yours.*

"Thank you, baby," I said instead.

"You did your big one up there. I've said this before, but this is your true calling. Kids just love you. You're a star, Letitia Vincent."

"I feel like you have to say that because you're my man."

"I'm not a bullshitter." We exchanged a knowing glance. "Okay. I *am* a bullshitter, but I'm not bullshitting about *this.*"

Esme approached with a timid smile. "Can I steal her away for a minute?"

"Yeah. She's all yours," Rustin said. My eyes followed him as he walked away, looking for a conspicuous place to hide.

"Letty, that was so good," Esme said.

"Thanks. It's just reading."

"It's an experience, one that these kids will remember for a long time."

"Most children don't remember anything before the age of six."

"I forget how rebellious you are," Esme joked.

"Girl, it's been too long, and standing here, I don't understand why."

"You know how life is—plans to meet that never materialize because of work, family, or some man."

"Are you still with—" I started.

"No, and we will not be speaking his name."

"Ouch."

"Yeah, secret girlfriend-and-kid ouch."

"Tell me you're lying."

"So now I'm celibate because men ain't shit," Esme said.

"For sure."

"Not you agreeing with me when just minutes ago you were cuddling up in a man's arms."

"It's new. It's great, but it's new."

"I'm really good at reading men—not men who *I'm* interested in, but other men—and he is head over heels. He's probably picked out an engagement ring already."

"God, I hope not," I said. "I just want to enjoy this newness for a while."

"It's so good to see you again. I've been meaning to call you."

"Yeah, we need to have drinks, but for real this time."

"Letty, we miss you and the energy you brought here. The children's section hasn't quite been the same since. I know you're with *Jellybean Junction*, and I'm so very proud, but I have a position available for you if you're interested."

"A job?"

"Director of children's entertainment," she replied. "You'd be overseeing branch activities across the boroughs. You'd curate books for story time with the help of your staff. Coordinate story-time events that are magical and one-of-a-kind experiences. You could even bring Wags out of retirement. He seemed to miss the limelight."

I used to hate going to the library because reading was always a struggle for me. It was my father who'd taught me there was so much more to the library than just physical books. My local library had forged my love of audiobooks and music, and when I was officially diagnosed with dyslexia, the library became a safe place to explore reading.

"Whoa, Esme, this is a lot to process. You mentioned a staff. I've never been in charge of anyone but me."

"I know I'm springing this on you, but I'm just eager to have you back."

"I would need to think about it."

"Of course. I can email you the job summary outlining the responsibilities, along with the compensation package."

"Yeah, that would be great."

After the library, Rustin and I went our separate ways with a plan to meet back at my place later. When the bell rang, I buzzed him up and was waiting at the door for his arrival.

"Hey, pretty lady."

"Hi."

"Why are you all smiles?"

"Two reasons." I pulled him inside and could feel him survey the lack of process of getting my apartment in order in anticipation of my mom and sister's arrival. "I'm happy to see you, and I need you to explain this." I dropped a copy of *Vanity Fair* magazine on the kitchen counter. "Are you kidding me right now?"

"Where'd you get that?"

"The newsstand across the street from the studio. You know I like physical magazines, but I stopped in my tracks once I saw this cover and your face looking back at me. Rustin, that's you."

"Yeah, it is."

"When the hell did you take this?"

"It was a while ago. I was starting to think the story got shitcanned."

"Look at you. You look so handsome."

"It's a trick with lights and mirrors."

"I do have just one question." I grabbed the magazine and flipped to page eighty-two, which I'd dog-eared. Placing it back down, I aggressively pointed to another picture. "Why are you shirtless?"

"Please put that away."

"And did they oil your chest for this?"

"I would like this to end."

"Is this what it feels like to date Michael B. Jordan?"

"You get one last joke."

"Okay." I needed to make it a good one. "Can you sign my copy? Make it out to Letty, and it should say, 'This thirst trap is just for you.'"

"And you're done."

I giggled at his embarrassment. "Has Omar seen this?"

"No, and it better stay that way." His smile faltered, and he resumed eyeing every box-crammed nook and cranny. "Isn't your mom coming tomorrow?"

"Yes."

"Letty, you haven't made a dent."

"I moved the boxes."

"From one corner of the room to another."

"Baby steps."

"Fuck baby steps. You need to kick into overdrive."

"What's the point?" I tossed my hands in the air.

"You don't have a headboard or room for the three of you to comfortably sit."

"I have that beanbag."

"Maybe your mom is always criticizing you because of shit like this. There's not even a TV."

Heat flamed up my neck. "I watch my shows on my laptop."

"I don't know how to say this, baby, but this is giving unstable, paycheck-to-paycheck, Ramen-noodles-for-dinner poor."

"I'm going to text her and say I have a family emergency, and she has to stay someplace else."

"How's that going to work when *she's* family?" he asked.

"No one asked her to come here."

"But she is, and now we have to stay up all night to get the place ready."

He was irritated with me. "You don't have to stay. You can fucking go home."

"You know what? You have all this smoke for me, but you can't say shit to your momma."

"That's different." I wasn't prepared to rationalize my complicated relationship with my mom.

"It ain't. Grow a pair, tell her how her actions affected you, and set some fucking boundaries."

How was this all *my* fault? "It's not that easy."

"You're an adult, and you're making this too fucking hard."

"And she's my mother!" All the air was sucked out of the room, and tears streamed down my face. My voice was shaky, and I could barely make out Rustin's shocked face because of all the tears. "It doesn't matter how old I get—I'm still her fucking child. She knows what the fuck she's done and makes no attempts to correct it. I am not going to be the bigger fucking person. I was eight, and she made me feel like I didn't matter. She was my fucking world, and then she blocked out the sun and took away any shred of light. When the twins were born, she stopped wanting me."

"I don't think that's—"

"*Don't* tell me a mother would never and make more fucking excuses, because I've already done that, and I know with every fiber of my being that if she could've packed up my shit and returned me to sender, she would've." I was a mess—my makeup smeared, snot running from my nose.

"Come here."

I collapsed into his arms like a marathoner at the finish line. "Fuck my mother, and fuck Madison." Even my sweet baby sister was catching strays. "No, I don't mean that. Not Madison, but one hundred percent my mother can get fucked."

"I'm sorry for giving advice you didn't ask for. If it's fuck your momma, then gang gang."

"We ride at dawn."

"Circle the neighborhood a couple of times."

"And then *pow, pow, pow, pow.*"

"Oh shit, we're shooting? I thought we were gonna throw some eggs, fuck up the flower beds, put the mailbox flag down."

"I'm a rebel, I'm a bad girl." I raised a disinterested shoulder. "It's probably how everybody thinks it's gonna end."

"Is there anything I can do?"

"You could hold me tighter." We stood in the middle of my studio in an embrace. When I finally unglued my face from his chest, my defiance turned into bone-chilling fear. "Oh my God, this place *is* a disaster."

"Yeah. I tried to tell you."

"She is never gonna let me live this down, and she's gonna go home and tell my father I'm living in squalor because of the mismatched sheets and grocery store bag in lieu of a proper trash can. Do you know how much trash cans cost? *Do* you?" I collapsed on the bed, wanting to curl up in the fetal position and soothe myself until I stopped caring.

"What time do they get in?"

"I'm picking them up at three in the afternoon."

"Leave it up to me. I'll take care of this place."

"I didn't take you for an arsonist, but it's kind of hot." I giggled at the unexpected pun. "Get it?"

"There will be no fires."

"What are you going to do? The place is spotless—it just feels like I'm getting ready to move out rather than in. And who says you need cohesive home décor? It's all a scam setup by HomeGoods."

"Why HomeGoods?"

"Have you been there before? It's all junk, but still somehow you leave having spent no less than two hundred dollars. Let's talk about something else. You didn't tell me about Imaginex. How did that go?"

"Their campus is nice. Nothing like our studio."

"Maybe when it all comes crashing down, Imaginex will swoop in and buy us out."

"Uhm…maybe…Who knows? Imaginex or an angel investor."

"Maybe you could talk to them now that you're on the inside of the mouse."

Rustin nodded thoughtfully, taking a seat next to me. "I don't want you worrying about your mom's visit. It's, what, three days? What the hell can go wrong in such a short span of time?"

"I feel like you just jinxed me."

CHAPTER 26

Rustin

I CALLED BOTH Brea and Omar, informing them I would be working remotely today. Letitia had left her apartment hours ago, and I was sitting on the floor in a virtual team meeting for Thread and Thespian. While I rattled off directions to my staff, Letty's place was being transformed. I told her I'd help, so I'd enlisted a staging company to come in and give this place character and curtains.

"Do you prefer neutral bedding or bold?" a redhead with a high, messy bun and clipboard whispered.

Muting the video chat, I said, "Neutral bedding with big, bold pillows and a funky throw blanket." They had a large truck parked downstairs filled to the brim with décor and furniture items. If the Curated Room didn't have it, your ass didn't need it. Letty had no clue I was doing this. She probably thought I was going to outfit her place with office furniture and call it a day.

Truthfully, when I'd offered my services, I didn't know where to start, but when I woke up—or rather, pretended to wake up for Letty's benefit—I realized there was a service provider for every occasion. And I was right—a quick Google and scan of the reviews led me to the Curated Room.

"You know, there is such a thing as spreading yourself too thin," Omar voice said through my earbuds.

"My bad." I focused back on my laptop screen and realized it was no longer a group meeting but a one-on-one.

"Where the fuck are you?" he asked.

"At Letty's."

"Why?"

"Long story."

"Okay, if you two are playing hooky to fuck and nerd out, I respect it."

"I'm literally working."

"Yeah, and I imagine Letitia is sprawled out on the bed in nothing but ass cheeks, waiting for round two."

"Don't imagine my girl naked."

"In my imagination, she's not naked. There's an *explicit content* bar over her naughty bits."

I sniffed.

"So, when am I gonna get that final draft of the play? Our meeting is fast approaching."

Omar knew he was walking a tightrope. As a creative, I could be very temperamental, and talking about the status of a work-in-progress was often met with big emotions.

"Yeah, it's good. Coming along." I didn't have the heart to tell him I had nothing. At meetings like Cinevault, I could bullshit through it, but this was different. A play needed to be a fully drafted, cohesive idea, not sleep-deprived ramblings. I was lying to Omar and Letty. After my writer's block confession, I'd decided it was best to spiral in silence. At night, I lay next to her in bed holding her tight, creepily sniffing her hair because staying up all night drinking coffee and popping Adderall was frowned upon.

I didn't want her to worry about something that was just a part of my writing process. I'd be the first to admit that said process was toxic and included mini freak-outs and my saying the most fucked-up shit to myself. It was a bit of a love-hate relationship I had going on. I loved the way my brain worked and my ability to find solutions. I hated the self-imposed pressure and nagging fear that I would die and no one beyond my immediate circle would remember me—which should be enough, but nothing was ever enough for me.

"Do you need anything from me—number two pencils, that fancy pen you claim is better than any other pen?" Omar asked.

"The Kaweco Sport is what all these other pens pretend to be, and it fits in my pocket."

"Rus?"

"Yes?"

"Are you good?"

"Am I… Of course I am."

"We don't have to do everything, you know. We have Imaginex and Cinevault. We can ease off the gas for a bit."

"What are you saying?"

"I'm saying I love you, and you don't need to bleed yourself dry for us."

"Have you *ever* known me to pump the brakes?" I asked.

"No, but we were poor and hungry."

"I'm still hungry."

"And I respect that, but we have access to a different reality now. We don't have to go this hard."

"So some other brothers can catch us slipping? I appreciate the advice, but I'm fine. Maybe a little tired, but that's what ashwagandha is for."

"You're not gonna tell me you love me back?" Omar half joked.

"I love you, and sitting next to you in Statistics 101 was the best thing that ever happened to me."

Omar tried to hide his smile. "That's what up, king. You know I've always got your back."

I'd never had a brother, but Omar was the next best thing because we'd chosen each other.

Had I fallen asleep on Letty's freshly dressed bed and was now waking up to voices on the other side of the front door? I was supposed to be out of here hours ago. Running to the window, I seriously considered escaping by transforming into a parkour athlete. I could hear Letty making apologies in advance for the state of her apartment.

"Just want to say work has been really busy, so I didn't get to—"

"Letitia, can you just open the door? It is very hot in this hallway," an older female voice said.

The key was jiggling in the lock. Maybe I could hide in the closet. *Fuck!*

The door swung open, and Letitia said, "Welcome to my…" No doubt stopping short because she didn't recognize the place with a gallery wall and small entry table with a lamp and catch-all bowl in the long hall.

Her mother was the first to enter the main space, and when she spotted me, she screamed like I was covered in blood and toting a machete.

"It's not *that* bad," Letty said, assuming her mom was reacting to the apartment.

Standing next to her mother, she barely acknowledged me, so transfixed by the apartment, which looked like something out of *NYC Living,* a YouTube show that took you inside New Yorkers' homes.

"Who is this man?" Her mom was clutching her purse to her chest.

Letty broke out of her trance. "Oh, sorry. Uhm. This is Rustin. Rustin is my…boyfriend. Rustin, this is my mom Eloise and my sister Madison."

"Does he live here?"

"No. He lives in Brooklyn."

I stepped forward. "It's so nice to meet you both. I've heard such nice things."

Letty's sister was the first to break the tension. "Hi, Rustin. Nice to meet you. Wish I could say the same, but Letty's been keeping you a secret."

"Not a secret," Letty said. "Rustin is amazing. He has a show on Broadway."

"He's an actor?" Letty's mom turned her nose up.

"I am, but I actually wrote the musical."

"What musical?" Madison asked. "Letty turned me into a theater kid because she loved it so much, and as the baby sister, I wanted to be just like my big sis."

"*U-Turn.*"

Eloise's demeanor shifted. "*U-Turn?* Aunt Debbie…" She rested her hand on my arm. "Debbie is my sister. She saw your show last year and raved about it. It's the one with puppets who are a little naughty."

"That's the one."

"And you wrote that?"

"Yes, ma'am."

"Good for you."

Letty stared up at me, shocked at how quickly I'd tamed her mother. I tossed my arm around her shoulders.

"Letty, your place is so nice. I love these curtains." Madison walked around the space, stopping to touch damn near everything.

"Thanks. Me too." Letty flashed me a look, questioning how I'd been able to do this.

"This apartment used to belong to Tiggy Chandler," I announced.

"Wait. I didn't know that," Letty said.

Tiggy was a famous cozy mystery writer that middle-aged women like Eloise went up for.

"Yep. She lived here in her twenties and likely penned some of her first few novels here."

"How quaint." Eloise appeared to appreciate the space with new eyes.

"Please sit. Is anyone thirsty? I don't have much, but—" Letty opened the fridge and found her wine box, plastic container with questionable contents, and various condiments replaced with fully stocked shelves of any drink you could think of and a simple charcuterie platter from Trader Joe's. She slammed the fridge. "Rustin, could I talk to you for a second?"

"Sure."

She grabbed my hand. "Make yourself at home," she told her family. "There are drinks in the fridge. We'll be right back." She dragged me from the apartment and up a flight of stairs so we were safely out of earshot. "Rustin, how?"

"I just had the groceries delivered. No big deal."

"Where did you get all the furniture and stuff?"

"Delivered."

"What did you just call 1-800-Dial-a-Favor?"

"Baby, do you hate it?" If I'd made things worse, I'd never get over it.

"I love it, and I love you. You didn't have to do all this." She kissed me while still talking. "And Tiggy. I didn't know my place once belonged to Tiggy Chandler."

"Oh no, that was a lie."

"What?"

"I made it up. I spotted the book peeking out from your mom's purse."

"You lied to my mother?"

"White lie."

"What if she Googles it?"

"She's not going to. She's going to tell all her friends and book club that her eldest lives in the same apartment that *Death by Lemon Tart* was written in."

"That's kind of genius."

"I'm an evil mastermind, remember?"

"You're *my* evil mastermind."

"Sorry for still being here," I said. "I fell asleep. My plan was to be out of your hair. I'm gonna pack up my things and leave."

"You can stay."

"No. I want you to get some focused time with the family, but if you're up to it, I'd like to take you all to dinner before they leave."

"They'd love that."

Back downstairs, I packed up my laptop. "What are your plans while you're here?"

"Tourist sightseeing stuff," Eloise replied. "We're rather basic, I fear. We'd hoped to see a show while here, but we didn't book in advance, so almost everything is sold out."

"Which one were you hoping to see?"

"*Hamilton*." Madison blushed.

"Consider it done. I'll email Letty the confirmation information when I get home."

"No, Rustin. You do not have to do that. I'm sure I can search Ticketmaster and find something," Letty objected.

"Yeah, in the nosebleed section. It's cool. I got you."

"That is so kind of you. Such a nice boy," Eloise said.

I smiled at Letty, taking pleasure in the fact that middle-aged white women still loved me.

I texted Letty the ticket confirmation around midnight, and to my surprise, she responded.

Letitia

You're such a nice boy.

Rustin

Shut up.

Letitia

Thanks for the tickets.

Rustin

Where's your mom and sister?

Letitia

Sleeping. I'm in the bathroom.

Rustin

Was it a good first night?

Letitia

It was eventful, but let's not
talk about that. Send me a pic.

Rustin

Of my dick?

Letitia

Yeah.

Rustin

I've never done that before.

Letitia

I don't believe you.

Rustin

I'm semi-famous with trust issues.
The last thing I need is for my dick to
be featured on TMZ.

Letitia

Pretty please. You send me
yours, and I'll send you mine.

Rustin

Okay. Give me a minute.

In that minute, I jacked off to waken my limp dick to attention.
After snapping the picture, I hit send.

Letitia

Why's it hard?

Rustin

Because the first rule of dick pics is never send a flaccid dick.

Letitia

I didn't know that. Guys are weird. It's a solid 9.4.

Rustin

Wait. We're rating the pics?

Letitia

Yeah, for shits and giggles. Better lighting would have put you over the top.

Rustin

Reciprocate.

The thought of having a picture of her I could reference in a pinch excited me. When my phone dinged, my heart stalled in my chest. Letty had sent me a photo of her bare nipples and an outstretched tongue.

Rustin

Motherfucker.

Letitia

You like it?

Rustin

Very much.

My hand slid to my dick.

Letitia

What would you rate it?

Rustin

Perfection.

Letitia

It can't be perfect.

Rustin

Okay, 9.99, only because it's never as good as the real thing.

Letitia

I'll allow it.

Rustin

FaceTime?

When her face lit up my screen, my breath escaped my lungs. Letty was sitting in an empty bathtub, floral headscarf wrapped around her head, still naked from the waist up. "Hi." Her voice was a whisper.

"Hi. Let's fuck."

We both eagerly shed the rest of our clothes.

"What did you think when you first met me?" she asked.

"I thought your ass was phat in them jeans."

"And what if I'd asked you to slap it?"

"Okay, I like this. I would have escorted you to the nearest restroom, pulled them jeans over those thick thighs, and buried my face in between them cheeks."

Letty bit down on her lip. I could tell she was working her pussy from the glint in her eye. "I would've been unable to contain my moans. I fear the whole bar would've heard us over the music."

"I'd just keep going teasing that hole. Can you handle a finger?"

"Yes. Put it in."

My dick was practically throbbing as my hand coasted over it. "You feel so good. Do me a favor and touch your ankles."

"You just gonna spread me open like that?"

"My own personal buffet. Help me hold them cheeks open. Do you think you could tolerate something bigger?"

"Give it to me, Daddy."

"First the tip. Does that feel good?"

"Yes." Letty stuck two fingers in her mouth, and then her hand disappeared.

"Good girl. Take all these inches."

"It's so big." Her voice was breathy and low.

"Do you think you can ride it?"

"I can try."

The sounds my voice pulled out of her made me beat my meat faster. My head lolled back, and all I saw was her face, as if she were actually in the room with me.

"Rustin, baby, I love you so much. You make me feel so safe."

"I always got you, baby. You're my person."

"Fuck. Take me."

Our words slowed, replaced by intense, prolonged eye contact, and our making funny faces into our phones. My toes curled, and my left leg stiffened as cum burst free, hot and satisfying. The whites of Letty's eyes were all I could make out—the camera was too close and shaky.

When she finally came back into focus, I asked, "Are you good?"

"I've never been better. You fuck me so good."

"That was all you."

"Nope. You definitely momentarily possessed my body. I can practically still feel your dick."

"I wish you were here right now."

"Maybe I can slip away while they're at *Hamilton*." There was a knocking on the other end, and Letty pulled her tank top back on. "Yeah?" She wasn't talking to me.

"What are you doing in there?" her mother asked.

"Uhm, scrolling on my phone." She sounded like a fifteen-year-old.

"I was looking for some aspirin."

"Just a second." Letty's face came back into view. "Sorry. I have to go. Love you."

"Love you too. Sleep tight."

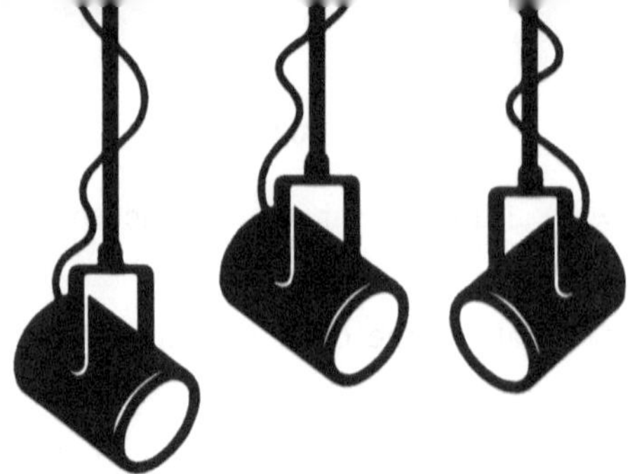

CHAPTER 27

Letitia

MADISON'S ARM WAS hooked with mine as we walked around the MoMA. "Why didn't you tell me about Rustin?"

"Why didn't you tell me you were actively planning a wedding?"

"Not actively. I refuse to get married until I graduate."

"Then why are you going dress shopping?"

"That was all Mom, and you know it. Back to Rustin. He's nice, I like him."

"I like him too."

We stopped at a painting, and I leaned in to read the summary. Unfortunately, it was just a blur of words. I squinted, hoping it would help. "Looking…looking…for…Langston. Ark, Arch—"

"Archival." Maddy was used to helping me make out the words I had trouble with, and I offered a grateful smile. Your siblings are your first best friends, and I loved the twins deeply. My acrimony was reserved for my mother. On the surface, my childhood had been picturesque, but when you lifted up the swath of peeling wallpaper, there was chipped paint and mold.

320

"Archival…archival footage of the Harlem Renaissance," I read.

"It says it's a movie, and we can watch it for free."

"It would be a nice break from walking in circles. Let's wait for Mom to catch up."

"What is she doing?"

Our mother was in an unusually long conversation with a fellow guest of the museum. They'd found commonality in a brooch my mother was wearing, and now they were trading secrets. No doubt my mother was bragging about something—"I'm here with my beautiful daughter, newly engaged and making straight A's in her classes at college. She makes me so proud. The other one lives here playing make-believe with dolls and works every last one of my nerves. She's adopted." I couldn't hear the conversation, but my mental reenactment was probably spot-on.

"Mom said you're working at Tiny Crowns," I said to Maddy.

"It's part time, after classes."

"I thought you hated the idea of pageants. You said they were misogynistic and center around the male gaze."

"I still believe that, but when you need money, sometimes you have to make exceptions."

"I thought you were on an allowance."

Maddy shrugged. "It's been put on pause. I told Mom and Dad I wanted to learn to take care of myself."

"Why? Life is hard enough as it is. If I had parents willing to subsidize my lifestyle, I'd jump on it."

"You do. You're just too proud to ask."

"Asking for money isn't the same when you're my age. When you're twenty-seven, that request is followed by questions—*Where did your paycheck go? Are you on drugs? I hope you're not out here blowing your money partying. Are you sure you're not on drugs?*"

"Don't act like you couldn't call Dad and have money CashApped to you."

"I could, but I try not to take advantage."

"Dad would do anything for you. It's clear who the favorite is."

"Are you talking about me?" I pointed to my chest.

"Yeah."

My words were sprinkled with laughter. "No, I'm not."

"Letty, you are one hundred percent Dad's favorite, followed by Mason and then me."

"Dad loves you."

"Yes, of course, but you are his heart and soul."

It was so weird how we'd all grown up in the same house but had vastly different views of our childhood. "You're Mom's favorite."

"That's not a good thing. As her favorite, I get the brunt of her scrutiny. You and Mason are lucky you both moved away. I'm kind of regretting the decision to stay close to home for college. Do you know she just showed up on campus in May? No call, no heads-up. Just her waving from the door to my fermentation science class."

"Why were you in a fermentation science class?"

"Because of a boy."

"You're engaged."

"But I'm not married yet."

"You whore," I teased, clutching an imaginary string of pearls.

Our mother joined us, shaking her head. "I must admit, I don't get half this stuff."

"Art's subjective—everyone gets something different. We get what we need from it," I said.

"Letitia"—my mother dropped her voice—"I can see your nipples."

It was cold in the museum, and my nips were pronounced, but I didn't see how that was my fault. "Mother, it's just nipples, and we all have them."

"You should take my cardigan."

"It doesn't go with my outfit."

"But erect nipples do? It's not ladylike." She fussed with the straps of my dress.

"Could you not?" I pushed her hand away.

"Letitia and I were thinking about watching the Harlem Renaissance movie," Maddy interjected.

My mother scanned the informational sign. "Forty-five minutes. We don't have forty-five minutes to watch people dance and sing. We came here for art, not that."

"That *is* art," I said. "Living, creating, and community are just as much a part of the artistic process as anything else." My mother's idea of art was a macaroni portrait. She was only here so she could brag to her friends and appear cultured.

"Why are you always so emotional?"

"Letty's passionate, Mom. There's a difference," Maddy said.

"Always trying to be different. Nipples with piercings. Why can't you just fit in?"

"Because I don't fit in, and I never have," I said. "And I don't know why you'd want that. I don't have to be like every other girl who went to Wepawaung Valley High School. Since when did being unique become a bad thing?"

"There's unique, and then there's whatever this is you're doing. Leaving home, working for public television making peanuts, and hanging with unsavory individuals."

That last one, she was just pulling out of her ass. She'd met two of my friends, Brea and Rustin, and both were far from unsavory. "You don't have the first clue about my life."

"I know what you tell me and your father."

"I only tell you the good things, and still you find fault. Nothing is ever good enough for you."

"That's not true. I think your place is lovely, and I like Rustin. But if you want to keep him, you need to get your act together."

"My act *is* together. I just bought a home with no help from you and Dad. I have a job I love with coworkers who value me, and I'm living my dream—something you'd know nothing about."

"We all have dreams, and then we grow up," she said with a sniff. "It's high time you do the same."

"If growing up means being married to a man who tolerates you and children who can't wait to get away from you, then you're doing a bang-up job."

"Letty, maybe we should go for a walk." Maddy tugged on my hand.

"You're just mad because I don't need you, and I haven't for a long time now," I continued.

"Well, maybe if you consulted me, you wouldn't be living in a neighborhood with music playing at all hours of the night and random people trying to sell you bootleg Coach purses," Mom replied.

"That's Harlem. It's what makes the city great. I'm sorry the gentrifying HOA isn't working fast enough for you."

"Letty, I just want what's best for you."

"No, you want what's best for *you*—a perfect, sanitized family where everyone never steps out of line. Well, news flash: I don't want your life. I want mine." I started to walk off, circling back. "And for the record, Rustin *loves* my erect nipples."

Maddy covered her face in her hand to conceal her laughter. I headed for the exit. This was a mistake. I should have let them tour the museum alone, but the morning had started out on a high note, us laughing in the kitchen over scones and bagels. I'd forgotten my rule—small doses of my mother so as not to overdose. Concentrated contact resulted in adverse side effects, like mood swings, loss of appetite, and a reduced will to live.

I hadn't made it three blocks before my phone rang. It was my dad. "Did Mom tell you to call me?"

"No. I was just thinking about you. Wanted to see how the visit was going."

My mother had called him complaining. I was sure she'd called me *your daughter* the entire time because when I was being difficult, I belonged to my father alone.

"It was great. We were at the MoMA, and then your wife started picking on me." I took brisk steps down the busy street like I was late for an appointment.

"I'm sure she didn't."

"She did. She mentioned my nipples."

"Excuse me?"

"Never mind."

"Where are you now?"

"Walking down the street, contemplating veering into traffic." A passing car honked, confirming it may be a good idea. A quick hit-and-run. I'd be posted up in the hospital with a broken leg. You can't run through a person's flaws when they're in critical but stable condition.

"Stop it."

A heaviness washed over me. I tried to be a positive person, but my mother slowly picked at the emotional scabs that hadn't quite healed, and when she did, a flood of doubt came with it.

I needed to find a safe place to cry. Tears were imminent, and I couldn't walk and cry at the same time. I turned off a busy street to one lined with trees and charming brownstones, then stumbled to a stoop with pots filled with colorful flowers and took a seat.

"Dad…" My voice cracked. "No. Forget it."

"You always do that, stop yourself from saying the thing. Just say it."

The words burnt and choked me as they passed my lips. "I don't think she loves me, and I don't know if she ever did. When I'm around her, I just feel like a disappointment. The etiquette classes, the prayer circles, the therapy sessions—all so Letty could be a better person. Because Letty didn't fit in, Letty didn't laugh at the right jokes, Letty was slow. Her siblings could read better at eight than she could as a sophomore in high school. Maybe Letty's mom was a drug addict, and that's why she's so delayed."

"No one ever said that to you."

"No, but they whispered it in the living room over tea or in the car when I had my headphones on and they thought I wasn't listening. She had conversations with the principals and school counselors practically setting me up for failure. *Just want to give you a heads-up—Letty's dumb, so don't expect much from her.*"

"Sweetie, I didn't know you felt this way."

"I don't know, maybe I don't. Maybe my glucose is just low." Lying, pretending everything was fine, was a whole lot easier than being honest. Honesty hurt people, made people cry or feel sorry for you. I wasn't looking for sympathy. I just wanted someone to validate my feelings and confirm I wasn't crazy.

"Letitia, adopting you was the best thing that ever happened to me. You made me a dad, and I love you for it."

"You don't think I'm dumb?"

"Never have, never will. I just want you to be happy."

I was bawling on a stranger's stairs while people walked by laughing with their iced lattes and designer dogs. When a mother and daughter passed hand in hand, I cried harder. On the other side of the phone, keys jingled and a car door opened and closed. "What are you doing?" I asked.

"I'm driving to you."

"Dad, no."

"My baby girl is hurting and needs a hug."

"Dad, please do not leave the driveway. I appreciate your papa-bear instincts, but Mom and I need to figure this out. And while I'd love one of your hugs, it will have to wait until another day."

"Are you sure? It's no trouble."

"It's impractical."

"Are you still crying?"

"No," I lied.

"If you need me, just call and I'll come running. I love you, kiddo."

"Love you too."

I found myself at Rustin's door hoping he was home. When he answered, relief kicked in.

"This is a nice surprise." It took him seconds to spot the tears on my face. "Wait. What's wrong? Have you been crying?"

"Yes, and I've eaten, like, three hamburgers from Burger Hut. They were disgusting, and the fries were cold," I said in the middle of a sob.

"Burger Hut did this to you? Which one?"

"Huh?"

"I will burn that bitch down." The fact that he joined me in my delusion with little to no provocation was not lost on me.

"I knew arson was your go-to."

"What happened at Burger Hut that's got you so upset?"

"No. It's my mom. The burger shit just kind of pushed me over the edge."

Rustin pulled me inside, and after I relayed my afternoon, he was caught up. "Some people are just bad with expressing affection. Maybe your mother is one of them."

"*BZZZZT!*" I recreated a buzzer sound to indicate a wrong answer. "My mother doted over the twins."

"Okay. She sees you as different, that's clear, and maybe she didn't know how to parent different. It's not uncommon that kids who don't conform are shoved into an uncomfortable box in an attempt to reshape what makes them special."

"Yeah, I was in a box, and she didn't care if it poked me or left bruises, as long as I was contained."

Rustin massaged my scalp. "I'm sorry that happened to you."

"It took me a long time to unwrap myself from that. I like who I am—by no means am I perfect, but I don't want to be. That shit is overrated. Take you, for instance—you're brilliant, and you see the world as others don't. Everything holds a story for you, and I love you for it. You're not idealistic, that's for sure, you're a realist, but you see the world for more than what is on the surface, and not many people can do that. It's a gift—your gift."

"Maybe your mother does and says the things she does because she's jealous."

"No."

"Hear me out. She followed the rules, got married, started a family—even when it was difficult to conceive—and she works, tithes to the church. On the outside looking in, her life is enviable— three beautiful kids, a husband, a job that allows her to travel—but having all that still isn't enough, because what about *her* dreams, *her* passion? And now she's watching her daughter break all the rules and succeed. At the end of the day, our parents are just people who got knocked up."

"Are you saying my mother at the core is just a girl?"

"I guess." Rustin moved from my head to my shoulders.

My eyes focused on his mural wall—the blank mural wall. "What happened to that?"

"I painted over it."

"Why?"

"If you want to make room for something new, you need to let go of the past." It was like he was speaking about my life. Maybe my mommy issues were holding me back. "I know when *my* mom meets you, she's gonna love you."

"Meets me?"

"It's kind of the natural progression of things. Meet a girl, fall madly in love, get the stamp of approval from the parentals."

His wanting me to meet his parents was a big relationship step I was more than ready to take. "I bet your mom is really nice."

"She is. A bit nosey, but nice."

"Nosey I can handle. I just hope she's okay with me asking questions about what you were like as a child."

"I already told you. I was shy, introverted, always talking to myself."

"No, that's how you see yourself. I'm looking for an unbiased opinion."

"From my mom?" His eyebrows crept up his forehead. "Good luck with that."

I leaned into him nuzzling my face into his neck. "Thank you for listening."

"Anytime. And if you ever need me to fight a few battles for you just say the word."

"You'd tell my mother off?"

"Yes, but nicely because I respect my elders."

"I think you're right; she and I are overdue for a chat. We both know something's off and we just keep avoiding it hoping it'll go away. Well, it's been twenty years and this rift between us has just grown bigger. I don't wanna continue to walk on eggshells with my mother."

"I think talking is a good start." His hand slid up and down my arm.

"Yeah, because what we're currently doing is obviously not working. I'm mad at her, she's disappointed in me and we can barely say two words before one of us takes shit the wrong way."

"You've got this. And I'll be here if you wanna talk afterward."

"Thanks."

"No need to thank me. This is what boyfriends do."

Caressing his cheek we locked eyes. "I'm grateful to have you in my corner." Knowing Rustin would have my back no matter the outcome made what I had to do next a little less daunting.

After a trip to the bathroom, I returned to find Rustin dumping frozen fries in the air fryer. He smiled at me and said the unexpected: "I think you should talk to your mom."

Back home, I was surprised to find my mother outside my building smoking a cigarette. "When did you start smoking?"

"I've always smoked—just hid it."

I shuffled from one foot to the other. "How was the rest of your day?"

"Where have you been?"

"I needed space, and I didn't think you'd miss me."

"Of course I would. I came here to spend time with you."

"You came here for Kleinfeld and Dylan's Candy Store."

"I came to see my daughter to make sure she was okay. Maybe buy her silverware."

"You were gonna buy me silverware?"

"Or whatever else you needed for your new home."

Fuck, I really *could* use silverware, and my mother only bought the good stuff because the shit went in your mouth. "Mom, I'm sorry about the stuff I said at the museum."

"What about what you said to your father?"

Fucking snitch. "I was just upset, venting. I didn't mean it."

"You told him I didn't love you."

"Because you don't, and it's fine. I get it—I can be unlovable. That's probably why I was put up for adoption."

"Letty, oh my God, you can't believe that."

I gave a quick nod.

"Do you remember our first meeting?"

"No. I was three."

"You walked into the room and hid behind the legs of one of the staff members. I held out a Ring Ding, and you slowly inched from behind that lady's skirt until you'd taken it from my hand."

"That tracks. My love language is food."

"I told you my name, and you spoke yours—Letty—and my heart melted. You were so beautiful, a little thing with these big, brown, curious eyes. And I thought, why would anyone ever want to let you go? When they told us we could officially adopt you, I bawled my eyes out. I was so happy the little girl with big eyes was going to be a part of our family."

"Okay, so when did that joy switch to regret?" I pushed a tear from my cheek.

"Never regret. I never regretted adopting you. Where do you get these thoughts?"

"From you and the way you've treated me. 'Letty, remember, no swimming at the pool party because your hair will curl up.' 'Letty, why can't you be more like your sister?' And don't get me started about the consultation with the plastic surgeon for a nose job."

"Wait a damn minute. You asked me to take you."

"I was *thirteen*. You were supposed to tell me I was perfect and didn't need a new nose, not validate my dysmorphia."

"I was trying to be supportive. That's all I ever wanted, was to keep you safe. You don't think I understand how hard it was for you growing up in that community—people smiling in your face but behind closed doors calling you names or making assumptions? I get it, and I thought if you fit in, then it would spare you from bullying and feeling like you didn't belong."

"It made me feel ashamed and like who I was wasn't good enough."

"I was doing the best I could. No one gives you a handbook on how to raise a Black child in a predominantly white community." She lit another cigarette. When did my mother become a chain smoker?

"Why is nothing I do ever good enough for you?"

"Because there are just some things about you I don't understand, and the only way I can think to keep you safe is to keep you close."

"You're not keeping me close. It's making me close off. I don't call you because I can never just get an 'I'm proud of you,' or 'How exciting.' There is always a criticism—always notes."

"That's how my mother was with me."

"And how'd that make you feel?"

"Horrible. Your grandmother was my first bully."

"Then why are you doing it to me?"

Her head jerked back, like this was the first time she was seeing the correlation.

"I want to fix this. Us. I know it'll take some time, but I'm willing to try if you are."

"I would like that," I whispered, drained from being emotionally bled dry.

She brushed my hair from my cheek. "Letty, you have such a beautiful face. Why do you insist on covering it up with all this hair?"

"Mom. This isn't a fresh start, just more of the same."

"Sorry. I will work on it." She tilted my chin up. "I know you won't believe me, but I have always loved you, and nothing and no one can change that. You're my special girl. I tell my friends about my beautiful, brave daughter who moved to New York all alone to pursue her dreams—working at *Jellybean Junction*, winning an Emmy—"

"The show won an Emmy, not me."

"As a part of the cast, that win is as much yours as anybody's. And now you've bought your first place, and it's the former home of Tiggy, no less."

Wow, this lie had legs.

"I'm so proud. *So* proud."

"Thank you, Mom."

It had taken years to get us where we were, and it would no doubt require a few more to change the tide, but I was grateful for the conversation and the possibility.

CHAPTER 28

Rustin

"I COME BEARING the good stuff." I had two iced coffees in my hand.

"Is that a salted-caramel cream cold brew?" Brea asked.

"You know it."

She stretched her arms, gesturing with the *gimme* fingers. "Just what I needed."

I handed her a cup. "Look, I don't have much good news, but I do have coffee." Closing her office door, I took a seat.

"Thanks. It's much appreciated. I've been staring at my screen reviewing the fundraising numbers, hoping they would magically change."

"That bad, huh?"

"We did well. Any other year we'd be patting ourselves on the back and popping open a bottle of champagne." She took the first sip of her coffee, and the caffeine had its intended effect.

"The cast was flying economy and road-tripping around the country attending these fundraising events. I thought we'd have more to show for it," I said.

"We raised more than last year by a few hundred thousand. That's respectable, and in spite of it all, we should be proud."

"I can get on board with that."

Brea let out a sigh. "You know if you asked anyone on the cast or crew why they choose to work at *Jellybean Junction*, they'd each have a story to tell. If you told me in college I'd be working at a public TV show, I would've scoffed. As you know, I grew up in an affluent neighborhood, and things have generally come easy to me. But this job—this place—has taught me so much about myself. I'm resourceful—I don't take no for an answer. I learned to sew because I wanted to be able to help mend the damaged puppets. And I love this place and what we do, even though half of them work my damn nerves—your girlfriend included."

We shared a laugh. "I'm sorry, Brea. I wish I had better news."

"So, lay it on me."

"Ratings from this season's first few shows—episode one was twenty-six percent better than past seasons."

"No doubt because of your name pulling in viewers."

"After that, we see a dip, with episode three being our lowest-performing episode in over eighteen months."

"But all of our changes haven't even made it to screen yet. Next week's episode will feature the new-and-improved Grumpy Gus."

"I fear we are running out of runway and grace."

"That's not fair." Brea plopped her hands into her lap.

"You sound like Letty."

"She's right. Have you told her?"

"No, God no. She just brought an apartment, you know."

"So I've heard." Humor was the only thing keeping us from breaking down. "We're not going to make it this time, are we?"

"I'm sorry. I feel like this is all my fault."

"It's not. You tried. That's all anyone can ask."

"Yeah, but I don't usually fail."

"Failing is good for you. It builds character."

"What are you going to do?" I asked.

"Maybe take some time off to really consider that question. I could tell Letty if you prefer."

"No. I want her to hear it from me. I want her to know that no matter what, I've got her back."

"Make sure there's food available. She has a better temperament on a full stomach."

"Give me the weekend, and then we can tell the others on Monday."

"Sounds like a plan." Brea tipped her cup in my direction. "It's been nice working with you, Rustin."

"Look, if you ever need anything, I'm a phone call away."

"I just assumed you'd change your number after this."

"I was planning on it, but you're friends with Letty, so it would be awkward at the wedding."

"For sure, because I'm gonna be the matron of honor."

"This was nice." Letty beamed at me.

"I wanted to take you some place you'd never been."

"Well, I can say I've never been to the Trailer Park." She popped a now-cold fry in her mouth.

The Trailer Park was a restaurant in Chelsea. Its décor was tacky, in a cool way. There was zero empty real estate because every wall, table, and archway was decked out in a kitschy style. I'm talking framed pictures, rest-stop signs, and Christmas lights. Even the ceiling was lined with some type of chandelier—it wasn't glass or plastic, but it was certainly a fire hazard.

"Esme reached out again," Letty said.

"Oh yeah? She wants another stacked story time?"

"She offered me a job."

"When?" I asked.

"At the library event."

"And you're just telling me now?"

"Yeah, because at the time, I wasn't considering it."

"And you are now?"

"Is that a bad thing?"

Given the fact *Junction* was ending, it was almost as if God had realigned the stars just for her, and I got it—because if I could, I'd do the same. "I just kind of feel like everything is falling apart," I replied.

Her features were marred with concern. "In what way?"

Staring into her brown eyes as she looked to me for an explanation, I knew I had to fix my attitude real quick. "You know what, scratch that. Let's start over. Tell me again like it's the first time."

Her eyes smiled before her mouth did. "Esme offered me a job at the library."

"Oh my God. As she should. Who doesn't want Letitia Vincent on their roster? Esme recognizes a good thing when she sees it, and you, baby, are the best there is."

"That was better."

"I'm proud of you."

"I don't know if I'm gonna take it. Maybe I could negotiate part time when *Junction* is on hiatus."

"About that."

"Yeah?"

I hated that I had to be the one to ruin this moment. The food and crowded location were one hundred percent by design. I'd wanted Letty to be happy before I dropped the bomb. My hope was that some of the residual merriment would help soften the blow.

"You know I had a meeting with Brea yesterday."

"Yeah. Big Q1 planning session."

"Less planning and more reflecting."

"On?"

"I'm sorry to have to be the one to say this, baby, but it's official—we're going to be canceled."

"What does that mean? Let's implement plan B."

"We are well past plan B. I was at plan Z."

"Our Obi Wan Kenobi." Her voice had a distant quality. She reached for my hand, and when she finally looked at me again, her eyes were stormy. "I'm sorry, Rustin. I know how hard you tried to make this work."

"It feels so anticlimactic. All the long hours, the cast racking up frequent flyer miles. Saying the same spiel over and over, hoping guests would cut a check. It shouldn't be *this* fucking hard. All that for Harold to call Brea and me on a Friday afternoon and tell us our next three shows would be our last."

"That's only a few weeks from now. How do we tie up loose ends? I don't even have everyone's number. How do say a proper goodbye?" Tears fell from her eyes, the gravity of it all finally setting in. "What… How are we…" She was sobbing now, and I felt useless just sitting there rubbing her back.

A waitress witnessed Letitia's shoulder-shaking cry session and approached our table. "You're an asshole." She pointed directly at me. "Sweetie, you are way too good for him."

"No, this isn't a breakup," I protested.

"She's the prize, and you're just a stupid guy. Bullets have been dodged tonight."

"No, it's fine. We're fine," Letty said in the midst of tears.

"If you need me, I have a taser in my locker." The server tossed me one final look, telling me she was ready to throat-punch me at the slightest provocation.

"Can you stop crying so I don't get beat up?" I joked, which elicited a pathetic laugh from Letty.

She grabbed the paper towel roll from the table, ripping off a sheet. Dabbing her eyes, she said, "Have you ever been fired from a job?"

"No, 'cause I've only ever worked for myself."

"It sucks. It's like someone telling you you're not good enough. It can really do a number on your self-esteem, and then on top of that, you have to revise your résumé and apply like it's your job because, technically, now it is. And when you're not applying online, you're taking Excel courses or going to networking events. It's exhausting. And all you really want to do is grab some snacks, curl up into a ball, and hibernate, but you can't even do that without the fear creeping in—fear you'll never find work again. That you'll lose your apartment, have to move back in with your parents, and run into Camryn Voss, the popular girl from high school who's now a nurse who wears cool scrubs and buys eight-dollar Frappuccinos."

"It kinda sounds like *If You Give a Mouse a Cookie*."

Letty gasped. "I love that book."

"I promise, you will never have to tolerate a catch-up conversation with Camryn Voss. We'll make it through this together. Whether you take the library job, explore other options, or take a break, I've got you covered."

"Rustin Hayes, are you offering to make me a stay-at-home girlfriend?" she quipped.

"I guess I am."

"That's very sweet, but you're right, this time I have options. It doesn't make the pain any less, but I know I'll be okay because we have each other."

By the time the check came, Letty's mood was much improved. She was bopping her head to the loud music with a slight smile. No doubt her mind was racing, calculating probabilities, despite the uncertain factors. When I joined *Junction*, I went into it with the understanding that no matter the outcome, I'd be okay. And while I was saddened by the results and what could only be classified as a black mark on my pristine record, today I was better than okay because I had Letty's love as a parting gift.

Back at my apartment, while Letty showered, I shot off a few text messages—first to Jackie.

Rustin

We are a go. Let's put together an aggressive offer. Send me a draft once complete.

Apple Jacks

Hi, Rustin. Always all business.

Rustin

Sorry. Hi, how's the family? How long until I get a draft?

Apple Jacks

Will Monday morning work, or do you want me to forgo sleep?

Rustin

Monday works.

Apple Jacks

And don't call me before 9
sniffing after it.

Rustin

You are the best money mover around. I owe
you.

Apple Jack

You have no idea. Did you talk
to Omar?

Rustin

He's next on my list.

Pulling up my message thread with Omar, I sent him a text.

Rustin

Don't hate me.

The Plug

What do I have to clean up
now?

Rustin

I wanna purchase the rights to Jellybean
Junction.

My phone rang, and I headed to the balcony. "Hello."

"What the fuck?"

"I know, I know, but just hear me out."

"Was this your plan all along?"

"No. It was more of a contingency plan in case of an emergency."

"The show may be canceled, but something like that isn't going to be cheap."

"I know, but Jackie has crunched the numbers."

"You pulled Jack into this?"

"I was just tossing around hypotheticals. You know I like the big picture. Best to gather all the possibilities."

"And did you ever think about looping me in?" he asked.

"That's why we're speaking now."

"What are you proposing?"

"Sixty/forty."

Omar laughed. "Fifty/fifty."

Now it was my turn to cackle. "Fifty-five/forty-five."

"Deal."

Omar and I had agreed years ago that we'd never let the money fuck up our friendship. Our negotiations were never heated. We'd learned to eliminate emotion and just talk numbers until the matter was settled. I couldn't close this deal without him.

"Great," I said. "Jackie is sending over the proposal on Monday. I'll ask her to copy you."

"Gang gang."

When Letty returned to the living room, she was wearing a tank top sans bra and pink-and-white-striped boxer shorts with her hair already tucked in for the night under her silk head scarf. "Hey, do you remember the coffeemaker?"

"At *Junction*?"

"Yeah. Will you still have my back?"

"Baby, I can buy you another coffeemaker."

"I want that one, and you promised you'd be my witness."

"Okay." When I beckoned her with my outstretched hand, she walked toward me, and I pulled her on my lap. Immediately, I planted a cluster of kisses to her bare shoulder.

"When are you going to tell the others?" she asked.

"Monday."

"Then what?"

"I don't really know. We do have three more episodes to film."

"Those will be the most melancholy three episodes ever." She rubbed the back of my neck thoughtfully. "When are they coming to pick up the furniture? My mom and sister have long gone."

"It's fine, take your time. If there's anything you want to keep, just let me know. But there's no rush—it's set up for auto-pay each month."

"Top two all-time boyfriends, and you're not number two." She lingered over my lips before finally offering up a slow kiss that threatened to steal my soul. "I want you to fuck me like one of your French girls."

"She asked DiCaprio to draw her, not fuck her."

"I took some creative liberties."

"This is actually the perfect segue for me to give you something."

"You bought me a gift?" she said.

"Reduce your expectations. It's just a silly little something."

"Gimmie, Daddy."

I pulled a box from a side table drawer and tossed it at her. Letty removed the bow to reveal the embossing on the top of the box.

"Van Cleef isn't silly."

"Open it."

She opened the box but didn't utter a word. Shit, she hated it. I'd even enlisted Jackie's opinion before purchasing it.

"Rustin, are you fucking *shitting* me?"

It was Van Cleef's signature clover motif, a simple gold necklace with mother-of-pearl inlay. Letty typically wore several necklaces at once, and I thought this one would complement her everyday go-to stack. "If you don't like it, we can exchange it."

"Like? No. I love it."

"Thank God."

"Rustin—" I recognized that tone. She was going to tell me it was too expensive and far more than she deserved.

"Listen to me: I love you. You're my entire world, so no, it's not too expensive. It's actually not enough. Your love language is food, and mine is gifts and daily orgasms."

"A simple man," she joked. "Will you put it on me?" Letty stood, and I clasped the necklace around her neck in between pecks to her soft skin.

She flipped around, tossing her arms over my shoulders. We swayed to nonexistent music. Her gaze was soft, as if she didn't have a care in the world. I liked to think I was the reason for her serenity. "You're my everything," she said.

I hadn't always known Letty was the one, but in this moment, any sliver of doubt was obliterated. "Everything," I whispered.

Sleep was still elusive. While Letty softly breathed next to me, I stared up at the ceiling. So many good things were falling into place. Letty, deals with Cinevault and Imaginex. And, if I was granted God's favor, I'd soon own *Jellybean Junction*. All this good shit, and all I could think about was the bad parts—failing the show through my inability to save it, and this fucking new musical that was like an anchor around my neck, never allowing me to fully relax or catch my breath.

I'd promised a new project, and now I had to deliver. After a quick tally, I'd found I had forty-three handwritten pages. That included set sketches and random dialogue that didn't yet have a home. My throat was tight, and my chest was heavy. If I was being one hundred, I hated much of what I'd captured. It read like I was *trying*. I needed effortless, and it was giving desperate.

Letty rolled over, cuddling up to me. "Are you asleep?" She yawned.

"No."

"Is it the new musical?"

"Yeah. It's horrible. I'm just putting lipstick on a pig." The realization that I'd been wasting my time these past few months pissed me off. "I'm going to throw it into the incinerator right the fuck now." I attempted to get up, but Letty wouldn't let me budge.

"No you're not."

"The crazy thing is, I have so many funny and bittersweet stories about growing up in Brooklyn and navigating fame."

"Then lean into that."

"My thoughts are so scattered, like they're ricocheting back and forth against my skull."

"Have you ever considered a one-man show?" she asked.

"What, just me and my stories?"

"You could sing too."

"Aren't I a little too young for that? Shouldn't I live a little bit more before I take to the stage and regurgitate the particulars of my life?"

"You make the rules, so you can do whatever you want," she said. "Consider it Rustin Hayes, Chapter One. You could play the harmonica." I didn't know how to play the harmonica and wasn't sure if Letty was serious or if these were just dreamy, delusional ramblings. She yawned again, turning toward the window. "It doesn't have to be a musical. It's your story. Tell it your way."

"Letty, you might be a sleepy-time genius."

There was no response—she'd already drifted back to sleep.

Jumping from the bed, I stumbled downstairs to the living room, grabbing a spiral notebook. On the floor, I opened the first blank page, and the words spilled from my brain onto the paper. Stories of helping my grandmother cook while she told me neighborhood gossip. Or the fear and confusion I experienced when my grandfather passed. My first kiss with an older woman. I was in seventh grade, and she was in eighth, and we were in a summer art class together. I included the funny anecdote about getting cursed out by Keith Lee. And Letty—there were several stories about her, basically me expressing my awe for ten minutes straight. She continuously breathed life into me, and for that I would be forever grateful.

CHAPTER 29

Letitia

I HANDED PHOEBE a hardcover book. "What's this?" she said.

"It's a yearbook. I made it myself. It has pictures of the entire cast and crew and behind-the-scenes images from over the years. There's one in here with you and a huge afro. I think it was the seventies."

Flipping through the pages, she laughed at select photographs from the show's history. "I remember him." She pointed to a fine white man with a full beard and feathered hair. "We fucked nonstop over the course of one delightful weekend."

"Glad I was able to unlock that very specific memory for you."

"This was very sweet, Letty. Thank you."

"I'm handing them out to everyone as a parting gift." The last few words stuck in my throat.

Phoebe pulled me into a hug. She smelled of shea butter, lavender, and incense. I'd resolved myself to the fact that this was really happening, and this was my last week with this incredible group of people. But despite my acceptance, I still found myself tearing up occasionally. The costume room was already sparse, as fabrics and other items had already been moved or sold off, making this all too real.

"Would you sign my yearbook, Letty?" Phoebe asked.

"Me?" I pulled away in surprise.

"Yes. I want to always remember you."

And here came the waterworks. "I love you, Phoebe. You are the most interesting woman I know, and if I can be half as self-assured and full of life in my sixties, I'll have done something right."

"I love you too, kiddo." We exchanged yearbooks, signing our farewells.

I found Stanley in the breakroom, and without thinking, I walked up to him and threw my arms around him, burying my face into his cardigan. His familiar earthy, sweet, and spicy aroma from the pipe smoke we all complained about was now a source of comfort.

"Why are you hugging me?" he asked.

"Because I'll miss you."

He pushed me off. "Don't."

"Won't you miss me?"

"I don't think I'll get an opportunity, since I've been hired at your boyfriend's studio."

"Rustin hired you?"

"Don't sound so surprised. I have a Miffy."

Why was this the first time I'd heard of this? Rustin hadn't mentioned anything. "What will you be doing?"

"Don't rightly know. It's all hush-hush, but he told me it will perfectly align with my current skill set."

"Wow. Congratulations." I fished a yearbook out of my overloaded tote bag. "Here's a *Jellybean Junction* yearbook. Don't leave without signing mine."

Stanley walked toward the door. "Letty, you take care of yourself."

"Yeah, you too." I leaned against the counter. This was in my top three worst days ever.

My eyes landed on the coffee machine. Yanking the cord from the wall, I emptied the water reservoir and claimed my inheritance. "Come to Mama."

Brea was in the archive room packing up old VHS cassettes from years-old episodes. Everywhere you went in the building, it felt like death—as if Big Momma had died unexpectantly and now the family was left behind to sort through her belongings. I hated this.

"Here you go." I handed her a yearbook.

She ran her hand over the cover. "It came out beautifully. I'm so happy you did this."

"Me too." I hopped up on a dusty counter. "Did you know Stanley is going to Thread and Thespian?"

"What? Wow."

"Yeah. He said Rustin offered him a job."

"Doing what?"

"He acted like it was so top secret that even he didn't know."

"Well, he's an accomplished puppeteer."

"Yeah…"

Brea turned her attention from the tapes to me. "But…?"

"I'm just wondering why Rustin didn't offer *me* a job."

"You took the job at the library, remember?"

"Yeah, but I was open to entertaining other options."

"Maybe he wants to keep your relationship separate. It's healthier that way."

"I guess. Where are these tapes going?"

"Don't know," Brea replied. "I was just asked to box it all up and ship it to some warehouse in Brooklyn."

"I hope they properly archive all this stuff. It would suck to see it be lost."

"They probably won't. It'll most likely sit in the warehouse until there's a fire or it gets auctioned off, and by that time, the tape will be degraded or damaged by rodents."

"So this is it, everything must go?"

"Yep. At least we have the farewell party to look forward to."

"I'm liable to cry the entire time."

Brea gave my hand a squeeze. "At least I'm not losing you."

"No. Who else is going to feed me?"

"I think that's Rustin's job."

"Oh, best believe he feeds me every night."

We both leaned into a conspiratorial fit of giggles.

Rustin had rented out Electric Lemon, a rooftop restaurant on the twenty-fourth floor of the Equinox hotel, for the farewell party. Every corner of the space was a social media viral moment waiting to happen with water features and impressive art pieces. I'd chosen to sweep my hair into a natural updo to showcase my backless cocktail dress. Rustin was in a suit, no tie, and he was the finest man on that rooftop. And in New York that was saying a lot, but I was willing to admit I was totally biased. Currently, he was rubbing my neck while Sandra shared a harrowing delivery-room story.

"I know we all think our jobs are important, but I think you win the prize hands down," Rustin said.

"I have a sensitive stomach, so it would have been a no-go for me," I said.

"I thought you hadn't thrown up in years."

"And I'd like to keep the streak going, thank you very much."

"It was really nice for you to host the farewell party," Sandra said.

"It's the least I could do, seeing how I was the reason the show got canned," Rustin said.

I swatted at his arm. "Don't say that. You did all you could. We were essentially on life support when you showed up." The thought of his carrying the weight of the cancellation unnerved me. We'd all worked hard, but luck just wasn't on our side.

"Letty's right," Sandra added. "You and Brea both need to let this go. It's not one person's fault—it's a collection of bad breaks that led to this."

"We had a good run," I said.

"Legendary run," Rustin agreed.

"Speaking of Brea, I'm off to find her," Sandra said.

"Check the bar," I teased as she walked away.

Rustin rubbed his thumb against my skin and somehow caused my pussy to water. "You okay?" he asked.

"I'm good. A little sad, but I'm not currently crying, so I'll consider that a win."

"It just sucks that all these good people are now unemployed."

"All but Stanley."

"What?"

"He told me you offered him a job."

Rustin's expression was one of surprise, as if he hadn't expected me to know that bit of information. "Omar hired him."

"At your direction, I'm sure."

"Yep."

"Why didn't you tell me?"

"The last few days have been hectic. It must have slipped my mind."

"I thought you didn't like Stanley."

"I don't, but he's a good puppeteer. Baby, I think the photographer just arrived. I want her to get some pictures, and we have to capture one final group photo for posterity. I'll be right back." After kissing me, he rushed away.

My intuition was screaming that he wasn't telling me everything. Yes, Stanley was immensely talented, but hiring him didn't make sense. What was he going to do at Rustin's studio but get on everyone's nerves? Maybe I was just raw from the emotions of this week, but my antenna was extended.

Eight—that was how many mini gougères with smoked salmon, caviar, and prosciutto I'd eaten, and now I was leaning against the wall trying not to bust a seam.

"Hey, buckaroo." Rhodes approached in her sensible orthopedic shoes, which right now I was envious of.

"Enjoying yourself?" I asked.

"As much as one can when they're being forced into retirement."

"You were going to retire at the end of the season anyway."

"Yeah, and that was on my terms. This isn't."

"I'm sorry."

"No need to cry over spilled milk. I have a gift for you."

"I love gifts. How'd you know?" She handed me a gift bag with squiggles all over it. Pushing the crinkly tissue paper aside, I pulled out the Wendy Whimsy puppet. "What's going on?"

"I heard you are going back to the Brooklyn library in an expanded role."

"Yeah. That's right."

"My puppeteering days are in the past, but Wendy has so many more stories to tell, and I'd like you to help her tell them."

"Rhodes, Wendy is your baby. I couldn't."

"If you don't, she'll just sit on a shelf and collect dust. Don't deny a dying old woman her last wish."

"You're not dying," I said.

"It's a slow death. It should catch up with me in approximately fifteen to twenty years."

Tears streamed down my face. "I promise you I will give Wendy a good home where her stories can soar. Thank you for entrusting me with her."

"I couldn't think of a better caretaker. You've got something special, Letty. Don't ever let anyone steal your shine."

After he'd worked the room reminiscing and telling stories, the clinking of glass quieted the rumble of conversation, and Rustin took center stage.

"This night has been bittersweet. Life rarely turns out the way we plan. When I joined this team, I hoped for a long and prosperous run, and six months later, we are shutting our doors. While my time has been brief, I've grown to appreciate each and every one of you. Sometimes goodbyes are really just see-you-laters, and I hope this is the case for *Jellybean Junction*."

Shouts of "Hear, hear," "Gone but not forgotten," and "*Jellybean Junction* forever" could be heard amid applause. Several eyes landed on me.

"Go ahead and start us off, Letty," Brea said.

I beamed with pride, and with sob-filled voices, we all sang the *Jellybean Junction* theme song one last time.

The RideX home was a silent one. I was sure Rustin assumed my lack of conversation was due to the finality of it all, but I was carrying the one and multiplying, because shit wasn't adding up. When we walked into his place, I was ready to share my work.

"Why didn't you offer me a job?" I asked.

"You took the library job."

"Your studio could have still extended an invitation for me to interview."

"Do you want a job at Thread and Thespian?"

"No, but I would have appreciated an offer."

"Where is this all coming from?"

"What the fuck is Stanley going to do there, and why did I have to hear it from him and not my boyfriend?"

"I don't normally disclose business and hiring information until it's finalized," he said.

"Sure, I get that, but I'm not a *Daily News* reporter. I'm your girlfriend."

"I planned to tell you all of this. I'm just waiting for a few additional pieces to fall into place."

"Tell me now."

"How about we sit down?"

I followed him to the couch.

"I have great news," he said.

"Well, you're in luck. I happen to love good news."

"I found a way to save *Junction*."

Rustin was a fighter, and I'd just knew he would come through with a three-pointer in overtime with five seconds on the clock. "How?"

"I bought it."

"You *bought* the show?"

"Yes. *Jellybean Junction* is now a property of Thread and Thespian Studios. We still have to sign the paperwork, but it's a done deal."

"When did you decide to do this?"

"It was kinda the plan all along."

My vision blurred, and heat whooshed up my neck and face. Rustin had been playing the long game. This was never about saving the show—it was about enriching himself. "So, were all your proposed changes just platitudes?"

"No, of course not."

"But if the game plan from jump was to acquire the show, then earnest attempts to save it would be counterintuitive to that goal."

"No, you misunderstand. The plan was to keep the show on air. Plan B was to purchase it if plan A failed."

"One thing about me is I'm a really good judge of character, and I'm pissed because I knew you were hiding something months ago, but I let your big brown eyes and fake sincerity cloud my better judgment."

"Fake sincerity?"

"You lied—to me, Brea, and the entire cast," I said. "This was always about Rustin Hayes and his divide-and-conquer agenda." I was going to be sick. This whole time, I'd just been a pawn in his quest to gobble up intellectual property.

"I never had an agenda."

"We both know that's a lie."

"Letty, would you stop? It's me. This is a *good* thing."

"For you."

"For us."

"I get it now," I said. "Stanley is for continuity. You hired him for his historical knowledge. Wow, that's insidious." A lump formed in my throat at the realization that, from hello, this had always been his end game. Phoebe, Brea, me—we were all just collateral damage.

"You're overreaching."

"No. This is me filling in the blanks you chose to omit." The finality in my voice hinted at where this conversation was headed.

"Oh my God, Letty, don't do this."

"You lied to me." The first tear was followed by a flood of others. Our entire relationship, he'd been hiding this from me. I'd shared my deepest, darkest secrets, and he had never so much as *hinted* that purchasing *Junction* was a possibility. I'd been right to be suspicious from the very start.

"I was trying to protect you," he said. "I didn't want you to get your hopes up if it all fell through."

"Or maybe you just didn't want me getting in the way."

"Are you fucking kidding me right now?"

"It's all coming together—the overexaggerated praise, the gifts."

"I meant every word I've ever said."

"Yeah, but it's all the shit you didn't say." I stood, heading for the exit.

"You don't have to leave. I'm willing to talk about this until we're on the same side."

"That's the thing—I could never be on the side of a capitalist asshole. Don't you have enough?"

"Please don't leave mad."

"I think—" My voice was barely above a whisper.

He clutched my face, forcing me to look at him. "No, baby, please."

"We might need some space." Tears were streaming down my face.

"I don't want that."

"I need it."

Rustin's shoulders shrank. "Okay. I'll give you as much time as you need."

"I'm sorry."

"I'll be right here—right the fuck here—when you're ready to talk."

"Goodbye, Rustin."

"Not goodbye—it's just see you later."

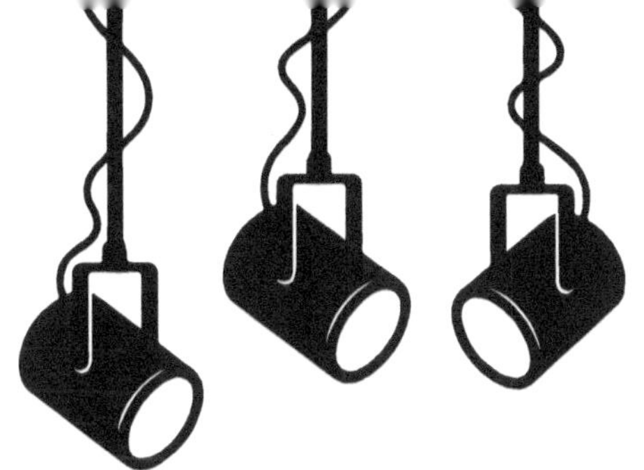

CHAPTER 30

Letitia

Eighteen Months Later

"HEY, GIRL, HEY." Esme breezed into my office on the third floor of the Brooklyn Public Library's art deco building.

"Hey. How's it going?" I asked.

"Busy as ever. I haven't had a bite to eat, and it took three hours to make it to the restroom because I was constantly being interrupted."

"Bright side, it's Friday." Which for me meant very little, since I worked half days on Saturdays for my story-time series.

"That's the only thing keeping me going." Esme plopped into my guest chair, and I couldn't help but admire her style. She seemed like the type of woman who had her shit together, mixing vintage thrift-store finds with high-end pieces. I knew if I toured her closet, I'd be drooling over the eclectic mix of designer brands. Esme gave off curated vibes, as if she were the orchestra conductor and everyone else was just trying to keep up.

"What's up?" I asked.

"I reviewed your suggested summer reading list and loved it, which is no surprise. I'm a girl with impeccable instincts, and I knew you'd thrive in this role."

"Thanks. I appreciate it."

Esme seemed to linger, grazing her fingers over trinkets on my desk.

"Is there something else?"

"Before you say no, just hear me out."

"Okay." I cast her a suspicious glance.

"I wanna set you up on a date."

"No."

"Letty, you're supposed to be open-minded."

I pretended to zip my lip.

"His name is Simon. He owns a recycling company."

"A garbageman. You want me to go on a date with a garbageman?"

"First of all, garbagemen make beaucoup bucks, so don't be so quick to judge."

"Go on."

"He's thirty-two, no kids, which means nada baby-mama drama."

"What's he look like?"

"Looks aren't everything, but he's fine as hell, and when I showed him your picture, he practically went feral," Esme said.

"You're showing my picture to strangers?"

"He's not a stranger. He's Simon from Green Cycle Solutions."

"I appreciate you looking out, but I'm good."

"Letty, it's been more than a year, and the only way you're going to get over an old man is by finding a new one to fuck."

"I don't *want* to get over it," I said.

"You broke up with him."

"I did, and it sucked. Yes, I've moved on, but—"

"I get it. You don't have to explain anything to me, but you're amazing, and it sucks that you're in your prime, and you're sleeping alone. I'm not suggesting you fall in love. I just want you to get fucked."

"What about you? Maybe you should take some of your own advice."

"Trust me, I've been fucked—just not in the way I'd have liked. I'm on a sabbatical from men. This is my year of discovery. The year of yes. Just not to men, sex, or situationships."

"So why don't we spend your year of shadow work making new memories sans men?" I asked.

"Is that a no to Simon?"

"Hard pass."

"Do you want to get drinks tonight?"

"Now *that* is something I can enthusiastically say yes to."

Esme left my office, and I focused my attention on the stack of children's books on my desk, and by focus, I mean staring at them until I was cross-eyed. One thing I'd been trying hard not to do was say his name. Because if I heard it, a rush of what-ifs would flood my brain. Rustin had lied to me and, however unintentionally, used me. I hadn't seen him since telling him I needed space. A week later, I'd sent him a text message.

> *I'm sorry. I can't do this. I feel betrayed. And maybe you were just trying to protect me, but this whole thing seems calculated, and I don't like being played. I wish you nothing but the best, I really do, but this is where I get off.*

Right after hitting send, the three dots appeared then disappeared, and that was the end.

Did I miss him? Yes, every damn day. Was I putting on a brave face? Also yes, but I doubted anyone believed me when I claimed to be fine.

"This is nice. I never thought I'd see the day when you would be hosting guests in your apartment," Brea said while eyeing the charcuterie board.

"We all have to grow up some time."

"How's work?"

"I love it. I've never had this much creative control. Being allowed to curate reading lists for the kids all across the city, and then there's the story-time series, which has taken off."

"I saw the feature in *Essence* magazine—*Story Time with Letty, Wags the Fox, and Friends.*"

"Last Saturday, Colman Domingo read to the kids." I beamed.

"That man's voice is perfection. He could read me a bedtime story *any* time."

"What about you?" I asked. "How's my godson, and why isn't he here now?"

"Sandra said I should take advantage of some much-needed girls' time, but he's fine. We finally got him to sleep through the night."

"Brea, that's great. I know it was a struggle for a hot minute."

"I was sleep deprived for the first six months."

"News like that calls for wine." Hopping up, I pulled a bottle from the fridge. In this past year, I'd made this place my own. My first step at liberation was contacting the Curated Room and having them pick up their shit. Don't get me wrong, I'd loved all the design choices, but my place reminded me of *him*, and I needed a clean slate so I could start making new memories.

"I will drink to that. Shit, truthfully, I'll drink to anything right now." I handed Brea a half-filled glass, returning to sit next to her on the area rug. "So what else is new?" I snagged a red pepper cracker from the board.

Brea cleared her throat. "Did you hear Rustin was nominated for several Prism Awards for his one-man show?"

Would it ever stop, the pang in my heart at the thought of him? "That's great."

"Wasn't that your idea?"

"Doesn't matter where the idea came from. He punted the ball and ran with it. Is that correct? I don't understand how soccer works."

"Clearly because you're talking about football."

"Aren't they one and the same?"

"Yes and no. Stop changing the subject. Have you thought about sending him a congratulations text?" she asked.

"No. Why, did you?"

"I did."

I mean this with the utmost respect, because I loved Brea down, but…*bitch*.

"What the fuck?" I said.

"He's my friend."

"Whose side are you on?"

"I've always got your back. That will never change."

"Did he respond?"

"Yes. He said thank you."

"No, bitch, I need verbatim."

Brea pulled out her phone, retrieving the message thread. "I said, 'Congratulations on your Prism nominations. Very proud of you, and well deserved.'"

"And he said?"

"'Thank you. Surprised more than anything. I heard you welcomed a baby boy, so congrats back. Hope everyone is doing well.'"

"Who's *everyone?*"

"I assume Sandy, me, and the baby."

"Oh yeah, for sure that makes sense. Was that it?" I didn't know what I was expecting.

"Yes." She worried her bottom lip, deliberating whether or not to push.

"Brea, don't look at me like that. We agreed I did what was best for me."

"You were really upset. I just wonder if time has provided new clarity."

"I made my choice, I stand by it, and I don't appreciate your wanting to circle the block on this particular decision."

"I don't want to argue. I just want what's best for you."

"The truth was what was in my best interests, and Rus... He couldn't give me that."

CHAPTER 31

Rustin

"SUITS HAVE ARRIVED." Omar was at my front door holding a garment bag.

"Since when do you make personal deliveries?"

"Since my boy got nominated for five Prism Awards." When I stepped aside, he came in and draped the custom Armani suit on the couch. "You might be the only playwright to have two plays receiving nods in the same year."

"Kinda overkill, don't you think? People are going to get sick of me."

"It's been ten years, and it hasn't happened yet. And anyone who claims you're overrated is just jealous."

"Who said I was overrated?"

"I think it was Oona who mentioned something," he teased.

"Lies. Your daughter loves me."

Omar surveyed my messy living room with a judgmental eye.

"I know what you're thinking," I said. "I'm just in the final read-through for the script. *Strings of Legacy* has to capture all the key points." Our first project with Cinevault was a documentary of the history of puppeteering in Hollywood. Once I approved the script, production would begin.

"Are you close?"

"Yeah. I've got, like, ten or twenty pages left. I was thinking at the end credits, we could include various puppets talking in the style of a documentary. Could be funny."

Omar gave me a thumbs-up before taking a seat. "Have you been working on an acceptance speech?"

"The chances of me winning are slim to none."

"Negro, you're favored to sweep. Vegas has you at two-to-one odds of winning."

"Who's betting on Prism Award nominations?"

"Theater kids have gambling addictions too."

"Watch the theater-kid slander. You're one of us, remember?"

"No, I'm a movie buff, similar but with way more swag." Omar was a man of many talents. Not only was he deeply involved with my projects, he had a shit-ton of ventures of his own. Most notably, he was a film critic. I'm not talking sitting in his man cave waxing philosophical over cinematography. He was renowned, and Aspect Ratio, his podcast and social media empire, had more than fourteen million followers. If Omar liked your film, it was the equivalent of a Roarsome Work sticker from a first-grade teacher. I'm talking bragging rights in perpetuity.

"Maybe I'll just play it by ear," I said.

"Don't do that. You're bound to have a grand mal seizure if you win, and then I'll have to go into damage control. Write a damn acceptance speech."

"Yes, Dad."

"So, I spotted Letitia at a coffee shop in Brooklyn."

"Did you two speak?" I asked.

"No. When I noticed her, I snuck out like a bitch. Didn't even wait for my drink."

"Was she alone?"

"Yeah. I think so."

"Did she look like she was doing good?"

"I can't call it. She was at a table staring at her phone."

"Yep."

"You know you could just call her," he said.

"No. She made it very clear she didn't want to hear from me, and I'm gonna respect that."

"But it's dumb."

"Are you calling me dumb?"

"Rus, some people are just meant for each other. That's you and Letty."

"Well, apparently the fuck not!" I punched my palm with my fist.

Omar fell silent. I didn't want to talk about her. I'd established a tolerable habit of pretending she never existed—just a really long dream that now felt like a nightmare. It was the knowing that hurt the most. Knowing she was walking the same streets, possibly dining in the same restaurants, and was perfectly fine with never seeing me again.

"You good, bro?"

"No." My response was curt. I hadn't been good in months. I didn't work without Letty. She was like an update that had been downloaded into my DNA, and then malware came in and corrupted it all, and as time passed, all that was left was blurry, frayed edges of what once was.

The Prism Awards were held in the David H. Koch Theater at Lincoln Center for the Performing Arts, an impressive space filled with stars from both stage and film. It was an honor to be nominated, don't get me wrong. I definitely wanted to win because I was a competitive bastard who thought I was better than everyone else. But being here was great too. I'd brought my parents, who had agreed not to embarrass me with stan behavior.

We'd already won lighting design for our play. But now, we were getting into the big categories—best lead actor in a play and best play, both of which *This Scene Wasn't in the Script* was up for.

"Try to act surprised when they call your name," Omar said from his seat behind me.

"Do you think he'll actually win?" My mother sounded shocked. It wasn't like I didn't have an entire case dedicated to displaying my many trophies and awards.

"I'm gonna need you to have some faith in me," I joked.

Award shows were like a family reunion, where the family members were dysfunctional and phony. We all wanted the same golden trophy, and when someone said, "Good luck tonight," oftentimes they were internally thinking the opposite. I was constantly having to remind myself to dial up a smile and not look constipated—to just remember that by midnight I'd be back home eating leftover curry chicken. No after-parties for me—the curry chicken from Everything's Irie would be the highlight of my night.

Glancing at my father, who was nodding as the orchestra played a classical version of Jay-Z's "Big Pimpin'," I reached over to adjust his crooked bow tie. "You enjoying yourself?"

"Do you think you can introduce me and your mother to Angela Bassett?"

"I don't know her."

"Just tell her you're Rustin Hayes."

"And when she looks at me like I'm stupid and says, 'Who?' then what?"

My father swatted my words aside. "She knows *of* you."

This event was live, and I knew friends, family, and staff were watching, anticipating a win. I'd done my best to tamp down expectations since I'd been nominated, saying things like, "It's a stiff field of nominees," and "This is our first year with *This Scene Wasn't in the Script*. It hasn't really found its audience yet."

That last one was a lie. Each show in the past six months had been sold out, and I was now kicking myself for agreeing to this level of onstage commitment. The thing about a one-man show comprised of your life stories was that there was no understudy.

But I had to admit, it was great to be back on the stage and to feed off the energy of the audience. The fact that I was on stage alone, except for a section that included puppets, was vulnerable and freeing. I'd always been scared of being clocked as an impostor, and now I was front and center, baring my scars, and people were laughing with me and singing along.

Denzel Washington walked out onto the stage to loud applause. He was a lover of the stage, and despite all his success in Hollywood, he still considered himself a stage actor. After a self-deprecating joke, he read out the names of the five nominees for best lead actor in a play. Polite applause followed each name.

My mother dug her fingers into my arm. Good thing I was wearing a suit jacket, or her nails might have drawn blood.

"The Prism Award for best lead actor in a play goes to…" Denzel fumbled with the envelope. When he opened it, a knowing chuckle rang out. "Rustin Hayes for *This Scene Wasn't in the Script.*"

From that point until I reached the stage, everything went sideways. My mother flung her arms around me, and I vaguely remember hugging her back while my dad vigorously smacked my back. Omar was mouthing, *I told you so.* I had to recover quickly—no one liked it when the winner lingered in the audience. On the way to the stage, I was pulled into hugs by fellow actors and actresses.

When I reached the podium and was handed the award, the heft of it threw me off guard.

Omar shouted, "Yeah, boy!"

I exhaled a long breath in an attempt to reset. "Wow. I did not expect to win this. If you know me personally, you're probably calling BS right now because I'm normally confident as all get-out, but this play was a passion project for me. A year and a half ago, I was in the worse writer's slump of my career, and my confidence was at an all-time low. When you accomplish what I did at nineteen, you often question if you deserve to be here.

"A valued friend at the time said, while still half asleep, 'Why don't you do a one-man show?' Mind blown, earth shattered. That night I wrote everything but the songs for *This Scene Wasn't in the Script.* Sometimes we give up on ourselves, and it's our circle of friends and loved ones who breathe life back into us. This award is as much theirs as it is mine. To my parents, thank you for allowing me to be the awkward Black boy. To my brother from another mother and business partner, Omar, it don't shake until Mendoza signs off on it. And finally, I want to thank Letitia Vincent, a brilliant puppeteer who reminded me why I'm so passionate about this art form and that love, no matter how brief, is worth it. Thank you, Prism, for this honor."

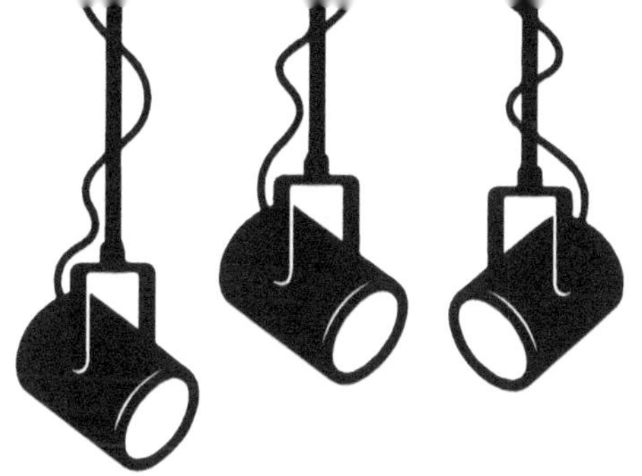

CHAPTER 32

Letitia

AFTER MY SATURDAY reading with Letty and Wags, I'd decided to treat myself. The weather was a perfect eighty-two, which meant ice cream and vitamin D were in order. I headed to Pier 57 at the marketplace. I couldn't decide, so I got salted-caramel ice cream, a lemon-filled cronut, and a lavender iced latte. From there, I headed to the rooftop park. I'd been here several times since Rustin first introduced me to it. I loved it for the views and was actually learning to appreciate the silence.

Living in a major city, you grew deaf to the noise pollution you were subjected to. The honking and screeching of tires. The never-ending buzz of conversation. The sirens of emergency vehicles and cat-callers trying to capture your attention. Up here on the roof, there was none of that. The serenity of it allowed me to think. I'd been working on a business plan for a puppet workshop for kids. I'd learned you should at least be planning for your next big career venture, and I was hopeful one day a dedicated space for a workshop would be the move.

I enjoyed a spoonful of ice cream, nodding enthusiastically, confirming I'd made the right choice.

My phone dinged on the table.

Mom

Can't wait to see you.

Letty

I'm looking forward to it.

Mom

Your father said you're super aggressive at bingo.

Letty

I'm there to win the cash prize. I don't play games.

Mom

Dad says hi. Don't forget to pack a suit. We might go to the beach.

My mom and I weren't perfect, and truthfully, I didn't know if we'd ever get to that, but when she called, I actually answered, and I liked to think that was progress.

Most things were fixable if you were willing to put in the effort. Over a year had passed since Rustin and I last spoke. I'd wanted to call him so many times. When I landed my first big celebrity for story time, Keke Palmer. When my new couch was delivered—my first that wasn't a hand-me-down or scooped up from off the street. The joy I felt when Brea's son was born. I took my role as godmother very seriously. That kid could always come to Auntie Letty when his mothers were tripping.

But as the months past, it became harder to believe we could just pick up where we'd left off. And on Rustin's part, he'd never once tried to call or text me. Not at Halloween to say, *Witching you a happy Halloween,* or coming through at Thanksgiving with a turkey emoji. Shit, at the start of May, he could've sent the played-out meme of Justin Timberlake telling me it was gonna be May.

But no, it was motherfucking crickets. You had to laugh to keep from crying, was what Brea said. I hardly ever laughed anymore. I mean genuinely. Happiness was no longer my default. It was now a role I played so my friends and family didn't worry about me and flash me the *are you okay?* stare. I wasn't, and right now, I didn't think I ever would be. I'm not saying I was going to be like Rose on the *Titanic,* pining over a lover who'd died sixty years ago. Yes, I was hurting, but if I'm seventy and still talking about the one that got away, I give you permission to slap me.

"Is this seat taken?"

I looked up to find Rustin blocking my sun.

"Yes. I mean, no." Was I hallucinating? Was the sun hotter than I'd first realized, and now I was in a fever dream?

"Hi." He claimed the wire chair across from me that was bolted to the concrete to prevent people from tossing it over the edge.

"What are you doing here?"

"This is my spot, so…"

"Are you implying I'm encroaching on your territory?"

"It depends on what set you claim."

This seemed like a trick question. "Theater kids? Is that a correct answer?"

"*Ding, ding, ding.*"

"Good, 'cause I thought I was going to have to get initiated."

"The initiation would've been performing a show tune, by the way."

"I would've picked 'The Trolley Song.'"

"From *Meet Me in St. Louis*. Good choice."

It was weird how, after all this time, sitting across from him seemed like the most natural thing in the world. "Congratulations on your Prism Awards."

"Oh, you heard about that. Thanks. Did you happen to catch any of my speech?"

"Brea showed it to me on YouTube."

That was a lie. I'd watched it live like the rest of the world and was rendered speechless when he singled me out.

"I meant every word. If not for you, I'd probably still be waking up bleary-eyed each morning."

"Glad to hear you're getting more sleep."

"For the first few months, I'd wake up in the middle of the night reaching for you, but you were never there."

"Rustin—"

"Can I just get the chance to properly apologize? You were right about everything. I should've told you what I hoped to do once things got serious between us. I just thought I was making shit better. I guess it's the savior complex in me, and I hate losing. So, walking away from *Junction* was never going to be an option for me. But I should have told you. It was selfish of me not to."

"I'm glad *Junction* has a new home, and for my part, I can admit I might've overreacted."

"Really?" he said.

"Don't press your luck, Mr. Hayes."

"Sorry."

"I still stand by the belief that it all felt covert, and I thought we weren't keeping secrets from each other."

"You're right. My judgment was flawed on that one."

I shrugged. "It all worked out in the end."

"Did it? 'Cause you and me still feel unresolved."

"Some things are better left in the past."

"While others continue to bleed into the present. Your being here at the same time as me is not some coincidence. This is feeling like fate—fate leading us here for a second chance."

"A second chance at what?"

"To get this shit right," he replied. "I never stopped loving you. Not a day passes when I don't think of you and hope you're doing well, and since this may be the last time our paths cross, I'm going to lay it all out."

The sting of an impending cry was all too real.

"You are the one for me. I've never felt loved or seen like I do with you, and frankly, the thought—the mere thought—of you looking at another man the way you used to look at me makes me want to crash out. I'm talking posting cryptic quotes about not knowing what you have until it's gone and getting your name tattooed on my forehead."

"Not your forehead."

"In Comic Sans."

My unexpected laughter was like a match igniting hope inside me.

"Just tell me you've missed me a scintilla as much as I've missed you."

I breathed out a sharp, shaky breath. "Not all day, but every fucking day." Tears slipped from my eyes.

"Let me fix it. Allow me to prove to you I'm the same guy you fell in love with. We can take it super slow. I won't rush, no pressure. I just wanna be near you again."

"I don't want that."

Rustin's face was marred with sorrow, like I'd just inflicted irreparable harm. "Oh, okay." His words almost crumpled as they left his mouth.

Reaching for his hand, I hoped to repair his heart. My chin trembled. "I don't want to take things slow. I've missed you so much it hurts."

Rustin pulled me from my chair and into his arms. "Baby, I'm so sorry. I never meant for any of this to happen." He stepped back, now cradling my face. "You have to believe me. If I knew I'd lose you—"

"I know. I'm sorry too."

Rustin's eyes dropped to my lips, and our bodies did the rest, erasing the gap between us until his lips made contact with mine. I practically evaporated from the heat of it all. His hands were all over me. It was obvious kisses weren't enough. We each wanted to be closer, and were lucky there was no one else on the rooftop because what we were doing was bordering on NC-17. Rustin's hands on my breasts, in my hair, creeping up my thigh. The harder he pressed against me, the more pronounced his dick became.

"God, I love you so much," he said.

He was breathless, and forming sentences was difficult for me. "Same, always, never…stopped."

When we finally paused for air, Rustin said, "I have so much to tell you."

I beamed, thinking the same. "I've been keeping a running list on my phone just in case."

Reclaiming our seats, he locked his fingers with mine. "Tell me everything."

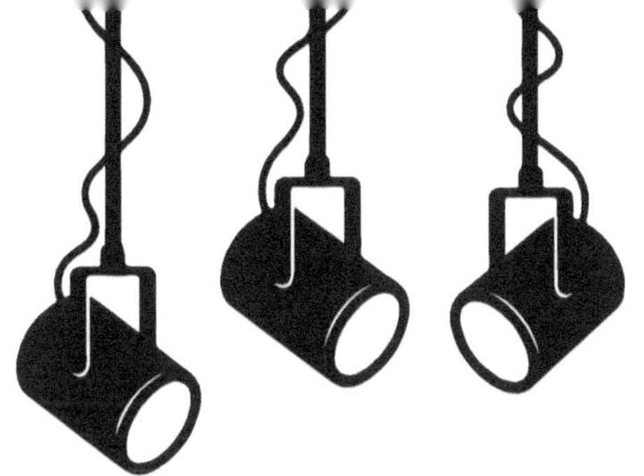

EPILOGUE

Rustin

Six Months Later

THE STUDIO WAS packed with creatives from every sector— television, literature, film, and visual art. When I purchased the property for Thread and Thespian, I'd found it included a green space tucked away in the back of the building, with lush, fully grown trees acting as shade and offering up privacy. A faux waterfall muffled the sounds of living in an urban environment and colorful vegetation welcomed you from the moment you entered the space.

We were gathered for the soft relaunch of *Jellybean Junction*. After acquiring the show, I'd known I wanted to breathe new life into it, and right now, the hottest market was online. So we were starting out small but ambitious, with shorts and videos no longer than five minutes. I'd hired up-and-coming puppeteers who were hungry and looking to make a mark. And under Stanley's guidance, they produced tons of fresh and innovative ideas.

The goal was to eventually flip our social media presence to a network or streaming deal, but this was chess, not checkers, and deliberate and calculated baby steps were the move.

"I cannot believe this space is just hidden away smack dab in the middle of Brooklyn," Brea said.

"That's what I love most about this city—it's full of surprises," I said.

Letitia approached with two drinks and three lemon pepper chicken skewers in her hand. "Is that all for you?" I asked.

"No. I got you a drink too."

"What about the chicken?"

"Now, *that's* all mine."

"Damn."

"You know she's greedy." Brea left us to go mingle with the former cast and crew from *Junction*, whom she hadn't seen in a while.

"This turnout is amazing," Letty said.

"Why are you surprised? My rolodex stays stacked like my bitches."

"Do not get knocked out at your company event," she teased.

"I could see the headlines now."

Life could be hard, but choosing to love Letty every single day was easy. She matched my nerdy sensibility. We never ran out of things to talk about, and when the restaurant got my order wrong, she made them take it back and fix it. My little enforcer. For years, people would talk about how they fell more in love with their partner each day, and honestly, I'd never gotten it. But now I did. Because without fail, every fucking day, I was finding something new to love about this woman.

Her love was more than I deserved, and it was important work, ensuring she was cherished, supported, and taken care of. And that was what I planned to do until God called me home.

There was a clinking of glasses, and Omar was holding a microphone, so we should all be scared. "Gather 'round and listen up." The guests complied with laughter. "When I met Rus in college, I had no idea this fucker was going to change my life. He is always trying to enlist me to sign up for one of his hare-brained schemes."

"Hold on now. You like my ideas," I shouted.

"Most of them. People don't view entertainment as important work, but getting people to laugh, cry, or learn is a gift. And my brother from a Brooklyn-born mother has a talent for knowing what people need. *Jellybean Junction* does great work, and I'm proud the work is now being created by Thread and Thespian. Rustin, come on up here and share a few words."

I weaved through the crowd, only letting go of Letty's hand to claim the mic. Omar and I exchanged daps, and then I turned to the guests in attendance.

"My girlfriend once said *Jellybean Junction* is an institution, and I agree—like Lenox Lounge in Harlem, the A.I. Friedman art store on Eighteenth Street, or Cup & Saucer on Canal. Do you know what all these iconic places have in common? Each one closed for various reasons. We can all agree that at one time, they were New York establishments that fell by the wayside. And *Junction* is no different. The show is iconic and legendary, but it was also failing. As creatives, we've all felt the brunt of the changing landscape in media, art, and entertainment spaces. It's up to us to protect and historically preserve our stories.

"Thread and Thespian purchased the rights to *Jellybean Junction* because I know the story isn't over. There's more to learn, new friends to meet, and amazing places to discover. Now, I don't have any kids yet, but I sure as hell don't want to bring any into a world devoid of educational programming such as *Junction*. So it's my honor to present to you *Jellybean Junction Shorts,* available free on our social media platforms with exclusive content hosted on Patreon for paid subscribers. I'm excited to share what we've been hard at work on, so let's roll the clip."

There was a round of applause and cheers as the trailer for the new format started. We'd highlighted everything that made the show great, including some returning favorites like Aaliyah and Jabari. When the video presentation ended, I closed my remarks with, "Same great neighborhood, same friends, while making learning fun again. Thank you all for coming. Now you can go back to getting drunk on my dime."

"That was great." Letitia tossed her arms over my shoulders when I came off stage.

"You think?"

"Don't act modest. You know you killed it."

"I couldn't have done it without you."

"You're right. You couldn't have." She playfully shoved me.

Since reconnecting six months ago, we'd been inseparable. She'd read children's books to me at night, asking my opinion on whether they were good enough for Story Time with Letty and Wags the Fox. My answer was always yes, because Letty understood her audience. It took a special person to tap into what resonated with kids, and Letty had a natural-born talent for it. Her role as director of children's literary entertainment was one she took pride in. She'd also assisted with the relaunch of *Junction*, lending her voice and puppets to the show.

A woman in a polka-dot dress with chunky jewelry and lashes caked in mascara approached us. "This is all so incredible. You must be so proud."

"We are so grateful to be able to give *Junction* the second chance it deserves." Letty squeezed my hand.

"Rustin, you've been a busy bee—your one-man show is a masterpiece. I sat in my chair riveted, just hanging on your every word."

"Thank you, I appreciate it."

"So, do tell, what's next for you?"

Letty and I looked at each other with smiles. "Just this, us," I said. "Constantly, perpetually, and endlessly—until Rustin and Letitia are all anyone can remember."

"I think that's your best plan yet." Letitia beamed.

Book Club Discussion Questions

1. Letitia and Rustin both love Jellybean Junction, but they have very different visions for its future. Whose approach did you agree with more at the beginning of this story, and did that change by the end?

2. The novel explores what it means to fight for creative work that feels personal. Have you ever held onto something (a job, a dream, a relationship) long after it became difficult? What kept you there?

3. Letitia is fiercely protective of the show, while Rustin is more willing to risk change. How do their personalities shape the way they approach love as well as work?

4. Workplace romances can be messy, especially when power, passion, and pride collide. Did you feel their relationship crossed any lines, or was it inevitable?

5. Humor plays a big role in how Letitia and Ruston connect. Which scene best showed their chemistry through banter, and why?

6. Strung Together pulls back the curtain on the behind-the-scenes labor of children's television. Did it change how you think about the media you grew up with?

7. Trust is a major theme in the novel; trust in a partner, in yourself, and in the work you create. Where did trust break down most, and how was it rebuilt?

8. Letitia fears Rustin has an ulterior motive for joining the show. When did you start to believe his intentions, and what finally convinced you?

9. The show itself functions almost like a third main character. How does Jellybean Junction shape the emotional stakes of the story?

10. If you were in charge of saving Jellybean Junction what would you do differently than Letitia and Rustin?

About the Author

KASHA THOMPSON is a contemporary romance author. She writes authentic love stories that examine the complexity of falling and staying in love. Her books center Black love with relatable characters, humor, and spice. Kasha was born and raised in Brooklyn, New York, but she currently resides in California with her husband.

Also By Kasha Thompson

Working Through It
Figure of Speech
Holding Back the Years
Last Night a DJ Saved My Life
Sight Unseen
Jamaal the IT Guy
Christmas with Kris Kringle

The Las Vegas Ramblers Series
Defensive Stance
Jump Ball
Double Dribble

The Birch Sibling Series
Love You a Little Bit

www.ingramcontent.com/pod-product-compliance
Lightning Source LLC
Chambersburg PA
CBHW020902060726
47591CB00004B/1045